Can a cut-throat reiver escape his nefarious past with the help of the only woman he's ever loved and a promise he never dreamed he'd make? Falca Breks will find out on a journey through a wilderness more dangerous than the squalid city of his birth, toward confrontations with not only enemies past and present but also himself—and the lure of two things that could make him the richest and most powerful man in the Six Kingdoms.

ALSO BY BRUCE FERGUSSON

THE SIX KINGDOMS SERIES

The Shadow of His Wings

The Mace of Souls

SUSPENSE

Morgan's Mill

The Piper's Sons

Two Graves for Michael Furey

PASS ON THE CUP OF DREAMS

A NOVEL OF THE SIX KINGDOMS

BRUCE FERGUSSON

A Lucky Bat Book

Pass on the Cup of Dreams
A Novel of the Six Kingdoms

Cover Design by Joe Calkin

ISBN 978-1-939051-49-3

LuckyBatBooks.com

10 9 8 7 6 5 4 3 2 1

BOOK ONE:

GOLDEN-EYES

Chapter One:

THEFTS

FALCA BREKS would have bet all of what little money he had that the phaeton was following him.

He'd first noticed the blue and white carriage as he left his Slidetown lodgings in the abandoned spice warehouse for the last time, taking only a broad-brimmed hat he'd recently plucked off a drunken caravaner outside the Glass Anchor.

True, phaetons were common enough in this part of Draica, where bogland had been drained and channeled into canals long ago, the marshfangs hunted to extinction except for a few mating pairs in the royal bestiary on Cross Keys Island.

Draica's affluent districts held the heights, offering views of the harbor, the still-damaged Colossus of Roak and, distantly, the Isles of Sleat, but they lacked distraction. So Heart Hill dandies and festaloons from Beckon often came down in phaetons from those wealthy enclaves to purchase scrape from Timberlimbs before buying slides with the swallows of Galore Street brothels, the better ones in Falconwrist, or going to a bloodsnare den in Catchall to listen to ghorgens play their aulosts.

Phaetons had once meant coin in Falca's pocket by way of fisting mottles—Timberlimb refugees—of their proceeds from selling scrape and the more potent rife. He was out of the business now, but the habit of marking these sumptuous carriages hadn't faded entirely.

This particular one kept turning with him as he walked familiar streets, taking a turn here, a shortcut there. He glanced back frequently yet never saw the driver stopping the high-wheeler to let out some caped keelcat eager for the evening. The phaeton passed several brothels and dens he once frequented and as many he hadn't.

The Skullsroll marked the unofficial boundary between the Limb ghetto and Slidetown, and this uncommonly sunny day for late spring had brought out the throngs. Lines of clothing, flapping in the breeze, sagged between tenements. Vendors hawked their wares from stalls and carts lining both sides of the street. An itinerant thedral touted his from a portable feretory crammed with supposedly holy Pelagian icons and crude statuettes of the Erseiyr. A competing thedral dressed in a more gaudily barbed cilice had nothing to sell except a louder rant proclaiming the superiority of the salvation he offered. To Falca it was only more evidence that empty barrels made the loudest sound.

He passed a cripple in a wheeled sled pulled by a large nob-ear mongrel that had stopped to slurp water from a puddle left by yesterday's rains. A pale ghorgen hurried by him, both arms wrapped around a writhing leather sack that contained his bloodsnare.

Falca wasn't far now from the settlement house where he'd be meeting Amala and Gurrus. He paused by a stoneskin doing brisk business sharpening swords, knives and axes on his belly where his roughy was less coarse. The phaeton was still following, the rumbling of its iron-shod wheels a harsh counterpoint to the music of a nearby flinarra. Falca decided that if this was a boil, better to prick and drain it sooner than later.

Poash's cart was up ahead near the corner of the 'Roll and Gullshead Lane—at least it had been the last time Falca saw the old man. A stop there with the fruit-monger would offer the chance to be proved wrong if the carriage passed by. If not, he could always dart down the side street should the odds prove daunting. A phaeton could carry four, and Falca could have filled a dozen with the enemies he'd made over the years, from Heart Hill to the Valor Canal and on to the quays of Catchall; festers like Saphrax and Lambrey Tallon, in particular. At least those two were now where dogs couldn't bite them: Saphrax in Gebroan, and presumably dead by now; Tallon in one of the prison hulks along the River Rhys east of Draica.

Falca quickened his pace when he saw the cart.

Poash had once been a sailor on a merchant galliot. With the doldrums of old age he'd given up that trade for a monger's cart of fruits and spices. He had teeth of assorted colors and only one eye that worked; the other socket bulged with a plug of polished dawnstone. Still, he was quick enough with the long, sharpened cane he used to rap knuckles and poke away the twin-tailed eloes Timberlimbs trained to leap onto vendors' carts and snatch what they could in their out-sized jaws.

When he began stealing from him as a boy, Falca learned to favor a move to Poash's blind side, getting the moments he needed to pilfer and scamper down the 'Roll. He became such a deft and persistent reiver that Poash made a deal with him: be his second eye for an hour or two in exchange for a ripe redbelly and, if he'd done well, a dash of tart sinnot to cut the sweetness.

Falca kept stealing from him anyway, but he nabbed enough of his thieving ilk to make it worth the monger's while, even without the stories he liked to tell as much as Falca liked to hear: of wicked Sandsend in Gebroan and the Shelter Isles; the Flaggy Shore where kraken shed their skins; and of fabled, far-away Milatum, the jewel of Keshkevar.

Poash saw him approaching, swatted away a sniffy eloe as he shuffled around the tilted side of his display cart. Falca glanced back down the street. The phaeton had stopped not far away, perhaps because several adolescent Timberlimbs were climbing the spokes of the front wheels, shoving packets of scrape at the driver, spreading their fingers to indicate the price as the driver kept batting away the offers. But the Limbs wouldn't have been able to mount the wheels if the carriage hadn't already stopped.

"You've added flowers since I saw you last," Falca said, brushing a hand over harlequin roses and meadowbride.

Poash nudged aside Falca's hand with the cane. "Word had it you was dead."

"Ah, just away."

"So I see—a hat now but no gloves. Not that I missed you, mind."

"Yes you have. Who else would believe those stories of places you've never been to?" Falca picked over the fruit, selecting two fat-stem golos.

"Two?" Poash said. "Fer that cob I used to see you with—whawuz his name?"

"Saphrax. We had a burr, why I've been scarce."

"Not him. The one always had the whetstone hangin' from his neck. Tallon, was it?"

"Another burr; before the other."

Poash shook his head. "F'only you could sell those you'd have enough to stock a cart twice the size a' mine."

Falca had missed a worm-hole in one of the golos and picked another.

The carriage was moving again.

"You don't like golos f'I remember," Poash said. "Who for, then?"

"Her name's Amala. She likes 'em, so I've found out." Falca gave him two reives. Poash stared at the coins as if a seagull had shit his palm.

"Now there's a sight. Since when you decide to start payin'?" Poash put the coins away in his safekeep.

"Since you started putting out fruit worth buying."

"Which ain't it. Allays tole you they taste better when you pay for 'em."

"You were wrong about that," Falca said, and then grinned. "Oh, you mean your fruit?"

"Yah, like I was talkin' Galore Street, ya ditchie. But this woman a' yours; bring her by sometime. I'd like to see the mare what put a tail to your flies."

Falca had to laugh at that one. "She won't be doing that here. We're going away."

Poash turned a redbelly to hide a bruise. "Y'allays wanted to see Gebroan."

"I did. Now we're heading out to the Rough Bounds, with a Limb."

The monger snorted. "Whadda you know of the Bounds or mottles, besides fistin'em here for their scrape money?"

The phaeton rumbled past. Falca turned to see the gilded *D* carved in the middle of the door panel. *So that's who it is,* he thought, and put the fruit back on the cart. "Maybe later," he said.

"Later? You just paid for 'em."

"We have trouble."

"*We?* Uh unh. Your ruck ain't mine. You take it somewhere else."

"Sorry, Poashie. It's already here."

The phaeton had stopped again. The driver on the board reached around and tapped the curved roof of the carriage. Falca didn't see the near door swing open, but he figured a second man would be getting out on the far side, just as the first must have done down the street.

He'd used the same grift more than once and not far from here with his own deeks, Saphrax and Venar, and as Lambrey Tallon's before them, but they'd never worked out of the phaeton of a wealthy Heart Hill patroon like Havaarl Damarr.

The first man would be waiting for the second to get out. They'd close together, two halves of the vise. And there he was, in a black hawksbill cap with a pouting red feather, short sword at his side, a rock in the stream of passersby.

"Need your cart," Falca said to Poash.

"An' I'm tellin' you; not here!"

"No time to argue." He shoved the monger away, grabbed the cart's handle. Poash struck awkwardly with the cane, stinging Falca's back as he pushed the cart into the street toward the first deek. Poash cursed as fruit and flowers tumbled to the paving bricks.

People scrambled after golos, redbellies and melons, grabbing handfuls. The monger swung his cane at the worst offenders—to little effect since he was trying at the same time to redeem what he could of his business.

The hawksbill deek shouted—"Trass...now!"—but found himself blocked by all those swarming around the cart, bending over to snatch fallen fruit, pelting each other with ruined squashers.

Falca drew his falcata. The first man held a ballocks dirk in his right hand, a leather knockon flout in the other. He backed away, hoping to gain time for his companion to bull ahead through the ruck. Falca had no intention of letting that happen.

The man had no length to keep him at bay, though he favored the longer knockon with its head the size of a golo, and used that to parry the falcata to the outside—once, twice. The third time gave Falca his chance. When this Trass stopped his darting, searching glances behind him, Falca knew the man was ready to make his move.

As Trass turned, eager with the dirk, Falca pivoted away, and with the same motion swung the falcata over the man's right arm—cleaving hand from wrist. He spun, losing the caravaner's hat, ready to face the other deek, ignoring the screaming Trass who'd dropped the flout and fallen to his knees. Blood spurted from his stump. He clamped his wrist with his good hand, trying to stanch the flow. The other man was close enough to have done that for him, or grab the knockon Trass had dropped. He fled.

As Falca picked up his hat, the deek looked back one last time at his moaning companion—and toppled over a woman behind him who was bending low to pick up a twined sheaf of meadowbride. She kicked him before he scrambled to his feet and escaped, leaving the hawksbill cap he'd lost in the collision.

Falca kicked away the knockon. A young man dropped the redbellies he'd nicked, scurrying away with the greater prize of the flout. Falca plucked Trass' severed hand with the dirk and shook it off into the deek's cap.

Lord once again of what little remained on his cart, Poash shook his head in disgust at Falca—who shrugged: *what was I supposed to do?*

Trass stumbled away, his bloody stump tucked into his belly. The man had come prepared for a rap n' rip, a useful tactic on a crowded street—if you had both a deek with spine and an unsuspecting mark.

As Falca expected, the phaeton was waiting around the corner on Gullshead Lane, out of the way of those heading toward Rushes Bridge that spanned Wolf's End canal at the far end. The driver leaned against a wheel, cleaning his nails with a sliverheart.

Falca walked on and idled on the far side of a short queue of people waiting for the services of a street eddy who sat behind a makeshift stall, reading or writing for others, depending on the transaction. Falca waited to make sure Trass didn't come back to the phaeton from whence he'd emerged, to beg for help from a furious Havaarl Damarr.

He gave it a while longer, then took the opportunity of an approaching chandler's cart to move down the lane, keeping on the side opposite the phaeton, unseen by the driver. Once past the carriage he crossed the street and waited until Damarr's man finally sheathed the sliverheart.

Falca set the hawksbill cap down and strode up behind him, quickly mating the falcata to his neck. The driver reached for a larger dagger. Falca pressed his keen edge harder below the throat lump, drawing blood. "Leave it, or you're dead." The man's hand fell away. Falca took the dagger out, belted it and pulled him away from the carriage, past the pair of horses.

"See the fingers curling out of that cap over there? They belong to one of the men you've been waiting for. If you want to keep yours you'll run for the bridge ahead. No stops or shouts." The driver nodded emphatically.

Falca pushed him away. He wasn't worth killing unless he did something foolish here. Down the lane, he could scream to the High Fates for all Falca cared. The driver ran as he was told, weaving through the crowd, looking back only once.

Falca chased away two gulls eager for the prize within the hawksbill cap. A peek around the other side of the phaeton assured him that Damarr hadn't the space to fully open the carriage door to escape that way.

He suddenly thought of another way to work this, his last fist in Draica. He'd killed men for less than what Damarr had tried to do. Well, he couldn't kill this one, much as he wanted to, and the patroon's wealth and plumage wasn't the reason. Still, he might as well get a song out of the man along with the shine.

He stopped a passing cart filled to its reeking brim with brown coal, told the elder of the pair on the board that he needed a driver to take that phaeton—"see it over there?"—to Heart Hill, since the patros within had been abandoned by his own. The coaler didn't believe him; it wasn't necessary he did. The man upped his price for the services of his son. Falca threw in Trass' dagger and that, along with two reives, was enough persuasion.

Once the coaler's son had the phaeton's reins, Falca gave him another reive—"that's for you alone"—and told him to wait until given a signal. He walked to the side of the carriage, singing a tune—"Larks on the Bough"—that he and Amala heard a flinarra play in Rhysselia's Garden; a courting song though neither of them knew it at the time. He spitted Trass' hand with the driver's dagger, slid it off into his caravaner's hat and rapped twice on the phaeton's side.

From the way the inner curtain drew back, Falca knew where Damarr was sitting and kept back just enough to that side. The paned window partially slid back on its groove. Unless Damarr stuck his head out he wouldn't be able to see who it was outside.

"It's done then?" Damarr said. "Breks is dead?"

Falca offered the bloody evidence, hat and hand, in a way that blocked Damarr's view should he lean forward more to look out.

"Excellent. You've done well, Trass."

Falca soured his lips. "Cut my *sheek* he did."

"So what? I'm paying you well. Here."

Two pouches chunked against the bottom rim of the window. Falca stuffed them away.

"And that falcata—you took his sword for me, as I instructed?"

"Oh, *yesh*."

"Well, give it here," Damarr said, and wriggled his ringed fingers outside the window: three rings, speckled with gold, sapphires and rubies. Not so long ago, Falca would have lopped off the entire hand and prised the beauties later. He sighed—such a waste—and smacked the flat of the falcata on Damarr's hand with a chink of steel on rings. The man shrieked, jerking back his hand. Falca tossed Trass' through the window, a fish to the basket.

He stepped ahead so Damarr could see him, and waved to the coaler's son on the board, shouting: "Take him to Raven's Gate." The youth whooped, the phaeton lurched ahead, the clatter of hooves and wheels vying with the shouts and curses of Havaarl Damarr; a song, all of it.

✼

POASH HADN'T MUCH left to sell; then again he didn't have to, not for the rest of the year; not after what Falca gave him from one of the two pouches. "Careful," Falca said, "or your eye'll pop out."

As he walked away the monger called after: "Yer forgettin' something, bullo." He threw him a golo, which Falca caught at the knees. "Which is for the woman—if yer still going t' her."

He pocketed the golo, took the 'Roll, the falcata resting and ready on a shoulder should Trass' deek have found his belly and come back with friends to finish the ruck. But Falca was thinking not so much of that unlikely possibility as what Poash had said: *If yer still going t' her.* As if the old monger suspected that Falca might change his mind, given the weight of the gold splendents and silver lucras in the inside pocket of his tunic—more coin than he'd ever reived in any one fist.

Falca took out the golo, hefted it. A year ago he might have eaten it on his way to the quays of Catchall, to book passage for Milatum with but a third of what he'd stolen, and see for himself if that city matched the sweetness of his dreams.

He had the fancy that Poash might already have met Amala, that she once bought a golo from him on her way to or from the settlement house. Had the old monger sighed, watching her take the first few bites as she walked away? Her golden hair would have been long then, as it was when Falca first saw her very near here: possibly the one mark that would get him, finally, to Gebroan or Milatum, away from the rain and stink of Draica and the corners he could never turn without assuming someone was lying in wait for him, to keep him from ever slipping the bridle of his birthplace.

And she did, but not in the way he'd thought.

Sure, Poash had a very good point: *Whadda you know of the Bounds, or mottles besides fistin'em here for scrape money…*

Well, unless he left he'd never know if he'd amount to anything more than a Slidetown ditchlicker. Keeping his promise to Amala and a young Timberlimb named Frikko, who died in Gebroan, was the best way to find out; maybe the only way.

He put the golo away and walked quickly, as if someone—or something—was still following him. Soon he came to Furrow Street, not far from the settlement house where Amala waited for him with Gurrus.

Perhaps after the Rough Bounds they might journey on to Milatum, far to the south. But wherever they went it would not be back to Draica, even if Falca had decided to kill that wattle-throated patroon after fisting money the man paid to keep a Slidetown ditchlicker from taking his golden-haired daughter away forever.

He could have done that, all right, with Amala none the wiser. She had no idea how much he'd taken from the hidden kist in the warehouse. He was a good liar, but he had no wish to become a better one; not now, not with her. Nor did he want to forever keep the secret that he'd killed her father.

There was this as well: let Havaarl Damarr always wonder why she saw a cage in the future he'd planned for her. Let him keep a wound that would never heal: the outrage and disbelief that his only daughter wanted to leave as much as the man he tried to kill.

Chapter Two:

THE KINNET AND THE CUP OF DREAMS

A BLOCK AWAY, Falca collared a skiver in faded red livery and buckle chasers. The mildewed leather pannier strapped across his chest marked him as an errand boy for lesser merchants and burnfingers.

The messenger patted the pannier. "Easy, bullo. All I got is dockets'n waybills."

"You'll have a coin if you deliver a message to Shipshole," Falca said, using the other name for the settlement house, once a maritime guild hall.

The skiver scrunched his pocked face. "It stinks, that place."

"You want the shine or not?"

"Didn' say I wouldn' do it. Who's there?"

"Her name's Amala. Golden hair, cut short. Green eyes. Her ward's in the back, past the staircase to the gallery."

"What's to say, then?"

The skiver sighed impatiently when Falca asked him to repeat the message, then held out his hand for the coin.

"She wears a broken swan's-wing brooch," Falca said. "Bring it back to me here and you'll get your siller."

Falca watched him long enough to make sure he headed in the right direction and hadn't decided that the promise of a coin might not be worth enduring the walk past old, sick or dying Timberlimbs stretched out on pallets from one end of the hall to the other.

It was a necessary caution. Havaarl Damarr might have third slewdog who knew him by sight and was waiting by the settlement house to prevent him from seeking refuge there should he have escaped the other two. Falca didn't consider a third likely but couldn't take the chance of being seen with Amala, being followed to a hiding place and having its location reported to an angry—and humiliated—father before the moons had risen with the night.

He didn't have to wait long for the skiver's return. The exchange was made, reive for brooch. Before he left, the messenger said: "If she was *my* ringaround, I'd buy her better, if'er husband won't. That one's worth it."

And he'd be wasting his money. There was nothing in the Six Kingdoms that Amala would prefer over that broken swan's-wing brooch, not even Cassena's Nimbus, one of Roak's legendary gifts to his children. Falca pocketed her keepsake and crossed Furrow Street, to Piper's Alley, the shortest way to Ringwater Square.

The Timberlimbs made baubles like Amala's brooch from eloe hair, stiffening the thin weave with blood and Roak-knows what else, and then deftly painting them colorfully. A sharpened eloe claw served as the pin. They cost less than what Falca had given the skiver.

But Amala's brooch had been one of the gifts offered by Limbs who gathered, day after day, outside the gate to the Damarrs' Heart Hill residence, while inside the manse she lived as an empty, her soul lifted by Saphrax after he found his calling as an acolyte of Maradus and his cult of the Crucible.

Falca hadn't been there for the Limbs' vigil; he'd been in Gebroan, where Saphrax had taken the crystal mace that held Amala's soul, trying to recover the mace before it was added to the Crucible of Souls. Only later did Ellele, the woman hired by Havaarl and Serisa Damarr to care for their daughter, tell Amala and Falca the story of the swan's-wing brooch.

The father, angry at the reek and incessant keening of the Limbs outside his gate, had ordered the gifts trashed, but Ellele had saved one. She gave it to Amala, a play-thing for her hands. With an empty's constant hunger, Amala had immediately tried to eat the brooch, but Ellele snatched it from her after the first bite. The day after Falca returned with the mace and restored Amala's soul to her body, Ellele gave her the bitten swan's-wing as a parting gift. She'd worn it ever since.

Falca told her of how close she had come to remaining an empty for the rest of her life. A Timberlimb named Freaca had saved his life in Gebroan and thus Amala's by sacrificing her own at the Crucible.

Freaca—Frikko he called her—had journeyed west, far from her home in the Rough Bounds, with little else but innocence and a belief that she might find help in stemming the Wardens' destruction of her homeland. Amala and Falca were determined now to go there, to find her kin with the help of Gurrus, the old Limb priest who once knew her, and tell them of her heroism—if any still lived.

Falca had no intention of letting Havaarl Damarr prevent him from keeping that promise.

THE LAUGHING LOUT, locally known as a gathering place for Myrcian exiles and traders, fronted the eastern edge of Ringwater Square and Sciamachon's Fountain. Falca had never stayed in any of the rooms above the tavern. He'd been there often enough in the past, however; not so much for the ghorgen aulosts, but to hear stories of places he might never see. His last visit was a particularly eventful occasion, resulting in Falca being able to do much more with the exquisite falcata Amala had given him than admire its beauty.

He could have met Amala and Gurrus at the fountain, yet with the waning day they needed a place to stay for the night, where her by now smoldering father could not find them. The Lout had the advantage of being near Roak's Gate and the King's Way—the only road to Bastia, the city closest to the ever-expanding Banishlands bordering the Rough Bounds.

Falca stood by the fountain's rim. Two lovers waded in the water, hand in hand, mimicking the tiered dawnstone sculptures of young men and women descending through the *shusshing* cascade. No doubt the pair had the legend in mind: twice wade for the birth of girl; thrice for a boy. Closest to Falca, children played at boats in the calmer water.

Soon after the lovers left, happily drenched, he saw Amala arrive in front of the tavern. Gurrus sat next to her on the board of the jaunting cart. For a moment Falca felt as if he was seeing her for the first time. She was like an extra hour to all the days of summer and it wasn't enough to assume she knew that by now. The words were hard to come by but he'd find them, most likely when he wasn't trying. Maybe that, too, was a reason for leaving Draica—and not by sea.

He didn't shout or wave in acknowledgment as she paused to look around for him. She drove on, turning a corner, to presumably search for the tavern's stables off a back alley.

He kept watch on the Lout while they were gone, waiting by copperleaf trees at the corner of the square, and longer still after he saw them return.

Amala's right hand was lost in the folds of her black duvelin, close to the dagger she always kept hidden within.

He left the trees when he was satisfied neither he nor they had been followed. Gurrus saw him first, tugged at Amala's sleeve and pointed at Falca. Her hand slid away from the dagger.

It had only been two days since last they'd met yet it seemed like a month to him.

"Kushla," he said, embracing her tightly. The settlement house Limbs called her kushla—sun-thicket—as well, but they stopped after Falca adopted the endearment.

Gurrus looked away as he kissed her. Limbs were uncomfortable with this sort of intimacy in public, not that they used their lips in private, either; they preferred kellowing, a rubbing of wrists that released musks of varying degrees of fragrance depending on the moment and the partner.

Falca offered him the traditional Limb greeting: "Many breaths."

Gurrus smiled, nodding in return, appreciating Falca's effort in Tongue, though it was closer to "your feet stink." He responded in Arriostan, which he spoke well, thanks to Amala: "Yours are mine."

She squeezed Falca's hand. "So…?"

"Tell you inside."

"I have something for you as well, kahyeh."

That was her endearment for him in Tongue: my heart.

They crossed under the Lout's sign, whose top edge was frosted with the leavings of Draica's famously plump gulls and spanners.

THEY GOT THE last available room on the third floor, which would at least mute the piercing elations of the bloodsnare's pale ghorgen who was setting up for the evening's aulost in front of empty ale casks stacked high by the front windows, a customary precaution for the later hours when patrons, bored with conversation and games of three-star, got rowdy.

Falca had to pay extra for Gurrus, and to stable the horse and cart, but the flap-eared proprietor included a flagon of leg-up, some bread and redrind cheese with the price of the room. The stairwell was poorly illuminated: two of the three lunelings hanging from wallspits were dead.

A musty smell pervaded the tiny room whose ceiling Falca could touch without fully stretching his arm. For the money they got a single luneling with the usual soiled nightcloth to hang over the spit; a sleeping pallet on uneven floorboards; a pisspot or washbowl—he didn't know which—atop a three-legged stool; and a small table that leaned off-kilter by the window. The room did, however, offer a useful view of the square and the nearby fountain.

As Amala latched the door, Falca opened the window to get a better look at the square, just in case.

"Thank you, that is better," Gurrus said, assuming the room's smell was as offensive to Falca as it was to him. There was no one out there loitering suspiciously, only people filling jugs or pots with water at the fountain, and the children still playing with their tiny boats.

Falca slung off the falcata scabbard, emptied his pockets on the table.

From the pile Amala plucked her brooch, snagged it back on.

"That skiver thought you were my ringaround," Falca said.

"Did he now?"

"He couldn't believe I hadn't bought something better to please you and shame your husband."

"Oh, *him*...that poor, unfortunate man. If only his cudgie matched this endowment." She hefted one of the chunkier pouches, let it drop with a thunk. "But you now...*you*...If I'd known you had all *this* stashed away, well, I might insist on something better."

Falca nudged his safekeep. "This is mine, clippings to nails."

"The others?"

"From your father."

"*My father?*"

By the time he finished telling her all, Amala had shifted past the twilight shadows of the room to the window. Falca settled in on the pallet, knees up, back against the wall. Gurrus scratched his belly, as if the crawlies in the room had already found him.

"If he had hurt you..." Amala said.

The whisper had an edge to it, something Falca could almost feel rather than hear. He'd heard that edge their first night together, when he realized he'd been the mark, not her.

Amala picked up the golo, turning it over.

"That's for you," Falca said.

"My father's lucky you didn't kill him," Amala said, putting the golo down. "He'll try again."

"I expect he will. The question is how many more slewdogs he'll send after us; he knows we're for the Bounds."

Gurrus plucked the golo from the table, filling the ensuing silence. "I have heard these…golos are now grown in orchards where once there were villages high in the trees of Kelvarra," he said, giving the Limb name for the Rough Bounds. "Klesket villages, some Kaikurra—do you mind, Amala?'

"I'm not hungry."

"Falca?"

"It's all yours."

Gurrus tossed the golo out the window.

Amala sighed. "The one named Trass was a friend of my brother's. That's what this is about, too. I should have known my father wouldn't believe you didn't kill Alatheus in Gebroan. I never should have suggested that dinner when I told my parents about our leaving for the Bounds—all of it."

"We were hoping for the best," Falca said. "That's no more a coddle than assuming the worst."

"Perhaps it was…the lifting…and I forgot just what a wankspit my father is."

Falca smiled, for a moment wishing the man himself was listening at the door, and certainly blaming Falca for teaching Amala a word crude enough to shock her mother. He'd be wrong.

"If so, you didn't forget for long," Falca said. "That's why you told him later you'd come to your senses, sent me back to where I belonged…where I wanted to go before we met. We thought surely he'd believe that."

"Well, he didn't."

"It's done, but I should have been more careful going to the settlement house to see you. Your father must have posted a watcher near there with me in mind, or maybe he was concerned for your safety going to and from Heart Hill—it amounts to the same thing. His suspicions were confirmed."

"So we let him keep them."

"Keep something he already has? I'm not following you."

"That's because I just thought of the idea. Why not let him believe what he always has about you, that his opinion of you—and my brother's before—has been proven in a way that not even I can doubt: you took his money. And you didn't show up at the settlement house and I…hmmm…I was frantic to find you but couldn't and must now face the certainty that you sailed into the sunset, with a spanner's wing for a smile as you watched the towers of Cross Keys fade in the distance beyond the stern of a galliot bound for Milatum, with more than enough left of the money to—I don't know—do whatever it was you were going to do there."

Falca held up a hand. "I don't like this at all."

"Oh, but *he* will. The way to make him believe is for me to go home, lock myself in my room for a week, furious at him for bribing you to leave, and just as angry at you for taking it. He'll turn from my door very satisfied. Better to let me think it was boot-money not blood."

"What about Gurrus and I?"

Amala shrugged. "You wait a few days, time enough for my father to recall the men—more than two this time, I'd wager—that he's hired to watch the road. With me at home, why would he keep bearing the expense? I know him. There's a reason why he's one of the wealthiest men in Draica and it's not just because of my mother's family."

"Then what?"

"You and Gurrus take the cart to Virenz and wait for me there."

Falca remained skeptical. "Even to Virenz the road isn't safe."

"No less so than from Virenz eastward. And the stages carry guards. I'll slip out of the house before dawn, take the first of the day. By the time my father and mother realize I've gone, I'll be halfway to you both."

Falca couldn't talk her out of it, and perhaps he didn't try as hard as he could have because it made sense the more he thought about it: playing to the holes in her father's heart. Still, he felt uneasy about the plan.

"You said you had something important to tell me?"

"I do. After I saw you last, Gurrus had a kesslakor."

Falca rubbed the scar on his jawline. "Which means?"

"Something like 'between the mist'—or fog."

"There's naught between a fog except maybe a path through it," he said.

"Just so," Gurrus said. "A kesslakor is a kind of path."

"Which I'm no farther down. Maybe there's a fog between my ears."

"It's a vision," Amala said.

"Oh, one of those," Falca repeated, suddenly wanting something in his hands. He found it, along with the whetstone in the small pouch he'd sewn onto the falcata's scabbard.

"Why do you remove your sword at the mention of this?" Gurrus asked.

"To sharpen it; a habit, nothing more," Falca said. "As yours is to conjure visions, with sweethand or scrape to put the keener edge on them—so I've heard."

"We mehkas use those, yes. But this time I had no sweethand or even krael to part the mist. This kesslakor was the most powerful and vivid one I have ever had, before or after I was taken from Kelvarra by the shitcatchers to the dunghill of Bastia and then to this bigger one."

Falca rasped the stone along the falcata's edge as the ghorgen's aulost began below, muted but still piercing.

"I never heard of this…krael either, unless you mean the coin. It sounds…useful," he said, glancing at Amala. "Better than sweethand?"

She matched his furtive smile. Their first night together she'd given him sweethand, which Limbs said puts eyes in your hands.

"It is nothing," Gurrus said. "Merely something mehkas use when the need arises."

Falca kept sharpening. "So this…kesslakor…this vision?

"I saw a great victory. Not the story of a mere ambush of Warden shitcatchers that our soldiers later embellish in the village hovens. I saw thousands of Kelvoi killing Wardens by a wide bend in a river, near a stone palisade bigger than the one here, the Cross Keys bastion of your child-king. I was told that to make this victory come to pass, an artifact sacred to the Kelvoi—a kinnet—must be brought to the Isle of Lake Shallan, deep within Kelvarra, territory which the Wardens have yet to despoil. The kesslakor was no dream."

"Vision or dream," Falca said, "what's the difference?"

"There is one. The voice that spoke to me was my father's, though he chose Sky many years ago."

"Sky?"

"If one is fortunate to reach elder years," Gurrus explained, "he or she chooses Sky or Water as a way to end the life. It is a much anticipated and longed for ritual."

"I heard the voice of my own dead father once, in Gebroan—at least I think he's dead," Falca said. "But yours…where did he say you—we—are supposed to get this kinnet?"

"He did not say because he knows."

"Gurrus, you…ah…you need to spoon more of the meat from the stew here," Falca said.

Gurrus squinted at Amala, rubbing his silvery shoulder flange. "What does that…"

"Em, it means Falca doesn't understand," she said.

"I have the kinnet," Gurrus said.

"Where?" Falca asked. "The settlement house, the cart? There's nothing in this room."

Gurrus stood and loosened his belt, took off his loose shirt and unwrapped a cloth from around his scrawny belly. Something fell out, a tapping on the floor. He quickly retrieved what looked like a bit of food and put it away in a pocket. Holding the cloth high over his head, the kinnet still lay in a few folds at his feet. Falca could have spanned its width with one hand.

"It's a blanket," he said. "And it doesn't look like it could keep anyone warm."

"It may look like a blanket but it's not," Amala said, taking the kinnet from Gurrus and passing it on to Falca. "It's not woven."

He rubbed an edge. The kinnet had the feel of the supplest leather; dense yet thin as whisp. And moist. Gurrus' sweat? He didn't smell the Limb's musk, so where did the moisture come from? Falca handed the kinnet back to Amala.

"It is but one segment of many, twenty-two, to be exact," Gurrus said. "Each part of the Tapestry—the Keta—is called a kinnet."

"A tapestry? Gurrus…are your eyes so different from mine? There's no coloring, no stitching of events or words."

"Yet they are there," Gurrus said. "I saw the Tapestry myself, though only once, when I journeyed to Shallan with my father who was a mehka before me. Those of the Kalalek clan there who guard the lake and Isle reveal the Keta only for certain rituals and then only briefly."

"So…what does this Tapestry show?"

Gurrus shook his head.

Falca frowned. "You said you saw it."

"I saw the Keta, not what is on it."

"Then how in Roak's name can you be certain there's something on it?"

"I know, Falca. You wish me to—what was it?—spoon the meat for the stew? All I can say is that I know the Kalaleks are lying when they say the Keta is a record of our history, in words and depictions; that they made it themselves."

"If that's the case," Falca said, "why wouldn't they show what the Tapestry reveals, however that's done."

"For the same reason the most wealthy among you do not readily dispense their riches; they would not be so powerful if they did."

"True enough. But still, you must have wondered what's on the Tapestry, what these Kalaleks don't want anyone to see."

Gurrus smiled. "Yes, I have wondered about that."

"So…no one but these Kalalek liars have ever seen it, yet it's important to return this kinnet to make the Tapestry whole again. Hmmm…" Falca looked at Amala. "I need help here. What am I missing?"

"Nothing more than most of us," she said softly. "Why do so many revere the Erseiyr, a creature few have ever seen, at least in the skies above Lucidor. Why do so many of us want to believe in something that cannot be seen, touched or heard?"

The only answer Falca had to that was the falcata's sharpness. *That* could be seen and touched. And heard. He drew the whetstone over the edge.

The kinnet still seemed to him something that could be mistaken for a stable blanket. He had one more question for Gurrus: "If this kinnet is part of the Tapestry, how did you come to have it?"

"I should not have the kinnet, but I do. What is important now is that it must be returned, the Tapestry made whole again, if the kesslakor is to be fulfilled. It does not matter if you remain unconvinced about what someone saw within himself, and the importance of what he would return to where it belongs. You go with love and a debt to Freaca, to a place where you and Amala would likely die without my help.

"I will need yours. What is more foolish than an old mehka who thinks he might return alone on that road, through all the Warden shitcatchers who first brought me and so many other Kelvoi here to rebuild the canals and that Colossus damaged in the last of your wars."

Amala handed the kinnet to Falca.

"What am I to do with this?" he said.

He was about to give it to Gurrus, to wrap around himself as before, but Amala touched his arm. "Why don't you stretch it out widely and"—she leaned forward to whisper in his ear—"grip it tightly as you do—well, you know, kahyeh."

"Amala…it's all right. If Gurrus must return a blanket, we'll do that. We're for the Bounds, anyway."

"Please. You must see this."

She picked up his falcata from the floor. "There is no edge finer than this in all of Draica. If there was it would have found you long ago, and we'd never have met that day." She angled the falcata over her thumb, a mere twitch, but enough to draw a bead of blood.

"You've made your point."

"Not yet I haven't." She sucked on her thumb. "Stretch it tighter. Shoulder's width—that's right. Ready?"

Falca kept his head back as she swung the falcata down on the kinnet with both hands. The kinnet dipped slightly in the middle—he felt the force of her strike as his hands jerked inward.

He couldn't believe his eyes.

There was no cut."

"A poor attempt," Amala said. "The ceiling is too low for a proper cleave."

"No, you struck well. There should be two blankets now, not the one."

Amala dropped the sword on the pallet and took the kinnet from him, folded it once, twice, then again. "You try now," she said, slid out her quillons dagger at her belt and handed it to Falca. "Give it your best stab. Here." She pointed at the center of the folded kinnet she held over her belly.

"Oh, no," he said.

"Don't worry. You won't ruin me for the children we shall have someday."

"I won't do it." He threw the knife at the door, where it stuck.

Amala walked over and yanked the dagger free. "Then I will," she said.

Falca vised her hands. "No more."

"The floor then," she said, and put the kinnet down by the corner of the pallet.

"All right, to end this."

He and her father had given her daggers after the lifting, but she had since carried only the one he gave her. He took it now and kneeled down. He put his thumb over the end of the hilt and stabbed with enough force to pierce the lamellar armor of a Warden's ruerain or finest chainmail—and certainly the floorboard underneath.

Amala knelt by him, brooch in hand, and slid the thin, unbroken wing between the dagger's point and the kinnet. She took the dagger from his hand, gave him the brooch, and struck again. She leaned over, the dagger an awl now, and when she nodded at Falca he passed the swan's-wing under the dagger's tip as she had before.

She sheathed the blade, plucked the brooch from the kinnet where he'd dropped it and pinned it back on the linsey cloth of her duvelin. Falca grazed his hand over the kinnet, feeling her breath and the kiss she gave him but no puncture in Gurrus' kinnet.

HE COULDN'T SLIP over though Amala and Gurrus had, hours before. He rose from his side, sat on the edge of the pallet, elbows on knees, heels nudging the falcata tucked close in on the floor. Amala didn't stir, not even when he turned to caress her thigh. This was a change, too. Before the lifting she'd been almost as light a sleeper as he. Now, she slept heavily though her breathing was as soft a sound as the distant rustling of the fountain's falling water.

Maybe his restlessness came from the moons or the fountain's dawnstone sculptures, from the light that sifted too generously through the window that Gurrus insisted they leave open because he needed better air to mask the stink of the seed and soil of all the others who had stayed in the room before.

But Falca knew his trouble sleeping had a different source: what Amala had wanted him to do. Stabbing her in the belly, with the kinnet her only protection? *Don't worry. You won't ruin me for the children we shall have someday...*

Was this edge to her merely a keener one he hadn't seen yet, or a consequence of the lifting, like her lapses in memory? And then there was her plan: reasonable enough, but if they separated now they might never see each other again. Havaarl Damarr saw her as the most prized jewel in his hoard and thus one to retrieve at all costs. He was the kind of father who regarded his daughter's right to her own life as a theft from his own.

Still, sweet sleep had always been a dice roll for Falca. For a while when he was a boy, his mother and father had solved the problem by putting a cup by his pallet—thinner than this one—that he shared with his brother Ferrex who never had a problem slipping over.

The cup had a crack which made it useless for drink, but his mother, Ephea, told him it was good enough to hold a night's worth of dreams, the best sleep coming when you dreamed.

Usually his mother, a fierce woman from the Isles of Sleat, had little patience for nonsense. So that was why Falca, just shy of eight years old, believed her when she told him he would find his dreams out there, though all he saw beyond the window of the room was the Corry Roads—the junction of the locally-used

Stemon's Canal and Motessin's Moat that cut through the heart of Lucidor. Long into the night came the shouts and curses of the Moat's canalers loading or unloading their corries' freight.

You'll be fine with somethin' tucked close, Falca, to hold your dreams…

Every night either she or her husband, Barla, would make a brief show of dipping the cup in the open window and sometimes pretend to sip a measure for themselves. Ferrex didn't need help to sleep, but he wanted his own cup. Falca didn't mind that the one they gave him wasn't cracked.

Ferrex was dead now and with him the cup he'd used to beg in his usual spot on Furrow Street, holding it in the stumps of his wrists. Falca's cup was long gone, too. He'd smashed it to pieces only months after his father disappeared and a day after his mother evidently fell, jostled by a passing phaeton off the crowded Rushes Bridge, the highest in Draica.

He would never believe she'd jumped, taken her life, abandoning her sons, doing what her husband may have done even though she'd been sick the day before, coughing up what looked like blood to Falca. She said it was only beets in the cush they had for dinner.

He was surprised that the kinnet still lay folded where Amala had left it on the small table by the window. He'd heard Gurrus moving around earlier and assumed the old Limb had wrapped it around himself. Had he left it out so Falca could further ponder its mystery, as if Amala's unsettling demonstration hadn't been enough proof of its remarkable properties?

Whatever it was, Falca intended now to hang it from the bent rod above the window that probably hadn't borne a curtain in years. As he unfolded the kinnet his wonder came with a price: if Wardens in Bastia discovered this…stable blanket that weighed little more than a similar length of whisp yet could blunt a dagger strike, they would be very eager to find out where there was more.

Before he slung the kinnet over the rod he noticed something on the rim of the fountain. Though his nighteyes were good he couldn't discern what it was—but he had a good idea.

The kinnet was no blanket but it could hang like one and helped block some of the light coming into the room. That wasn't the only reason why Falca soon felt the pull of drowsiness not long after he lay down on the pallet next to Amala. It was what he'd seen left on the fountain rim, something that worked as well now as the cup of dreams his mother and father always left by his pallet long ago.

The burr he'd had about Amala's plan had vanished. He was sure she'd see the lean to the idea he'd suggest in the morning because it would let them all leave Draica together, without a scent for more of Havaarl Damarr's hired slewdogs and streetbusters to follow.

Chapter Three:

THE SHADDEN

HAVAARL DAMARR LOOKED out the alcove windows of his second-floor muselair, thinking that if he were twenty years younger he'd go after Falca Breks and kill him—instead of having a shadden do it for him.

It wasn't so much the money he'd save, which was considerable, though he could easily afford the expense of a shadden. Nothing could equal the pleasure of personally taking the crouchalley's life as Breks had taken that of Damarr's only son in Sandsend—never mind Amala insisted he hadn't killed Alatheus. Who could believe her? She hadn't been there; she'd been *here*, at the family's Heart Hill manse, an empty, to use that crude term, her soul lifted by an acolyte of that accursed Gebroanan cult.

Serisa called it a sickness then, yet it was nothing like the illnesses—feigned or not—that now kept Damarr's wife in her rooms so much that a day could pass without his seeing her.

Amala was cured, evidently by Falca Breks. But who had originally been to blame? The same man who had known the acolyte and was taking her away to the Rough Bounds to supposedly help the mottles; in effect emptying her again of a proper life. The gutterwipe who grew up by the quays and canals of Draica, stealing from his betters in good neighborhoods and bad, extorting scrape money from Timberlimb refugees, now wanted to help those worthless creatures in their forest wilderness homeland? What rot!

Damarr had four more men watching for them but still they'd slipped away days before, with Breks no doubt plumping the idea of stealing Damarr's favorite horse from the stable behind the manse *and* his beloved jaunting cart, a wedding gift from his old comrades. Either that or Serisa had secretly paid someone to get rid of the cart, as she'd long complained he preferred its ride over hers.

Roak's balls! If he had those twenty years back again he'd kill the ditchlicker for that outrageous theft by the 'Roll alone.

As much as his gold Havaarl Damarr hoarded memories of his exploits commanding the Draican Greys. To be sure, most of his men hadn't been much better than hazels pressed or levied for the fyrd, but there had been older Wardens among the Greys' officers, who'd known Alatheus from his brief service with the Wardens in Bastia. And plague take those fleaks who whispered behind his back that his greatest achievement had been to marry the third and last daughter of a prominent Draican family, one of the First Twelve.

Yet the fact remained that what he had now was wealth, not quickness of foot or sword-hand. Since Breks had escaped with his daughter there was only one solution: a shadden, someone named Stakeen who would be arriving very soon, when Erisa's Campanile sounded the noon hour.

An old comrade, Bokan Shull, to whom Damarr had gone discreetly, arranged the meeting. "It will cost you," he'd said. "If you want the best, that is."

"Of course I do. This is my daughter's future." Damarr knew Shull had his own daughter whose prospects were such he'd probably pay to have her taken off his hands, hence the sly thrust at Damarr's well-known miserliness.

Citing confidentiality, Shull refused to give more details, only that this particular shadden came highly recommended by another friend who'd used Stakeen for an especially sensitive matter involving someone in the upper echelons of Cross Keys. Shull knew these things, which played no small part in the success of his business of provisioning—fleecing was more like it—the commissary of the royal fyrd.

Havaarl Damarr, however, was a man who had to see for himself where his money was going. So through another contact—the proprietor of an exclusive Falconwrist bloodsnare den—he arranged for the services of a quay-stomper named Tarx who had reputedly never lost in a hundred Catchall prize fights.

And there he was now, striding quickly for a dock-heave his size across the greensward opposite the Damarr manse. Another man, not that much smaller than Tarx, seemed to be trailing him. Both stopped together at the oval fountain within the green, where the golden-haired Damarr twins once played.

He usually kept the muselair's quarrel windows closed because the air in Draica could be foul even on Heart Hill in late spring. But he dropped the window latch now, pushed open the nearer half to better view the fountain.

They were together all right. Tarx stood, arms crossed, the fighter waiting for the bell to ring, which would indeed be the case. The second man had sat down on the fountain rim, fidgeting with his skimmer cap, until Tarx cuffed the back of his head to get him off. The ganger tightened his wrist leathers, crossed his arms again, oblivious to others nearby, including children playing a game of tail-the-robie, and a woman feeding gulls and red-tipped spanners from her hand.

Two for the price of one? If Tarx wanted a deek for this, so be it. Nothing had changed except the odds for the shadden.

Tarx was supposed to wait by the fountain until Damarr had concluded his business, then attack the shadden as he left with the payment of gold. Damarr hadn't met the shadden to discuss the disbursement, but he should have no problem with it: one-quarter now; another upon the safe return of his daughter along with the Breks' severed hand and his falcata; and the remaining half when Amala confirmed to her father that no one, Stakeen or anyone else, had violated her on the journey back, which would be insult to the injury of what Breks had already done.

The ganger's payment would be that initial payment plus whatever else of value the shadden might be carrying. Though not as expensive as a shadden's full price the sum was dear, probably what Tarx could make in a dozen fights, yet well worth it for Damarr to know if the shadden's skill was not as promised.

The arrangement was more than enough incentive for Tarx to perform well, and undoubtedly the reason he felt he could afford the deek. A mere beating would not do; he was to kill the shadden. Otherwise, there could be repercussions for Damarr. There would be none if the shadden killed Tarx, of course.

He left the window to get the gold coins from the chinkwell underneath the fifth floorboard behind the large escribore where his children had often done their lessons with the squint-eyed Keshkan tutor. Serisa had chosen him but Damarr could hardly understand the man given his quick, lilting accent. But he'd been Amala's favorite of all the tutors they'd employed, perhaps because he filled her head more with the wonders of Milatum than sums, spelling and recitation. Damarr should have dismissed him sooner than he did.

He had his own burlbright gallery-desk where he managed the household accounts and corresponded with his two mistresses in Slacere and Virenz, keeping their existence as discreetly as he did his ledgers meticulous. He figured five gold roaks for the shadden's first quarter but took out enough silver for what he needed for the den tonight as well as a gift for Elua, who would be arriving tomorrow from Slacere to stay for a week at an apartment in Falconwrist he kept solely for his dalliances. She had more expensive tastes than his other mistress, but also a better gift for flattery; a skill she supposedly learned, among others, at a school for heteras in Sandsend.

He finished counting the money and hefted the shadden's pouch. Then he heard, distantly, the chiming of Erisa's Campanile. He sat at the desk, dropping the pouch to the floor—a tinkling *thunk*. No sense in showing it until the concluding moment. On his desk next to the stack of ledgers and inkwell were the strutter and flowers that Lannid Hoster had brought as gifts for Alatheus and Amala the day before. Recently graduated from the renowned military academy at Skene and summoned to Bastia by his father, the Warden Allarch, Lannid had not known Alatheus was dead.

The sweet Gebroanan leg-up he'd brought as a gift for Damarr and his wife had been consumed during his unexpected visit, mostly by Serisa, who was now in her rooms at the far end of the hall. Damarr didn't expect her to emerge until the dinner hour.

If he hadn't been waiting for the knock at the muselair door he might not have heard it.

"Yes?"

The servant, Cerrux—a timid replacement for Sippio who had died with Alatheus in Gebroan—entered, knuckling his brow. "A Shar Stakeen is here to see you, patros."

"Very well," Damarr said, dismissing him with a flick of his hand.

He positioned himself to the side of the wishbone chair behind the desk and turned to the window one last time to make sure Tarx had left the greensward and was ready to intercept the shadden on the street when the time came. He had, but the ganger seemed confused, looking to his right, then left. At his side, the deek's arms were raised, palms up, as if feeling for rain that wasn't falling.

Damarr heard the door close behind him, turned and sighed impatiently. He'd specifically told Cerrux he had a very important meeting at the hour.

"Excuse me," he said, "but I'm expecting someone else momentarily. My servant will arrange a more convenient appointment."

"I believe we already have one, citizen Damarr."

She was the woman who'd been feeding spanners at the fountain. She looked behind her and thus didn't see his flush of anger.

This one's the shadden? he thought. A waste of time and money—and more expense since he most certainly would pay the ganger to teach a lesson to Bokan Shull, who no doubt had already shared this comedy with Cross Keys courtiers at the Grotto Garden.

She was tall, wore high, tight-laced chasers he'd never seen a woman wear before. Her black hair fell only to the neck of the russet spring cape. The cut-off blue tunic was unadorned except for an embroidered sunburst above the crossed leather straps that held two daggers in their sleeves. He saw no scars on her face or the bare, sinewy arms, which only made him more disgusted. Besides the daggers the only hint of utility about her was ring-less fingers.

The woman had obviously been born to better sun that Draica's—her complexion had nothing of northern paleness. A purlie bower indeed, if you liked dark eyes and brows to match but…a shadden? Beauty wasn't going to kill Falca Breks.

"Is something wrong?" she asked.

Wrong? he thought. *Besides the fact that Bokan Shull claims the best shadden in Draica feeds birds by hand and is almost as young as Amala.*

Damarr cleared his throat. "You're not what I expected."

She smiled. "Perhaps that's one reason why I was referred to you."

"Indeed." He brusquely gestured for her to sit.

"I prefer to stand."

"As will I—this shouldn't take long."

"A brief matter, then, that requires my services?"

"The matter is straightforward enough." He told her what it was, and about what he knew of Breks from his informers.

"So you say this Falca Breks has been tutored by Starris Vael?"

"For three months, evidently payment for a debt incurred in a brawl at a tavern frequented by Myrcian traders and exiles. The instruction began soon after my daughter gave Breks a very expensive falcata."

"That's quite remarkable," she said. "Not the short time; the instructor. He must be getting on in years, but he is the famously wayward son of Dalkan Vael. I'd be curious to hear how Breks persuaded the son of a Myrcian Sanctor to teach him the falcata. That's not a blade for spindle-wrists. Perhaps you know."

"I don't; I never heard of either of them and I don't care who…"

"You should, if the son is half-again as skilled as the father. Dalkan Vael was reputedly the best bladesman in Myrcia's Garda at the time of the Skarrian invasion, before his unlikely ascension to the Cascade Throne."

Damarr knew what she was plumping: the more difficult the task, the greater the fee. "You seem easily impressed for a shadden."

Stakeen shrugged. "Your daughter's…unfortunate choice may have moved up from fists, dirks and sliverhearts, and developed a liking for a longer length, but the edge can only follow the hand and eye. Those are not so easily whetted in three months."

She stepped close enough to the desk to brush her long fingers over the flowers.

"Your daughter like flowers?"

"What has that to do with killing Falca Breks and bringing her back?"

"Nothing regarding him, but I have to return with her. It would be useful to know some things about her," she said, rearranging the flowers. "That's better. Harlequin roses and sunsbreath are my favorites as well. "

"They were a gift to her from a possible suitor."

"Expensive. As is the price to bring her back for him."

"And that would be?"

"Sixty gold roaks."

Damarr felt the sudden pulsing of a vein in his forehead. "You must be joking! That is…quite unacceptable. I could hire twenty men for that price."

"The price is firm. It's unfortunate you didn't inquire about my services earlier while Breks was here and thus spare yourself the expense of my pursuit and the return."

He stared at her, on the verge of dismissing her and immediately going out to hire ten men for half her price. Ten should be able to take Breks and his three months of lessons with some aging Myrcian bladesman.

He got up to face the window, giving her his back. The outrageous price was almost as much of an affront as what Breks did to him by the 'Roll.

Then again…

Would it be worth an expensive afternoon's entertainment to see from his window this arrogant young woman spill her blood on the paving bricks? Possibly. And so much the better that she was probably Myrcian given the slower cadence to her speech and what she knew about the family Vael.

"Very well," he said. "Sixty."

"You understand this requires more than the removal of your daughter's lover."

The woman might as well have stabbed him with the strutter Lannid Hoster forgot to take with him. "Lover? There's no possible sentiment that can be attached to Breks. He's a ditchlicking muckleshoot who…"

"Abductor, then. Regardless, I'll be bringing back a distraught young woman and as these things go, quite possibly against her will. I might need to…soothe her."

Damarr frowned. "Soothe my daughter?"

"With certain remedies familiar to shaddens. They'll not harm her but should make the return easier and quicker. I assume that's acceptable to you."

"As long as she's not harmed in any way."

"Of course. Now, I'll need you to describe your daughter and Breks."

She listened as Damarr did so, then smiled. "That will do." She plucked the strutter from the desk and ran the length of it through her fingers. "Another gift? For your son, perhaps?"

"It was supposed to be. He's dead."

"My condolences." She tapped the bronze-tipped point on the floor, then put the strutter back on his desk though not where she'd found it, to Damarr's annoyance.

"One more matter," he said, moving the cane to where it had been. "The strutter and the flowers were gifts from Lannid Hoster, the youngest son of the Warden Allarch in Bastia. He may complicate your efforts at some point. Do not harm him or there could be consequences for me here. Is that clear?"

"It might be if you explain."

He did so, though it irked him to have to recount the details of his wife's meddling—innocent meddling since she was unaware of the shadden but a bother nonetheless. Serisa was no judge of men—and that had to include Damarr himself since her choice of husbands had been her father's, not hers. She'd asked Lannid Hoster to do what he could to bring Amala back, and he accepted the request without hesitation. In Damarr's estimation, Maldan Hoster, who would be escorting his younger brother to Bastia evidently, was a better fit for Amala and with the same pedigree.

Stakeen said: "This Lannid should not present a problem if he's as awkward as you say he is. No doubt he'll be occupied by his duties in Bastia, which is where I should be able to recover your daughter, if not before. Now, I don't believe we've discussed the payment arrangements."

He told her. "I assume this is acceptable to you."

"It's not. I require half now."

"*What?*"

"And the other half when I bring Amala back with the hand of Breks—you want the sword hand, of course."

"Sixty is outrageous enough—you push this too far," Damarr said. "We're done here. I'll make other arrangements. You may go."

The shadden smiled. "You think you're going to lose the clinkers?"

"What are you talking about?"

"Your men out there. You wouldn't be the first to test a shadden though it rarely happens to my male brethren. I've taken that into account in the price and its parceling. If you're unhappy with my requirements perhaps you'd prefer to put your daughter's fate in the hands of Lannid Hoster."

"I have other business with those men out there."

"If ours is finished, as you say, why not summon them to begin the other now? There's room enough in the hall below for us all to pass with pleasantries."

He glanced back at the window. There they were, a few steps away from the gate of the manse, waiting. Stakeen went on, talking to his back. "It's up to you, citizen Damarr. I can leave empty-handed, of course. I'll still have to kill your men out there though you surely wouldn't object to that. But I'll spread the word about you to the better of our ilk. You might employ a lesser shadden for a more agreeable price—and less certainty of your daughter's return. However, the longer she's with her lover—excuse me, her abductor—the greater the chance for unfortunate events to occur, such as a plumper belly, or temptation for those twenty men you'd send to bring back your daughter."

Damarr whirled to face her. "*Enough!*" He snatched up the pouch of gold from the floor, added more from a desk drawer and his pocket—all he had without going to the chinkwell, and he wasn't going to do that. He dropped the pouch with a loud chunk on the desk. "There's twenty-eight in there."

"Not the half, but I'm not unreasonable, and these are my favorites." She took the pouch, then plucked a harlequin rose from the vase, sliding the stem—thorns and all—underneath a leather strap. "Consider consoling yourself with the thought that necessary decisions can only be the wisest ones."

"I'm not paying you for your thoughts. Now get out and bring me the hand of Falca Breks, his sword and my daughter." He gave her his back again, hearing only the faintest tapping of her bootheels and the soft clutch of the closing door. He pushed the window all the way open, the better to see how quickly Tarx would become the richest dock-heave in Catch-All—at least for the month it would take him to gamble, drink and fuck his way through twenty-eight gold roaks.

She might take down the deek but Tarx? Not a chance. The very dear entertainment he'd just bought would not last long.

The deek picked at his nose. At least Tarx was looking around.

Damarr fidgeted. Where was the woman? She should have been down there already. He waited longer still, until he realized the moment had passed, that he'd paid for entertainment that wasn't going to happen. All he had to do was go down and ask Cerrux to get the sickening confirmation: his recent guest had gone out the other way that led to the side street and the stables where Breks had stolen the horse and jaunting cart. Shar Stakeen would be striding away, laughing at him for the fool he surely was.

And he had no recourse. He couldn't very well go to the local magistrate, to lodge a complaint about a shadden—if even she *was* a shadden.

He'd been swindled, humiliated again, and in a way almost worse than what Breks had done. It almost seemed as if they were in league.

He seized up, fuming, and when he slapped the table hard enough to ripple the water in the flower vase, he saw that she'd stolen the strutter as well. He fought the urge to sweep the desk. Back at the window again, close enough to feel the recoil of his panting breaths, he forced himself to calm down. He was letting what Breks did to him cloud his thinking.

Would Shull have pushed a joke this far, sent him someone who wasn't a shadden?

No. And a shadden wouldn't take his money and not fulfill the contract. If she did that she'd never get another in Draica. Reputation was everything to these fixers. Also, Stakeen had to know he had the means to hire another to find and kill *her*.

But where *was* she?

Damaar saw Tarx, the patient beast, standing by one stone column of the gate, keeping his eye on the door and the short brick path leading to the portico of the manse. The deek leaned against the other column.

Moments passed and still Damarr didn't see the shadden. He had to confront the fact that she had indeed played him for a fool, leaving the Fates to decide her consequences. He cursed at the thought of having to go down there now, call them off, and having to shine the ganger's palm with as few coins as he dared.

Then he saw her, on the edge of the greensward, not far from the street. She was kneeling, as if wiping mud from her boots, the harlequin rose still tucked at her cross-strapped breasts.

She could have been halfway to Tidesback Street but there she was. He leaned forward on the window sill.

Roak's Bones!—what is she waiting for? he thought.

A phaeton clattered by, blocking his view. If it blocked his, then it surely would for Tarx and his deek should they turn from their vigil at the gate. So that was it: she wasn't taking any chances that the pair might wonder if the woman they'd seen going into the house was more than just a female visitor.

The carriage passed. Stakeen slipped by, striding directly for Tarx, steps away from the gutter on his side of the street. She held the strutter behind her in her left hand, a stiff leash for an absent dog. Her right hand moved to her belt—and there it was: the glint of steel.

Damarr felt the catch in his throat, caught between a desire for Tarx to humble this woman, yet wanting to see if she was worth the outrageous price. On the verge of shouting a warning he swallowed hard instead.

The ganger sensed her presence now, turned, saw the knife too late. The pointed rungs of the iron fence to either side of the gate obscured part of Damarr's view. But she had to have thrown the knife; she hadn't yet closed on Tarx—and why would she? She must have found the soft throat because he staggered back, hands high and tight. She darted at him with a second blade, a quick slash, the strutter at her side, pointing away, and leaped back, spinning toward the deek as Tarx fell, gurgling, to his knees.

The deek turned to run. She tripped him with the strutter, tumbling him to the bricks. He tried to scramble up. Damarr thought he might escape as she took a moment to belt her second dagger. She grabbed his hair, pulled him back, pounded his head on the paving bricks.

Damarr was sure she'd use the blade now.

She plunged the strutter's tip into his mouth.

The deek jerked his head wildly from side to side, trying to spit out the slim bronze gag, his feet kicking, hands quivering around the strutter. Stakeen rose, rammed home the curved top, a last churn of the butter.

Tarx lay by the gate, inert.

Damarr gushed out a breath; he hadn't realized he'd been holding it. He ran a sweaty palm through his thinning hair. Surely she would leave now, hurry down the street. Passersby who hadn't already fled clustered by the fountain, whispering as they stared at the bloody scene.

Stakeen wasn't finished yet. Damarr couldn't see her slicing the flesh and tendons of the deek's outstretched hand—the gate was in the way—but he did see her impale the severed hand on the tip of a fence rung. She stepped back over to Tarx and, with a single stroke, removed an ear. She flung it with a back-hand throw to the edge of the green. Gulls quickly descended upon it.

She watched them for a moment as she wiped both of her daggers on the ganger's red and white-checked trews, then left. Passing the deek's body, she brushed her fingers over the strutter, much as she had the harlequin roses. The one she'd taken was still intact—as if nothing had happened. By the time he lost sight of her at the corner of his property, the strutter had ceased rocking like a harbor buoy.

He knew he had to go down, sooner rather than later, to have Cerrux take the hand from the fence before his fragile wife chanced to see it. But the hand was a token of a prize to come. He'd paid for it dearly, so he enjoyed his purchase a while longer, wondering what sort of men Shar Stakeen took for lovers if, in fact, that was her preference. He shuddered.

The Red Feathers, Heart Hill's private constabulary, would have to be summoned to take the bodies away. Someone may already have gone to find one. Chances were slim that anyone connected a tall woman seen going into his manse with the same one who killed two quay-stompers because no one saw her come out. No one, least of all the Feathers and Havarrl Damarr, cared what had happened to a pair of gangers in Heart Hill, except that they were dead.

Two spanners chased away the smaller gulls pecking at the ear she'd thrown toward the greensward. One of the spanners made off with it, harried fiercely by the cawing second as they dipped and swerved, until the ear fell splashing in the moss-rimed fountain.

Damarr whispered: "I sought a brick-layer and got a sculptress."

If he'd known before what he would witness he would have gladly paid the sum without protest to ensure Amala's return. Here was artistry that in its own way rivaled aulosts of the finest ghorgens in the most exclusive dens.

And it had been a private performance, without a bow at the curtain call. She had more than proved her skill. He realized he was lucky because, of course, a shadden would rarely do more than was necessary to fulfill a contract. He doubted she would bestow flourishes for the death of Falca Breks. It didn't matter; Damarr wouldn't be present to witness a mundane killing.

But if he'd known he would have asked this shadden—and paid extra—to bring Falca Breks back alive, so he could watch her perform again and not have to imagine the one hand for the other spiked on the fence.

Chapter Four:

THE GRAYLOCK

FALCA CAUGHT THE tickler in mid-air.

"You want it?" he said to Gurrus, who was walking next to Amala on the towpath.

"Why not? Thank you."

Falca shook his fist as if he was rattling three-star dice instead of an insect the size of his little finger. Gurrus accepted the stunned tickler, pinched off a yellow wing to eat.

"Now you've seen his quick hands," Amala said. "Once, before I knew he had them, he bet me a lucra that he could pin a fly—no tickler mind you—to the wall with a sliverheart."

"You lost the bet I assume?" Gurrus said, and ate the other wing.

"She did and I didn't eat that one, either," Falca answered. "Even the dog spits these out after he catches them." He thumbed at the whiskertail, Kazy by name, that the corry's master, Harro Scapp, used as a mouser. The dog had darted ahead, ready in the reeds should Scapp succeed in shooting for dinner one of the black-neck swans gliding along the canal.

Amala gave the mule's rump a sharp tease with her prod but saved a little for Falca. "Surely if a spoiled Heart Hill quiver like me had the belly to eat one yesterday—they're quite good." She licked her lips.

"They're clever is what they are. They only bother the one who won't eat them. You see any around Gurrus?"

"Em, well, it seems then you have the answer to your problem," Amala said, winking at the old Limb.

"You two," Falca muttered, and took off his caravaner's hat, wiped the sweat from his brow. "I'll wait. There must be plumper ones in the Bounds."

"There are, wikkano, and much tastier," Gurrus said, "but with some you have to remove a barb before you eat them, otherwise you will die; not like these." He popped the rest of the tickler, his sixth of the afternoon, into his mouth. Falca winced at the crunch.

Gurrus had given him a towpath name—wikkano—which, in Tongue, meant "thinks as he walks." The name wasn't so bad considering all the others Falca had been called. And what he'd been thinking off and on for most of the afternoon, was that if he'd known he'd be walking to Bastia staring at the arse-end of a canal-boat mule named Casso, he might not have suggested the Moat as an escape route, and Roak piss on the merits of the idea, to which Amala had immediately warmed.

Oh, he could see the wisdom of getting his legs here rather than in the Bounds, which was about a two-day journey east from Bastia, according to Scapp. Yet they'd only been gone three days from Draica now, and already Falca's feet suffered from loosened seams in his chasers. If the blisters got much worse he'd have no choice but to toss the boots and go barefoot until he could get another pair.

He'd never done so much walking in his life, not even in Gebroan. In Draica he knew the shortcuts to get from this alley or quay to that canal embankment or street. There was no shortcut to Bastia, however, and he'd had plenty of time to realize that one shortcut after another was the sum of his years so far, at least until he'd met Amala. And what about after the Rough Bounds? No more shortcuts, either, to Milatum or wherever he and Amala went after they found Frikko's kin and then returned the kinnet to the Isle of Shallan.

He couldn't go back to what he knew best. Neither could he see himself in some honest trade, counting the days as regularly as Casso twitched his tail back and forth to discourage pestering ticklers.

They'd relieved Scapp on the towpath at noon, as the last of the morning mist cleared from the Moat. Normally, the corry's master and his sister, Doula, had a swale to help them but the man never showed up at the Roads for the departure from Draica—the reason why Falca had been able to secure a working passage on so short a notice.

It was now the middle of the afternoon, and they had to walk the mule until dusk when the corry would stop for the night, to anchor safely in mid-canal along this stretch of the Moat where the forest to the north closed in tightly—what Scapp called "springin' close".

Snagwolves and the bolder flenx had been known to attack mules and men on the towpath. Flenx mostly prowled at night but even so, Falca kept his falcata at the ready.

For the past hour they'd been walking along woods of boxbarks and hack-hards, whose branches hung over the towpath and, in places, the canal itself. Where the forest gave way they passed by skillet-flat farmland. To the south rose foothills of the mountains separating Lucidor from Myrcia. Summer beckoned but snow still capped some of the peaks.

The hills to the north, rising above woods or fields, were unmistakably man-made, crowned by strongholds or estates and, not far back, the Cassenite fhold. Scapp said there were a dozen of these hills along the Moat's route, formed from earth hauled out to carve the canal. The hills were called Motessin's Fists, named after the Lucidorian king who'd ordered the canal dug to the depth of a lance and thrice as wide.

Scapp had chided Falca for never having heard of Motessin's famous decree: Myrcia had a great river through its heartland, and so would his kingdom, for commerce and defense. His subjects would create theirs as they'd created Draica, where once there had been only fens and the hillock dens of marshfangs.

Falca wasn't impressed. Commerce was one thing; defense another. Motessin must have had the wits of a dock bollard since it didn't seem likely a narrow canal and a few hills would prove much of an obstacle to the Myrcians if their next invasion came through the southern mountain passes. In the last one they came by sea and knocked the ballocks off the Colossus of Roak in Draica's harbor with their siege engines before proceeding to level half the city.

Harro Scapp finally got their dinner. A loud "*Yahhhh!*" rolled over the canal, followed by a piercing whistle. Kazy plunged through the reeds along the bank. Retrieving the black-neck swan he paddled toward the corry, the arrow wobbling above the water. Amala paused to watch Scapp haul in both dog and dinner. He stepped away as Kazy shook himself and barked proudly.

"Someday I'd like to have a dog, and one that can do that," Amala said.

Falca thought of the one she once had, Shindy, but said only: "That means one of us will have to learn how to shoot like our friend Scapp."

Since her lifting Amala was prone to forgetfulness. Just yesterday, as she kissed him goodnight, she slid her hand over the stubble that didn't quite hide the scar on his jawline. "It's healed well, the scar; what he did to you in Gebroan."

She meant Saphrax, the most brutish of all the scapers with whom Falca had worked the west-end streets of Draica, before he became an acolyte of the Spirit-Lifter cult.

Saphrax wasn't the one who'd cut him. Sippio, her brother's gillie, had done that on a winter's day in Draica, with the edge of a skate, before her lifting. Amala once knew Sippio had done it, but she'd lost her memory of that and other events such as the death of the dog who'd been with her when Falca first met her.

It was better she didn't remember what happened at the home she'd been sharing with her twin brother near Raven's Gate. Saphrax killed Shindy, who had tried to protect her. Then the hulking fester lifted her soul into the crystal mace. Falca arrived too late to stop the process and saw Amala, an empty now, stabbing away at the carcass of her beloved pet with the scissors she was going to use to snip the stitches she'd earlier sewn to close the slash on Falca's jaw.

He wished he could forget the memory of her stuffing bloody chunks of the dog into her mouth. All he could do now was thank the High Fates—and Frikko—that she was with him now on this hot, dusty path alongside a stinking canal, as eager as he was to share the coming coolness of the night air, the constellations so rarely seen in Draica, and perhaps a few fingers of Harro Scapp's scorchbelly.

The mule was getting tired, the towline to the corry scything through reeds and sinking deeper into the canal. Amala stopped the mule while Falca freed the rope tangled in a branch below the bank.

Doula had tied off the corry's rudder and was sweeping with her 'scoom' by the short ladder leading up to the roof of the bow cabin where passengers slept who could not be accommodated below. The scoom was a peculiar domestic scepter that had the usual bristles of a broom at one end, and a nicked, blunt-bladed scoop at the other. Amala suspected she used it to squash mice in the aft cabin and slide them into the cooking pot. How else to explain the small bones they found in the evening stew she served up on the first day?

Scapp's plump prize promised relief from their other fare of neaps and hanches, and fish Doula invariably managed to burn. Her brother may have felt the same since he was singing as he plucked the swan's feathers.

The corry's master took a minstrel's pleasure with his boisterous, "capstan voice" he called it, a relic from his seafaring days when he helmed the fastest packet on the Draica-Slacere run, or so he claimed.

Falca thought the mule hit more notes with his braying than Scapp did with his. He'd just begun a tangy ditty called 'Tail Taddle', that required another to fill in the chorus, the cruder the better. Falca knew the tavern song and offered a few of his favorite responses, but he let it go after a while. His lewd duet with Scapp was awkward enough—towpath to boat—and then there was Gurrus asking him questions about whether certain lines of the chorus were physically possible to duplicate.

"Em, well, it's a song, Gurrus; anything's possible in a song," Amala said, and gave him an example that caused Falca to smile. But that was it for the towpath duet. Scapp kept on by himself, and a hearty effort it was—perhaps because the somber Crake family was no longer aboard.

They'd left in the morning, at the bridge where the Virenz road headed north, to take their young daughter to the Cassenite fhold and offer her to the Vasper, the cult's patriarch. She'd been crying when they got on the corry in Draica, and she wept when her mother combed her long, dark hair for hours at a time by the hatchway to the cabin where the family had spent two days of the passage. "A ritual for one," Amala had said, "and it's not for the poor girl."

So they were gone, the Crakes. No more did Falca and Amala have to listen to stern scoldings rising from the cabin below.

"...And you repay us with your whining after all we have done for you?"

"Are you so dense you cannot understand we are doing this for you?"

"How many times do we have to tell you? Only the Vasper can judge if you're the true One."

On the first night out from Draica, the mother pounded on the roof, shouting shrilly: "Quit your basting up there. She'll learn the rut soon enough"—as if Falca and Amala were sweet-at-the-bellows instead of sleeping.

Falca didn't think Amala awakened in time to hear, but she had: "Children—we think they're ours, kahyeh. They're not. We only borrow them for a time, no more."

The sleepy words were enough to keep him awake after she'd fallen back to sleep. He wondered where she'd learned the lesson; it couldn't have come from her mother or father. Then he realized it had.

They continued on now, three abreast behind the mule, soon to greet Falca's favorite time of the day, when the lowering sun lost its glare and shadows appeared; when a deepening golden light seemed to bring the world into sharper relief.

The dusk would bring an end to the path, at least for the night, and Falca could rinse the dust from his throat with scorchbelly he'd bought from Scapp. He and Amala would take turns swabbing the other's feet with cloths soaked in canal water and, no doubt, Gurrus would again mention the Lake of Shallan where they would no longer have to skim water for bathing and boil it for drinking. As if that was the sole reason for going there.

Casso suddenly balked on the path, twisting his neck, eyes wide and white. Amala steadied the mule as best she could and managed to pull him back and closer to the bank of the canal, almost to the reeds.

Falca saw no movement in the forest verge, nothing ahead except the tangled rootball of a fallen boxbark and the remains of the trunk Moatmen had axed to clear the towpath. Yet something had frightened the mule. Whatever it was had to be lurking, crouching on the far side of the boxbark, ready to pounce.

He wiped his sword hand to dry the sweat and gave the boxbark trunk a wide berth, keeping his left shoulder toward the tree should a flenx, impatient to begin its hunting for the night, spring out. Best greet it with a quick, sweeping strike. If he tried to impale the flenx its headhorn or claws might gore him first.

He was dead if there was more than one. Amala could swim—and take Gurrus with her. But The Moat offered no refuge to someone who couldn't.

It wasn't a flenx.

A man sat in the lee of the boxbark, head lolling against the crook of a shorn branch. At this distance Falca couldn't tell if he was sleeping or dead. He had no weapon except for the hilt of a long hunting knife poking out from his belt. Falca waved for Amala and Gurrus to come ahead. He moved close enough to see the slight rise and fall of the man's breathing.

The others were soon at Falca's side. "A nasty cut, that," Amala said. Blood soaked the left arm of a long-sleeved doublet sliced down from the shoulder to reveal the wound. Amala shooed ticklers away with her prod.

"Someone got him good," Falca said, "but not here." He nodded toward the forest. "He's been running and a lot was in his way—look at the trews." The man's graying plaits were frayed out, as if he'd forced his way through brambles.

"And *those*?" Amala said.

The graylock had three splotchy scars on his face—one in the middle of his forehead and on each cheek. "Whenever he got them," Falca said, "it wasn't recently."

"How can a wounded man frighten a mule?" Amala said.

Gurrus breathed deeply through his nose. "I can smell it. Kudu."

"Kudu?" Falca said.

"You call them bloodsnares."

"He's too old to be a ghorgen consort. They don't live long enough to lose their hair up front like he has."

"He won't live much longer if we don't get him to the corry," Amala said.

The graylock's eyes fluttered open. "No," he whispered. A beetle scurried across the palm of his bloodied right hand. "Jus'...water...please..."

Falca nodded. "We have that." To Amala: "I don't have much left in my 'skin."

"I do," she said.

"Not too much at first," Gurrus cautioned.

She nodded and knelt down in front of the man, uncorked the waterskin. He opened his eyes again when he felt the first drops trickle on his lips. He licked his lips. When she gave him more, he said: "Flu-ree?"

"Is he saying a name?" Falca said.

Amala leaned back. "Em...I think so."

He blinked his eyes, as if trying to see more clearly, then breathed deeply, almost a sigh it seemed to Falca. He closed his eyes again as Amala gave him more water.

Harro Scapp shouted from the corry, asking what the problem was.

"I'll get Casso going," Amala said.

"We'll give him more water and catch up to you," Falca said.

"Maybe he'll change his mind about the corry."

She left and didn't see the graylock shake his head, a slight yet unmistakable response.

Falca persisted: "The corry's not far. You won't last the night here...the flenx."

"No," the man said again, and turned his head away. An arm slid off his belly, revealing something that glinted at the corner of a pocket in his leather trews.

Falca should have left then and joined Amala, who was now just passing them, looking over in their direction as she led the braying mule past, almost in the reeds. He waited a moment longer...and pulled out a pendant on a golden chain. The graylock stirred at the intrusion, but no more.

The pendant itself was long and thin, with bird's-eye rubies, emeralds, and a blue jewel Falca had never seen before, each gem set within the finest gold filigree.

It was so small in his hand, so easily hidden. He closed his fist around the pendant. The graylock clearly didn't want them to take him to the corry, whatever the reason. If he wanted to die, that was his choice, wasn't it? The flenx would savage him in a few hours, leaving nothing except gnawed bones and this treasure for someone else to take.

They wouldn't need it in the Bounds, but what about after? Falca had never held such a prize and couldn't even begin to think of what it might bring them in Milatum.

Rob a dying man? Not too long ago he wouldn't have thought twice about stuffing the pendant into his pocket, so why hesitate now to take what this rough-hewn graylock—possibly once a prisoner given those hideous scars—had undoubtedly stolen? It had to have once belonged to someone of such stature he or she might whisper and a king would listen…

"Falca…we should go now."

He'd forgotten about Gurrus, who waited a moment longer and then began walking down the towpath, leaving him to his choice. The graylock had already made his.

Falca closed his hand one last time around the beauty before stuffing it back in the graylock's pocket, swearing softly, thinking he'd be a scut one way, a fool the other. He placed the waterskin by the graylock's right hand. The blunt, scarred fingers stirred when he nudged the 'skin against them.

"We're on a corry named *Cock-a-Manger*," he said. "We won't be far down. There's still time to change your mind before it's too late."

He left quickly, before he changed his own.

*

EVER SINCE LEAVING Draica they'd had a fourth companion—the certainty that Amala's father had hired more men for the pursuit. Yet as Falca thought about it, the more he discounted men like Trass and his deek, wankspits who might see a better profit in selling Amala to some skinner in Virenz or Nostoy instead of returning her to her father. Most likely it would be a shadden who could be trusted and, unlike Havaarl Damarr's first hirelings, would know what he was doing.

There was a time when Falca had thought of becoming one himself. But however lucrative, it was a life devoted solely to killing and you thus lost choice in the matter. For a shadden, reputation was everything, and Falca had long loathed burdens of any kind. A shadden had to prove himself capable of killing anyone, even a child old enough to remember your face, who might peek into a room the moment after you'd killed his father or mother—whoever the target was. It was all or nothing. Take away choice and you weren't the one who decided to pull the bowstring, draw the spiddard or thrust the dagger; you were only the arrow, dart or blade.

The dog's barking woke him up that night, and within moments he was kneeling at the rail of the cabin roof, falcata in hand. The moonlight was enough to glimpse someone walking away down the towpath in the direction they'd be taking at daybreak, and he knew this one was no shadden to give up so easily. Or was he?

The dog, chained to a bolt by the aft cabin, roused Gurrus and Harro Scapp, though not Amala. Scapp came forward but didn't climb the ladder to the fore-cabin roof where Gurrus and Falca were, since Kazy had stopped barking.

"Two legs or four?" Scapp said.

"Two. On the path," Falca said. "He's moving away."

"Alone?"

"Most likely." Unless Havaarl Damarr had hired two shaddens.

"Eh, give it a while, just in case," Scapp said, and left.

Falca tapped Gurrus on the shoulder. "Stay here a moment."

"It could be the…graylock."

"Unless it isn't. I want to check the other side of the corry."

It's what he would have done if he was out there with someone else: move silently around the boat, holding his breath beneath the foul canal water, while the other lulled those aboard by walking away, to make them think all was safe.

He kept a step back from the rail. No one surfaced. So just the one. Who had it been? The graylock might have heard him before, and recovered enough with the water given him, but he was in no shape to attempt a swim to the corry anchored in mid-canal.

Falca was still there when Gurrus called out softly from behind him. "I found this on the deck by the corner of the cabin, near the bow. It is the one we left the graylock."

"That's odd. Why would he return an empty water skin?"

Gurrus handed it to Falca. "It is not empty."

Chapter Five:

SLASH AND NOD

SHAR STAKEEN NEEDED another horse.

Not long before sunset the one she'd ridden from Draica pulled up lame: a split hoof. She hoped to find a replacement at the beacon tower ahead, however she managed the theft. Since Virenz she'd ridden around three of these fortified royal waystations and elsewhere on the road passed a detachment of cavalry, no doubt in pursuit of bandits or tollbreakers, so the horse she needed could be at the next tower.

Her problem now was whether she could get to it before dawn robbed her of opportunity. Shortly after nightfall she'd seen a flare from this tower to the east that came low over the horizon, brighter than the most prominent stars, even those of The Bellows, The Anvil and the Silver Trail. But darkness made it difficult to judge distance, and the brief signalling had not occurred again as she led the lame mare along the road by the light of the Sister moons, Cassena and Suaila.

If she couldn't steal a horse from the tower's stable she could always take one from a traveler, or poach from a farmstead during the day. That, however, meant walking through the night, time lost after she'd ridden so hard to catch up to Breks and Damarr's daughter, who couldn't be that far ahead.

Much later she left behind a vale and the urge to steal a draft horse from the nearby farm. She might have done that had there been only one dog, but she'd heard at least two barking, scrabbling furiously at the enclosure, evidence they were not chained. She could kill one or two easily enough; a third would be on her as she did. The risk was too great, especially when an attack would rouse the farmer. Moreover, she needed a fleet horse, a cavalry mount, not a field plodder.

The road left the vale and curved up past high fields, disappearing into the blackness of upland forest. The night was cool but it wasn't long before she was sweating from the steep ascent. This had to be the biggest hill yet since the Cliff of Virenz. If a tower did not crown this summit, surely the next. Yet by that time dawn would have arrived.

The forest closed in ahead, funneling stars toward the road. There was little light to reflect the eyes of snagwolves or flenx but she knew they were not far, tracking her stink and step, and the mare's. The forest was only two spits away to either side of the road.

Stakeen held the reins tightly in one hand, dagger in the other. Head bobbing nervously, the chuffing mare wanted to break and run; Stakeen wouldn't let her. She'd bought the horse, Mally, in Castlecliff with part of the proceeds of her first contract, for the return to Draica. She'd ridden no other since then. But the mare was bait now, not just the means to relieve Stakeen of the burden of carrying panniers.

She stopped only long enough to remove essentials from them. She carried Damarr's gold on her, as well as the two daggers sheathed at boot and belt. But now she took out a waterskin, draping the strap crossways over her shoulder, and tucked her vials of slash and nod in a pouch. Those could not be easily replaced, nor could the spiddard and agonette she hooked to her belt.

She walked fast enough up the hill to lengthen the distance between her and the horse. The column of stars between the trees grew in breadth and depth—the summit could not be far away.

The mare whinnied in terror, bolting to Stakeen's right. She let the reins fly from her hand, snatched a second dagger from her belt, and backed away, weaving the blades before her. She knew better than to turn and run; that would only signal fear to the flenx—and they *were* flenx. The snarls were too high-pitched for snagwolves.

Mally bleated and snorted as she tried to escape. Two of the beasts had already gored her, flank and rump, with their headhorns. They were writhing black masses against the mare's light chestnut color. One fell off; another took its place. But the dying horse carried them away from Stakeen. More flenx bore in for the feeding when Mally finally collapsed.

The shadden backed away slowly, ready to gut any late-comers to the crowded feast. They growled and yelped, fighting each other for the choicest portions. Stakeen heard the ripping of sinew, popping tendons, clicking of fangs on bone. Gradually, the sounds faded until there came only the snuffling of muzzles buried in flesh.

She kept moving back slowly, occasionally stopping to listen for the tapping of claws on headhorn: the signal a flenx was about to attack. Finally, confident no flenx were stalking her, she turned and walked on, her breathing calmer. At the crest of the hill she slid the daggers back in their sleeves.

The forest in the immediate vicinity of the tower had been cleared but there was a newer cut across the road. Stakeen knelt behind a stump, keeping low to observe the tower. She had excellent nighteyes—better than Tranch's. And Cassena helped, higher and brighter in the night sky than Suaila.

This station, its tollgate lowered for the night, seemed larger than the others she'd skirted, though still absent an outer wall and thus the room for horses. A lower building on the far side had to be the stables. The signal tower itself rose half again higher than the foundation, with half its girth. She marked the darkened arrow loops on the first story of the facing wall. Light shone from a few windows on the second. Torches burned from two stanchions flanking an entrance braced with iron straps and a huge round shield stamped with the royal marshfang seal of Lucidor. Below that gleamed the local lord's: three bronze wolves' heads on a striped field of yellow and red. A long set of stone steps led up to the oaken door.

That local lord probably hosted a modest retinue of cavalry in return for a cut of the royal tolls. Not counting the tolltaker and signalmen, Stakeen estimated a garrison of a dozen, including the one guarding a calesse: the smaller, nimbler Lucidorian version of a Myrcian war wagon.

The horses were stabled for the night. A lone sentry, his back to the light, sat on one of the calesse's two long yokes that reached almost to the steps of the tower entrance. There was no way she could approach without him seeing her first, yet he'd have to be dealt with quietly. Given the low light, the stitched iron discs of his Warden's ruerain, and the proximity of other soldiers who might hear a scream, a dagger throw was not as suitable an option as it had been for the bigger of Havaarl Damarr's hirelings.

Stakeen took out two vials. One contained slash, so named for the blade-like petals of the shrub from which it was made. She hadn't much of this left from what Tranch had given her as a parting gift, but she needed some now, not wanting her weariness to beget a mistake.

The stems had to be soaked, hence the water-filled vial. She took one out, slid the bitter bark off with her teeth, chewed it thoroughly, swallowed, flicked the husk away.

She decided to use the spiddard instead of the agonette, unhooked it from her belt, then ratcheted the whiskers to tension, a soft *snick-snick-snick* the Warden could not possibly hear. Slimmer than a tavern trencher, the spiddard could propel a dart accurately and powerfully enough to penetrate leather or a thick, quilted gamby at short range.

She uncorked the vial of nod, a rare substance found only in the Rough Bounds. A few drops diluted in a bucket of water made one drowsy; smeared straight on the tip of a fletched dart, nod could immediately thicken a man's tongue, stiffen his legs and arms. The less calm and relaxed the victim, the quicker the effect of the nod.

Stakeen fitted the dart in the spiddard's middle groove, placed a thumb over it so the dart would not dislodge until she was ready to shoot. Already she was feeling the effects of the slash: the torchlight seemed brighter, the odor from the stables more pungent. She knew now the sentry had been drinking, and where he'd stashed his comfort; she knew that some of the men in the tower were preoccupied with a game—the sound of clattering dice came faintly through a window high above. She also felt a pleasurable tingling below in her delta but there would be no slaking that tonight.

Staying low, she angled her approach to keep the calesse between her and the Warden. Reaching the battle-wagon, she tossed a spray of gravel to her side, to rouse him from his perch and prime him for the dart, then continued on around to the other side of the calesse in time to see him drawing his stagger-axe from the back scabbard. Stepping cautiously toward the sound he'd heard, the Warden was unaware he was moving with her in a slow dance that would be ending very soon.

Stakeen crouched on the lit side of the calesse, aware that if someone came out now she would be seen. The Warden returned soon enough, glanced back, shaking his head. He hadn't yet sheathed the double-headed axe but that crude weapon was of no concern to her. He stood a few strides from where she knelt, pawed his nose, sniffed. His stink was terrible, but she'd only have to endure it for a moment longer.

She braced the spiddard and fired…a snapping twig.

The dart stuck in the side of his thick neck, below the ear. He winced, shivered his head and slapped at what he thought was a biting insect—and came away with the dart. He dropped it, his mouth wide for the scream or shriek. All that came out was a moan that ended in a low, guttural stutter.

Stakeen hooked the spiddard to her belt and rose, stepping away from the calesse to block his path to the door, just in case. He tried to swing the axe but couldn't. She took the blade from his grasp as if it were a gift willingly given, before his frozen hand could drop it. She slid the stagger gently over the side of the calesse. The Warden had sunk to his knees, staring at her, still trying to speak before he toppled over. She picked up the dart, wiped the tip clean and put it back in the thimble quiver whence it came, and dragged him under the calesse. The nod wouldn't wear off for hours yet.

She hurried to the stables. She'd saddled a horse before in the dark but never while she held her breath—the slash heightened the reek of the muck. As she led the horse out—another mare—she heard a fierce round of shouts from the tower, a tumbling and crashing of tables or chairs. Carousing gotten out of hand? She was about to mount her prize when the tower door opened. There was no time to lead the horse back into the stables. If whoever was coming didn't notice that, they surely would hear her galloping away and alert the garrison.

She left the mare with a smooth stroke and calming whisper, and broke low for the dark side of the calesse, the nearest cover. The Warden stared at her, his lips slowly opening and closing, like those of a fish in a pool. She peered around, a hand on the nicked iron rim of a wheel. A man stood at the top of the steps before the door, holding a cloth to the side of his pudgy face, smoothing his rumpled hair with his other hand.

He wasn't one of the garrison—no uniform. But the taller, leaner man who soon followed wore the checkered green and black cape of a Warden officer. The man with the cloth said: "I suppose the captain paid you off."

"What if he did? The question now is, baby brother, how much you will give me to keep my mouth shut about this?" The tone of his voice, though light-hearted, had a thrust to it.

"I don't care if you tell father or not."

"Of course you do. I've told you that he instructed me to do more than merely bring you east; he wanted me to train you in more practical matters, but you resist."

"He knows where my expertise lies."

"You call graduating from Skene without honors expertise?"

"You've been a tenon since I went there, Maldan. Only when you've risen beyond that junior rank may you lecture me on expertise."

"I'm sure father will be lecturing you on the value of a man being able to defend his honor. I did it for you in there yet you insult me. I'm still willing to save you from his disappointment in you, though I won't take as payment one of those poems you've been scribbling every night since we left Draica."

"They're not poems and I didn't need your help. I could have handled the bastard."

The Warden laughed. "Believe that and you'll believe swallows prefer poems for payment. Lannid, you can't handle a drunken hazel yet you think you can take on that Slidetown cob who's run off with the quiver you've had your eye on for years, as did we all—at least when her brother wasn't looking."

"That's the last time I'm ever…"

"And even if you *could*, what makes you think you'll have any *time* to hunt for sweets. I suspect we won't be in Bastia for…"

"Will you *never* shut up? You make my ears ache as much as…"

"What? Your wee bruise? The scut inside would have done a lot more than smack your jaw if I hadn't intervened. The man's getting thirty lashes tomorrow; he's also being docked a month's pay—the same amount that's just fattened my purse."

"It's too much."

"Yes, well, the captain's lucky I didn't make it that for each of us. He detests Wardens as much as any in there, but the last thing the licklog wants is for the Allarch to hear that his youngest son was attacked by one of the men under his command. Father would make sure he'd be exiled to a posting in the north where he can't skim tolls, and the only women to be found are stoneskin greylas who'll scrape his cudgie bloody raw."

"I was talking about the lashes."

"You complain about lashes for a man who hit you? Do you think Cossum and Bovik would complain? Are you a Hoster? Are you even truly my brother?"

"I've wondered the same about you."

"Look, 'Niddy, hopefully this will be the last time I have to tell you that father *does* have plans for you, just as he has for me and Cossum, and once had for Bovik. Yours don't include fighting. I know that. But even so, you'd be well-advised to put a point on more than your quills. I may not always be around to help you if you insist on cheating at three-star or spill some other kettle."

"And for the last time: I wasn't cheating. I merely have a facility for remembering numbers and sets."

"Who *cares* if you were cheating! It's what you do if you get caught."

Shar Stakeen shifted to her other knee as she watched the elder brother go back inside.

Lannid Hoster kept tenderly touching his bruised face but he seemed relieved his brother had left. One of the stanchion torches flickered out, casting him more in shadow. He sighed mightily and turned to go back in.

This one? Stakeen thought. *This whining…strutterman fancies himself a suitor to Amala Damarr?*

If the father had him in mind for the daughter, it was no wonder she took off with that quay-side strappyjack.

Stakeen rose from her crouch, eager to get to the horse and away, then knelt again when Lannid Hoster stopped, called over his shoulder: "Kellot, bring me the books I left in the calesse."

He waited a moment, then: "The books and whatever's left of what you've been guzzling out here. I need it more than you."

She drew a dagger, just in case the strutterman persisted in fouling her escape more than he and his brother had already. They both deserved cracking slaps: the elder for his sneering bullying; the other for his mewling passivity.

"Kellot! Do you hear me?" Lannid Hoster shouted, and waited. "Put the damn jug away."

Stakeen scuttled back from the calesse's near forward wheel when she realized he was coming around to her side, grumping now about having to get the books himself. He climbed back into the wagon. The heavy springs squeaked as he rummaged about, finally muttering: "*There* they are."

He slipped as he stepped down from the calesse, croaking an oath, and the books fell with him. Gathering them up on his knees, he saw Kellot and sucked in his breath.

Stakeen was on him before he could shout an alarm. She clapped his head into the side of the calesse, then again, harder. He collapsed, senseless, on his side. She had a mind to slice his throat, the world better for one less fool. Damarr would never know who killed him but there was still a risk with the man. She contented herself with emptying a pocket of his winnings at three-star: a lucra, three silver eclats, and as many reives—a tidy sum, whether he'd cheated to get it or not.

The light of the single torch at the door was enough for her to see the title of the slimmest of the three books: *The Vales of Dramore.* The strutterman's poetry? She only looked inside because Tranch was living now in the most beautiful of those legendary glens south of Virenz, in a manse made possible by her lucrative years as a shadden.

She glanced at the book's formal printed dedication: *To my sister, who brings me home, wherever she may be.* Alatheus Damarr had personally inscribed it: "*And to my accomplice Lannid—now you know what I was doing aftwards.*"

The strutterman would regain his wits long before Kellot did, but the immediate signs would point to disgruntled mates of the soon-to-be flogged hazel, who wanted to teach the prissjack a lesson. Stakeen would be well away by the time the brother and garrison fit more pieces to the puzzle. Of course, they'd signal east and west, not knowing which way the horsethief had gone. But she would at least have enough of a lead to ride up on the dawn, then perhaps move off the King's Way to rest. As soon as she saw the horsemen pass by from the east she could resume pursuing Amala and her Falca Breks.

She walked the horse down the road until she felt safe enough to mount, and only then did she allow herself the whimsy of thinking that, with any luck, the Heart Hill harlequin rose would take off again with some other cob, only to have her father pay again for a second helping of kill-and-return.

Shar Stakeen spurred the mare down the hill, a swift shadow in the moonlight, exulting in the wind that reminded her of the only regret she had in following the way of the shadden: she couldn't keep her hair long. One thing she remembered especially of her father, before he'd died in the shipwreck a year before she'd gotten her blood, was her preference for him brushing her hair instead of letting her mother do it.

A much more recent memory was of Tranch cutting and braiding it tightly. At the time, Stakeen wondered why—until Tranch handed her back the most tightly woven length and told her that the last of a shadden apprentice's Fifty Tests would be to kill someone without using metal, wood, water or poison; common rope, stone, or flesh on flesh.

She passed.

Chapter Six:

A CHANGE OF PLANS

THEY TALKED ABOUT the graylock's gift on the towpath as the cool mist rose with the morning. Falca was of a mind that the High Fates had to have been in a drunken stupor at their Loom Eternal. Even revived with the water, the wounded graylock should have missed the corry with his moonlit toss.

Was he a criminal escaped from prison? That seemed likely given the arrangement of facial scars that could not have resulted from accident. Yet Falca had never heard of a renegade who repaid a favor with a pendant like that, regardless of the depth of gratitude. Why would an outlaw give up such a treasure he had to have stolen at great risk? Someone else might, of course. But a king, nobleman, or even some wealthy merchant was not usually found in a hunter's leathers at the edge of a forest, gruesomely scarred, wounded and desperate for water.

They got answers—a few—later that day.

Six mounted Cassenites stopped on the path shortly before noon, crowding them closely, the hammered service marks glinting on their steel helmets—the distinctive dreacon halos. Braided wire whips hung from their belt loops. Falca had seen these rat-tails when he was younger, and Cassenites could be found in greater numbers in Draica, before the cult was outlawed and forced out of the city.

Their cape-and-cowled leader said they were seeking a murderer, and gave a description that matched the graylock's.

"Haven't seen him," Falca said, "and we've been out on the path most days since Draica."

Amala bettered his lie. "If he was wounded, as you say, the flenx must have gotten him in the forest."

"He's alive," the dreacon said. "We've searched the forest."

They also searched the corry, shouldering past Scapp's protests. Falca knew now why the graylock hadn't wanted to be taken to the corry.

When Amala asked what he'd done the dreacon told her curtly she didn't have to know. There was, of course, the evidence, dazzling with jewels, inside the coarse waterskin draped over Falca's shoulder, within the dreacon's reach if he leaned from his saddle.

He glanced at the falcata. "If you see him, kill him, and bring his head to our fhold. You will be rewarded generously, as will you," he said, looking directly at Amala, as if sizing a haunch of meat for the table.

"Oh, *that*," she said. "I've heard of the Vasper's generosity. But I've already chosen." She smiled sweetly at Falca, forestalling words from him that might complicate matters or worse. After they rode on she wet her finger and gave the dreacon a crude alley gesture.

Falca had never liked the Cassies, either, though there was a time when he had a sense of wonder tinged with envy that a mere blacksmith's son could fool more than a few people into believing he was the incarnation of Vasperioc himself, the First of Roak's Red Hands, still searching after a thousand years for his lord's vanished queen. Cassenites believed that when the Vasper—Vasperioc—found her, so would Roak return, ushering in a new Golden Age to rival the old. Falca doubted it had been so very golden.

Such a clever blacksmith's son to convince so many he might find the reincarnated Cassena in the guise of every comely young woman or girl who came, escorted or not, to the Cassenite fhold.

Such a clever way to keep your cudgie well-polished.

Falca had grown beyond his wonder and youthful envy. Down to his bones, stripped of all else that beguiled, the Vasper was nothing more than a brothel spur.

Still, Falca well knew the lure of hope. The graylock whom the Cassenite dreacons sought was old enough to be the father Falca always thought he'd find again in Gebroan. And if the graylock was hunted for a theft, so was Falca—in Havaarl Damarr's mind anyway. But the man they'd saved along the towpath was luckier in one respect: he knew who hunted him.

✲

THEY CHANGED MULES early that afternoon, when the tops of Bastia's towers and walls showed as a faint, reddish escarpment in the distance. Doula replaced them on the path. Her brother Harro took a moment to suggest they leave the corry now.

"T'aint none of my business why you're goin' into the Bounds with the mottle, and I don't much care; you've paid his passage. But unless you hide him, soon as we berth at Bastia Roads he won't last long. Either the Shofet's fyrdies will take'm for the quarries, or the Wardens for augor feed."

Falca knew as much from what Gurrus had told him and Amala. The mehka had once been in the quarries, briefly, before being roped on to Draica with other Limbs for work there. Unlike Draica, few Limbs walked freely inside the walls of Lucidor's easternmost city. And if the citadel's garrison or the Wardens didn't make a claim on one, a Banishman in from the Borders would. Every other settler had lost someone to raiding Timberlimbs.

Amala thanked Scapp for his concern, adding: "There's also the matter of the toll I assume you'll have to pay to the gaugers at the Roads, who most likely would count a Timberlimb as cargo no matter his fate the moment he steps off the corry."

"Ah, well, that's part of it," Scapp said. "That goes without sayin', no?"

"You see our problem," Amala said. "Gurrus has told us that the lake reaches far to the north from the city, and beyond that lake are fens—it's a long way to the Rough Bounds that way. And we can't reach the Bounds any more easily by going south around the quarries; Gurrus won't go anywhere near there."

"Does the canal end with the Roads?" Falca asked.

"Well, no it don't," Scapp said. "Goes on through the city and keeps on past the sawmill, and meets the lake—what're you peelin'?"

"Seems we already have a place to hide Gurrus," Falca said. "Until we don't need it anymore. I don't think that's asking too much of a friend whose sister's burned every meal since we left Draica. Do you, kushla?"

"Not at all, kahyeh."

"I'll let you do it, for a price—and lose the Tongue while you're at it; this ain't Draica."

"So how sharp do gaugers look?" Falca said.

"Depends on which one's workin'." Scapp rasped at his stubble with the back of a hand. "All right, I have an idea, and because I happen to like you both—Roak knows why—I'll give it to you for free. But I doubt the Limb'll like it.

✵

THEY KEPT GURRUS hidden in the lee of the aft cabin as they passed the quarry quay to the south of the city. Along the canal scores of Timberlimbs were loading pallets of cut dawnstone onto a half-dozen corries bigger than theirs. Gangers shouted, cracking their whips.

Amala stayed with him. From where Falca stood with Scapp at the tiller, he could see only Gurrus holding his hands together, as if to quell the trembling. He might not be able to see the quarry, but he couldn't hide from what he remembered of it.

Gurrus had told them there had been a time, somewhere between distant memory and legend, when the lake and the citadel bluff at its south end had been part of Kelvarra, and the route of the canal through the city once a narrow valley between the bluff and the hills to the south. It was in this valley that Kelvoi found seams of dawnstone, which they traded to their brethren to the east. The dawnstone was used for the earbolls every male wore and, in a fine grade, to work designs into the flesh of their shoulder flanges and proud nasal ridges.

They were close enough to the city walls, and deep enough into the afternoon for the nearest tower to cast a shadow on a broad wishbone walk spanning the canal. The walk was supported by a middle stone island that divided the canal into two passages, and served as a means to drag the chains over the canal and secure them, to guard that way into the city. There were two sets of chains, spiked and coiled to either side of the walk in stone abutments. Like everything else, they were coated red and gold with dawnstone dust from the nearby quarries. Falca knuckled his itching eyes. Usually there was a north wind, Scapp said, which blew the dust south. Not today.

As they glided toward the wishbone walk, a west-bound corry emerged, so crowded with passengers that some had to sit under the rail, feet dangling almost to the water.

Falca asked Scapp: "Is that common, coming out of the city?"

"Never seen one *that* stuffed."

"Well, the weather's good."

"Yah, but the chain walk's empty."

"It usually isn't?"

"Something's going on. Should be swallows on it. I've seen'm, going on seven years now, a few spurs too, showing us what they have and dropping brothel markers to match later for a slide in Muletown. The fyrdies let'm go out the southwest gate, and use the walk, for favors of their own."

"So they're busy elsewhere."

"Which ain't right. Not all of'm."

Directly ahead, the brown canal water, tinged with dawnstone dust, merged with the blackness of the gate's arched maw. Doula hauled in the slackness of the towline and with the mule disappeared into the darkness. Falca would rather have scaled the wall of the gatetower than go under, but under they had to go, into a chill that made him shiver.

The ceiling seemed to press down; he could have kneeled on the fore-cabin's roof and scraped the tip of his falcata on it, or poked up into the succession of murderholes fouled with the nests of chittering birds. Prone to traps-and-squeezes, Falca couldn't help imagining the bared iron teeth of the cully—fitted to block both canal and path at either end of this passage—clattering down, sealing them in with far too many rats. Doula threshed away the squealers with scything arcs of her prod.

Amala used the darkness to take Gurrus below decks, where he'd stay until they stopped under the fourth of Bastia's seven bridges that stitched its eastern and western halves.

By the time she returned they'd left the darkness and the dank air of the passage for the smoky air of a city in a late afternoon bereft of a breeze coming off the lake. Falca was accustomed to the reeking peat-smoke air of Draica. And fires were always burning somewhere in the Banishlands closest to the Bounds so perhaps some of that had drifted to the east over the city. But there was something more cloying to this pall.

They soon got their answer to why there had been no swallows on the wishbone walk outside the city: there had been a fire in this part of Bastia—Muletown—and recently.

Dawnstone was a prized and valuable commodity, but it was too soft for foundation construction. Muletown, like most of the city, was built from timber hauled to Bastia's sawmills north of the Roads by augor teams or barge. The fire had been contained between the second and third bridges, and the canal had prevented it from passing over to the precincts by the quarry. But in between lay a wasteland of charred timbers, the side streets and alleys full of debris.

Soot-grimed urchins played at a game of jostles with the countless water-buckets littering the thoroughfare. A boy kicked a bucket past a woman sitting on steps leading down to the canal. She held another bucket in her arms, stroking the rope handle, rocking the pail as if she cradled a baby—or its remains. The kicked bucket clattered past her and splashed into the canal.

They were collecting corpses in the middle of the street fronting the route of the canal. People with rags over their faces poked through the ruins; others were hauling away the dead in carts and wagons.

The corry glided on.

The ruins of Muletown ended with the second bridge, the lowest of the seven. Falca and Amala, standing at the tiller next to Scapp, ducked together for the clearance.

Off to their left, statues of Roak and Cassena rose to a height rivaling that of the barbican that fronted the moat of the citadel rising from the bluff to the north of the square. The dawnstone sculptures faced each other, their outstretched hands holding a basin from which water cascaded to a pool below. Even from this distance, Falca could hear the sizzling of the falling water above the shouts of vendors hawking their wares. Wagons and trundle carts clattered on the pavement.

That noise gave way to the roaring of a crowd that had gathered for a prize fight. Raised stands surrounded the ropeless ring near the canal, at the edge of the square. One of the fighters tumbled off, a blow or slip on blood. Jeering spectators leaned away to let him fall.

"That ring," Falca asked Scapp. "Was it…the stump of a tree?"

"Only one left, inside the city walls, anyhow."

Between the third bridge and the busier fourth—the crowded King's Way bridge, Scapp told them—scaffolds had been erected on the embankment bordering the canal. Boys and young men, wielding sticks and knockons, batted at the bloody, dangling feet of four men hanging by their wrists from ropes knotted to the scaffolds. The men were long dead; "scolded," Scapp said, in the usual Bastian manner by having a stick and leather tourniquet tied around their face and tightened to crush the nose and pop out the eyes. Crows and spanners must have already pilfered that bloody fruit yet the mob kept shouting curses as if the men were still alive. Bigger dogs timed their leaps to the swaying meat of legs.

"The sooner we're out of here, the better," Amala whispered to Falca. He'd seen worse in Draica, though not this scolding.

Scapp said the men looked to be Myrcian: "See the spurroses stuffed in their mouths? You wonder what they did to get the spits n' banes. Usually the Myrcie traders are left to their business nowadays."

Except for two channels north and south, the Gauger's Thumb blocked the entrance to the Roads. The royal Lucidorian flag—black, green and white, with the red marshfang—and the Bastian black augor-on-gold, fluttered from a campanile that rose from a low building at the center of the diamond-shaped island.

Past the wishbone walks linking the Thumb to the opposite quays, the tow-path to either side of the Moat broadened tenfold, as did the canal itself, which curved around, diminishing in size, to continue on toward the eastern wall. Another bridge, this one widest of all, spanned the bulge in the Roads, linking the northern and southern quays.

On the towpath, Doula leaned against a bollard, waiting, as they all were, for the gaugers to finish assessing the cargo of two corries ahead of the *Cock-a-Manger*. Several westbound corries, freighted with timber, passed by without pause since tolls were not taken for corries leaving the city.

Falca and Amala took the time to bring Gurrus up and she explained the necessity of keeping him tied up. He understood, but complained about the tightness of the ropes when Falca bound him. He wouldn't loosen them. "Until we're beyond the walls, you're our captive, so start looking miserable and fearful."

Warehouses, shops and taverns surrounded the quays and lined the narrow streets leading to them, spokes to the wheel of the Roads. Merchants' signs hung from myriad portals: anvils and tools for smiths, carpenters and furniture-makers; jars for potters; candles and lunelings for chandlers; coiled ropes for rope-makers; scissors for garmenters.

When Falca saw another vendor's mannequin, he wished he'd kept his mouth shut a moment before with Gurrus. The mannequin had once been alive. The vendor was selling pouches and parasols made from the skin of Timberlimbs.

THEY WERE LITTLE MORE than a stone's throw from the campanile. Falca could scarcely hear its bell sounding the hour, given the rumbling of the wagons and trundles on the bricked wharves, the braying of mules, the clatter of horses' hooves, and shouts of dock-heaves—some of them stoneskins—loading and unloading cargo from the corries.

Mongers at their carts hawked fish and roasted meats, baked bread, scorch-belly and the less potent but sweeter moomaw—all of which reminded Falca that they would have to buy what they could from Scapp, enough to last them for a several days. They'd be well into the Banishlands then, and could purchase or steal more food from steads or settlements, even leather to wrap their feet when their chasers wore out.

He'd have to do the buying or stealing, however, while Amala and Gurrus stayed hidden. Once they were into the Bounds the mehka would have to guide them in getting what they needed so they wouldn't starve until they reached a Limb village beyond the pale of Warden incursions.

When the gauger was done with the corry directly ahead of theirs, he motioned for Scapp to move up. Doula prodded Casso to get him going again. The gauger walked up the mulebridge as if one arm was heavier than the other, and indeed he carried in that hand an assortment of measuring rods and a ledger. Scapp greeted him sullenly, since he'd earlier told Amala and Falca that gaugers were suspicious of cheerfulness; to them a pleasant demeanor meant you had something to hide.

Gurrus sat, roped and scowling, near the stern, between Falca and Amala as Scapp peppered the inspection of his cargo amidships with complaints the gauger ignored, both before and after he disappeared into the cabins fore and aft.

Falca thought he had ignored Gurrus as well, or overlooked him because soon after the pair came back up Scapp shined the gauger's palm near the mulebridge, then put away his safekeep, assuming the toll complete.

"We're not done, Master Scapp," the gauger said, walking past him toward the stern. "There's the mottle up there." He wiggled his fingers. "Five more."

"*Five*?" Scapp said. "For what? They're taking him to the sawmills to sell to the Banisher drovers."

"Just so. He may walk on two legs, but you've still brought a sack of feed into the city."

Scapp sighed wearily. "Ach, here's your siller."

"Not that it's any concern of yours, or mine either," the gauger said, pocketing the coins, "but your passengers won't have a problem selling the mottle, what with all those Banishers and their augors out there by the hills. I'm told a thousand of them, and more arriving each day."

"A *thousand*? What are a thousand stumpers doing outside the walls?"

"Protection, or so they hope."

"For what?"

"Didn't you hear? There's Myrcian Gardacs moving this way through the Bounds. Up through the mountains, from Castle Rising they say. They ambushed a Warden vexal out there, wiped it out."

Scapp whistled. "That's over 200 men."

The gauger sniffed. "247 to be exact; three escaped. Word is it won't be long before they reach the Banishlands. The Allarch summoned every last Warden from postings north and south; they're all assembled now at the castlet east of the city."

"Culldred's taking *all* four prossars?"

"That he is. The entire varrang. I hear he's moving out in a day to teach the bastards a lesson—better out there in the Bounds than here—so it looks like war again with Myrcia when the news gets back to Cross Keys. After he goes, the Moat and all the city gates will be sealed until their return, by order of the Shofet. For the time being it's business as usual, except for the Banishers outside the walls. No one's letting them come into the city, with or without their 'gors."

The gauger waddled back down the mulebridge.

A glum-looking Scapp came aft. "You heard that? I'm stuck here. I can't work up a load worth the return and get out of here in a day—there's a shortpole for you."

"You're forgetting the people wanting to leave for the west right now, my friend," Falca said. "But us? We've got thousands of Wardens and Banishfolk blocking our way to the Bounds."

"And we don't have much time to find a way through, or we're stuck here," Amala said.

"T'sakut," Gurrus whispered. "T'sakut kakor."

Scapp glared at Amala. "What'd he say?"

"Same as you, except the shortpole doesn't go in the water."

"If we are to die soon, I would like these ropes cut now."

Amala used her dagger. "No one's dying soon, Gurrus."

"Sakut kakor…Saket Roak's damned kakor," Falca muttered and went to help Scapp with the mulebridge.

Chapter Seven:

GIFTS

As THE SENIOR wife of the provincial governor, His Prominence the Shofet Gelfrey Lusurr, Lady Shahanna should have been sitting at his side on the dawnstone dais for this gathering in the great hall. The steward, however, had placed her—with Gelfrey's certain approval—toward the end of the long table, beyond his two other wives: Jansa the Sow, who'd already given the Shofet two squealers; and Melia the Bitch, who would be adding a third soon enough.

Normally, Shahanna would have complained, but not this day. The slight would only make it easier for her to slip away. In the meantime, she would have liked to converse with Culldred Hoster, if only to measure the man against his son. Unfortunately, the Warden Allarch was on the other side of her husband, loudly commenting on the present demonstration of stagger and skurr techniques in the middle of the hall between Wardens selected from the boisterous flanking tables.

So Shahanna was stuck, on the one hand, with the foul breath of Hanek Sarr, commander of the citadel garrison and royal fyrd, who was boring her with his less-than-enthusiastic opinion about the display of Warden axe and shortsword martialry as he kept glancing furtively at her cleavage.

And on the other sat the steward, Leko Frim, who groused to the chamberlain about how busy the recent days had been, what with the fire in Muletown and the shockingly bold assassination of the Vasper, which had brought to the city a delegation of Cassenite dreacons demanding that certain favors given discreetly in the past to a certain prominent official by the Vasper should now be repaid with help in catching his murderer.

"As if the Shofet doesn't have enough to worry about with these back-door Myrcians coming through the Bounds," sniffed the steward as he inspected the cut and polish of his fingernails.

Shahanna also had a manicure that morning but for different reasons.

Gelfrey was hosting this convocation for Culldred and twenty chosen officers, and an equal number of Sarr's, on the eve of the Wardens' departure for the Bounds. Cossum Hoster had told Shahanna that his father did not want a somber affair. And so it wasn't, not yet anyway, since the first course of the meal had yet to be served, and Gelfrey hadn't yet risen from his chair to remind everyone in his reedy voice about the seriousness of the threat to Bastia—and the kingdom, of course.

Hopefully, when the moment came for him to give that long-winded reminder no one needed to hear, she'd be impaled to his chamber bed by Cossum's glorious baster, which wasn't so much smaller than one of the rolled-up scrolls from which Gelfrey read his proclamations every month atop Motessin's plinth in Citadel Square.

Shahanna and Cossum had not been lovers for long. She'd heard of his reputation, but hadn't met him until the day he came, escorted by a fellow Warden named Farro, to the Shofet's residence by the lake, bearing a message for him from his father.

She happened to be in the gardens by the front gate as he was leaving. He could have hurried on his way with a nod and the usual formalities, but he sent his escort ahead after a brief introduction and lingered to watch her, as if pruning roses was the most important thing in the world.

"Surely," he said, "His Prominence the Shofet can afford gloves for his lovely wife to use in her garden."

That was enough to pique her curiosity. Roses had their fragrance; was this handsome Warden's reputation as well-deserved?

In less time than it took for a manicure, Shahanna agreed to a tryst at a certain canal-side inn. Cossum's gift to her that first time was a pair of gloves that fit perfectly. To be sure, he had the demeanor of a carpet-knight, with surprisingly soft hands for a Warden, neither calloused nor scarred. He was so very amusing, making her laugh as few men could, with his gift for mimicry. If his father hadn't been the Allarch, no doubt he would have found his way to an actors' troupe in Draica. His talents certainly seemed wasted as an officer in the last remaining varrang of the King's Own Wardens.

The next time was in the Shofet's own bedchamber, he being away at a villa on one of the lake islets, not far from the one, as it turned out, where Cossum said his family once owned property. There was little danger of Gelfrey hearing of the affair. He mostly ignored her these days, favoring her the least of his three wives. And the household staff—the steward excepted—liked her the best.

Some of that was sympathy for the way Gelfrey treated his senior wife. It wasn't her fault she was barren. It wasn't as if she'd *chosen* barrenness. And from the servants' point of view that made her a preferable mistress since she had no spoiled brats to torment them. Moreover, she liked to gossip about the other wives with them in the kitchens, and protected them on occasion from the wrath of the steward, his under, and the chamberlain.

She was older, yes, but attractive and bed-eager, yet Gelfrey still ignored her. Still, she was discreet with Cossum; she worried that Gelfrey might leave his considerable wealth to the wives who gave him children. And she'd overheard Frim saying with a sigh to the chamberlain that Gelfrey was considering taking a fourth wife. Who did her husband think he was at his age, the now-dead Vasper?

The most recent tryst was at the Tiller's Rest, because Gelfrey was back in the city now, busy with Sarr making preparations for defending the city should Culldred's imminent campaign fail to stop the Myrcians. The convocation might be the last time they would see each other, and she wanted to give him a gift for him to take: a ring of blueveil accented with emeralds bought at a Feckle Street jeweler off the King's Way.

Their plan had him arriving late; she'd excuse herself from the hall and they'd have one more time, an hour perhaps, to be with each other. "I intend to soak Gelfrey's bed," she told him. "You know where it is."

The steward and chamberlain were exchanging complaints about all the Banishmen who had left their steads and stouses and were now camping outside the city with their augors. "One can hear the keening of those disgusting beasts at all hours," Leko huffed. "It's no wonder some of our better citizens are leaving."

"At this point for lack of sleep," the chamberlain replied from his chair behind the steward's, "and not fear of the Myrcians out there."

Shahanna couldn't wait any longer. Already she was feeling the effects of the expensive Gebroanan wine—and the meal was only now being served. She excused herself from the table. Gelfrey didn't notice her leaving which was, she thought, the sum of the reasons for *why* she was leaving.

She feigned distress—fingers to brow—when her handmaiden caught up to her by one of the two spiral staircases behind the dais. Shahanna sent her back, assuring the girl she merely needed to rest a while.

The din of the gathering receded as she hurried past the solar, where the Shofet conducted most of his business, then the muselair and lastly his bedchamber opposite hers and those of his broodmares. The room would be locked, but she had the key. Things hadn't soured so much that he'd taken that away from her.

She undressed, leaving only the chemise of the finest whisp. Cossum preferred to finish the rest himself, sometimes slowly, sometimes with a violent ripping. She looked at herself in the mirror. Well, she might be considerably older than Cossum but he brimmed for her. "You're still a flicka to me," he told her. "You have to be the ripest, seedless fruit I've enjoyed in a long time." She didn't believe that for a minute—and loved every word.

His one complaint was her chatter, especially when she'd sipped too much wine. "You could talk the buzz off bees," he said. True, he was hardly taciturn himself, and she had to admit that he clearly enjoyed the sound of his own words more than hers, but he had a grin that melted her, reminding her of how long it had been since her husband had smiled at her.

She told herself not to waste what little time they'd have by complaining about the Shofet, or otherwise prattle on derisively about the often ludicrous consequences of his forgetfulness, short-sight and many eccentricities: how he only ate with a spoon every other day, and employed a servant whose sole purpose was to check his clothes for insects prior to dressing.

Cossum had been amused by her revelations, especially attentive when she told him about the tapestry in the muselair.

Back when she was a more regular visitor to Gelfrey's bed, she awoke one night to find him gone. Light shone through the crack in the partially-opened door to the adjoining muselair where he spent much of his private time. The room held little interest for her, but she was curious this night. She got up to have a peek, saw him emerging from behind the tapestry that filled half the wall by his escribore.

She had to stifle a laugh. It was the silliest thing she'd ever seen. What, had he been seized with fear of insects crawling behind the tapestry while sitting at his desk?

Cossum had stared at her, almost sternly, when she described what she'd seen, as if he was a magistrate to whom she'd brought an inconsequential marital complaint. For a moment she thought she'd gone too far in the telling of private tales. Then he smiled: "Perhaps he got lost on the way to his golden pisspot."

Shahanna heard the knock at the door.

THE LAST THING Cossum Hoster thought of before she opened the door was his father telling him: *You'll have to kill her, of course.*

After they embraced, she said: "Before I forget, and Gelfrey finds this in his bed…" She opened her hand to show him a ring.

"For me?"

"For you."

"It fits perfectly," he said, even before slipping it on.

"The blue is for your eyes, the emeralds for my own—so you don't forget me while you're gone."

He could smell the wine on her breath as he kissed her. Her eyes glistened, expectant. She closed the door—too loudly—but no one would hear; there had been no one in the corridor as he made his way up. Everyone was below.

He picked her up and carried her to the canopied bed with the Shofet's personal coat-of-arms to one side, and the Bastia augor crest on the other. She was still nuzzling his neck when he set her down.

"Hurry up," she whispered. "Take all that off; you need no ruerain here. Here, let me…" She grabbed at his belt, then the buckle. While she was doing this, giggling, he took one of the embroidered pillows. She noticed that but thought nothing of it since she liked a firm pillow under her hips when he took her from behind. This time he pushed her back, kissed her one last time, and quickly slid the pillow over her face and muffled protest: "Cossum…what are you…"

He pressed down. She struggled ferociously, kicking her legs, thrashing her arms, trying to pull the pillow off, yet unable to throw off his weight. He was a big man, as were all the Hosters. She lasted about as long as he thought she would, but he didn't expect his cudgie to still be hard when it was all over.

He wasted no time lifting her limp body up and over his shoulder. He took her to the wide, mullioned window, one of two in the chamber, sat her down on the sill. She leaned against him; he pushed her away, propping her against the window. He opened it, and as he pushed her through, the chemise caught on the latch and ripped, prompting the memory of how she liked him to do that. After he'd ruined a third dress during their last tryst, she said: "By the time you get back, I'll have more."

She landed on the narrow scrim of lakeside gravel. *Crump*...

There was little danger of anyone seeing the fall, except for Farro and his two men in the prouty rocking gently on the lake, and certainly not anyone in the hall where the windows faced the south and west, not north.

The Lady Shahanna would likely be found before Cossum and the entire Warden varrang of 4000 men left at dawn, but no one would be suspicious. The unhappy first wife of the Shofet had taken her life, people would say. Perhaps if she hadn't been barren...

She'd been diverting enough. He preferred women old enough to have refined their desires and she most certainly had, even before she told him about the tapestry.

He'd discussed that with his father, who came to the same conclusion he had: what else could the tapestry hide but a door...a door to a hidden chamber? And if you were the governor of Lucidor's largest province, in charge of levying and collecting taxes—much of which never got back to the royal treasury at Cross Keys in Draica—what would you keep in a secret chamber?

Culldred deemed the gamble worth the risk, especially since they were leaving so soon after the convocation. And if they were right, the Allarch would finally have the means to pay Furka Vat the remainder of his commission, with a fortune left over.

The Lady Shahanna had done her part well, getting Cossum into the Shofet's quarters. It was possible there was some other explanation for what she'd seen, but her life was worth finding out, and he couldn't spare the time for a slide in Gelfrey's bed, much less convincingly persuade her for one in the muselair or beyond. Whatever was in that room couldn't include a bed.

He moved quickly past the hooded fireplace. He'd brought lockpicks from Bashto, lead armorer of the First prossar, but he didn't need them for the door to the muselair. He bolted it behind him.

Across the room, two wooden augors, painted black and carved to half-size, flanked the escribore, as if it wasn't enough for the Shofet to have as many larger ones guarding the arched gate to his residence. The mandibles were too small to be menacing and one was broken off but the eyes, painted as red as the real ones, seemed to be watching him as he hurried into the room.

The Wardens had first brought the ferocious beasts from the Bounds, to sell to quarrymasters and to facilitate the clearing of the wilderness for their castlets up and down the Borders. Banishmen bred them now. Every stumper stead had at least one for heavy timber hauling and protection against Timberlimbs who were terrified of them.

Behind the escribore, just as Shahanna had said, the tapestry hung from a wall paneled in burlbright, depicting a motif of birds in blue, green and red and, prominently, an Erseiyr. The Shofet a secret worshipper of Erseiyrs?

The tapestry and augors dominated the muselair. A large tripod spyglass stood by a window ledge set within an alcove. Wall maps of the kingdom and province flanked the mate to the fireplace in the bedchamber. Scrolls, ledgers and leather-bound books filled shelves on another wall.

Cossum made sure a second door to the outside corridor was bolted. Slipping behind the Shofet's high-backed chair at the escribore, he drew his dagger and lifted the bottom edge of the tapestry…and grinned.

A door.

He bunched the tapestry higher, moved his hands to align the folds with the center of the door, and stabbed the heavy cloth to the paneling with the dagger. The door was made of hard shivernot, a single plank for the entire breadth and height, its dimensions crafted to the smaller Shofet but not Cossum; he'd have to duck his head to enter.

There was no key hole or handle. That made sense. A key could be misplaced or stolen, a lock picked. So there had to be a mechanism elsewhere, most likely hidden in the surrounding paneling. He pressed and grazed the paneling for hidden seams, but all he felt was the urgency of passing time. His father had said he'd make sure to speak at great length at the end of the convocation. Still, Cossum had to find the way to get in here, and soon, or he'd have to abandon his mission.

He went back to the middle of the room, to put himself in the Shofet's place: Gelfrey entering and deciding he wanted to go into his inner lair.

Where would he put the mechanism to open the door? In the room somewhere close to the tapestry, the desk? Why fumble between wall and tapestry for it? The Shofet would want to just slip inside and into the chamber. There would be a latch within, of course, so he wouldn't trap himself. When he was finished, he'd simply go out and over to the mechanism to close the door still hidden by the tapestry.

The escribore?

Cossum could see the desk wasn't centered on the door; the augors were misaligned as well. One crouched beyond the end of the tapestry, the other closer to the hidden door: guardians of the Shofet when he sat at his escribore.

Or…guardians of the tapestry?

Their painted red eyes bore into him as he stepped closer. The mouths were open, snarling. He noticed something, and it wasn't the difference in the carved mandibles. One of the tongues seemed…polished, unlike the other. Why would it be polished? What might have done that?

He put his hand in that fanged mouth, grasped the curled tongue, and lifted it.

Nothing.

He pushed it down.

A growling seemed to animate the beast. He snatched his hand back with a girlish shriek. The growling changed to a rasping sound…

The door to His Prominence, the Shofet Gelfrey Lusurr's secret chamber slid into the wall.

The room glowed golden-red: dawnstone. That provided enough light for Cossum to see, as he entered with a bow of his head, that the gamble had paid off—far beyond his father's hope.

On a small table to the right, by a cushioned settee, there was a small golden swan's-neck ewer with a jeweled chalice alongside. Another table held an earth-filled dawnstone trough of lunelings, the musty smell permeating the chamber. Along each wall there were barbs, from which Gelfrey could hang fresh lunes that would die slowly, providing him additional light to gaze upon his hoard. Cossum spitted two—all the additional light he'd need.

Black silk draped over dozens of pedestals and wall abutments showcasing the gold artifacts: a drum-playing skeleton presiding over a funereal scene; a goblet rimmed with leaf-nosed warrior bats; a hammered mask traced with emerald foliage; a double-headed serpent scepter; a ruby-eyed flenx pendant and another in a gripping-beast design; a stalker armlet; a bee-upon-a-thistle pin; a ribbon necklace decorated with pearl collets and rare blueveil…

He sifted through a chest of rings, torcs, bracelets and loose gems. By contrast, two larger chests brimming with gold and silver coins seemed ordinary.

Cossum knew where Gelfrey had gotten the shine, but the artifacts? Caravans from Helveylyn, smugglers from Myrcia or Keshkevar? The stalker brooch must have come from Skarria…

No more, he told himself. He'd come to steal this, not gape or wonder at the artifacts' provenance. He hurried to the window, to signal Farro and the two other Wardens in the boat, one of whom was an archer, the best in Cossum's prossar. All were men he could trust. The prouty was not that far away, the window a target that could be hit, despite the unsteady platform of the boat. Cossum set aside the standing spy glass and waited against the wall, thinking that the Shofet surely had not waited long before arranging the death of the one who built the secret chamber and devised the access.

The arrow hissed through the window, to thunk into a beam in the middle of the muselair's ceiling. Cossum pulled on the attached line to free the arrow from the beam, then began pulling up the heavier rope to which the line was knotted.

A small bale of double-lined flour sacks was also knotted at the end of the rope, and when Cossum had pulled that up, he untied it and went back to the vault with the sacks.

"Keep talking, father," he whispered.

The work went quickly. He swiped all the artifacts, save one, off the pedestals and abutments and into a single sack, not caring if they were damaged. The jewels would be prised off later, the gold melted down. He was more careful with the ribbon necklace.

He emptied the chest of jewelry and gems into another sack. The larger, heavier ones of splendents, lucras and roaks took longer. A few coins escaped the sacks. He couldn't spare the time to retrieve the strays. He would, however, have to take time to leave everything outside the vault just as he'd found it, so Gelfrey would not suspect anything was amiss—until he visited his lair again. Chances were that would not be until later in the evening, by which time his treasure would be safe in the Wardens' castlet outside the city.

Cossum filled six sacks. A single one would be enough to satisfy the contract with Vat. He could have filled each more fully, but he had to save room to tie off the ends of the sacks to the rope.

He dragged them from the vault to the window two at a time, not caring about disheveling the rugs. He lowered them, one by one, to the embrace of Farro and the others in the prouty beached on the narrow gravel strand not far from where the Lady Shahanna lay, ignored by all except for the water which had transformed her chestnut tresses into the finest filigree to float upon the lake's edge.

As Cossum made his way past the garderobe near the back of the hall, he realized he'd been lucky to have met no one on his way down. The convocation had come to an end. Separately from Sarr's men, Wardens were beginning to depart in varying states of intoxication. Redko Slange, a senior tenon in Cossum's vexal, lurched close enough for him to smell the wine on his breath. "Wherr you been, Cossie?

"Having better than what you got drunk on," Hoster said.

"Yah? Where'd ye get it?"

Cossum pushed him away. "Someday I'll tell you."

And he would, though in two weeks' time they'd know anyway, all of them—except his father's sixteen Red Hands, who already knew.

Without a doubt what Cossum drank above was better than what the Shofet had served below. In the vault he'd emptied the contents of the swan's-neck ewer—toasting himself, the Lady Shahanna and the hope that it would not be *that* long before he again slicked his baster.

On the way out he passed his father who was talking to the Shofet and the steward, both of whom had their backs to him. Cossum raised his newly-ringed hand in a fist, and nodded. His father smiled.

He went on into the pavilion, striding toward the gates, feeling a little clotted in the head. Whatever had been in the ewer was potent. Had the Shofet dosed the wine with a pinch of rife? Still, it was nothing he couldn't handle.

He patted the head of one of the stone augors and weaved his way through Wardens mounting their horses. One drunken officer fell off, to howls of laughter. Cossum felt like running, such was his exhilaration. That, however, wasn't something a Warden tenon, and the Allarch's son to boot, should be seen doing. Tenon? No, make that comitor. His father might be stingy with promotions for his sons. But after today, Cossum had no doubt he'd soon be wearing a comitor's cingulet, much to Maldan's disgust.

The street curled around to the docks of Charsen's Oath, where Bastia's most affluent moored their lake galleys, and where Farro and the others would be coming to pick him up in the prouty. Cossum trusted him completely; even so, Culldred told his son he should accompany the boat in the unlikely event the men were tempted to pilfer a coin or three.

The designated landfall was across the lake, past the citadel, on the eastern shore just north of the city's walls. The lake route would be much safer than taking a wagon-load of treasure through the entire city. Gates could be closed, pursuit could materialize should the Shofet discover, sooner rather than later, just how poor he'd become.

The nod Cossum gave his father was the signal for the Allarch to dispatch ten sworn men and a wagon to meet the boat.

Cossum could see the prouty approaching the end of the mole, and beyond, a lake galley coming in for the day. There was a time when the Hosters had their own double-tiered galley and a large villa on one of the islands off the western shore of Lake Meleke. The family made the day-long trip sometimes twice a month.

He'd been six years younger when they took their last trip up the lake, and five when his father sold the galley, villa and island shortly after his mother Heresa was abducted on an outing with three of her bodyguards and as many handmaidens. Culldred had been on a foray into the Bounds, hunting down Kezelix, a particularly troublesome Timberlimb chieftain.

The seven were never seen again. It was an outrageous crime, with hints of royal treachery since Heresa had an estranged sister who'd parlayed her beauty into a marriage to one of the King's regents. That was one rumor; others involved escaped Limbs, or bandits from the fens and krannogs at the northern and eastern fringes of the lake, or Banishmen still seething at The Clearances now generations past.

His mother's fate and the sacks of the Shofet's treasure were all of a piece, a glorious piece that few knew about, not even Lannid and Maldan, who were expected to be arriving shortly from the west.

But Culldred had to tell Cossum. What began as an off-hand comment to his father about Gelfrey's peculiarities led to the plan for the day of the convocation, and Cossum had questions Culldred had to answer. What need would there be for the Shofet's gold in the wilds of the Bounds, in the coming battle against the Myrcians? Surely they couldn't take it on the march. If all the Warden were going on the campaign, who could be trusted with guarding it in the castlet? And what of possible repercussions upon the return? There were many who despised the Wardens, who might spread rumors about the outrageous heist, rumors that in this case would be true.

His father's answer stunned Cossum.

As the prouty slid against the mole he walked ahead to greet Farro—a little unsteadily but here was a bollard to lean against—and think about how wonderful it would be to see his mother again after so long a time. He was sure she'd like the ribbon necklace and agree that the gift the Lady Shahanna had given him did indeed match the color of his eyes.

Chapter Eight:

MOON RIBBONS ON LAKE MELEKE

THE GAUGER HAD said business would be as usual for a little while longer yet, and so it was with the wagons Doula and the mule got stuck behind on the towpath leading to Finsgate. There were two of them, piled high with garbage, some of which slid off as gutterkin picked over the stinking refuse. The drovers didn't care, nor did the soldiers posted at the canal-gate farther up. Undoubtedly they had more important worries than fallen garbage, such as what would happen if the Wardens couldn't stop the Myrcians in the Bounds.

As the *Cock-a-Manger* emerged from Finsgate the wagons headed north on a road veering off from the towpath, creaking toward the lake and their destination: the municipal dump, more commonly known as the Sanctor's Piles. The garbage heaps lured so many spanners that it seemed to Falca as if snow had fallen.

They passed two other corries freighted low in the water with lumber from the saw mills ahead. Set on a low ridge at the belly of an inlet which funneled the breezes off the lake, three windmills rose higher than any tower of the city. The wind had risen with the waning day. White vanes, four to each mill, spun with a rumbling *whick…whick*. Rafts of huge logs extended far out into the lake. Teams of augors plodded around a capstan hauling in the chains that winched the logs up to rails leading into the mills.

The corry moved underneath a wide bridge linking the mills to warehouses and augor pens—ketches they were called here. Scores of men and beasts hauled lumber from the mills to corries docked at the canal-side quay, the last work to be done before the city's gates were sealed.

The Moat now curled around the far, eastern side of the mills. The vanes and top half of a tower by the lake's edge caught the lowering sun. The *Cock-a-Manger* slid into the shadows at the end, where a bridge, darkened by the base of the nearest windmill, arched over the Moat, and marked the turn-around for corries.

Doula halted the mule there, and began pulling in the slack, dripping towline as her brother guided the boat toward the embankment. Gurrus was up at the bow, sitting on his haunches, an arm around Kazy; the dog had taken a liking to him. Amala had already gathered the slingsacks of supplies they'd bought from Scapp and filled two additional waterskins. She took Falca's to fill as well, jiggling the graylock's gift inside, muttering: "If only it could make the water taste better."

Falca was standing by the mulebridge amidships when she returned and added the 'skin to their pile. He felt the bump and grating as the corry docked at the embankment.

"Doesn't look good," he said, pointing. "There's more of 'em than the gauger said."

The camps of the Banishfolk extended from near the lake's edge to the north, choking off the northern road, all the way to the hills to the east. They'd already started their fires, anticipating nightfall. Dogs yowled and barked. Staked out by the myriad crude huts and tents augors keened, rubbing their mandibles together to produce a piercing lament.

"We can't go through them," Amala said. "We can't go south—that's where all the Wardens are, ready to move out in the morning. And we can't go back into the city."

"No, we're out now." Falca scratched his bristly jaw. "Maybe we could go around?"

Gurrus joined them, the dog beside him, sniffing at the slingsacks.

"Around? How?" Amala said.

Falca thunked the rail. "With this. We've paid Scapp more to get us this far. A little extra and he might keep on, let us off farther north. No harm in asking him if he'd do that."

"Can't," Harro Scapp said.

They turned to see him standing behind them, just in from the stern. "Not that I wouldn' like the shine. But we couldn' get as far as you need to get past them squatters. No place to tow the *Manger* with that bluff out 'ere. See it?"

"I saw a small boat," Gurrus said.

"A boat? Where?" Falca said.

"Not far, on the other side of this bridge."

Falca led the way to the bow to take a look.

Through the arch of the towpath bridge flanked at the end by sentinel towers, they could see a boat gliding in toward the shore, soon disappearing behind the nearer of the towers.

"Hmmm…that would do," Falca said.

"Just the size for the three of us," Amala said.

Scapp huffed. "Didn't you see what's in that prouty? Groods. You try to buy it you'll be lucky them Wardies jus' take your money and let you keep your lives."

"Who said anything about buying the boat?" Falca said.

"No…you're not thinkin' of…"

"Unless they want to give it to us."

"Breks, listen a' me. There are four of 'em, maybe more in the east tower—whatever's outside the walls is grood business, always has been."

"You see any sentries in the tower?" Amala said.

"Well, no, but…"

"Seems they've gone to join the others with…what's the Allarch's name again?"

"It's Culldred—look they're Wardens, not hazels just press-ganged for the fyrd. You're both…"

"And only four of 'em," Falca said, "with a boat we need to get around a couple of thousand of those refugees out there."

"You're crazy, the both of you."

"Don't forget Gurrus; he saw the boat first." Amala said. "Anyway, if you have a better idea…"

"*Me?* You're asking the wrong man. I'm not—awp, there's Doula. She wants to get us turned around before dark."

"So would we," Falca said, and offered the corry's master six more coins from the pouch of Havaarl Damarr's money.

"That siller ain't worth a Scapp's hide, mine or Doula's, never mind the cargo which they'd confiscate. Anyhow, you done paid up for what you're taking."

"It's for your bow."

"You want my *bow*?"

"In case we need it—is the shine enough for you to buy another—and the arrows?"

"Well, yah, but that ain't the point. Roak's Bones—can you even shoot?"

"I've done a little," Amala said.

"Don't even try then," Scapp said. "The groods—they ain't swans liftin' off the Moat. You miss, they won't fly away." He dry-spit the corryman's ritual Threes—*ptuh...ptuh...ptuh*—to ward off bad luck. Falca wasn't much for superstition, but at this point, he figured anything would help.

THEY LEFT SCAPP and Doula where the towpath bridge rounded high over the canal. When Kazy began barking on the corry, Falca looked back and saw the *Cock-a-Manger's* master shaking his head before getting back on and hushing the dog.

The three of them kept to the brighter—and in this case hidden—side of the tower that rose from a low swell above the strand The top of its conical roof of dawnstone slate shone red in the last light of day. No challenge came from the battlements above or arrow loops. Amala had been right: the tower was empty, save for a pair of spanners ripping apart garbage or fish on the top of a merlon.

They passed the steps leading up to the door, moved around to the east side, and knelt down, unburdening themselves of slingsacks, waterskins, bow and quiver. The Wardens were not that far—a stone's throw away on the strand.

"Could you do it?" Falca whispered back to Amala. She had a hand on his shoulder.

"Maybe one, if I was lucky."

"One of the three is an archer—see him? So much for shooting them all."

The bowman and one other grood stood away from the beached boat. Another sat nearby, head over his crossed arms and a fourth was walking away from them, as if making an inspection of the empty strand. All but the sitting Warden had short-swords—skurrs—in hand.

"We all can't wander down," Falca said. "That beach is theirs for as long as they're on it. I don't think I could get close enough to draw 'em back here into an ambush so you could take a better shot or two."

"They might not come after you, either," Amala said.

"Not all of 'em."

"Could we not simply wait for the shitcatchers to leave the boat?" Gurrus said. "Surely it has served its purpose in bringing them to the shore."

"Well-tipped, Gurrus, but we don't know why they're here. They could be waiting for someone else to arrive."

"Deserters from that castlet?" Amala said.

"Not likely, not Wardens."

To their right the northern road snaked between the refugees' campfires, more of them now infesting the foothills beyond the road. Still, the Banishfolk were not close enough to see them by the tower. Directly ahead in the distance, Falca could see the passage between the rocky, wooded islet and the headland that had prevented the corry's use at any price. There were flecks of firelight on the bluff, which meant Banishers had assumed control of a place they could defend if the Myrcians defeated the Wardens in the Bounds.

It also meant the three of them couldn't just walk along the shore to get around the Banishers already in the area—even if they waited until nightfall to get past the Wardens by the boat.

Amala had seen where Falca was looking. It wouldn't have been the first time she knew what he was thinking: "We need that boat, kahyeh," she said. "And we shouldn't wait to try and get it. The night might not better the odds."

"I agree."

"But you can't swim."

"I won't have to."

It took her only a moment to realize what he meant: "Of course; why didn't I think of that?"

"You did."

"We'll have to leave everything here."

"Either we're alive to get all of it...or we're not and it won't matter."

"What are you two talking about?" Gurrus said.

"We're going for a walk in the water," Amala said.

THEY SMEARED THEIR faces—and Amala her golden hair—with handfuls of muck scooped up from the shallows. They each found their depth, with Gurrus closest in. Only their heads could stay above the water.

Falca was farthest out. Amala held on tightly to his right hand, at arm's length, ready to pull him in should the shelving suddenly drop off sharply. They couldn't risk any thrashing about or splashes the Wardens might hear.

Evening insects flitted and buzzed close to the surface of the lake, tickling and crawling over their faces. Falca didn't dare brush the pests away or duck his head into the water for a moment's reprieve—the Wardens might see the sudden movement.

So far, so good. The two groods closest to the partially beached boat were still facing away, looking inland, near enough now for Falca to hear indistinct snatches of talk. He dropped lower still, bending at the knees, so that the water lapped around his closed mouth. Amala and Gurrus did the same.

Falca stepped more carefully now. A slip here and the men would surely hear the splash. They passed the point where the Wardens might see them with but half a turn, and stopped directly behind the boat.

Gurrus was the closest to the stern and waited for Amala, then Falca to join him—she on her knees, he on his belly, straining to keep his head above the shallows. He slid over to his side so he could signal with his hands for the next: Amala to the left; he to the right. Falca pointed to Gurrus and silently tapped the planking. Gurrus acknowledged with a nod that he was to stay. Amala took out her quillons dagger. Falca checked his side one last time. The archer was still there. He would have to be dealt with first, so he couldn't pick them off as they escaped in the boat.

Falca couldn't see the other two and could only hope they were still where they'd been last: about a dozen paces beyond the nearer two, facing away, one kneeling, the other at his side.

Slowly, very slowly, he slid the falcata free of the scabbard.

Distantly he heard the rumbling of the windmill vanes, the keening of augors. And closer, much closer:

"…Still, 'twas a lucky shot, Quisky, through tha' window."

"From a rocking boat at that distance? More than luck, Farro. 'Lease ye can do is gimme the nod fer the bet if naw the siller…"

That's it, Falca thought. *Keep talking.* He crept ahead on his belly, the falcata bridging his hands, secured by his thumbs. He was so close to the boat the point of his sword almost touched the side. His elbows dug painfully into the rocks and gravel of the strand.

"Which I'm good fer it; I'll pay up."

"Yah? With what you lost at three-star last night? You had yer chance in the boat; a little pilfer I said, with none the wiser."

Falca rose to his knees, gripped the falcata. He could spit and hit the tattooed numbers on the shaved back of the grood's head. He had the bow in his right hand, the curving end resting on the gravel, string out. Falca drew back the falcata…

"And we're all lucky I didn' let you do't. A little pilfer while the tenon's puking over tha rail? How'd ye explain the shine when they searched us—and they will—where *are* they with that fucking wagon?"

Falca made sure of his footing, and sprang, twisting hard to put his weight behind the sweeping strike. The archer whirled as the falcata snapped the string and continued on into his neck above the protective ruerain flange. The archer collapsed to his knees, a hand at his neck flooding with blood. The grood he'd been talking to darted to the inside, close by the boat, to deny Falca's right hand. He saw Amala, but that moment of distraction, and a curse, was all Falca needed. He struck the Warden in the thigh, to the bone.

"Falca, behind!" Amala's shouted.

He spun away to his left. The third grood's strike narrowly missed him—Falca felt the vicious whisper—and instead sheared off half the ear and split the skull of the second.

Amala feinted a lunge with her dagger, delaying for a moment the Warden's recovery, giving Falca time for his own. He backhanded the falcata into the grood's knee, the weight of the angled blade shattering bone, shivering his hand. The Warden dropped with a scream, and began scuttling away on two hands and a leg, trailing the useless other. Falca would have gone after him but the last Warden—the tenon?—was closing on him now.

Falca easily avoided the strike that met the stones of the strand with a *clang*. This one was drunk or sick; he almost fell backwards as he straightened up, raising the skurr weakly. Falca allowed him the foolish charge, and had he himself not been tiring, would have lopped off the tenon's sword-hand, instead of giving it a bloody hinge. The skurr clattered to the gravel. The Warden seemed to stare at a ringed finger of his dangling hand. Falca took him by the ruerain flange and belt and hurried his head into the prow of the boat—a solid *thunk*—and yanked him away, to fall over the archer moaning his last. Falca snatched up the Warden's skurr and tossed it into the boat; an extra blade might come in handy.

He was catching his breath as Gurrus splashed through the shallows and onto the strand. Amala gave him the dagger to kill the three Wardens if they were not already dead. She ticked her head toward the fourth who was hobbling away toward the northern road and the Banishers. "He worth going after?"

"Can't waste the time," Falca said. "It's getting dark; he won't be able to see where we're taking the boat. We have to get our supplies. And quickly—they were waiting for others to arrive."

THE SPRINT TO the tower and back exhausted them. They tossed the panniers and 'skins over the rails. Grunting and chuffing, they moved aside two of the three Wardens to rustle the wide-bellied prouty off the strand. After they turned about the bow, Amala helped Gurrus into the boat; then she and Falca slid over the side in turn.

"There are sacks in here," Gurrus said.

Falca and Amala sat down at the two benches, reaching for the shipped oars to fit into the locks. The sacks were spread out along the keel: four between the benches and one each tucked in the bow and stern. "Flour sacks," Amala said. "Why would they be carrying flour sacks?"

"Not flour," Gurrus said, from the bow. "Something just poked me when I sat down on this one."

ONLY UNTIL THEY were far out into the lake did they stop to rest. Falca hung his wrists hung over the oar. "There they are," he said, nodding toward the shore. "The ones they were waiting for. See the torches?"

"I think so. They're hard to make out with the campfires beyond," Amala said.

"I saw two torches, those points to the north of the mills a moment ago. Now there are four. They're lighting more from the others—there's another one."

"It seems like they're spreading out," Amala said.

"Looking for the boat."

"Can they see us?"

"Probably not. The moons are bitten and the groods are blinded by their own torches. But they won't search the strand for long."

"Out here then…tonight?"

"Without a doubt, once they get the boats to do it. They won't wait for the dawn. The sooner we get past the headland the better. They'll be looking closer in for a beached boat, thinking the Banishers were the ones."

"They also don't know we're going." Amala said.

"If I was them, I'd look first around the city and then the western shore of the lake. They won't look north of the headlands. What use is treasure where it can't be spent?"

"Why not empty this boat now?" Gurrus said. "We would be able to move faster, no?"

"Gurrus is right," Amala said.

"So he is," Falca said, "but…let's not take the time now. We've had our rest. Better to lighten the boat closer to that channel we saw earlier, when we stop for another.

Amala may have understood, if not Gurrus, why Falca didn't want to dump the sacks now. She didn't press the matter, took up her oar with Falca and began rowing. They kept on until they came to the channel between the wooded islet and the bluff, guided by the glow of the Banishfolk fires on the promontory.

They shipped oars. Falca slit open one of the sacks—a small cut with the Warden skurr, yet big enough for him to take out a gold lucra…only one. "There's no point in opening up the others," he said.

Amala said nothing.

He still couldn't comprehend the fact of what lay at his feet. He'd measured his whole life with pouches and shined palms—a coin here, two there—until the graylock's gift, anyway. But here was something that might as well have dropped from the sky, a gift from the Sisters.

Where tha ribbons a' tha full moons cross a field on a cloudless night, with the Silver Trail in the southern sky, there ye'll find yer riches, boy…and look sharp because there's but a single night of the year it happens…

It had been a useless, even cruel thing for Barla Breks to say to his young son: cloudless nights were not common in Draica. And in Catchall, where the family had lived by the tanneries long enough to develop coughs and rashes—before being evicted and moving on to the tenement near the Corry Roads—how was a boy supposed to find moon ribbons that crossed a field, and know which night of the year was the one? Or perhaps his father had become so desperate with the traps-and-squeezes of his own life that he'd come to believe the legend, and left Draica—left them all—to find the fabled field.

Even if the moons had been full, the lake a field, this wasn't the one night because they couldn't keep the Wardens' gold; or rather, the hoard of the one from whom they'd stolen it.

He turned the coin over and over, rubbing the stamp of some dead king or queen with his thumb. "Wherever they got all this," he said, kicking at a sack, "they were waiting for someone else to bring it home."

"Home being…the Warden Allarch, this Culldred?" Amala said.

"And four thousand groods."

"That's the burr, isn't it?"

Falca nodded. "Taking all this to the Rough Bounds? Something else is going on, unless he means to ransom a victory instead of fighting for it."

Gurrus was at the bow, to keep watch for outcrops of rock in the water—even at his age he had better nighteyes than Falca. And he saw one now. "We are drifting toward the isle—see that rock ahead? Not the one beyond that has the shape of a flenx head."

It was a shelving, crevassed spur in which a straggling sapling had somehow found purchase. "All right, then," Falca said. "Before I sink us all." He tossed the coin—a faint *plunk*. Or was it a giggle from one of the High Fates?

The boat rocked as Amala helped Falca dump the sacks overboard.

They resumed their places and began rowing. Falca eased off so the boat turned away from Gurrus' flenx-head rock.

Sacks of flour, that's all they were, he thought, and began rowing harder. The boat moved more quickly, the only sound the dipping and splashing of the oars, the creaking of the locks and, as they passed by the headland, the keening of the augors high above.

Chapter Nine:

RAIDERS

FALCA OPENED HIS eyes to a brightness that had no source. He turned to nuzzle Amala next to him, but she was gone from the bedroll they'd shared for the night on a hill above the lakeshore. Gurrus was gone, too. The falcata, which he always kept unsheathed at his side, was gone.

He scrambled to his feet, ignoring the stiffness and aches from hours of rowing. Mist enveloped him. His sudden fear seemed almost as palpable as the skeletal trees surrounding him.

Where were they?

He knew they wouldn't have taken his falcata and gone on without him, abandoning him, not willingly. Was this one of those visions Gurrus called a kesslakor? For here was the fog and he was in the midst of it. But didn't visions provide answers not mystery? And where were the voices? Weren't there always…

Then he heard them: somewhere below, not far away.

"We couldn't have sunk the boat with only the dagger."

"No one will see the boat now to mark our landfall."

"We should go back now; it's good we let him sleep for a while longer. We'll have our breakfast on the move."

The disembodied voices came softly to Falca. He'd heard another almost as clearly: his father's, in Gebroan, when he was sure he'd found him at last; and Frikko's too, after she died, though for all he'd understood of Tongue, she might have been a girl playing a stick across a fence.

Another voice came to him, the softest yet, just before Amala and Gurrus appeared out of the mist: *I know what you fear. If only it were as easy to sheath that fear as it is the sword for which your father named you. But heed this: better the path ahead, for all that could befall you and those with you, than the way behind. That retreat has no destination except a burrow snug with laments and regrets for what could have been…*

GURRUS SCENTED THEM FIRST.

"Horses. Many of them, approaching quickly."

Falca looked back, smelled nothing but the scrubbed-out forest to either side of the meandering track they'd stumbled upon earlier in the morning. He heard little save the faint knocking of axes somewhere ahead. Still, if Gurrus said horsemen were coming, they were coming.

"Falca, over there," Amala said. "Till they pass." She pointed at the nearest of the huge stumps that dotted the rising, scavenged land here. They quickly left the rutted trail. A few hours before they could have taken only a few steps away and not be seen. Now, all that was left of the fog was a misty lacing in the treeline beyond the cutting, wreaths that swirled slowly to the east with the breeze that had carried the smell of horses to Gurrus.

They crouched behind the stump. Two saplings rose from its rot. They could have spread out, hands to hands, and still not spanned the width of the stump that had been sawed off beyond Falca's height. He breathed in the dankness of decaying wood and flowers growing from a broad notch that had once supported a Banishman's sawing plank.

They were hidden well enough but still not far from the track. They couldn't risk continuing to the dense forest where the less impressive heirs to this giant had yet to be felled. They didn't want to chance the open ground, tromping through the brush and ferns and salal that shrouded all but the tops of the myriad smaller stumps. The next closest giant—Gurrus called them kelvastas—was even bigger than theirs.

Falca unsheathed his falcata. Amala, huddled next to him, gripping the Warden's sword. As they'd walked, he'd given her a few lessons in its use, the rudiments of what Starris Vael had taught him.

He heard no thundering of hooves—the track was not fit for pace. Soon enough he heard them talking. He dared not peek around. Two, four…ten horsemen? However many, all that mattered was that they move on and then he, Amala and Gurrus could decide how best to move around the Banisher stead, or whatever lay in the vale below.

The riders didn't move on.

Someone cleared his throat: "Wespy, g'on ahead, see what we got."

Falca turned, sensing Amala's tenseness. She was biting her lip. Her face was smudged; he grazed it with the back of his hand. She mouthed: *Wardens?*

He shook his head. They couldn't have ridden north so fast. Nor could they have discovered the boat, much less seen them in the fog that had lasted most of the morning.

After a few minutes one of the riders said: "Well?"

"Four quivs in tha' field, an' one not worth tha taking."

"That's my nod t'make, not yorn."

"Tha one's scarce more'n a titter, Vocar; s'all I meant."

"Still shine, Ticker, still shine. Men?"

"Cuttin'…over there, past tha ketch fer tha 'gor. Two I saw."

"Good."

Another voice: "So we net three—four, I mean; that'll make nine with what Quire's gotten."

"Eight. Yer scassin' the one he ain't gonna sell. 'Salt for his beans', he said."

"He will, an' shut yer reekhole, Ticker."

"Only countin' what won't bring us nothin' in Baster."

"Save yer spit for the quivs down there. You know what t'do. Take Jovall with you."

"Me n' Ticker…wisha…thass all?" the other said.

"Any more, the stumpers might break fer the trees to save their own arses. Seen it before, an' we canna have that."

"'Cause they might see us and we're s'posed to be Myrcies, right Vocar?"

"Just get down 'ere. Let the stumpers get close but not too close before soundin'. Got it?"

Falca heard the men ride off, then…boots, a scuffling.

"Whar you goin', Cassop?"

"Whut d'ye think?"

He noticed a beetle with pincers longer than its body scuttling down from his shoulder. He stayed still. Amala flicked it off.

The boots scuffed closer. Falca wiped dry the palm of his sword hand. A branch snapped, then another. After a moment he saw the end of the pissfall.

Falca let out a silent breath. The rider wouldn't be coming any closer to do his business.

Someone laughed. "You piss like my brother stutters."

"Least I have one worth holdin'."

Another: "Might's well leave it hangin', Soppie."

Vocar: "None a' that; not 'til we get back an' Quire sees what we brung."

A horn brayed distantly and the riders took off with a yipping and hooting soon matched by the beat of hooves.

When that faded, Falca said: "We can't stay here."

"Where, then?"

Falca pointed to another of the giant stumps, whose canted scalp rose to the level of the ridge. "It's east, anyway."

The cut woodland brimmed out to a knoll stubbed with small stumps and piles of logs waiting to be hauled away. They passed hummocks of wild grass and ferns that hid the ruin of the logging, and stopped near the kelvasta stump crowning the ridge. Looking back, Falca was satisfied they couldn't be seen from the track they'd left. He crept ahead, Amala and Gurrus following. At the edge of stacked logs near the crest they slumped to their bellies…as women below began screaming.

Surrounded by two dismounted raiders, one had already been netted, a gray cocoon writhing by the pen where an augor strained at its stake. Near the tilling field, another with a hoe slashed at a horseman. A flung net fouled the crude weapon before she could strike again, and they were on her.

A third, child in hand, tried to escape toward the forest and the men. Two more riders, a net slung between them, bore down on the pair. Snared, the woman fell, and tried to free herself even as she held the child. The riders wheeled sharply back to cinch their prize.

Other raiders had blocked the two men from the women, and further separated those two from each other. There were gaps between the horsemen; the men could have fled toward the forest verge where they'd been working by a trundle cart. They didn't. One had an axe, the other a canthook to parry the riders' swords, hobblers and spiked augor prods—a ferocious clanging of iron.

The younger of the two men had the axe. He knocked aside a prod, charged the rider. In his frenzy, he gave his back to another rider who spurred ahead and cut him across the waist before he could kill the other. The stumper fell, twisting one way until the first rider's prod smashed into his face, spinning him in the other with a gushing of blood.

The older man had kept his back to a wide stump, refusing to be drawn out. A raider lay in front of him, his horse trotting away. Another screamed as he held a partially severed arm, stumbling past a dying, twitching horse. But now that the younger man was dead more riders closed on the elder. He couldn't fend off all the prods and swords.

He didn't see a rider dismount and creep up behind the stump. Falca wanted to shout a warning to him; he bit his lip instead. There were too many of the bastards; at least a dozen left. He felt Amala's hand grip his arm just before the stumper fell from a sword that cleaved his shoulder.

The leader—this Vocar—swung his sword-arm as if smiting something else in the air: "No!" he shouted. "Not yet. Take'm to the ketch while he lives."

They dragged him by his boots. Amala, then Falca turned away. The screams of the man being fed to his own augor came soon enough, like no other Falca had ever heard.

Gurrus had his head down; he hadn't been watching. Falca knew why: he'd seen it all before in the Rough Bounds. When Falca looked again, the riders had assembled by the Banishers' dwelling, a cabin built atop the stump of a kelvasta.

"Check tha stouse," Vocar shouted. Two of his men dismounted, raced up the steps cut into the flaring trunk, put their shoulders to the door and crashed through, to the faintest of screams within. While they were gone, others made sure of the ropes that bound hands and feet of the netted women and child draped over horses and cinched tightly as saddles.

The two reappeared. Vocar yelled: "Anything else?"

"Nat but graylocks, which they're dead."

"Good. Yerra, them scattin' Myrcies'll pay for this!" Vocar chortled. They hurried down the steps and mounted, the last of the raiders to leave.

Falca, Amala and Gurrus waited a few minutes before coming down from the ridge, passing close enough to the pen to see the severed foot, still in a boot, by the gate. The augor's muzzle hung off its mouth where the raiders had cut it so the beast could feed. The 'gor stomped in frustration, trying to use its serrated mandibles to get the bloody muzzle off, but they couldn't curl back far enough.

Smoke still curled from the reekhole in the roof of the stouse. Falca gave little thought to why the raiders hadn't torched the dwelling. He was in no mood to step over the dead within, to rummage among the stumpers' belongings and food.

Falca stopped by the body of the dead young man. Whirring insects lifted off one bloody, staring eye.

"Falca, you're not going to…"

"No, I mean to bury him, not poach his pockets."

"I'm sorry," Amala said softly.

"Don't be. There was a time I would have—so a shallow grave; won't take long."

"I would like to help," Gurrus said.

The offer surprised Falca: "A day before, if he'd seen you passing, he would have tried to kill you."

"Without doubt. But he deserves a better fate than what the night will bring."

"Well, that's what I was thinking, too."

He and Amala carried him to the field where the women had been tilling. Gurrus carried his axe. They put him down on the green barley and Amala went to find the hoe, to make the digging easier, giving a wide berth to the augor ketch. Falca and Gurrus set to work deepening a furrow, he with his falcata and Gurrus the axe.

"I am surprised you would use that," Gurrus said.

"The soft earth helps; I'll bring back the edge tonight."

"You mean that sometimes you must use what you have."

"Yes, I s'pose that is what I meant," Falca said. He could have used the Warden sword, didn't know why he hadn't.

They made better progress once Amala came back with the hoe. Falca hadn't thought before that he had soft hands, though he'd often worn gloves in Draica for street work. Yet soft they were. If a night at the oars wasn't sufficient evidence, this scraping and scrabbling was. Finally, he stood. "Not as deep as it should be, but it'll do."

They gave the young man his grave and mounded the soil over him. Falca wiped his sword free of dirt and moisture, sheathed it. He placed the axe on top of the mound and headed with the others toward the trundle cart near the forest.

They could use the cart to keep Gurrus hidden until they reached the Bounds; Amala too—a tight fit, but the discomfort paled next to the possibility of meeting more of these raiders. The cart was closer to the track leading east, well away from the northern the riders had taken with their captives.

The men had been lopping branches off young felled trees, sawing them to useable lengths to stack in the cart. They quickly emptied it, and tossed in a leather gamby one of the men had presumably taken off to work. They'd need it to drape over Gurrus, to fool a casual eye.

Amala boosted him up over the board. As she and Falca each lifted a rail and began pulling, Gurrus said: "Someone has been in here, and not long ago."

"It's the gamby," Amala said.

"I do not think so. The taint is strong. Someone else."

"So it is," Falca said. "It's all that's left of the one we didn't bury."

TIMRIT SLOAT WAITED until he could no longer hear the creaking of the cart, then emerged from his hiding place in the forest verge.

Before, watching them from his belly as he hid behind the cart, he'd thought they were going to finger Covall's pockets for something to steal—what he was going to do after the riders left—but the three buried him, the strapper using a sword the likes of which he'd never seen before, to carve out a hole for Covall. It reminded Sloat of the time his pad smacked him for playing in the dirt with a dagger: "Doona make me gripe again, boy—nat but wood, rope or flesh for a blade."

He had the same nicked dagger now, but it wouldn't have done him much good preventing them from taking the cart; the big man had that crooked blade. So he'd scuttled away, the cart shielding him from their sight.

He fled not because he was afraid, not him. He'd just never seen the likes of them, that's all. He still couldn't believe what he'd seen. Digging a grave for a stranger with an axe, sword and a hoe? And keeping company with a Limb? Sloat had seen plenty of mottles in his twenty-odd years; either dead, soon to be, or skinned and hanging from stouse poles. But alive like that?

Sloat left the woods to get the axe on the grave hump, thinking that Covall hadn't been *that* brave. He would have done the same, too; sure he would, it'd been his family. But he wasn't going to get himself killed for those who weren't kin, not even to save Maela.

He'd only come over to help with the cutting and finally quit the debt to Covall, and maybe sneak a quick slide with Maela, his older sister, like he'd done the week before. All he did was shove her against the stouse where the others couldn't see—to get her kindled, that's all. But she would have none of it—calling him a slackhoop, a sawrider; saying he was as lazy at work as he was between her legs.

No, he'd been canny to stay behind when Covall and his pad took off. He didn't know why the riders hadn't come after him; they must not have seen him loading the cart with the scantling wood Covall and his pad, Tavis, had piled for him as they argued about the decision to stay; the son saying the only thing worse than Wardens was the lack of them now; the father griping that wasn't him talking it was his mother—"so go then, an' save us tha mouth to feed."

Covall had a temper and the old man the canthook as well, so Sloat kept his mouth shut. He'd heard it before. His own pad had said the same thing for why he'd been left when his mother and younger brother left for the camps outside Baster; told him he was on his own now.

Sloat felt better with the axe in his hands, and a fine axe it was, with a new shaft. They should have taken it, too. There was nothing worth stealing in the stouse—he'd been in there. The most valuable thing Tavis had to his name was his daughter, and maybe the cart. Now that was gone, too.

He leaned on the axehead, shaft and butt pressing down on the earth they'd pampered over someone they didn't know, feeling the edges of the blade—which gave him the idea.

They couldn't have gotten far pulling the cart. They'd have to stop somewhere for the night, wouldn't they? With an axe, dirk and darkness, how hard could it be to bury Covall's pride in the strappyjack while he slept. The mottle was an old one. And the woman…

Any man who'd use his sword to scrape out some kindness for a dead stranger was a fool who didn't deserve a woman like that. Sloat liked long hair on a woman, yes he did, the longer the better, like Maela's; reins for the rut. But he'd make do with a quiver like that. What's more, that short golden hair couldn't be as greasy as Maela's.

The cart would be an added prize. He could take the woman anywhere he wanted with that. Stash her in there, bound hand and foot, save him the trouble of dragging her along behind him; keep her from running, she tried to escape. Find some stumpers willing to trade a night's worth of slides with her for a mule or swayback and he wouldn't have to push the cart.

Maybe he'd just keep her just for himself. It wasn't likely he'd ever tire of that sweet milk, but he could always sell her in Baster if he did; get ten times the price the riders would probably get for Maela.

He put the axe to his shoulder and began walking quickly after them.

Chapter Ten:

THE HOLLOW HAND

AS THEY APPROACHED the village, Amala left Falca at the wicket of the cart and joined Gurrus within—a crowded fit. She gave him more room by draping her bare arms over the side, head lolling for anyone to see. It wasn't too hard for Falca to affect the weariness of a man whose woman was plagued and dying; he'd been pushing the cart all day.

Early on, the only Banishers they'd met were the occasional horseman or family heading toward Bastia. But what if they encountered riders like the others?

Gurrus suggested spotting Amala's face and arms with koskava juice to feign disease. Along the way he'd seen thickets of koskava, common enough in Kelvarra and much favored as the shrubs produced early. The berries were also prized for skin-staining competitions during the mid-summer festivals when young males and females chose their mates.

The ruse was at least worth the sweetness of the extra berries they ate: keep a diseased woman in plain sight and it wasn't likely riders would want to ransack the cart, discover Gurrus hidden within, or even bother with the poor husband of a dying woman.

They couldn't avoid this mostly deserted village of timber-and-daub dwellings; the track they'd been using had led to a road—what passed for one in these parts—and it seemed to continue on to the east.

Four youths were playing a game of dirks, seeing how close they could stick knives to skulls set at both sides of the road. Falca pushed the cart between them, ready for any consequences of interrupting the game. One of the boys to his left knelt, tapping his dirk on a skull, whispering something to his companion, but did nothing more.

Two elderly Banishmen sat on the edge of a nearby communal well. One was sharpening the blade of a cut-shaft hobbler against a stone horse-trough, the other squeezing a boil on his cheek.

Falca was relieved that none of villagers offered to help when the cart's left wheel got stuck in a deep hole. He had to get behind the cart to rock the wheel free. Amala obligingly moaned, as if the motion added to her misery.

The man with the cut-hobbler pointed it past the well: "Take'er to tha river an' be done wi' it; t'aint far as ye go."

Falca nodded his thanks, as if the old man had relieved him of the decision. He took up the wicket's wooden bar at the front of the cart and began pushing. When he looked back he saw that the men at the well had been joined by a third.

No one was following them, but they kept on as they were, with Gurrus hidden, until the tracked dipped down again, and nothing could be seen anymore of the miserable village. Only then did Amala get out. Gurrus stood up in the cart to stretch; he'd been half-buried under Amala's legs. He dropped back down, however, since there were stouses here and there among the cutlands and fields, though the closest dwelling seemed abandoned.

The track rose again. From the noggin of this hill, they saw the stitching of a river through swatches of forest. As dusk would be coming soon they decided to camp somewhere by the river, away from the track. The bridge ahead seemed stoutly built, though narrow, and had only the spindliest of rails to prevent a fall into the river. The current churned the water white around outcrops of rock and two timbered piers supporting the span.

Amala saw a place upriver, on the far bank, where sedge and brambles partially hid the ruins and collapsed wheel of a grist mill: a defensible refuge for the night—if it came to that.

If they hurried across the bridge now, Falca would have enough light left to fashion crude spears from saplings. He figured there was a reason why Banishers preferred their hobblers: to control augors from a distance and keep predators at bay.

Still, their biggest danger now might be fatigue, an ensuing deep sleep abetted by the *shusshing* constancy of the river.

Falca lifted the rail of the wicket, about to push toward the bridge—and stopped.

A man in a hooded black mantle walked slowly along the riverside track, coming up from the south, clearly heading for the bridge. He carried a hobbler on one shoulder and a bulky pannier slung over the other. A belted longshank blade reached almost to his knee.

"Might as well let him go first," Falca said. There was little point in hurrying to get over before he did. He'd seen them now, yet evidently judged a man and a woman with a trundle cart to be of no concern and continued on his way. He was halfway across when two horsemen approached the bridge from the other side.

The riders were likely heading to the village and so would be passing closely by them. Though there were only two, Falca said: "Best the cart now, kushla."

She was about to get in when the man on the bridge brushed his hood back and shouted at the horsemen: "Bear off. Wait till I'm over."

If Falca could clearly hear him surely the riders could, yet they ignored what seemed more a warning than request. One yelled back: "Bear off yerself, old man—into the water." They spurred their mounts ahead to ensure that would happen. Soon came the brisk *clip-clip* of hooves on planking. There was scarcely enough width to the bridge to accommodate the horses, much less the lone traveler, who kept walking toward them, as if he was returning home after a day's fishing in the river, his hobbler a pole upon his shoulder.

The riders had their own at the ready. If they didn't skewer him first, the horses would trample him. They were almost upon him when the man stopped.

"If he doesn't jump now…" Falca said.

"Maybe he can't swim," Amala said.

The horses suddenly whinnied, forelegs rising, then stamping down, and rising again, bucking off the men, separating them from their hobblers. One rider fell directly into the river, helplessly splashing as the current swirled him away. The second dangled for a moment, his ankle caught in a stirrup. His head cracked into a railing post as his horse backed up with the other, snorting and stamping before he, too, splashed into the river and was gone.

The traveler resumed his walk as if nothing had happened, ignoring the riderless horses trotting away.

Falca nudged Amala. "You thinking what I am?"

"The graylock?"

"He was tall enough."

"Well…he *was* still alive the morning after. They *did* call him 'old man'. Too bad we couldn't see his face before he went on the bridge."

"If I had dreacons hunting me, I'd surely want a hood to hide my face."

Gurrus had peeked over the cart. Falca asked him: "You catch any 'snare stink?"

"Kudu? Not from here."

Falca scratched his jaw. "Towpath mule or horses, they might as well have met a wall."

"How likely is it there are two men walking around who can do that?" Amala said.

"Only one way to find out."

NOT FAR FROM the bridge, Sloat cursed as he watched the four of them move on down the track together, the strapper at the wicket; Sweetmilk and mottle to either side of the tall one.

What a skinning waste! Never mind half a day following them, hanging back far enough so they wouldn't see him skulking from stump to stump, and occasionally getting too close when eagerness got the better of what little patience he had. But he didn't think they'd seen him.

He'd have no quiver now, no shine for her later if he tired of her, and not even a cracking cart to make the day worth his while.

What happened at the bridge was very strange. Longshanks hadn't even taken out that stumper's toothpick he carried, much less braced the hobbler to spit the horses…just stood there.

Sloat had been so sure the three would stay near the river for the coming night, and let the other one move on. But the strappyjack crushed his hopes when he pushed the cart ahead faster than he'd done all day, and shouted loudly: "So the dreacons didn't catch you after all."

Then they began talking, like they knew each other.

Longshanks changed everything. Now, two men could take turns keeping watch while Sweetmilk and the mottle slept.

Maybe he was giving up too easily. Hadn't the strapper been pushing the cart all afternoon? Had to be tired. He might stand a watch but he could fall asleep and if he did…

And the other one moved slowly, or had come a long ways. Had to be tired, too. And he did look to have some years on him. If one didn't fall asleep, the other might, or get drowsy enough. So Sloat could get one with the axe and the other with a dagger swipe across the throat.

His footfalls echoed dully on the bridge planking, and soon the hissing river was behind him. He slowed to a walk when he caught sight of the cart ahead. It disappeared where the trees wept low over a bend in the track. He began loping again.

He rounded a bend in the road. The cart was gone.

All he saw was a millstone, cracked in half, leaning against a stump. The track continued on, a thin wedge between the trees. No cart.

There came a faint creaking off to his right, past the broken millstone. He noticed ruts, wider than the cart's leading through a ragged break in the forest. He hurried ahead, slowing only when the sound of the cart came more distinctly.

Then, ahead: voices…the burbling of a creek…splashes. *They'll be stopping here for the night,* Sloat thought.

He slid among the trees to begin his vigil once they made their camp—but they didn't. The voices, the cart's rumbling soon grew fainter. He followed the sounds through the thinning woods…

They were going to be stopping all right—at a stouse in the middle of a clearing.

It was no derelict, abandoned by stumpers gone to Baster: smoke wafted from the reekhole.

For all the luck he'd have getting into this one and surprising them, he might as well have knocked on the Shofet's door.

The stouse was larger than Covall's, or at least the mothering stump was—big enough for the stairs to be planked in a curling rise along the flaring girth, leading up to the trap door of the hoarding that expanded the platform of the living quarters. Nor had Covall's stouse a fancy cistern at the top, to catch rainwater that dripped off the roof. Or music—at least that's what Sloat thought he heard. Couldn't be the keening of 'gors in a ketch; there wasn't one in the clearing.

The sound rose and fell, like no other he'd ever heard, as strange to his ears as what he saw happen on the bridge.

The burly stouser, a graylock by his looks, was yanking out the topmost planks for the night, pulling on a knotted rope at the ends. He paused with the last and called out a name when the cart and four weren't even halfway across the clearing: "*Ossa*? Shave my hairy arse, it *is* you!"

He ducked inside the door. Soon after the trilling stopped a girl came out, a white band over her eyes. Somehow she found the railing, and began jumping up and down as the old stouser shoved the stair planks back into their slots. He hurried down to embrace Longshanks and greet the others.

Sweetmilk went up the stairs, followed by the mottle—to Sloat's astonishment. The stouser gestured to the cart and went over to smack the axle pin with a mallet, the loud rap resounding across the clearing. Soon, the strapper and Longshanks were carrying the wheel up the steps, and with it Sloat's hopes for the cart, a theft to salvage the day. There was nothing else he could steal. He could see the opening of an outbuilding, but there was no wagon much less a mule to pull it.

The stouser removed the last three planks, moving up a step each time, and slid the planks through the opening of the trap door. After lowering and barring it, he leaned the planks against the wheel the others had left, and went inside the stouse, taking the axle pin with him.

Darkness had fallen by the time Sloat got back to the bridge, but he was not too tired to vent his anger on the railing, hacking at it with the axe, as if the bridge itself had spawned Longshanks, the man who'd ruined his plans for the night.

Exhausted from his rage, he decided against going all the way back to the village and instead trudged off the bridge, heading toward the ruins of the mill he remembered seeing not far up the river.

In the morning he could look for the horses that had sauntered away, though with his luck snagwolves would already have shitted out what they'd eaten of them. Still, the riders surely had drowned, their bodies wedged on river rocks. Maybe he could find something in the pockets, a few coins for his trouble. Cassena and Suaila hung well over the tops of the trees, draping the river with their ribbons. He cursed the Sisters, whose brightness only reminded him of the golden-haired quiver who should have been his tonight.

Amala woke up with enough of start to stir her man.

Falca murmured: "Kushla?"

She was breathing as if she'd run down the steps to the stouse and back again. "A dream…not a good one."

He turned closer to her and she felt his cool fingers brush her cheeks. Was it warm in here or was it her? He slid his arm around her waist and began rocking her. It helped to remember how surprised she'd been to discover she liked that the first time he did it.

When he ceased she knew he'd crossed over again. She tried to join him but every time she closed her eyes they opened within to the dream…

Four Wardens gathered around a huge fire, from which rose cinders and sparks that seemed to merge with the constellations. She didn't know why Saphrax wore the ruerain but there he was, towering over the others. Falca, Gurrus, the graylock and the girl lay nearby, but they weren't dead. Falca knew where she was, knew she was watching from beyond the pale of the fire, hidden from the Wardens. He shook his head, as if telling her to go while she could, that she had no chance of saving them and the girl. All around her there was a thundering, the rushing of water that had neither source nor destination. The sound stopped as Saphrax pulled the girl up by her hair, and said to Falca: "If you won't tell us where she is, I'll cut out the girl's eyes, and save the rest of her for later; you can watch that, too." He skimmed a dagger over her eyes. "The choice is yours." The sound of the rushing water resumed louder than ever, masking her screams as she rushed from her hiding place, sword in hand, to kill Saphrax…

She thought of waking Falca up again, rousing him further—that would surely get her away from the recurring dream. But Gurrus was sleeping close by, the graylock not much farther away in front of the door.

They were one thing; the girl another. Surely Sovay would awaken in her bed behind the curtain next to her mother and father's little room. It would be hard to make love quietly when she and Falca hadn't for days now. She ached to have him inside her; even now she felt a quickening blush in her loins just at the thought of it, and the things that would have to wait until there was no one around to hear.

She kissed him on his hand as she slid from under his arm, got up, and sat down at the table close to the hearth. The scent from Ossa Vere's pipe still lingered: no cheap Lucidorian solo. Myrcian sot. The graylock was Myrcian, born in Castlecliff he'd said, and not much more.

Boket's snoring bleated from the room. His wife, Vessa, was going deaf so at least she didn't have that to bother her. They were both older than Vere, though still lively. Amala hoped that vigor would be enough at the wicket of the cart, when they left in the morning for Bastia with what little they had.

Vere was willing to accompany Falca and Amala to the Bounds, and he knew a quicker and safer way than the track, so the cart wouldn't be needed for Gurrus. The cart was their thanks for the hospitality, yet Amala wondered about their journey. What had Boket said at the table earlier, over the meal, while Vessa and Sovay were unrolling thick blankets for their guests to sleep on? "There's been those what covered tha distance with less. We've two pairs of eyes and ears 'tween the three of us, and my one hand to caress my purlie wife."

Luckily, the hand that was missing was not his carving hand, so Boket had crafted wooden replacements which hung from their straps on the wall like trophies: one a fist; another flattened like a trencher; and two more with curled fingers and thumb, so he could hold shafts or rope.

At the beginning of the meal—stumper hasmore stew—Vere had given him a new one, specially made in Draica. When Boket asked why the palm and outsized fingers were hollow, the graylock plunked the pouch of coins on the table. "Is there a better place for you to hide these?"

Were there better, more trusting people than Boket and Vessa, who'd not hesitated in offering shelter for all, and had left the hollow hand on the table? The coins were mostly smaller gold lucras; they spilled out from the wrist cuff that lay near Sovay's doll and kalo, the Kelvoi musical instrument that had widened Gurrus' eyes as much as the kinnet had Falca's. The doll and kalo were the only things she wanted to take with her in the morning.

At first Amala thought the hollow hand and money were debt-pay, for Boket and Vere evidently had been friends for many years, working the trade in bloodsnares culled from the Bounds. But she and Falca learned that the couple had wanted for some time to take their daughter away to Draica since the Banishlands, especially east of the river, was no place for a beautiful young girl. How could she be wary of the looks being given her if she couldn't see them? Boket and Vessa said this while Sovay was away from the table playing her kalo for Gurrus.

Falca and Amala exchanged glances: Draica was hardly a refuge. They said nothing, however. There was some confusion on Sovay's part; she thought Vere—whom she obviously adored—was going to go with them to Draica. He said he couldn't do that; things had changed since he saw her last.

He hesitated when the girl asked him what had changed, saying only that he hoped tell her when he saw her again. Tell her what? That he'd done something that set men after him? Amala suspected it was more than the business with the Cassenites. She sensed he had other business besides bringing back more bloodsnares to sell to dens in the cities of the west.

Boket and Vessa put Sovay to bed, and followed not long after. Gurrus soon fell asleep. Over what little remained of the scorchbelly, Amala asked Vere who the name belonged to, the one he'd murmured by the towpath. She didn't remember it but Falca did.

Flury.

The name was his daughter's, his only child. In his delirium he must have thought Amala had been her, leaning over him, giving him water.

"There's a resemblance?" Amala said.

"None that I'd recall after so many years. When you're half in the hold your mind can play tricks on you."

He thanked them again for saving his life—twice, including the dreacons the following morning—and toasted them with the last of the scorchbelly. "May you both live to wear out your last pair of boots."

"You already thanked us," Amala said.

"That? The value of that to me was in the taking."

"I almost did," Falca said. "It has to be worth the price of the corry you tossed it on."

"I might have tossed a skillet."

Amala said: "Em, there're places where that opinion would make you more of a outlaw."

"Well, it seems you know your skillets—and an honest man," Vere said, pointing the stem of his pipe at Falca, who smiled.

"I've been called many things so far," he said, "but never honest." And Falca, her Catchall ditchlicker played a hunch that never crossed her mind. "Ours wasn't the only skillet you took from the Vasper, was it?"

It wasn't. Vere had cashed the other in Bastia for the lucras on the table.

Amala looked over at him now as he twitched in his sleep. Troubled by his own bad dreams? Of his daughter and the woman who gave her birth? The murder of the Vasper? What? His hands? He never took those gloves off: not at the table; not to pack his wolf's head briar with that sweet-smelling sot; and not to sleep.

Amala picked up Sovay's doll, so unlike the fancy ones her parents had once bought for her. Normally the girl would have taken it to bed with her, but not tonight. "He needs company," she said. "He doesn't get much besides me."

She'd named the doll Shangles, made it herself from straw and twine, used the biggest buttons Vessa had—one blue, the larger brown—for the skewed eyes. To Amala, the beauty was not only in the making of the doll itself, but also that Vessa had let her do it, for surely the needle pricks would have bloodied her fingers, kept them sore for days.

Sovay said to Amala: "You have yellow hair, don't you?" It was a lucky guess, but Amala asked her how she knew.

The dark-haired girl with the linen band around her eyes, a girl on the cusp of womanhood who looked nothing like the elderly couple, held up the doll. "Shangles told me."

Amala took the pendant from the waterskin, put it in a skillet she found hanging on a peg. She left the skillet next to the hollow hand and kalo which had so entranced Gurrus. He hadn't heard its music for a long time, listened to anyone play it so well, and he'd told the girl just that, leaving aside the question of where she'd gotten it.

Amala lay down next to Falca and drew his hand around her waist. In his sleep he pulled her tightly to him. Soon after that she found a better dream waiting for her.

Chapter Eleven:

CULLDRED'S BOOK

MY SURVIVING SONS were at my side for the farewell pyre. Maldan's demeanor befitted his rank. Lannid's slouching and restlessness, however, were an embarrassment to me. He may be a Warden by right of birth, but he clearly hasn't the desire or aptitude to become one—which is also his brother's opinion. Lannid might as well have been a common hazel; some farmer's or shopkeeper's son levied into the rabble of the Shofet's fyrd.

Except for my youngest son, no one else in the four prossars ranked behind us moved or coughed though the smoke swirled thickly with a change of the wind over the gyrus grounds.

He and Maldan had arrived, tardy and squabbling, at our castlet east of Bastia the morning after the murder, and upon hearing the news from me insisted on taking part in the hunt for their brother's killer. I sent both with fifty men to search corries along the Moat and especially the Roads, to no avail. Five hundred more—half a prossar's strength—searched fruitlessly to the west of the city, along the shores of Lake Meleke and in the city itself.

It is night now. Through the west window of my chambers I can see the embers of the pyre, the blackened husk of Cossum and the others murdered with him. It is the eve of my long-planned departure, but I will at least be leaving knowing that he received the traditional Warden honor of the twilight farewell pyre. My own father never had such and deserved it more. I relented in bestowing the honor for Cossum and the other two because I chose to believe the sole survivor's report of the treachery involved, the matter of Cossum's impaired state, and the delay of the wagon and escort caused by mobs of Banishers demanding food.

As is our custom, I waited until the setting sun blessed the sword and axe mated hilt to shaft on the plank where he lay. Cossum's skurr had not been found with his body. Undoubtedly, his killer stole it. As no one—not even Maldan and Lannid—knew about what else had been stolen, this was judged in the ranks an insult to Cossum second only to his murder.

Rumex Talga, a comitor of Cossum's prossar, the Third, offered his sword for the pyre and so it was done: the pairing of stagger and skurr. Below him lay Teket Murr, the optio who had escaped with the murderer's name, description and that of his unlikely accomplices. Talga and the ten sworn men I had ordered to meet Cossum and the prouty, encountered the optio on the road where it turned south to our castlet by the bridge over the canal. The wagon that should have borne the Shofet's hoard carried Optio Murr instead.

All involved had been sworn to silence, under threat of execution, but there is no need for that now. Cossum and his picked men are dead, the Shofet's treasure gone. The optio's ruined knee would make him useless in the coming battle against the Myrcians. He couldn't bear to be left behind so I honored his request for self-sacrifice. There will be no such battle, of course; at least not for a considerable time, but Murr's uselessness remained the fact. He gave me the name of Cossum's killer; Lannid, unexpectedly, has provided much more.

Evidently he knows the furless cur, Falca Breks, by name and reputation—and the woman. He confessed to more than a passing interest in her for some years now, having made the acquaintance of her brother at Skene. It seems the woman's father had asked Lannid, before he left Draica with Maldan, to see if he could bring the daughter back without this Breks, who is nothing more than a guttering street thief. On the face of it that request is preposterous. Lannid? Yet he insisted it was made. If it seemed strange the pair would be with a mottle, Lannid informed me that the father told him they had planned on going to the Rough Bounds, to help those low creatures who dwell on high. Lannid was convinced the three should be followed there.

Since he knows nothing about the Shofet's hoard, the question of why a scavenging mongrel like Breks would let go of such a bone did not fall to him to answer. My youngest son doesn't yet know how much more useful he will be now that the Shofet's treasure is gone—and with it Furka Vat's last payments. I shall have to have Vat killed as soon as I arrive, since there is little left to pay him. Lannid will finish what work remains. That may be like asking the deaf to dance to music since he did so poorly at Skene, but dance he will.

Has this Breks hidden the Shofet's treasure somewhere along the closest shores, at a location he will remember for later, upon his return from the Bounds? He must have; how could he, a woman and a mottle take all of it with them?

Unfortunately, it might take weeks to find it if ever I could. Hundreds of my men—a thousand—would be required. So how to explain that diversion when we, a full varrang of 4,000 Wardens, are supposed to be marching east into the Bounds to meet the dire threat of a Myrcian incursion, never mind protecting the progress made to date with the extension of the King's Way into the Bounds.

No, the only course is to hunt down this ditchlicker and force him to reveal where he hid the Shofet's treasure, and come back later for it. And yes, there is the matter of vengeance for my son.

I had several candidates in mind to lead a small band to track down Breks. I was initially inclined to choose Comitor Jossar, also of the Third, who had performed so well in the extermination of the remnants of Kezelik's clan. But I have given the task to another officer. I soon found out why he came to me and volunteered.

The man is well known to me, of course. When Bovik was a comitor of a vexal of the First, he recommended the Warden's promotion from scav to tenon, a rare double elevation in rank. Years ago, I was honored with the same advancement, so that certainly got my attention. Then, six months later, this new tenon earned another promotion after a mottles' ambush not far from where our riverboats were built and currently await us. It was the same clever ambush that killed Bovik, five other officers and almost half of the men. This brave Warden took over what was left of the vexal, and though wounded himself from a stingvine, brought back the body of my eldest son.

For this I awarded him a comitor's cingulet and subsequently chose him as one of my Sixteen, the only Wardens I have allowed to venture to our destination and return. He has made two forays, the latest with the news for which I have long planned. Only the Sixteen know of what awaits us; not even my four basileii know, as there is always a danger of loose tongues in the higher ranks, where gossip can be too readily equated with fact. Not even Lannid and Maldan know. Bovik knew but he was by nature taciturn and secretive. I had to tell Cossum in order to proceed with his heist of Gelfrey's treasure.

I was initially hesitant to accept this comitor's request. Now that the secret work of the Sixteen is done, my desire is for them to become my personal bodyguard. Roak himself had his Sixteen, one from each of the ships that brought him and Cassena to this land over a thousand years ago. The Red Hands he called them. So I shall have mine, and I do not mind confessing that he was my inspiration for the number.

Still, this comitor deserved his request to be honored for the services he has rendered me to date. I can manage with but Fifteen for the time it takes him to find Breks and continue on in our wake through the Bounds. As I had to know the cut and fit of my own Red Hands, I knew of how this man came to us—the heirs to the foul legacy of Cross Keys' treachery and betrayal following the War of the Return with the Myrcians, whose assault on Draica the Wardens had done so much to repulse.

This comitor endured five years in a River Rhys prison ship, and save for the royal writ I managed to procure to yearly cull prisoners, he most surely would have died there. Four hundred were to be executed that year due to overcrowding. We chose fifty, dividing them into groups of five and, as is the Warden custom, took only those who were victorious—one way or another—for the subsequent training year.

What I did not know until tonight, when Comitor Lambrey Tallon informed me, was that Falca Breks as much as put him in that prison hulk.

Tallon is strange to look at. His black eyes seem to float above the white below. Perhaps because of the unsightly consequences of rife—that all too prevalent prison currency—he speaks little, chooses his words carefully. While this makes some men appear to be excessively cautious or timid, with him it lends an air of import to what he does say. He suggested there was no point in waiting until dawn to leave, and I agreed. Riding while Breks is sleeping will shorten the hunt. There are no decent roads through the Banishlands, except for the King's Way but if, as Lannid says, Breks and the others are for the Bounds, it is likely they will take the northern road.

Tallon understands that Warden honor is at stake, as is that of its Allarch for a personal loss. He also understands the importance of not killing Breks and the woman until he has gotten from either the location of the Shofet's hoard. Seven of our best trackers left with him and my sons.

Maldan had wished to command the detachment, to prove himself, as his rank of tenon galls him. But until he has learned to control himself better, that is where he shall remain. I would have preferred to keep both my sons with me, yet could not refuse their desire to avenge their brother. I am hopeful both will gain from this hunt for Breks; with Comitor Tallon as the bridle for Maldan, the spur for Lannid, and protector of both. I told him to treat the two like men, not my sons, and tell them what he deems necessary about our purpose as long as he does it well into the hunt.

Sons cannot be coddled and sheltered; even so, I have lost my two best and I would not want to lose any more until Bovik and Cossum are…replaced. Heresa will be distraught over Cossum, her favorite of the four, and I would be surprised if she did not wear to the end of her days his ring around her neck—and also the exquisite blueveil ribbon necklace that was found with him, no doubt his choice of gifts for the mother he hadn't seen for five years.

Heresa has done remarkably well; that is apparent from the reports of my Sixteen. Then again I knew she would. No other woman in the Six Kingdoms could have done what she has, before and after the ruse of her departure. Her idea to conjure a market for ladies' parasols made from cured skins of Timberlimbs has proven whimsically brilliant, contributing in no small way to the sums we have needed for our purpose. My agents tell me the fashion has spread beyond the provinces to Draica, and even to Castlecliff in Myrcia.

And, of course, she gave me my sons. Yet the blunt fact is that only if it had been possible to combine them into one, would she have breeched a suitable heir.

Lannid has the deft hands of an artisan, and I expect and hope he will soon lose his tavern potman's belly. But though he has the extraordinary wit to have devised the code in which I am writing now, he will never have the iron of a soldier.

Cossum was the handsomest and most amiable of my sons, with an admirable streak of cunning, but he was foremost a carpet-knight. If he had spent more of his time at the training lists and not in bedrooms he would still be alive—and I'd be gazing upon that whinny Gelfrey's entire treasure now and not merely a necklace and ring.

Though Bovik couldn't match Lannid's intelligence, or even Cossum's for that matter, he demonstrated a skill for leading men—and possibly more than that, given his indifference to women.

And Maldan? He has the brawn and temper best suited to take easy offense in a tavern ruck and prevail, yet he will always fight alone.

I would be content with but one heir to choose from, but who is to say that six are out of the question, the same number of children that Roak sired to seed kingdoms to come.

CULLDRED ADDED THE pages to all the others in the waterproof sleeve of Limbskin, now almost as thick as his wrist. Before sealing it he brushed his hand over, thinking for a moment of speckled Selila, the courtesan he would miss the most.

He'd begun the book a year after Heresa left. Never had a week passed since then, wherever he was, that he could not find the time to write an entry. Some of the pages were stained with blood—curious how Limb blood dried to a purplish black on paper. Some of them were wrinkled with his own sweat, others torn. Yet all that told a story, too.

He did not want the story to end, but it would have to at some point before he died, because he had to transcribe the code, leaving out what was not necessary or illuminating, what might sully his reputation and thus the pride of his heirs, so that others in edificias far and wide—and one in particular—could copy his work, study it and marvel: *this was Culldred Hoster and this is how he achieved his dream*…

And from the edificias the word would spread. Roak himself had bequeathed his Six Gifts but there had been a Seventh, so the legends said: a book of his life and conquests that began in the fatherland of Arriosta across the Farther Water.

That gift had been lost.

Culldred's would not. He would not let it be lost, nor allow it to be read by others until he chose the time. And he had to write it himself. Other kings and Sanctors fell prey to false and spiteful words written by others after they were dead, and sometimes before. That would not be his fate. Embellishments to his life and deeds were one thing; lies another.

It had taken him months to gain enough fluency in the code to write and read it without pause, as easily as Lannid with his verse. Lannid had developed the code he called "gliff" while he was at Skene, specializing in the study of fortifications.

The gliff began as a way for him to trade insults and gossip about detested instructors and fellow students with a friend there who had later died in a training accident. An instructor had found and confiscated the last exchange, however, and sent it to Culldred, demanding to know what it said. The necessary lies of his response had saved Lannid from getting expelled.

Looking back at the episode, Culldred judged the gliff to be the highlight of his youngest son's years at Skene. Realizing its potential, he and Heresa insisted Lannid teach them gliff. Lannid seemed to have forgotten his creation—it had been a whim, no more—but Culldred and Heresa hadn't. There was little chance the messages they sent to each other via the Sixteen would fall into the wrong hands, but if they had the gliff would have confounded both eyes and mind.

Before Culldred pinched out the candles for the night, he glanced at the latest and last message from her: *All is ready here, at long last. I await your arrival, my love, to resume our days together.*

Well, a month or two should suffice for those days. It wasn't a matter of her presumed bedswerving. After all, it had been five years, and there were on site over 300 Wardens, the vanguard necessary to prepare for the full complement of their brethren. Culldred would be surprised if Heresa, given her appetites, had not found among them a head or three for her pillows. He would certainly miss a few of the dozen he'd enjoyed, some more discreetly than others.

But she had served her purpose. He was in need of someone younger now to provide him a better brood of sons from which to choose his heir.

CHAPTER TWELVE:

PURSUIT

AT FIRST THEY wouldn't let Shar Stakeen leave, these two doordogs stationed by the King's Way gate. They told her it was for her own safety, there being all those Banishers camped outside with little to do but snatch a woman and take her horse—and what *was* her business out there that couldn't wait until the morning?

"Information about the man who murdered the Allarch's son," she said, "and I have to get it to him quickly."

If she'd heard the news only an hour after her arrival in Bastia that afternoon, these guards would certainly know, undoubtedly having seen hundreds of Wardens passing through all day. The bandy-legged guard shrugged and opened the lesser footgate. She asked how far the castlet, and he told her an hour—less if she sweated the horse—straight ahead past the fork of the road to the north.

"Mind the grood sentries," he said.

"Which they're a foul lot," the other guard said.

"Festers all," said the first, and closed the footgate behind her.

She spurred her mount ahead, thinking that a dose of truth always spiced the lie. She did have information that the Warden Allarch would find useful: not only the name of his son's murderer, but also the likely direction he'd have taken in the boat he stole.

Stakeen, however, had no intention of sharing this with Culldred Hoster. She might share the purpose of seeing Falca Breks dead, but Havaarl Damarr wasn't paying her to return a daughter violated by Wardens—or her corpse.

She rode on toward the beacon of a fire, no doubt arising from the Warden castlet. What else could account for so bright a burn except Wardens stoking some ritual to mark their departure? That fire remained her only companion for this night except for the shaved moons which cast illumination enough for shadows. The horse's hooves clipped along rhythmically on the King's Way road—timbered now, not paved as it was leading into Bastia.

BEFORE, EVEN with the time lost because of the lame horse, Stakeen had been sure she could make up the distance and catch the pair before they reached Bastia. After all, they'd been traveling in Damarr's jaunting cart—hardly a chariot for races—but either they'd abandoned the cart, taken horses, or they'd gone off the road.

So she figured either they were in Bastia for the stepping off to the Banishlands bordering the Bounds, or would be shortly. She decided, reluctantly, that she'd have to hire a few deeks, give them the description of the pair, and have them watch the other gates, while she stayed by the King's Way gate, the main route out of Bastia to the east. Time was of the essence, given the imminent closure of the city. If Breks and his woman left by one of the other gates, her bought eyes would hurry to tell her and within an hour or two she'd have them.

In a crowded tavern close by Citadel Square, she expected to find what she needed: a few pairs of eyes that weren't yet ale-shot, in exchange for a coin now and more later when the sighting was made.

She got what she needed, without the expense of deeks.

There was a reason why she'd seen so many Wardens in the city, and the tavern potman seemed surprised she hadn't heard the news; it was all over the city. Some outlaw by the name of Breks, a woman and a Timberlimb, no less, had murdered three Wardens, including Cossum Hoster, the son of the Allarch himself, and took their boat outside the city at the end of the Moat. "That's two now Knob-nose has lost," the potman said.

She listened to the barkeep and his worthies pluck the feathers of rumors from this fowl.

"A boat? Thass what sticks fer me."

"Boat's got nothin' t'do with it. Coulda been anyone's. They was on watch for Warden deserters, is what they were."

"Which ain't like no grood I saw."

"Banishers they were, I'm guessin'."

"With a mottle? Yer crocked."

She left them arguing about other news: the Shofet's first wife had been found floating in the lake. Had she jumped to her death? Was she pushed? Either way, there was agreement that three wives were too many headaches for one man, even if you could afford them.

Outside, Stakeen gave the tavern's reivebane a coin for watching her horse. She mounted, thinking that here was more proof—as if the connection to the son of Dalkan Vael wasn't enough—that Amala Damarr had run off with someone more than a common reiver. Three Wardens killed and a fourth evidently wounded? And only an old silvered Limb and pampered Heart Hill nelly to help him.

It seemed obvious Breks had killed the Wardens for the boat, yet surely not to go back *into* the city or west across the lake. So why then were the Wardens looking west? By now, Lannid Hoster would have told others where the three were going. But perhaps he hadn't arrived in Bastia.

The mottle had to be at least part of the reason for their destination of the Rough Bounds. And who despised the Limbs more than anyone else? Banisher refugees now crowding the hills outside the city.

The direction *had* to be north. They must have taken the boat to skirt the rabble, landed it somewhere north of them, and then proceeded east across the Banishlands to the Bounds. If their intent was to go south, they wouldn't have wanted the boat.

Stakeen found a stable to feed and water her horse and replenished her supplies of food and water, enough to last several more days out there. Surely that's all she'd need before she overtook them.

THE FIRE AT the Wardens' castlet had dimmed as she approached the junction of the King's Way and the northern road. Scudding clouds made the moonlight fitful. The cooling air carried the stench of smoke from campfires infesting the low hills. The absence of those fires marked the road as a rising, twisted black ribbon.

The presence of the refugees, the raspy wailing of augors, the howling dogs, only confirmed to Stakeen her reasoning, as it must have to Falca Breks and Amala Damarr.

The shadden, too, would have preferred a boat to take her around; no sense in taking chances with this lot. And with any luck she would for the return with the daughter: they'd have beached the boat somewhere on the lakeshore to the north.

For now Stakeen had to go through these Banishers. She was wary, not worried. The horse was rested for a run. Augors and dogs would be staked for the night. And how many fleet horses could the refugees have for pursuit? She'd heard the stories about these descendants of crofters cleared from their lands in the north for supposedly aiding Helveylyn borderers. Throw in criminals, smugglers and mutineers into the mix, and you had a people whom Cross Keys deemed more useful in buffering a wilderness than displaying on a gibbet, though exile usually proved as fatal as the gallows.

That was a long time ago and now the Banishers were poor gully farmers and loggers with little need of quick horses to plow fields, pull stumps, haul timber or even a lighter load of cured Limbskin.

Stakeen was about to spur ahead for the run when she heard the horses behind her, and not just a few. She quickly reined hers off the road, to the rotting remains of a stump almost as wide as the road itself. Behind it, she leaned low in the saddle. The staccato beat on the timbered road grew louder—and then the horsemen passed, at a pace fast enough to make loose sails of their capes.

Wardens.

The first three carried torches; the last the leads for two spare mounts. She waited until the torches had disappeared over a rise in the road before following.

There could be only one reason why ten Wardens would be traveling so fast, away from all their brethren who were to meet the Myrcians in the Bounds: Lannid Hoster had arrived in the city to set them in the right direction to hunt his brother's killer.

Stakeen was surprised the strutterman was with them, and further surprised he could ride at such a pace and not fall off, with or without a torch in one hand. His presence would only make the odds better for her when the time came for a reckoning with the annoying Falca Breks, who was making this retrieval less profitable for her with every hour he remained in possession of the daughter and both his hands. If he could kill the son of the Allarch and two others, nine Wardens and the whiny strutterman should not present a problem for a shadden if she was canny about it.

The Wardens were a boon for her passage through the Banishers: let them clear the way if need be. This was their territory, not hers—not yet.

But she had to keep close to them.

If they found Falca Breks before she could deal with them, they'd take turns with Amala Damarr—even the strutterman might be goaded to spill his muck before they killed her.

And the other half of Shar Stakeen's money would be gone, and with it her reputation as a shadden who had yet to fail.

Chapter Thirteen:

BOKET ON THE BRIDGE

THE SUN WAS already high over the clearing when they finally left. Ossa and the others had departed earlier in the morning, taking the trail to the east that Boket himself blazed when he had both hands and a son to help him do it.

Even the Timberlimb helped them fill the trundle cart. Vessa had given Ossa and his companions more supplies, including clothing and spare boots they could use or work the leather for a better fit. But she was merciless with what she and Boket took, because only her husband could be at the wicket, pushing the load ahead; she would have to keep Sovay's hand as they walked. She made plain her worry that the greater part of Boket's legendary stamina was his memory of it.

They paused by the creek that had watered them for so many years, to fill three jugs, enough to last until they reached Bastia. Boket also had his stoppered flenx horn of scorchbelly. He'd killed the beast himself on the very trail Ossa was on now. The hollow hand was heavy with coins, but he could still push with it almost as well as he could with his right. The wicket bar, snug between thumb and forefinger, bore the weight well.

It was best not to look back—but Sovay did, holding up her doll until Vessa gently tugged her away. The cart creaked amiably; the bowls, cups and utensils rattling in their sacks, and so Boket wasn't sure of the sound when it came. He stopped at the cart not far from the track.

"What is it?" Vessa said.

"Horsemen, up from the bridge."

Boket's hollow hand hid gold and its sleeve Amala Damarr's 'skillet' pendant. But outwardly the three of them weren't worth the bother to raiders, be they Tosk's men or Skiptoe's. There wasn't much to take from an old man and woman with a blind daughter worth little on the market, and a cart full of belongings the same as everyone else's.

They stayed put, not that they could have done anything else, being so close to the track and the marker to his stouse: the cracked millstone carried all the way from Kipe's mill when the river rose that year in a flood terrible enough to make an island of their home.

Soon enough they passed: Wardens, heading east with spares, at a pace fast enough to flutter the green-checked cape of the lead rider. Only two of them glanced in their direction, and then they were gone.

Boket cursed. "Yerra, there's nat we can do."

"I know," Vessa said, sighing.

"Do what?" Sovay said. "What's tha burr, pad?"

He paused a moment, then: "Oh, someone's after someone, but it's not where we're going, child."

He pushed at the wicket, turning west toward the river and bridge, thinking that the groods couldn't be after Ossa, unless the Cassenites had hired them away from Culldred to look for the Vasper's assassin. Boket knew well what had happened; Ossa told him a year ago what he intended to do, and so he had.

No, they were after his towpath friends who'd run afoul of Wardens leaving Bastia, and though they never gave the marrow of what they'd done, surely it had to be a chokebone for the Allarch to send these men so far away from the hunt for the Myrcians.

And without a doubt, these hounds were set to the chase, upon the asking, by the village slackhoops and idlers, for Ossa's friends would surely have been seen passing through with the cart.

They weren't far from the bridge when a lone woman approached, sitting tall in the saddle of a mare carrying dusty panniers, with an odd, trencher-like contraption poking out from under a flap. It took only heartbeats for Boket to know she wasn't from anywhere around these parts. If there was a Banishwoman, married or not, who would dare take a road alone, much less a track as rough as this one, keeping her arms bare, dark hair short and boots long, Boket would have heard the gossip about such a foolish if fine-looking quiver, the man who'd tamed her, and the ones who couldn't.

She reined in her mount. Her blackpool eyes flicked from Sovay and Vessa, to the cart, and lastly to Boket's wooden hand at the wicket rail. She asked if Wardens had recently come this way.

Vessa replied that they had.

"If ye hurry ye could catch 'em," Boket said. Something about her made him wish she would do just that. Was it just that this woman shouldn't be here?

"And how far to the Bounds, friends?"

"A long day's ride, that," he said and moved on with a push at the rail. He was glad he did, because his back was to this woman when she said: "Have you by chance seen a man and a woman hereabouts—he with a falcata; she with yellow hair? They may be accompanied by a Timberlimb."

Boket swallowed hard. Out of the corner of his eye he could see Vessa glance at him, Sovay now closer at her side. He turned by half, forcing a crease to his brow, which at his age wasn't so hard.

"Canna say I have."

"Nor I," Vessa said. "We've just taken to the road."

Sovay held up her doll. "He hasna seen them either, ladyhorse."

The woman smiled faintly. "No, I don't suppose your doll would have," she said softly, and spurred her horse down the track.

"Ye did well, Sovie," Boket said.

The girl shrugged. "Shangles tole me ta stay mum 'bout 'Mala and Falcer, so I did."

Boket and Vessa said no more about it. No good could come of Sovay listening to their suspicions and fears about the woman. And there was the possibility she was something else: perhaps a friend of the pair hoping to catch up to them before the Wardens did, and warn them. After all, she *had* asked about the groods.

Boket had almost convinced himself that's what it was—until they got to the bridge.

The body lay athwart the planks, toward the middle, blocking the span, an axe by his curled fingers. *If he's sleeping or drunk,* Boket thought, *then I'm as young as he is.*

He told Vessa and Sovay to keep back by the cart, and called out anyway: "You there!"

He went closer, didn't bother to nudge him. He was dead all right: a crop-eared stumper Boket had never seen around here before. Blood trickled down between his reddened, open eyes from a hole square in the middle of his forehead, between wisps of greasy hair. More blood seeped from a belly wound, soaking his tattered trews.

The stumper hadn't been dead for long and Boket looked around, not that he expected to see the killer hurrying away. If a local man had done this he would have taken both the axe and the dagger still sheathed at the stumper's moldy belt.

They were lucky; that was one way to look at it. Had they come along earlier, this one might have given them trouble, perhaps even ended their journey before it began. Scrawny and no doubt hungry, he might well have tried—for the cart and food within, if not an old couple and a blind girl. So surely, when the lone, comely woman rode onto the bridge, he probably could not believe his luck.

Even if he hadn't his own axe in the cart and belted dagger, Boket wouldn't have wanted the taint of the dead man's. He tossed the axe into the river, dragged boots and body to the edge and rolled the stumper off, to a second, louder splash.

Boket had no doubt now who the woman was.

And they could do no more about her than they could have the Wardens. Ossa's friends—the Draican lovers—were on their own, and Boket felt a weary sadness as he trudged back to his waiting wife and the girl they called their daughter. Never mind the 'skillet' pendant. He had enjoyed their company for the evening and would have liked to keep them as friends, to see again. The young man had a way of making you take stock in yourself, but that was how Boket liked it. And his woman obviously had more to her than outward beauty.

Falca had given them the name of a corry master named Harro Scapp, who could be trusted for passage to Draica via the Moat, if he hadn't left already. To get to the canal, they'd have to hire a boat to cross the lake, bypassing Bastia which was closed to Banishers. But they had the money for that. Amala had told Vessa of people in Draica who might help with Sovay, for she would need such…when the time came. He and Vessa wouldn't live forever.

They kept quiet until they were off the bridge. "They were right, weren't they?" Vessa said. "Her father did send someone to bring her back."

"Yes, an' they don't know the shadden's a woman."

"Man or woman, does it matter if someone can do…that?"

That? Boket thought. Vessa had seen only the body from a distance. She hadn't seen the head wound, which could only have been made by an arrow or some other point, and taken out after; yet he'd seen no bow with the woman. Whatever she'd used likely the stumper had blocked her way over the bridge. Moments before he died he was probably grinning at what he thought was his good fortune. The second wound was only to make sure. A careful, skillful woman, but that was part of her trade. He'd heard of shaddens. Now he'd met one.

Vessa walked closely enough to the wicket to rap on his hollow hand at the rail. "Bokie?"

"It does matter," he said. "When yer lookin' behind, expectin' someone else, and see a woman like that …it does. Yerra, it does."

Chapter Fourteen:

THE BARROW ON THE WHITE HILL

THEY FOLLOWED THE trail that wound through forested hillsides above the valley cutlands.

Ossa Vere assured them that taking the other wouldn't have been a good idea. Though the easiest way to the edge of the Bounds, that track went farther to the north to avoid sunken woodlands, and also passed through another village close to the rig—a fortified stead—of Gammar Tosk, who controlled much of the area.

Boket had cut the trail high in the hills to avoid the traffs that Tosk and his rival to the south, Broloy Steg, exacted from those crossing their territories, including the occasional 'snare hunter and the men who worked for them. Petty chieftains like Tosk and Steg prized bloodsnares almost as much as women for the Bastia markets. In the hinterlands, where Wardens were scarcer, they would take them if they could—including the dogs that pulled the small wagons stacked with crated 'snares.

Dogs didn't fear the taint of bloodsnares, and Boket's were sized and trained as well as he crafted the crates he once brought to the Bounds for Vere to load with his catch. But one afternoon he lost his hand, his son, his wagon and dogs in a chieftains' feud, and would have lost Vessa as well if he hadn't sent her to hide in the abandoned flenx den beneath a fallen tree by the trailhead. Though Vere hired others to replace Boket, he always visited his friend on his way to and from his hunting in the Bounds, and he always used this trail.

At a bend, where two flokas circled high over the trees, Vere stopped a moment and took out a coil of rope from his pannier. "Sometimes, Boket and I aren't the only ones up here."

Falca said nothing to this, though it struck him as odd, since Vere had told them that Boket hadn't worked with him for years. Odder still was the noose Vere quickly made out of the rope, despite his gloved hands. He pointed down at the stouse, the sixth they'd passed since leaving Boket's, then away to distant tendrils of smoke, where stumpers were burning off brush.

"Should have done this before," Vere said. "Stumpers don't always keep to the lowlands. We meet any on the trail ahead, we're 'snare hunters, heading to the Bounds. Gurrus is the bait we're going to use when we get there."

He draped the noose around Gurrus neck. "We see any ahead, one of you grab the end."

Far from being offended, Gurrus stroked the rope reverently, as if Vere had bestowed an honor, and told Falca and Amala that the rope was made of flessok: a tough, stringy moss that hung in great lengths from many of the trees in the Bounds. The Kelvoi braided flessok into ropes, then thicker cables.

"Those who braid and knot the cables," Gurrus said, "are the most esteemed of any of us, perhaps even as much as mehkas. My brother was such a one. I have not seen or held flessok in many years. Without it our villages and roads could not exist."

The trail broadened slightly as they went on. Falca looked back on the trail, to make sure it was clear, then walked ahead to ask Vere: "Gurrus will be… bait?"

"Something has to get the slithy beasts out."

The bloodsnares, he explained, hid in bolairs of the bigger trees, or bark fissures that were sometimes deep enough to bury an arm up to the elbow. They waited for prey to pass beneath and could spring out to a surprisingly long distance from the tree. They were easy enough to kill in a bolair but almost impossible to coax out—unless you wanted to become prey yourself. They hunted infrequently so it wasn't practical to wait for them to do so, hence the bait.

"You either have to trap and stake out something you've caught yourself, and net the beasts as they feed on it," Vere said, "or you have to bring the bait with you—and it has to be alive."

Amala, a few steps behind them with Gurrus, asked him if he always used Limbs for bait.

"I once did. Sometimes I'd have to climb a village tree ten times as high as that bridge was long where we met again. Paying a Kaikurra or Klesket chieftain for a shunned, sick or dying member of his clan was much easier than trapping an augor, snagwolf or flenx. 'Snares won't always come out for smaller prey like forras or kirries.

"Kleskets *would* do that," Gurrus muttered. "Kaikurras are not much better."

"If not Limbs, what?" Falca said.

Vere shrugged. "Sometimes myself."

"Just you?" Amala said.

"A man has to be very quick."

"Wouldn't it be better if two worked together?" Falca asked.

The Myrcian gave him a fleeting smile, the first Falca had seen from Vere since he greeted Boket at the stouse. "That works well on the streets of Draica, with the prize of a lady's day-necklace or safekeep. But not in the Bounds. The full price, not halved, of a healthy, wild bloodsnare puts a fell mark on the one you'd trust to work the net and light a flare to get the thing off you. It's not so much different than what a ghorgen does when an aulost is over."

A fallen copperleaf blocked the trail. As they ducked under—Gurrus didn't have to—Falca thought about Vere's lucrative trade, trapping bloodsnares and selling them to the dens of Draica, where most of the money was. A wagon-man would take his share, though, and there was the subsequent expense of the corry passage. Vere said that canal-boat masters charged double—sometimes triple—for a load of 'snares since the towline had to be twice the usual length, and mules could never be brought aboard the corry and thus were vulnerable to predators at night. Dogs couldn't pull a wagon all the way to Draica; horses and men wouldn't for different reasons. Still, it had to be a highly profitable—and dangerous—business.

"So where's your wagon-man; the crates and nets?" Falca said.

"Didn't I tell you at Boket's? I'm out of the trade."

"Why's that?"

"They've begun raising the 'snares now. Give 'em a roost, a pig or robie below once a month, and you put hunters like me out of business. Many ghorgens are buying now from the farms—mostly outside of Draica, but I heard there's some near Virenz and Nostoy. Not only do these cost less; they're also less poisonous than the wild ones, so a ghorgen can make more money since he's living longer. The Consort's Guild makes more money. Everyone makes more..."

"Except for you," Amala said.

"Well, that isn't the only burr. There's the aulosts: they're not the same. You raise a 'snare like livestock, it doesn't produce the same aulost as the wild. Sure, the ghorgens play 'em the same, but most don't care about the difference, and it won't be long before any anyone who goes to the dens knows it either."

The trail ascended more steeply and narrowly now. Falca could feel it in his legs. Yet Vere seemed to quicken his step. The wound on his arm, which had to still be bothering him, wasn't affecting his pace. Or had he enough of talking?

Falca fell back, and caught Amala's glance. He knew what it meant: if Vere wasn't going to the Bounds to hunt bloodsnares, why then? His purpose was none of their concern, nor theirs his, though they were lucky that he'd been willing to lead them on the trail. Presumably, they'd be parting ways once they reached the Bounds.

Still, there was something missing here. Vere could have stayed anywhere in the Banishlands. The Cassenite dreacons were no more as likely to pursue him here as Wardens or even a shadden were Falca and Amala. He felt confident that particular trail had ended in Bastia. As for this one, he couldn't get that word out of his mind: *bait.*

The valley below narrowed to the south, hemmed in by lower hills, and scabbed with cuts livid in the lowering light of the late afternoon. The trail still rose, veering off past a rocky outcrop. They stopped to drink from a rivulet coursing across the path. He and Amala were greedy with their slurpy sips. The water was colder and better tasting than any Falca remembered, or maybe it was just that he'd never been this hot or tired in all his days in Draica, if not Gebroan. Gurrus took but a few draughts, as did Vere, who went up the trail, disappearing around the rocks and talus of the outcrop, presumably to make sure there were no surprises around the sharp bend.

Gurrus slung the end of his noose over his shoulder so it would not get wet when they splashed through the little gully in the trail. Vere hadn't gone far. He leaned on his hobbler, his gloved hands closed to the wicked curve of the blade, seemingly lost in thought.

In the distance to the east rose a hill higher than others in the rolling terrain. Perhaps it was a trick of waning daylight, but this hill seemed bare of trees, not even cutlands. But there could be no mistaking the two white circles etched on the western slope. Within each circle, black kneeling figures faced each other; one clearly male, the other female, with exaggerated phallus and breasts. One arm of each figure reached high, the other low. Despite his weariness, Falca thrust an arm toward one of the circles on this strange hill: it easily contained his clenched fist. The circles were big.

Vere broke from his reverie and moved ahead, the butt of his hobbler tapping on the rocky trail. Falca couldn't take his eyes off the hill. Gurrus and Amala were already following Vere down the trail. He caught up to them, still wondering about the hill, but Amala was closer to Vere with the question.

"The hill?" he said. "That's where we'll be stopping for the night."

THE BARROW WAS made from the same white rock that had been cut away from the hill to form the shapes of the monumental circles and inner figures. It protruded out from the hill, below the rim of the southern circle, not far from the trail they left, and wasn't the only one. Falca counted a dozen more scattered around but none within the circle. They all seemed as empty as this one, that Vere said he'd used occasionally on his way to and from the Bounds, because there was a spring he'd found not far away, where they could replenish their waterskins.

Amala asked Vere: "What are those other things?"

"Cairns. They probably mark the entrance of looters' tunnels."

"This hill's a tomb, then?" Falca said.

The graylock shrugged. "No one knows, but some believe it's the tomb of a king that ruled this land before Roak and Cassena crossed the Farther Water. That's one explanation for this place, anyway."

"Another?" Falca said.

"Boket told me once that others believe the circles are a gathering place for souls to rise to the moons and reside there in eternity. He scoffed at that one, but it's a fact that Banishers avoid this place where no trees grow. I've also seen a monument of similar design in Milatum."

"And you don't scoff?" Amala said.

"I enjoy the flavor of legends as much as anyone—but not those. What's certain is that the Banishers haven't been in these parts long enough for them to make the circles or barrows."

"Kelvoi certainly did not," Gurrus said, "though I heard legends of a place in the west, where the Neksak once lived, where there was a hill, a wound upon the land that didn't heal. Now I've seen it."

"What I believe," Falca said, "is that we should make sure that barrow over there isn't occupied."

"Good thinking for a Draican, born and bred," Vere said.

"We have barrows in the city," Falca replied. "We just call 'em by a different name."

Vere made a torch of balled furze, stuck it on the iron end of his hobbler and entered the barrow and came out soon enough, proclaiming it empty. They all set about cutting and gathering what they could for the fire, mostly woody snowbrush and redstem—about all that grew here worth the taking, Vere said. The three piles wouldn't last through the night, but at least they'd have something to warm up the preserved meat that Vessa had given them.

The Myrcian started the fire at the barrow's entrance, ate some of the cheese they had, cutting away chunks of it with his longshank dagger—his Banisher's toothpick, he called it. But he took none of the meat, and little water; he seemed restless.

"While there's still light left I may as well make sure the other barrows are as empty as this one," he said. "We don't want any surprises during the night."

"Should we go with you?" Amala asked.

"No, it's something…there's no need of that."

Falca broke a stick of redstem and tossed it on the fire. "You sure? Amala and Gurrus will be all right here. Two of us out there are better than one."

Vere ticked a finger at Falca, acknowledging his meaning—the trapping of bloodsnares—and walked away.

Falca watched him for a few moments. "Something's not right. He had his mind set on this place for the night, but he seems to think there might be problems. So why would he choose it?"

"He seemed to me like a man who wants to be alone for a while," Amala said.

Gurrus was itching the holes where his earbolls once had been. "It is surely safer than somewhere along the trail, or in the forest."

"No doubt," Falca said. "But I'm going to follow him. The man walked as far as we have today, a graylock to boot, and you'd think he'd be for his meal and a pipe."

Amala put a hand on his arm. "Kahyeh…let him be. It could be as he said. So far we've no reason not to trust him.

"None at all." He squeezed her hand. "That's why I want to follow him."

He walked quickly up to the rim of the circle but didn't see the Myrcian below or ahead. He continued on, brushing through the grass and thickets of furze and snowbrush.

Then he saw him, a tiny figure below, passing by a barrow which appeared to have collapsed, so perhaps that was why he didn't stop to check it.

But there was another not far away, seemingly intact and Vere didn't even glance at it. Falca left the circle rim, hurried after, losing sight of him twice as he loped through the tangle of bracken, gaining ground on him. He could have shouted and the graylock would have heard him. Falca was thinking of doing just that—when Vere finally stopped at another barrow, this one larger than any of the others.

Falca knelt down quickly, obscured by the grass. Vere was looking around, though not yet in his direction. When Falca rose again, the graylock had disappeared.

He couldn't see the entrance to the barrow yet. Maybe Vere hadn't been lying after all. He was doing what he said he would be, at least with this one.

Falca hurried down the slope, unconcerned now about the Myrcian either hearing or seeing him following. Darkness had fallen more softly on this strange hillside given the whiteness of the barrow ahead. The lack of trees gave full measure to the stars and moons.

Vere was nowhere to be seen.

He's gone in, Falca thought, moving toward the misshapen entrance of the barrow. *And he's not coming out.*

There was a faint glow of fire within.

He settled into a crouch, picked up a chunk of the white rock bright as the Sisters above, and hefted it.

Why hadn't Vere told them there was someone else at this place? Falca thought of a few reasons, none of which eased his concern about the graylock's odd behavior.

A snagwolf howled from somewhere beyond the hill, and then came a more distant response as faint as the nearby rippling of water, the trickling of the spring.

At least he told us about that, Falca thought.

He had to know who was in there with the Myrcian hunter, and he wasn't going to leave until he found out. He tossed the rock aside and crept closer to the barrow's entrance, his hand on the hilt of the falcata.

CHAPTER FIFTEEN:

LAINETH

"YERRA, I was afraid ye wouldna return."

"I always do," Ossa Vere said. "I promised you I would."

"The fear wasna 'bout the promise," Laineth said.

She sat well back from the fire, a stack of wood within reach. Another rose behind her, almost to the height of the barrow. She drew back the hood of the cape he'd brought for her two years before, the finest he could purchase in Bastia. She'd told him once that she kept her hair long, dark as her daughter's, because the washing of it in the spring, and the brushing, gave her something else to do. When he visited her, it pleased them both for him to do that for her. This time would be different.

In her lap she had linen that Boket earlier had brought her. She'd stuck the sewing needles along the front edge of her cape where she would not lose them. They glinted in the firelight. Like her daughter with the doll, Laineth must often have pricked herself as she embroidered the linen bands her daughter wore. Boket would take them back with him, telling Sovay he'd bought them: a lie but also a promise to the mother who made them.

Vere had never seen any scars from the wounds, or those from the scissors Laineth used to cut the fabric. Never once had he heard her wonder why that was so yet her eyes remained sightless. Then again, perhaps she saved her self-pity for his absences, though he doubted that.

He used to visit her twice a year, on his way to the Bounds and for a briefer time on his way back since he had bloodsnares to bring to market. But he'd arranged with Boket and two other wagon-men with whom he worked to come every month and make sure she had enough food, supplies and firewood. Boket refused payment for anything. Vere paid the others well to leave what Laineth needed at the entrance of the barrow.

She didn't need the light of the fire in the shallow pit, or what little came in from the hole in the roof that he and Boket had made for ventilation. She could have sewed the bands for her daughter in the darkness and it wouldn't have mattered. She wore no band over her eyes; there was no point in that, not here. As with her daughter, there were no scars around her eyes, just a puckering of the eyelids that had closed around the emptiness beneath.

She put aside her sewing, placing it unerringly in the space between a drinking cup and a plate with morsels of food from her dinner.

"It's done?" she said.

"Yes."

She sighed deeply. "Wisha, it's so then, much as any beginning can promise."

"Sovay, Boket and Vessa left with the boon of a cart my companions no longer needed. They also suggested taking passage from Bastia on a corry, which should make a safer journey to Draica. Boket carries their money in a place—see if you can guess—that has no lid, lock or sides, but can greet a neighbor or chastise a sharp-tongued wife."

"A wooden hand. Hollowed out."

"I made it too easy for you."

"Ossa…"

"No, please…no thanks. I'm only doing what I can't do otherwise—you know that."

"And all the more reason to thank ye. May Sovie live to find out what ye've done for her."

"It's more than enough for her needs, even after Boket and Vessa are no longer around to care for her—the Vasper was very…generous."

"Ye were hopin' as much, as I recall. So tell me, how'd ye lick honey off that thorny vine?"

He smiled at that, remembering his last visit here, and what she said she would ask him to do if he was successful. "I happen to know a young woman," he began, "who must have sufficient honey or thorns—preferably both at the same time—or she tends to get bored. Luckily for me, she had little of either in her life when I confided to her my plans to go Vasper-hunting…"

They arrived at the Cassenite fhold pretending to be father and daughter. The young woman was rejected for trifling flaws: a bit too old; hair not dark enough. She summoned tears so convincingly Ossa half-believed she *was* disappointed at not being one of those selected by the Vasper for further…inspection, they called it.

Of course, he'd known she'd be found unsuitable, but not before he was loose in the fhold, hidden well until the night. He killed a blue-halo dreacon, stripped him for the uniform that would gain him proximity to the Vasper; coaxed a few baubles from the cult's patriarch before killing him, and shed the uniform after he made his escape.

Ossa didn't tell Laineth that he'd doubly stuffed the dying Vasper—mouth and arse—with skibbards taken from his nightstand, for what the pus-heart had done to Flury many years before, when she was a girl about the same age as Sovay.

Nor did he did tell Laineth the young woman was really a Draican swallow from a Galore Street brothel. For so unusual a request he had to buy her outright from the spur, but Vere would have paid twice what he demanded. Knowing the flute-girl as he did, and given what he'd later paid her, she'd probably already begun her own business in Virenz by now, though she had enough to get out of the trade.

Laineth undoubtedly guessed that his saucy deek wasn't who he said she was, however; he'd always been a terrible liar, which Flury's long-dead mother always said was one of his few redeeming qualities.

There was no need to tell Laineth how he barely escaped the fhold, and would have died if not for Amala Damarr and Falca Breks, a mercy which still surprised him.

"These companions," she said. "Friends of Boket's?"

"They are now. I met them by the Moat on my way to Bastia. As handsome and vaunty a pair of young lovers as ever made you remember how you wished it was. They did me a good turn. We met up again not far from Boket's."

Laineth smiled. "What're their names?"

"Falca Breks and Amala Damarr."

"Why would they be for the Bounds then? That's no place…"

"They killed some Wardens in Bastia."

"Yerra, *that* don't bode well for 'em."

"Nor the Limb who's with them. And they've come farther than Bastia. Evidently they had to leave Draica very quickly, so it seems the groods may not be the only ones hunting them. They've welcomed my wing, but I'm afraid they'll be on their own once we're into the Bounds—that can't be helped.

"They know 'bout ye?"

"Know what?"

"That you're dyin'."

A piece of wood fell away from the fire. Vere kicked it back in. Laineth must have heard the faint collapse; she reached over to the pile and gave the fire a stick of wood. "How bad now?"

"Laineth…"

"I want to know. Yer the man I wished I'd met after my first husband died; a good man, for all his poverty, who would've wished that for me…and Sovie. And I haven't even seen the color of yer eyes, nor ye mine. So please tell me, 'cause I've only the night. That we know."

"A month; probably less. The blisters have moved up my arms from my hands now. There's blood in my piss and shit. I'd be dead by now if I was a ghorgen, but I only handled the 'snares; they weren't feeding on me as I played 'em. It's why I couldn't go take Sovay back myself to Draica and find a place for us both, look after her."

Laineth drew him to her, hand to his glove, and they held each other. He stared at the fire as it burned lower. "Look for it anyway in the Bounds. Promise me."

She meant finding what had miraculously saved her daughter's life. It existed. It wasn't just the Eyes-of-the-Sun legend he'd heard rumors of when he first took to the Bounds, an outlaw far from the sea he loved, and scarred by the Myrcian Sanctor's spurrose Trice.

But he had as much chance of finding what would save him, as he did convincing Laineth that this should not be the last night of her life.

"I will," he said.

"For Sovie, too," Laineth said.

She had lived well enough in those days, the price of it her second husband. Traggo Steg treated her and Sovay scarcely better than he did the Timberlimb slave named Kakus. He broke the kalo Kakus made for Sovay, but there was a hidden, second one. When he was away, riding with his half-brother, Broloy Steg, Sovay brought it out for more lessons from the Limb, whose wrists and legs might have been bound in Traggo's absence, but not his quick fingers and mouth.

A Limb war band, on the way back to the Bounds, surprised them all at their stouse, killing Traggo. She saw his death from a window of the stouse, and if she felt no gladness, neither did she feel anger at what they'd done. They would soon be coming for her and Sovay, and she thought that it might be better for them both to die now, since Sovay was very sick, almost gone. A quick death would relieve her suffering, and Laineth's afterwards. She had no one else in the world.

But Kakus prevented his brethren from the killing, telling the chieftain the woman and the girl had treated him well, that the girl was eager and gifted with the kalo. Before they left with Kakus, he whispered to Laineth the whereabouts of something he'd hidden before his capture, that he couldn't and dared not give her before while Traggo was alive—something that would make Sovay well. He could say no more about where he'd gotten it, nor could Laineth give it to Sovay until after he left with the warband. He said only: "Crumble a piece and mix it well into a cup of water and have her drink it."

Laineth found it after a frantic search: a small carved box of bone containing six nuggets that could have been aged honey but were harder and without sweetness. She took one first, as any mother would.

Sovay was helping her dig the grave for her husband that evening when Broloy Steg came with twenty riders in pursuit of the Limb warband. Laineth often thought later how it might have been different if he'd come in the brightness of the day, when they might have mistaken the brightness of her eyes and Sovay's for something else.

But as the High Fates would have it, darkness revealed and did not hide—except Laineth hiding the remaining nuggets in her clothes when she should have been hushing Sovay, stopping her from blurting out, defiantly, that a Limb had given her something to cure her sickness.

They staked mother and child to the ground. Steg gouged out their eyes and tossed them into the grave, along with Traggo's body. He offered Laineth and Sovay to anyone. There were no takers except for one man, Hofer Nad, who was ordered to kill them after he'd had his fill, and burn their bodies. Steg and the rest left to continue hunting the Limbs.

Nad didn't do as ordered. "I know a ketch where ye'll be safe," he told Laineth and Sovay, and took them to the White Hill, leaving food and water. "I'll be back for ye," he said, leering.

While he was gone Laineth gave another of the nuggets to Sovay, thinking that if one cured her sickness another might restore her eyes. It didn't, and she gave her one more—until all were gone, along with their hopes.

Where were they supposed to go? The barrow offered protection from flenx and snagwolves but not from Hofer Nad. She managed to find a stick, sharpen it, and kept it close.

Nad returned a week later, bringing more food and water, marveling at Laineth's condition. "Which yer not bad at all, no mind the boley squints. I'll be tha handsomest strapper ever basted ye; whose to know diff'rent, eh?"

Laineth offered herself first to him, and when he was on her, as rooted in her as he'd ever be, she drove the stick into his left ear. Nad's scream was enough of a target for Sovay who had disobeyed her mother and come back inside the barrow with a rock. She hit him in the face. A moment later Laineth thrust the stick into his neck.

As careful as they were with the food he'd brought, they soon had no more of it. When Boket and Ossa stopped at the spring to replenish their waterskins, they saw the flenx-gnawed bones of the man Laineth and her daughter had killed and dragged out, and found them starving deep within the barrow, its entrance crudely staked to keep more flenx at bay.

There was no room in the wagon of crated bloodsnares for both, and neither mother nor daughter could walk. But there was enough room for the girl, so Boket took her on to his stouse while Vere stayed with Laineth, making her soup with water from the spring and animals he caught in the woods beyond the trail. After a few days she was well enough to walk. He said he'd take her to Boket's.

"No," she said. "An old couple with the burden of not one, but two? And what else would ye do with me? Take me to Baster, to beg on the streets, or offer myself to more like the other?"

Vere could not persuade her to go.

"Ye have your life," she said. "Would ye stay here for what's left? Best tell my daughter I'm dead, that her name was the last thing I said before I died. She must move on without me. She still has her life, such as it is now. Much has been taken from her; I wouldna take more by having her care for me the rest of the way.

"Wisha, I'd give anything to hear my daughter's voice again, hold her once more, but after? I've no right to ask more of ye. But I beg ye, Ossa, for her sake, tell her I'm gone."

"I'll be back. Something will be done," he said, and left.

Reluctantly, he did as she asked, but privately he made arrangements with Boket to supply her with what she needed, and then took his 'snares to market.

In the years that followed, as he went to and from the Bounds, he brought news of her daughter to Laineth, and to the daughter whatever gifts she'd made for the girl. He still didn't fully understand why Laineth wanted it this way. He persisted in telling her she should give the gifts to Sovay herself. What better gift than herself?

The last time he saw her he told her of Boket and Vessa's concern about the girl. They were growing older much faster than she was, or so it seemed to them, and the time would come when they would not be able to care for her. And Vere knew by then he had far less time than they did. Something had to be done—after he'd killed the Vasper…

OSSA KNEW SHE'D made up her mind, but still he persisted as they leaned against one another by the fire. He told her that he'd asked Boket and Vessa to wait for her in Bastia for a week, and then they could all go on together to Draica, with time enough to explain to Sovay why things had to be as they had for years now. He would take Laineth back to Bastia himself, though he couldn't continue on.

Falca and Amala could either wait for his return here, or go on without him. After all, he'd be leaving them soon enough after they left the Banishlands. He assured Laineth that there was enough money for them all to live well in Draica, to find a place where mother and daughter could live, with someone to care for them—before and after Boket and Vessa died.

"And live much longer than I want to, as I am?" Laineth said. "Kakus told me how Limbs, they're lucky, will choose their place and time to die, and ye have a place in mind for yours in the Bounds, no?" She added softly: "Some beautiful place ye've seen and would return to. "

"I may have said something about that."

"Well, this place is mine. Ye've made it as beautiful as any I could hope to see if I could, by knowing that Sovie has the means for care now."

She took out the dagger he'd given her for protection. The tapering blade glinted in the firelight.

"So ye won't have to use yours. It's time now. By now yer friends are thinking ye've swarped 'em. I would like to have met 'em, but it's just as well they're not here to see what they might not understand."

"They? *I* still don't understand. I'm not…Laineth, it doesn't *have* to be this way. You have a choice. I don't."

"Ye do," she said. "Ye still have time to find what could never give me or Sovay back our eyes but could heal ye—and maybe I have no right to ask ye to do this. I understand if ye can't or won't, but ye'll not stop me from doing it myself."

He took the dagger from her, and pushed the point hard enough so she could feel it through the woolen cape. He hoped the pain would bring her back, and his hope rose when she pushed the dagger away. But she opened her cape, brought his hand back, and closed the cape around the dagger. "So ye won't go back with my blood all over."

He could feel the dagger point at her skin, through the thin sark she wore underneath the cape.

"Laineth…you truly want this?"

His hand couldn't move.

"Truly?" he whispered again.

Her hands joined his around the dagger hilt. She moved the point so it would go up, into her heart.

"We'll do it together, then," she said.

Long before Ossa Vere came out of the barrow, Falca had sheathed his falcata. He knew he should have gone by now, to let them have their time. He couldn't. If that was a failing, it wasn't his first, nor would it be his last. He'd been a reiver all his life—the thefts large and small—but only now did he truly feel like one. It didn't matter that he left the entrance to kneel by the spring. He still heard them, the barrow chamber lofting their quiet words to echoes, and they echoed within him now, though all had been said, the woman gone. What he'd heard at the last wasn't her but him.

Falca stood up, prepared to announce his presence before Vere came too close, but whether it was the darkness, the burbling of the spring that masked his breathing—or what had just happened within—Vere didn't seem to notice him. He turned, as if he intended to go back in, but he didn't.

Falca saw something in his hands. It must have been the dagger because there soon came a scraping sound as Vere stood by the entrance, the top of which reached only to his shoulders. And soon Falca realized what he was doing: scraping at the seams of the fitted white stones around the lintel. Whatever the barrow—any of them—had once been, this one was now a tomb.

Vere, working steadily, his back to him, would not have noticed if he stole away, none-the-wiser at what Falca had heard, if not seen. But Falca called out: "You'll need help with that."

Perhaps Ossa Vere had noticed him before because he didn't turn around suddenly, only ceased his scraping. "All right, the two of us then," he said, and resumed his work at one end of the lintel. Falca was going to use his sword for the creases at the other end.

"No, not that," Vere said, as a father might to an inexperienced son. "The stone isn't hard but it still might nick that fine blade. Better this." He handed Falca the longshank dagger.

After a while they had loosened what they could of the seams around the lintel and began working the abutting stones free, Vere dropping one to the ground, and then Falca a second. The bigger lintel was harder work but they managed to loosen it, working at its ends and they stepped back as it dropped, cracking in half.

It was easier after that and before long the entrance was blocked except for a ragged opening at the top. Vere dropped the dagger into the barrow. Falca was about to return the blade he'd been using but the graylock said: "Keep it until you've had a chance to bring the edge back. And that"—he pointed at the opening—"we'll leave it, in case they're right about the legend."

Falca nodded. He didn't have to glance up at the Sisters. He understood: Laineth may not have left yet.

Together, with the light of the moons and the white rock of the hill to guide them, they walked back.

Chapter Sixteen:

WARDENS AT THE BOUNDS

LEANING AGAINST A huge stump, waiting for the scouts' return, Lannid Hoster thought about getting back on his horse, leaving his brother and Lambrey Tallon, and damn the consequences. He told himself he might have done just that—if his sore backside belonged to the man he wished he was.

At least he had noon sunlight above him where the tree once towered.

Beyond, where the track ended at a ravine, the Rough Bounds loomed dismally dense. In twenty years' time this edge of the Banishlands would be like the rest: a patchwork of younger woods and cutlands, the stumps nursing saplings or crowned with a stouse. There were few of these dwellings here; they'd passed the last miserable village not long after dawn.

Stumpers worked beyond the ravine at the base of a tree almost as big around as the salon of the Heart Hill manse where the pale and weary Serisa Damarr had asked him to do what he could "out there" to bring her daughter back to where she belonged.

Well, "out there" was here now—and no closer to keeping his foolish promise to Amala's mother.

He stared dully beyond Lambrey Tallon and Maldan, listening to the stumpers' rhythmic sawing. They stood on planks set in notches cut in the trunk above the flare, two at each end of the saw, with others ready to take over when they were exhausted. Teams of staked and muzzled augors, mandibles roped together, waited at a distance from their drovers. The beasts stamped their clawed hooves, and keened—which is what Lannid felt like doing, softly, so his brother wouldn't hear.

The stumpers sawed relentlessly. They'd paused only long enough to tell the Wardens that no, they hadn't seen anyone come this way, at least for the two days they'd been working the huge tree, a jiggo they called it.

The news, or lack of it, had put Tallon in as foul a mood as Lannid was now, though for different reasons.

The Wardens had been told at a village—those all seemed the same to Lannid—that their quarry had a cart and were on the track heading east, which continued past the ravine, Tallon said. He'd taken it once before with the Sixteen, whatever they were.

By now, however, they should have overtaken Breks, or seen an abandoned cart. Given the Timberlimb who presumably was still with them, there was no reason for the stumpers to lie.

Tallon had ordered scouts to the north and south to search for Breks, or at least find the cart he and the others might have left behind.

Maldan gestured for Lannid to come closer for some reason, perhaps to bear closer witness to the felling of the tree. Lannid stayed where he was. Earlier, his brother had chided him: "That far away, 'Niddy? The tree won't reach you when it falls. Where you're at you may as well be in Draica." Maldan shook his head with disgust at yet another obvious example of his younger brother's excessive caution.

Well, he might have only just graduated from Skene, but he still had an eye for measures, and could estimate height better than Maldan, whether it was a newly constructed tower or a...jiggo.

But that wasn't the reason why Lannid kept his distance, especially from Tallon.

He still simmered with anger—going on a day now—since Lambrey Tallon had told him and Maldan what he should have before they left, what their own father should have said long ago.

Oh, he'd left eagerly, having just lost a brother to Falca Breks. Amala was the ditchie's victim, too, not a willing accomplice to murder. He believed his father and Tallon wouldn't dare harm the daughter of a man whose wife's family was closely connected to Cross Keys.

Lannid had it all planned out: they'd find and kill Breks; Amala would be sent back to Bastia. And when the Wardens defeated the Myrcians, he'd return to Bastia, proudly accepting praise for his part in the campaign as well as avenging Cossum. These would be laurels of the kind he'd never won at Skene, and if at first they were given him by Havaarl and Serisa Damarr, surely Amala would bestow hers in time when she realized the mistake she'd made with Falca Breks.

But he'd been duped—never mind that Tallon said he was telling them now because the Allarch himself said it was time for them to know.

What could he do now?

Nothing.

How brave of his father—the Scourge of the Bounds—to assign a comitor to tell his sons the truth. That was bad enough, but it was somehow made worse that Maldan didn't seem to care.

Fooled…

Lied to…by his own father about his mother who had been alive all these years in some place named Scaldasaig deep within the Bounds, a place where his father and all four prossars were now going in an act of treason that surely had to trump any other in the long history of Lucidor.

There *was* no Myrcian incursion.

The annihilation of an entire vexal never happened.

Treason…that's what it was.

Lannid was not alone in his dislike of a child-king manipulated by corrupt regents, but treason was treason. And it galled him that Maldan saw this treachery merely as an opportunity, and scorned Lannid's outrage as henhouse clacking; prissy complaints made all the worse by his schooling. "But never mind that, brother," he said. "You'll likely be doing what you went to Skene for—building parapets, not pergolas."

He knew now why his father had insisted on his going to Skene. That was three years ago, and by that time his father's plan must have been well on its way—if his mother's faked disappearance was the crucial marker.

There was no way he could ever return Amala Damarr now—as her savior and devoted friend of her late brother, and son of a conquering Allarch—for the expected reward of her hand in marriage, or at least the father's approval of the only campaign in which Lannid wished to ride.

Amala may have been under the spell of Falca Breks, but in time spells could be broken. Surely she would have come to understand that she could no more base her future on defiance than he could design a loggia without columns, a citadel without towers, a city without gates, caryatids without heads…

Her life would surely be spared, but only so that she could serve as a barracks-swallow in this Scaldasaig, for barracks there would have to be for an entire varrang of Wardens.

Lannid almost wished now that they wouldn't find her and Breks. He felt guilty even thinking that; he'd liked Cossum the most of any of his brothers—well, envied was closer to the truth—and wanted Breks dead. But Amala and that gutter-cob were together; his fate could not be sealed without repercussions for her.

She couldn't have been any more than a witness to what Breks had done. And whatever punishment—if any—she deserved, could have been meted out, or so he'd thought, as payment from her wealthy father to his own.

She certainly didn't deserve the fate that would surely be hers if they found her and Breks. The scut undoubtedly treated her terribly—what else could a ditchlicker like him do? By now she must have realized how deluded she'd been about the man, what a colossal mistake she'd made. Still, she probably didn't consider herself a captive. Otherwise, she would have found her chance by now and escaped. He'd seen enough of Amala Damarr, with or without her brother, to know she would have seized that opportunity when it came.

But whether they found her and Breks or not, Lannid knew he'd lost whatever hope he'd had for her—and gained his mother back. He'd been a stripling when last he saw her, and now was a young man. He tried but couldn't picture much beyond her thin lips and buxom figure, and the hair she dyed to accent the violet eyes that were her best feature, eyes that had never seemed to be at rest except when Cossum was present.

He remembered that last day on the island of their villa on Lake Meleke, when she forbade him the honey he loved to slather on his bread, and took the book from his hands, telling him that too much reading would ruin his eyes, and pushed him outside to play with his brothers who were whacking their sword and axes at the parry-posts.

She must have known then she wouldn't see him for a long time. He realized now that she must have been concerned he'd grow up to be a weakling in her absence, as if a few dollops of sweetness every day would ruin him, make him plumper. She needn't have worried. Since they left the castlet he'd already lost weight; how could he not when all he'd eaten was dried meat and hard biscuits: the Warden campaign staples of grabble and grudge.

He never ceased his reading but he did lose his fondness for honey. When he saw her, he would make a point of telling her that she needn't have worried about him, that his eyes were still sharp. He wondered if she would even care after learning that Cossum was dead.

✵

THE NORTHERN SCOUTS returned—and not with good news, given the comitor's reaction. Lannid took some satisfaction that all of them—scouts, Tallon and Maldan—had to scurry away, horses and all, when the stumpers shouted a warning as they jumped from the planks. A cracking tore the air. The jiggo crashed across the ravine, shearing off branches of lesser brethren, one of which skidded close enough to startle Lannid's horse.

He felt the earth beneath him shudder, felt the gust of a violent wind that seemed to carry the smell of lemon. Something flew past him, to rap against the stump—a jagged fist-sized piece of bark that narrowly missed pulping his left eye. He picked it up and thought to take it for proof of the close call. He tossed it aside. No one that mattered would ever believe he hadn't moved when the behemoth fell.

Devoid of branches for most of its length, the jiggo bridged the ravine, angling away from Lannid. The dense foliage of heart-shaped leaves, ropy moss and branches at the crown formed a misshapen hillock through which smaller trees protruded.

Using the deep fissures in the bark as footholds and handholds, stumpers beetled to the top to begin the work of scaling the grayish-brown hide, shearing branches and splitting the jiggo into sections for augor teams to pull west.

Drovers collected small animals that had been shaken loose from the canopy, and began killing those not already dead—presumably to feed the augors later. One of the drovers spiked a dead bloodsnare and flung it, tentacles pinwheeling, toward the pile.

Not far away, Maldan punctured a sap boil on the tree and smeared the forward end of his sword with the sticky mess. Lannid knew what his brother was after; Maldan had told him as much before. If they had to wait for the other scouts, he said, he may as well use the time to see if he could catch a prize when the tree came down.

"I found Zeno in one almost as big," he'd said, asking Lannid if he wanted to help him look. Lannid refused. "You really need a pet; something besides your books," Maldan said. "We all have them, except for you."

And no one had pets like Maldan's. Bovik evidently had sported an eloe on his shoulder for a time. Cossum had his pets who were all probably still mourning him. His mother had Cossum himself. His father had those sixteen Red Hands.

His brother was now hunting for his pet along the underbelly of the tree, searching the ground, poking past the flutes of the bark with a stick, deeper into the fissures. He had his skurr ready.

He was looking, carefully, for a white rancer to replace the one that had died not long before they'd reached Bastia. Maldan got it the last time he'd been in the Bounds, carried it everywhere in a thick leather pouch, caught the mice himself to feed it.

Zeno…

What sort of man gave a name to a deadly insect as big as a hooly ball—not including the ten legs?

Lannid didn't doubt Maldan's claim that the thing had been undefeated in five gaming pits of Bastia and two in Draica—the reason Maldan had been late to fetch his brother for the trip back. Maldan was proudest of his pet's translucent yellow stinger the length of a middle finger. He'd only realized the rancer had died when the latest mouse he'd caught kept making a scratching fuss in the pouch…

An hour later, Tallon summoned Lannid from his distant sulk, and Maldan from the shadow of the tree where he'd still been pet-hunting when the Warden scouts returned from the south. From opposite directions they both walked their horses over to where the comitor and the others waited, mounted, impatient.

When Lannid glimpsed the blue gums that Lambrey Tallon so rarely displayed, he knew the scouts had been successful.

The slewdogs hadn't seen them, but four stumpers they met had—and not just Breks, the woman and the mottle. There was a graylock with them, who claimed Breks was his apprentice, the woman his wife. The stumpers couldn't know the man was lying. The Limb had a rope around his neck. 'Snare bait, the graylock said. The stumpers moved on, no doubt shaking their heads at the foolishness of bringing a woman into the Bounds, but 'snare hunters were known to be half-crazy from all the time alone in the wilderness.

"We have them," Tallon said, "if Kitso and Flesskie can find where they went in."

"Which we can, Comitor," Kitso said.

Flesskie nodded, scratching the shaven back of his head. "Those stumpers, they weren't too far from a trail that passes a mottle village we burned out a while ago, the year we finally got Kezelix."

"If this man's a 'snare hunter," Kitso added, "likely he'll know it's there, too. Runs under where the old track was, close enough anyhow, and down past a waterfall. The trail branches off, past the last of some pools. Couldn't have a better place to make camp for the night. S'where Limbs used to meet up. Th'Allarch got a lot of 'em there once."

"And so will we with our four now," Tallon said. "Let's go."

He turned in his saddle to Lannid, who had just mounted. "Whatever's ailing you, better you ride in the middle with it."

"'Niddy's worried he won't get his turn with Breks' quiver when we find 'em," Maldan said. "Or maybe that he will, since he's yet to spill his muck."

"The last time you spilled yours, brother—would that have been between two legs or aimed at your pet's ten?"

Maldan's reddened face gave Lannid a rare victory. But his triumph at silencing his brother soon faded with the pace set by Lambrey Tallon along the root-choked path above the ravine. What didn't fade was his guilt at hoping Lambrey Tallon would never find Amala Damarr and the man who murdered Cossum; not at the falls, not anywhere. He couldn't wish separate fates for them, much as he wanted to: they were together. And if found, they would share the same one.

LAMBREY TALLON PUSHED them hard for the rest of the day to gain the most of the trail Wardens had improved over the years. That lasted through the gloaming, the traditional time for Wardens in the Bounds to prepare for the night by clearing a camp and constructing the usual temporary enclosure of high stakes.

He kept them going, ordering one of the spare horses to be left behind as easier prey for flenx and snagwolves. With night fully drawn, Tallon abandoned the second spare for the same reason. And still they kept on, more slowly, moving by torchlight, until finally they stopped. As the men prepared the stakewall, Tallon heard Miggus whispering to Sulla: "Lucky we had the spares, or he'da left one of us."

He allowed Miggus the half-jesting, weary complaint—closer to the truth than the tracker thought. Tallon had done it before with the Sixteen, when Elcuin broke his ankle four days out from Scaldasaig on the return to Bastia.

After the meal, the comitor gave the sentry rotation, and they collapsed on their bedrolls, backs against the fire in Warden fashion, cradling their preference:

stagger or skurr. Lannid took his place next to Tallon, falling asleep by the time the comitor took off the whetstone from his neck along with the thought that if there *had* to have been a man left behind to distract flenx, *here* was the one. The comitor doubted the other Hoster would have protested vehemently.

He couldn't have done that, of course; not to a son of the Allarch. But another man certainly, if that meant an extra hour gained on Falca Breks while he was basting his quiver, or honing his blade—probably with the same whetstone Tallon had once given him as a reward for his particular help in that first fist in Slidetown. He could see him now, keening the edge with the same strokes Tallon had once shown his new deek.

He still couldn't answer the question of why he hadn't killed Breks for the attempted reive by the Valor Canal. True, he'd just lost his previous deek and needed a replacement. Sparing a life was one way to ensure loyalty. But Tallon held sway over half of Slidetown and most of Catchall at that point and could have had his pick of anyone. Was it the fact that Breks' attempt had been a clever one, and almost succeeded? Tallon couldn't believe the tall ditchie was working alone.

That was his first mistake: not killing him. The next was taking this fellow orphan under his wing, and that included flushing the gutter from his mouth, as the thedrals of the edificia in Slacere had scrubbed his before he fled to Draica after killing the one who'd tried to seduce him. Tallon dreamed of leaving the alleys and moving to places where better money could be had for two gutterkin who talked like they belonged there. Breks had the same dream, and Tallon was especially tormented by the possibility that his dream had too thoroughly nurtured Breks'—with fateful consequences.

The second mistake was as bad as the first: he'd taught Breks *too* well, should have realized early on that he was instructing the man to either be his own replacement or take his skills someplace else far from Draica. By the time Tallon decided his deek had to die, it was too late.

Breks was quicker—by a day—with his betrayal. He was nowhere to be found when the trap was sprung one drizzly night at a Falconwrist brothel. Tallon was hauled off by the Feathers, his cudgie still slick from the same swallow Breks had touted the week before.

Then came the five years in the worst of the River Rhys prison hulks. And all the smuggled-in rife he'd taken couldn't assuage his fury at Breks and his own mistakes…

Tallon tested the skurr's edge on a thumbnail…almost there. Miggus paced the small perimeter of the stakes as the comitor kept rhythmically rasping steel on stone.

Sure, it could be said that Breks had done him a favor. He'd risen rapidly in the Wardens to become one of the Sixteen, Culldred's chosen Red Hands, and the Allarch had hinted at another promotion for his ambitious comitor should this hunt be successful. His share of future conquests, however, could never wholly compensate him for what Beks had done to him. And never mind the ditchie had only been doing what Tallon himself intended. Until Falca Breks was dead, he always would be that one day quicker.

A favor? That was hindsight, the kind of sweets the High Fates so enjoyed dispensing.

Satisfied with the edge, Tallon draped the whetstone and lanyard around his neck, and cradled his sword, feeling the pull of sleep. Soon, he'd have the scut. The expectation of killing him came almost as powerfully as slaking a woman. It had to be a slow execution and that included Breks' quiver as well.

A Bloodwing? That was more like it.

Then he thought of a better way.

The deaths of two of the Allarch's sons had been a boon to Lambrey Tallon's advancement in the Wardens so far. Now, there was conveniently a third son who could still be useful, and not the plump one who alone of any of the men in the camp wasn't snoring.

Chapter Seventeen:

THE LEDGES

AMALA AWOKE TO the sight of kirries: two adults and two young, on a branch above where she and Falca lay, their amber eyes and red-ringed tails the brightest thing in the gauzy light of dawn. Were they wondering when these creatures below would be leaving so they could reclaim their home?

You're lucky we still have food or we might have caught you for dinner, Amala thought.

Gurrus had seen them first, the night before, their eyes anyway. Kelvoi bred them in pens for a ready supply of meat, their sleek fur, and the needle-like claws that had any number of uses. They weren't the only animals living in the dense forest canopy, but their meat was especially prized. Gurrus remembered the large ears, in particular, as very tasty when crisped. These kirries may have been descendants of domesticated ones who had survived the collapse of a ruined village.

Vere had known about this tangled hiding place off the trail the Wardens had blazed long ago. "It's safe enough," he said. "The groods are far to the south."

Their nest was pungent with rotting, mossy branches large and small, and quilted by a thick layer of leaves and broad tufted ferns they'd flattened the night before. It was so much more comfortable than the ground by the lake that first night, the floor of the stouse, and the stony ground of the barrow where they had talked long into the night.

Amala hadn't expected to sleep so well here in this cradle, whose protective sides were formed by fallen trees that had once risen high to support part of a canopy village destroyed by Wardens. A few Kelvoi might escaped to live on as renegades, but more would have been captured as slaves, and watched the Wardens flense the skins of dead mothers and fathers; sisters, brothers and friends. There was a lucrative market for Limbskins in Bastia.

Gurrus said they would have been Kaikurras, who never named the trees supporting their villages. Some of his fellow Tokanekes believed that was the reason for the demise of the Kaikurras, one of the more warlike clans of the west.

The day before he had pointed out the remains of the village: swatches of flessok hanging down, planking here and there, the drooping relic of a section of the canopy road that had once spanned the nearby river. But there wasn't much else to see after years of wind and storms.

Amala hoped she'd remember to tell Falca later that wherever they might eventually make their home, her wish was that it would be a place where they might hear waves crashing upon a beach somewhere; a swiftly moving river, a falls. For that's what she heard now: the sound of a cascade not far away that merged as one with the rushing of the nearer river feeding the falls through a break in these highlands.

The constancy of the roaring water was like a potion, but it had given her more than merely the best sleep of her life. The Wardens couldn't mute that sound as they had the voices of those once living high above here and in scores of villages elsewhere in the western Bounds. She had faith in Gurrus' kesslakor and in the remarkable kinnet they *would* return to the Isle of Shallan, to make the Tapestry whole again. Who knew if that might somehow unite the surviving clans of the Kelvoi.

But someday there might be Timberlimbs who would return here to reclaim what had been taken from them and make a new village among other trees. When they did, the falls and the river that nourished it would be waiting for them with a kind of music for them to hear once again, a sound that had no beginning and no end.

Falca did not wake as quietly as she. He rose to an elbow, smiling at her sleepily through a loud yawn that scattered the kirries. Amala got up, offering a hand to him. He grinned when she put a finger to her lips.

OSSA VERE PRETENDED he was asleep. He lay most closely to the entrance that was scarcely more than a hole underneath one of the toppled trees. Once out, there was a manageable jump to another and then down to the ground.

When they were gone he sat up, elbows on his knees. Gurrus roused, too. No doubt he'd also been feigning sleep.

"Those two might as well have banged skillets," Ossa said, shaking his head. Even now he could hear them whispering below—and Amala's soft laughter.

"They are young." There was no annoyance in Gurrus' voice. He seemed to understand Vere wasn't grumpy at being woken.

Ossa did feel sadness. He thought it more than likely the lovers would be dead long before they reached this Lake of Shallan. A person could do little about scent, but silence and a soft tread were crucial to survival on or off these trails in the Bounds, to help mask your presence from predators, and to give yourself a middling chance to hear them. Ossa had never told Falca he'd known he was outside Laineth's barrow before he emerged; he could hear his breathing by the spring.

And there was the sadness that he couldn't go with them, to keep them alive for a little while longer, before he was incapable of doing so. Better to leave them soon than give them the later burden of caring for a man who'd never live to see this Isle that was so important to Gurrus. He understood now a little more of Laineth's decision.

If only the Fates had given him the opportunity to see his own daughter sneaking away clumsily with someone like Falca…or a son stealing away with someone like Amala.

At least Falca took the falcata with him. Ossa supposed they'd be all right, for now, anyway. This nest was a fair piece away from the trail, which led to the falls and down past the succession of shelving rock to the pool at the end. He figured that's where they were going.

The falls and pool had once been a gathering place for Limbs and more recently a rendezvous for Wardens, coming into, or leaving the Bounds. But they were all south, the lot of them, moving to meet this Myrcian incursion. The danger of Limb renegades? Not many of those anymore; not here, anyway. Given the roar of the falls, Amala and Falca could make as much noise as they wanted, which was perhaps the idea.

"They'll be back soon enough," Ossa said, "shivering and wet." And smiling. If he'd had Rohaise with him—never mind the years—that's where she'd be taking him.

It wasn't the first time that Gurrus seemed know what he was thinking: "Once, we also would not have cared that there is nothing down there but slippery stone and chilly water."

Ossa was going to miss the Limb mehka, his gentle yet direct words, and even his oddly plump belly that he always seemed to be touching and rubbing, though Vere had never heard him complain of an ache.

THEY STOOD HAND-in-hand near the top of the falls, not far from the trail that continued down to disappear again in the forest. The river that fed the falls was only about half as wide as the one where they'd met Ossa, but the torrent of white water fell steeply. Amala could feel on her face the cool spray rising from the boiling below.

To talk would have meant shouting. They didn't have to. She had her smile and Falca his, as if he was stealing again—this time an hour alone with her. He told her he hadn't seen anything as beautiful as this place in his life. She hadn't either, not even at her mother's ancestral lake cottage north of Draica, where she'd spent summers as a child and learned how to skate in the winter.

Falca pointed at a russet bird with a bright blue tail trailing a skein of flessok from its beak, perhaps to bring to a forming nest. They watched it cross the gorge, from one side to the other above rocky shingles sloping down and away from the tumult at the bottom of the falls. These dissipated into myriad rivulets across the flat expanse of watery terraces shimmering in the sun. The bird stopped to rest on a branch of a tree angling out from the forest edge, and dropped the flessok.

Amala suddenly played the part, first giving a terrible imitation of a bird's call, then: "What was I *thinking*? It's early summer already; I've *done* the nest."

The russet bird picked the flessok strand up again and flew off, giving Falca his turn: "Oh well, I've brought it this far."

They laughed and went on toward the shelving rock that ended at a smaller falls. This one dropped to more ledges and a third set of falls, the widest yet, which emptied into a pool wreathed by early morning mist. Amala guessed the river continued on its way beyond a placid, lower pool and a trio of jagged pinnacles barbed with scrawny trees that had somehow found purchase in crevasses.

There, she thought, *somewhere down there by calm pool, the big one beyond the ledges.*

She tugged at Falca's hand. He needed no prodding and was soon ahead of her. They climbed down on all fours, grabbing hold of roots poking out of the eroded bank, but everywhere they kept well away from the slickest rocks closest to the roaring cascade.

Falca was quicker than she, even with the falcata he'd slipped into his belt. Twice he paused for her to catch up. Her only fear came near the bottom, where clouds of mist rose so thickly in places from the churned up water that she lost sight of Falca below. They swirled away as quickly as they'd enveloped her—and there he was waiting for her.

The descent was much easier once they reached the succession of sloping ledges that broadened out from beneath the higher pool into which the falls above thundered. Each ledge was no more than two or three steps down from the higher. Though water sheeted over the entire width of the ledges and more deeply in the middle, there were places along the edges where the water was shallow.

Branches littered the nearby bank; they'd have to go into the water to keep going down. Falca found a large stick and flung it out where the water was moving faster over the ledges. Seized quickly by the current, the stick disappeared over the little falls, but Amala caught sight of it lodged against one of the ledges farther down that rose up like thin tables from the water.

She wasn't going to stop here. How many sharp edges could there be, with all this water ceaselessly smoothing out the stone? Holding onto Falca, she took off her chasers, then supported him as he took off his. Carrying them in their hands, they waded in up to their ankles. She felt the chill and pace of the water. They moved ever downward toward the calmness of the pool.

When she'd looked down from the top, she'd seen but one large stony table besides the myriad smaller ones that lay as variously sized stepping-stones across the water, ending at the pinnacles. They came to this table peeking above the end of the little falls. And once Amala hopped up, she could see now that the table was divided in two; the larger portion separated from the other by a ragged fissure through which water quickened and surged to empty out into the pool.

She tossed the boots to the other side, took a running start and easily made the leap across channel. Falca did the same. They gathered up their chasers but found that they couldn't make the same carefree leaps for the remainder of the smaller stone ledges that lay scattered through the water all the way to the far bank, as they were covered with moss. Luckily, they weren't too far apart. Long strides got them across most of them—until Amala slipped, the consequence of her looking ahead to the place she'd been hoping to find down here.

Her legs spraddled out on both sides of the offending ledge. The moss that caused her to take a sudden seat also padded her ungainly fall. Falca laughed behind her. She gave him a coarse gesture that only made him howl more with delight since it was one he hadn't shown her before.

She climbed up to the last stone, bigger than the others, to wait for him. It was part of the bank, though flat enough and covered with patches of moss. The high rocky pinnacles sheltered their destination; she couldn't see the distant falls. Thick strands of flessok hung down from tree branches that reached half-way across the ledge.

Falca handed her his falcata, then his chasers. She set them aside as he paused to gaze back at the way they'd come, as if he was surprised at how muted the roar of the falls was down here by the still pool.

I'll give him something to look at, she thought, and shouted sweetly: "Oh, kahyeh…"

She pulls up her duvelin, plumped her breasts, and for good measure tweaked her nipples—not that they needed coaxing given the briskness of the early morning air and the chill from the water.

If she was satisfied by his lopsided grin, she was even more pleased when he, distracted by her bounty, slipped and soaked himself more than she had.

By the time he clambered up, she was pulling sheaves of flessok down, to spread over the moss. They added their clothes as well. She teased him further with a strand of flessok she draped over his eager cudgie.

Soon the only warmth they had was each other and then that wasn't enough.

Falca moved inside her, with her, more deeply and fully than ever before, kissing her, caressing her as if they were new to one another. Was this place the reason? Or was it the stolen time, the powerful urgency of the falls, the rushing water all around?

She would not let go of his hands. Her sense of time faded after she closed her eyes. When she opened them again, she glimpsed the bird, hoping it was the same one they'd seen before, who still thought its nest unfinished.

THEY LAY TOGETHER on the flessok and moss which they'd scrubbed down to the stone in places. Falca was still inside her, nuzzling her cheek, kissing her as she caressed his back to warm him. A green and gold petalutha fluttered by and she remembered Gurrus telling her that mehkas used the wings of petaluthas to hasten the healing of cuts and punctures.

Often they'd go to sleep like this, with him inside her, but they couldn't tarry much longer here; they had to get back. He said it with his eyes, and when he left her she ringed his cudgie with her fingers, tasting his slickness, a glimmer inside of her hoping that what wasn't on her lips might have seeded her. But that wasn't likely; this wasn't the most fruitful time for her. *And just as well*, she thought. The journey to the Isle would be perilous enough without the prospect of...that.

They crossed the stepping stones and the fissure of the large tabled ledge through which water sizzled and churned, to empty into the clear pool. The air seemed warmer here. Was it just the rising morning which had lifted the mist from the pool, or the clothes and chasers they'd put back on?

Amala caught sight of the fish in the pool. They couldn't help but linger, hand in hand, to watch them darting about, their red and gold belly bands easily enough seen through the pristine water. "They're plump ones," Falca said loudly. "We'll come back and catch some if we can; a last meal with Ossa before he leaves."

She wondered what this place was called.

Ossa and Gurrus hadn't mentioned a name. The Kaikurra must have had one, but they were gone, the memory of it lost forever. But she and Falca could give it one. Why not? They had to have one, if only for themselves, though a name wouldn't make this place any more beautiful.

She was thinking about possibilities as they turned away from the pool and saw the Wardens emerging from the forest.

Chapter Eighteen:

WARDENS AT THE FALLS

HE TOLD HER to go, run as fast as she could past the pool while he held them off.

She wouldn't do it, and Falca couldn't waste time to persuade her that she might have a chance if she bolted now.

One of the groods was an officer in checkered cape, paired off with a man who wasn't a Warden—no ruerain, green hooded mantlet and back-sheathed stagger. These two moved to Falca's left, to block a less likely escape up the ledges. Two more hurried to the right, to prevent Falca and Amala from sprinting past along the far end of the pool. That left four groods directly in front. Three more were coming out of the woods.

The only chance he and Amala had was to move back to the ledge by the pinnacles…give their backs to the steep bank beyond so the groods couldn't easily surround them…cut down a few struggling through the water and then…a final stand on the ledge? The Wardens would have to swing up with their weapons.

"Where we were," he said. "Keep behind me."

They stepped back, facing six of them now. The officer—why did he look familiar?—shouted out names, pointing his sword behind them. Two groods peeled off from the ends of the group.

They would be assuming he'd run, and he did, with Amala close behind—but not back across the fissure. He darted to his right, toward the Warden running along the edge of the stony shelf by the pool. The surprised grood had to stop to bring around the stagger-axe. Falca struck first, cleaving his left leg above the knee. He moved to his right, pulling out the falcata with the motion, sidestepping the screaming Warden's faltering strike. He finished the grood off with a thrust into his belly, withdrew, reached behind to grab at Amala and whirl her into the pool.

If he was going to die here, the better death was not drowning. She might have a chance if she swam quickly to the far shore of the pool. Amala was close but just beyond his reach. She'd grabbed a rock, hurled it at the other, closing Warden. He raised the flat of his stagger to deflect it—the ring of a bell—and avoided a bruise on the head, but not the falcata Falca buried into his neck above the ruerain flange.

He wrenched it free—a spray of blood; saw the others. In their eagerness to close, two had slipped; the others splashed ahead. Falca shouted to Amala: "*Go...GO!*"

Instead of fleeing she retrieved one of the Warden's staggers and turned, coiling for a strike. Falca's whistling back-handed blow caught the closest grood on the chest, where the ruerain armor was thickest, yet did little more than take him off his feet.

Falca parried another Warden's swing, but the falcata was no deliverance from the heavier stagger blade and it bore through, cutting into his thigh. He stumbled, fell, screaming less from the searing pain than seeing a grood ripping the axe from Amala's hands.

He felt the stagger blade at his neck as he lay curled on his side, his hands at his leg, bloodied. A Warden kicked the falcata away.

They shoved Amala down, one grood slapping her, then again, to stop her shouting Falca's name. He tried to rise and the stagger withdrew, replaced by a sword held by the grinning officer.

Back then he hadn't blue gums and a pitted face.

Lambrey Tallon.

JEKSEP AND KITSO stood to either side of the kneeling woman, not far away from where Falca Breks lay spread-eagled on his back, Sulla at the head, Striglis at the feet, skurrs at the ready. The point of Lambrey Tallon's sword made a scratching sound on the stubble of Breks' jawline below the scar. He was breathing hard, his trews steeping prettily with blood, but Tallon judged he wouldn't be bleeding to death any time soon, and escaping that way.

"Such a purlie bower you've brought here," he said. "So thoughtful to think of our needs. Now, where might the mottle and that graylock be?"

"The Limb…was 'snarebait. The other left…with his catch."

"Did they now? And yours? Those sacks in the boat you stole after you murdered three of our brethren, one of whom happened to be Cossum Hoster, the son of the Allarch."

Breks winced with pain, closed his eyes. Tallon snagged one eyebrow then the other with the tip of the sword, forcing them open. "Come now, Falca. The leg's not that bad."

"The sacks? How can you steal…what's already been stolen? I'm…surprised he managed the…theft of so much swag, drunk as he was."

"You soft turd," Maldan shouted behind Tallon, who stopped his surge ahead with an arm that caught him in the chin. "Not yet," he said. To Breks: "Where is it?"

"Let her go and I'll tell you."

Tallon laughed. "*She* can tell me, but it could go much easier for her if I hear it from you."

"She might…or not. She's…tougher than either of us. Let her go and… you'll get it from me in three days." He raised up, trying for a last look at Amala. Striglis shoved his head down hard.

"You're licking the barrel's bottom, Falca. Can't spare the three, much as I'd like to spend it hearing what I've missed since our Catchall days. She'll be telling me—or whoever's turn it is with her—in much less time than three days."

"Comitor?"

"Shut up, 'Niddy," Maldan said. "I know what you're going to say and…"

"The Comitor doesn't."

"*What*, Lannid?"

"Seeing as how this is more than…what I mean is, Amala's father…"

"Find your tongue!"

"Well, he's wealthy, the father. He'd pay hugely not only for her return but proof of Breks' death, but only if…of course…if she was…"

"What?" Maldan said. "Not basted two at a time, twice an hour till the sun…"

"A better sum than that, brother, unless you can replace the gold in a sack with your muck, and double it. She might well tell us…or she might not, knowing what will happen to her anyway. But surely if she knew she was going to the safety of her father's ransom. I'll take her my—"

"That's enough handwringing," Tallon said. "The ride to the Bounds has softened your brains."

"Has it?" Breks said. "You'd have to go with him. Why not? The man is right…the father would do anything to get her back…and he has. Better to pay you than others for her return. That and…what's in those sacks would more than make up for…ruerains left along the way west."

Tallon felt like slicing his throat for the insult, but that would be a mercy compared to what he had in mind. "You're still quick, Falca, but it wasn't a smart thing for you, of all people, to suggest desertion. You may have forgotten but I haven't." He turned to Maldan. "Give me your pitglove. You have a pet, I believe. It needs a run."

The tenon grinned. "So it does," he said, and handed the glove to him. "But Comitor, might I request the honor, on Cossum's behalf?"

"Denied. You heard the insult. As if a Warden's honor is so much slop to spill from a bucket. You can take your turn fucking the woman later on Cossum's behalf—and it seems your brother's as well."

Tallon put on the pitglove, one of the better ones he'd seen used in the gaming pits of Bastia, with overlapping scales of thinly hammered bronze. "Hold him down," he ordered Strigla and Sulla. "You too, Lannid. And you, Maldan, after I've got it out."

Carefully, Tallon dipped the gauntlet into Maldan's metal-lined pouch and withdrew the writhing white rancer. "Don't look away, Falca. Don't you want to see it? We had our own pits in prison but mostly for rats; nothing like this to bet on, nothing like you'll find in Bastia or a chieftain's rig in the Banishands. You have to get very close to hear the barb coming out of the sheath. Listen for it now."

He slid up the bottom of the trews, left leg, exposing just enough of Breks' ankle, and pressed the rancer into his flesh.

Breks screamed, bucked up, skewing Lannid back to his heels. Striglis and Sulla held on, forcing him back. "Keep him *down*!" Tallon shouted. The woman was screaming now. Tallon roared for Jeksep and Kitso to shut her up. The one slapped her; the other clamped a hand over her mouth. Kitso howled; she must have bitten him.

Breks was shuddering, exhaling staccato grunts.

Tallon tossed the rancer, watching for a moment as it scuttled away, up the terrain of the nearest body—Flesk's—and into the haven of his open mouth.

He bent low over Breks. "Can you hear me? Soon you won't be able to move, not even to crawl down to that pool and drown yourself, not that I'd let you try to escape so easily that way. There's no alley here, my old friend—did I forget to tell you we're not in Catchall or Slidetown anymore, marking phaetons and Beckon keelcats.

"I've seen my comrades die from these. You'll struggle for breath. Within the hour you'll start rotting from the point of the sting. Within two you'll be seeing what's left of your world through a haze of red because you'll be bleeding from your eyes. You'll feel the tickle of blood seeping from your ears.

Tallon slapped him. "Stay with me, ditchie. By nightfall your flesh might as well have been boiled all day like fowl in a pot. You'll wish that flenx will find you and put you out of your misery, but they turn away from the stench, understand. You won't be fit enough carrion for the flokas to pick at."

He leaned back and stood.

There was no blood in Breks' drool or eyes yet; there would be soon. His skin was already darkening.

"Kill him now, for Roak's sake," Lannid whispered.

If he hadn't been the Allarch's son, Tallon would have beaten him senseless. Instead, he picked up Breks' sword. It was too late now to ask him where he'd gotten such an exquisite weapon. "A fine edge you've given this," he said, feeling the shaking of Breks' hand as he etched a bloody line across the palm. "It's gratifying that you remembered what I told you once: keep a blade sharp enough to shave a quiver's poose."

He handed the falcata to Maldan, though he was looking squarely at his brother. "You can do those honors, tenon. It may help persuade her to tell us what the Allarch wishes to find out. You may keep it after, as compensation for the loss of your pet."

FALCA COULD SMELL the stink of his vomit as he lay on his side, breathing hard but not wanting to; he felt like he was sucking in shards of glass. The dizziness was worse if he kept his eyes open because of the blurring that faded in and out. He couldn't make fists of his hands, or move the stung leg. He felt numbness seeping into the other as well.

He couldn't crawl over to where he and Amala had crossed the stones, and quench his sudden thirst before moving on to tumble over the last of the falls into the pool, and drowning himself.

All he could do was to roll over on his back, wait for the next surge of sickness to rise and choke him, so he could drown in his own vomit instead.

Not yet. He had to see Amala one last time before the blurring came back to his eyes.

They were near the forest now, where the trees hung over the ledges below the falls. He glimpsed her through a seam between the Wardens guarding her and the others behind. The one Tallon had given his falcata, this...Maldan...was heading off more directly toward the forest.

Amala looked back at him. She must have shouted something because a grood shoved her ahead, threatening her with his stagger. Falca's eyes blurred but not from the poison spreading within him. He couldn't lift his hand to wipe it away, the only water he'd ever have again, but he could still feel it coursing down until the saltiness reached his lips. He didn't hear what she'd yelled out to him. The falls masked that, as they had the approach of the Wardens earlier. Nor could she hear his own words that ended with a spasm of coughing, yet they were clear enough within him.

A Warden at her side stumbled—the one who had shoved her before—then fell forward. Everyone seemed stunned...

Amala tore away from her guard as shouts pierced through the shushing water, someone yelling: "*Limbs*!"

He rose, his elbow shaking, to see her grabbing at the Warden's belt, and rising up with a longshank dagger, cutting the air with it in a tight arc...and again to keep Tallon and the Wardens' beside him momentarily at bay. Another grood had her now from behind, an arm around her neck—then stiffened, collapsed, fell away.

She was free; she still had the shanker. Falca screamed at her to run for the forest. The words came out a croaking whisper.

Tallon yelled, pointing up the ledges. "Striglis...Lannid, *get* her! Up here; the horses..."

Maldan was with them now, falcata in hand. The grood closest to Amala hesitated, as if he hadn't heard the command over the roar of the falls. Maldan shoved him aside. Amala seized the moment to slash wildly at Maldan across his face, ear to lips. Another grood seized her before she could strike again. An instant later this one, too, slumped away from her.

Shrieking with rage, Maldan stabbed Amala with the falcata—and then again.

Falca screamed: another whisper. His elbow gave way. He slumped to his side.

When he lifted his eyes again, Maldan was staggering away, his hand at his face, to join the last Warden and Tallon, who pulled Lannid away. The four of them ran up the ledges, splashing through the shallow water and into the forest.

Falca had to reach her. She'd fallen to her knees, was trying to get up, bloody fingers cradling her belly. He began dragging himself by his elbows, keeping on until the blurring came to his eyes, as if a sudden mist had descended. Then the world wavered, rippled and collapsed before him, all of it: the stone ledges, the now-silent sluicing water, and the mist-shrouded path among the trees.

Chapter Nineteen:

THE POOL

SHAR STAKEEN BRUSQUELY fitted one of her three remaining darts in the spiddard, in case the Wardens returned. That wasn't likely. Amala Damarr was dead; Breks dying. And for all the Wardens knew, Limbs hidden in the forest verge greatly outnumbered them.

So it was mostly anger that kept her hidden in a crevice of slanting rocks that broadened out to the ledge below. She had to let it subside before doing anything else. There had been few times in her life after becoming a shadden that she'd let anger prey upon her.

This was one of them.

Breks' woman—that unbelievably *stupid* bitch, that yellow-haired. . .*mat-girl*—had ruined everything.

Tranch had once told Stakeen she was extraordinarily quick and accurate with the spiddard. But what good had that done her here? She cursed herself for not anticipating that the woman might act irrationally, foolishly, what with her screaming, the slaps and taunts of the Wardens, and the sight of her prostrate, wounded lover. Her fatal action had caught Stakeen by surprise, distracting her aim at the last Warden who'd come running into the fray. Even then, Stakeen only missed his head—and the chance to kill him as instantly as the others—by a finger's width.

A near-miss.

Shaddens weren't hired for near-misses.

She'd failed.

Damaar's daughter lay curled up, facing Breks, one hand still at her belly, the other in a pool of blood.

It was almost as if she'd wanted to die with him.

Pitiful how he crawled toward her, as if he could have done anything to stop her from bleeding out once he reached her. He almost had.

If Breks wasn't dead, he would be soon; the Wardens wouldn't have earlier left him alone if they weren't sure of that. As a shadden, Stakeen was familiar with less conventional means of dealing death—in this case an archback or white rancer, more likely. No ever lived after having been stung by one of those.

Things had been working out so well: fewer Wardens for her to deal with, thanks to Breks; and then the boon of having them kill him for her…

Stakeen rose from her hiding place and scanned the deeper forest behind her. She couldn't hear anyone approaching given the noise of the falls; neither did she see any Wardens. They weren't coming back. All that mattered now was getting back to the horse she'd tied off in the forest, below where the Wardens had hobbled theirs farther up the trail, and putting this place behind her.

And go where?

She didn't want to return to Draica and face Havaarl Damarr with her failure—and a sullied reputation which might take years to fully regain.

She supposed she could go to another large city—Castlecliff or Milatum. Still, in the time it took to establish her reputation elsewhere she could repair the one she'd had in Draica. There was one other way she might mitigate this disaster: the last resort of arranging a fatal accident for Havaarl Damarr and his wife, and thus keep her failure a secret.

First things first. She had to retrieve the spiddard darts from the Wardens she'd killed, and while she was at it, Amala Damarr's swan's-wing brooch.

You'll know her by her beauty, her golden hair and a broken swan's-wing brooch she never removes, the father had told her.

If Stakeen decided against that risky last resort for the parents, the brooch would be the only thing she could take back to Draica to at least prove she'd tried to fulfill the contract.

Damarr would have to console himself with the hand of Falca Breks.

She unloaded the spiddard to save the tension, and laid it on the ground, put away the darts. As she was about to go down to the ledges to finish up, she saw a tall man in hunter's leathers, and a Timberlimb, coming down. They were burdened by slingsacks and the man a pannier and hobbler as well, yet they splashed through the rustling water as quickly as the Wardens had left.

She stepped back into the embrace of the forest before they could see her and took a knee, watching this odd pair approach. Was the Limb the one seen with Breks and his woman? But what was that terribly scarred graylock doing with a mottle? There was no gain in killing them—not yet. Better to wait for the hunter to leave after he looted the bodies, for surely that was his intent.

Breks' hand would be safe, and the hunter wouldn't want a broken swan's-wing's brooch made by Limbs on the streets of Draica, so Havaarl Damarr had said with disgust.

Still, she fitted another dart in the spiddard. The noise from the falls masked the *click-click-click* of the ratcheting tension. She didn't think she'd need her agonette for these two, but uncoiled it, anyway.

THEY'D SEEN THE end of it from the top of the falls, helpless to do anything except hasten down with the sickening knowledge that they might have made a difference if they'd left earlier. Ossa was furious with himself. This was the Bounds, not some greensward in Draica. He should have heeded the feeling that Falca and Amala were overdue in returning.

But he'd let the foolish thoughts of an old man sentimental about his own youth—and those times that should be savored because there were never enough of them—override his instincts.

Amala's blood was draining away over the gentle slope of the broad ledge toward the pool. Her green eyes stared beyond Ossa as he stood over the kneeling Gurrus. He didn't know why the Limb held his hand close to her mouth, feeling for her breath.

Amala was gone.

She fought the Wardens, preferring death over what they surely had in mind for her; a tough woman when she had to be, yet how easily she'd laughed with Sovay, asking about the doll, taking the time to talk to the blind girl even after so long and tiring a day…

A quick look at the dead Wardens scattered about Amala told Ossa they hadn't been ambushed by Limbs of any clan with whom he was familiar. The ones he knew used longer, more slender arrows than those protruding from the necks of three groods, and the left eye of a fourth.

Four arrows. Four dead.

The Limbs who had killed them, and forced the others to flee were probably tracking the survivors. If Gurrus hadn't been with him likely he'd be dead, too.

Falca lay on his side, stinking of vomit, his breathing heavy and halting. His eyes opened to slits when Gurrus whispered his name. He shuddered, as if the mehka had prodded him with something hot or sharp, and not a gentle laying on of hands.

Rivulets of sweat dripped down from his face, mixing with blood seeping from his nose and the bloody spittle that hung from his lips. The flesh of his hands, his neck, his cheeks was bruised, discolored. His left leg was tight in his trews, swollen badly; the right had been slashed by a stagger-axe.

Ossa knelt across from Gurrus. He knew the signs for this. The Warden sons-of-bitches could have finished him off quickly, but instead they'd used a white rancer or archback. He'd seen it before, the one time he'd gone into the Bounds with another 'snarehunter, Iolo Krex, who'd been stung on the neck as he leaned back to rest against a fallen tree at sunset, and died before the moons had risen for the night.

Stung in the lower leg, Falca might last longer than that, but Ossa wouldn't wish his remaining hours for anyone except the ones who did this to him and killed Amala.

Falca kept parting his lips, trying to say something. He might have been trying to sound Amala's name, or pleading for them to kill him….or begging for water, as Ossa once had by that trail along the Moat. He could at least give Falca that—before the mercy of a dagger through his heart. Gurrus nodded when he told him he was going for the water.

He got his battered cup from the pannier he'd left by Amala, and filled it under one of the myriad little falls of the ledges. When he got back, Gurrus had in his hand a reddish strip of something long as a finger and about as wide. Ossa asked him what it was, and Gurrus replied: "A parting gift in Draica from a fellow mehka named Juhu, should the need arise. He gave it to me at the settlement house where I met Amala. Now, Falca will have it with the water."

He broke the strip into pieces, rubbed those out into tiny flakes into his palm. He trapped the granules in his fist and released them into the cup, stirring the mixture with his longest finger until the liquid was an amber color.

"Please, Ossa; lift him up, by his shoulders. We need to keep his head where he can drink from the cup."

Falca's eyelids fluttered. He moaned as Ossa got behind him, and propped his lolling head in the nest of his gloved hands. Sweat sheened his face. Gurrus leaned over, opened his mouth, kept it open with the knuckles of two curled fingers. He tilted the cup slightly, enough for the liquid to drain slowly into Falca's mouth, so he would not spit it up.

"There," he said. "It is done."

"Quicker than this?" Ossa said, tapping the sheath of his longshank dagger.

"Not that, but quick enough, I hope."

Ossa would have given Falca his peace, as he had with Laineth, but in truth he was relieved he did not have to now. He gently lay Falca's head back on the shelving stone, and stood. "We'll weight them together for the pool below; we've naught the means to bury them, a vaunty pair, the both of them."

The old Limb nodded, or was it the rocking on his haunches? Ossa left, to let him be alone with the young man he called wikkano, who'd been with him from the beginning of a journey that had now ended, and perhaps for Gurrus as well since he'd be on his own.

On the far side of the broad ledge, half-hidden by pinnacles of rock, he saw the flessok he'd need to bind rocks to their bodies. His hands were hurting him—that seemed to be worse in the middle of the day for some reason. Perhaps it was the rubbing of the gloves on his blisters, but he'd tried doing without the gloves and that pained him more. The aching and occasional numbness in his legs, upper arms and shoulders was getting worse and there was still the blood in his piss.

The thought crossed his mind to join Falca and Amala here. He had less time than he'd told Laineth. He doubted he could make it far enough north to get to his own place, before numbness made his arms and legs useless. Besides the falls here and the rippling stairway of ledges, the inlet was the most beautiful place he'd come across in the Bounds, though he'd not hunted in the half of it. The one and only time he'd seen the inlet he hadn't ventured far. He knew it had to lead to the northern sea. What was the point then?

Now, he wished he had. The inlet was rimmed on the east by an escarpment, high enough for mating pairs of flokas to roost in the trees, and devour the basking storgons, some bigger than a Limb, that they caught in the waning hours of the day. If he got there, with no one to bury him, they'd have their fill of him, too. And so what? Did any mariner ever expect to be buried in the earth?

So here, then? With them? Gather enough flessok and rocks to weight himself, and slip into a pool of water not much larger than the forecastle of the *Flury*? But there was the promise he'd made to Laineth, and before he died he wanted get to the inlet he'd named after a woman he'd once loved so very much in Milatum, long after he saw her for the last time. He'd always thought Rohaise would have laughed at the name—*Roh's Water*—had she known. Which was, he supposed, the point...

He came to the ledge above a scattering of stepping stones, and knew this was where Falca and Amala had been, thinking they were alone. There was no other way to account for the carpeting of flessok over the patches of moss on the gently sloping stone.

He gathered up an armload and crossed the stones. Loose tendrils trailed in the swift water brimming around them. At the edge of the pool, a school of brightly colored fish turned sharply away from him.

There were plenty of shaling rocks for later. He cut lengths of flessok with his dagger, twisted them into ropes, ignoring the pain of the blisters on his gloved hands—three ropes each for Falca and Amala, to bind tightly around the flat of the rocks. He pulled aside two of these for Amala, lifted out a third from underneath a fallen branch.

He paused to rest a moment before he found the first and heavier rock for Falca, and had it in his hands when he glanced back at Gurrus—and dropped the rock.

SHAR STAKEEN COULDN'T believe what she'd seen: Breks sitting up, then standing, aided by the Limb as the graylock ran over, evidently as shocked as she was.

Now Breks was walking over with them to where the hunter had filled the cup. He knelt to drink. They knelt with him, each with a hand at his back, whispering words she couldn't hear.

This shouldn't be happening, she thought.

The Wardens wouldn't have left Breks unless he was dead or very close to it. Even if he'd somehow fooled them, he wouldn't have continued to feign death after they'd left, not with his woman lying nearby, nor after the arrival of his companions. And the graylock had walked away slowly to the far side of the ledges to gather a bundle of stringy moss and then rocks. Why else would he have done that except to dump the bodies into that glistening pool at the end of the ledges?

He was talking to the mottle who had his hands out as if he, too, was seeking some kind of reprieve.

What had the old Limb put in that cup of water the graylock had brought?

Everything would have been different if he'd given it to Amala instead of Breks.

Why hadn't he?

Either he hadn't enough for both, and had to make a choice, or it wasn't potent enough to bring back the dead.

Stakeen watched Breks leave the others and walk toward where she crouched, still hidden.

That's right; come closer, she thought. *I won't miss a second time.*

He looked away for a moment, up the ledges to the roaring falls, then knelt at Amala Damarr's side: an easy kill and well-deserved for denying Stakeen her own reprieve from failure. One dart each for Breks and the tall, scarred man with the gloves; a dagger throw or agonette for the silver-mottled Limb half his size.

She raised the spiddard and took aim at Breks. This would be no near-miss. He was leaning over Amala, his right hand brushing over her eyes, to close them, the same hand she'd be taking back with her to Havaarl Damarr.

Her forefinger closed around the splint, but she couldn't pull it—something was preventing her from making sure Breks wouldn't cheat death a second time…something she'd overlooked, yet had been in plain sight. Her hesitation alarmed her, until she realized the cause of it, and lowered the spiddard with a soft rebuke for not grasping the reason sooner. She'd seen it with her own eyes.

Forget the hand she promised Havaarl Damarr. Forget the balance of the fee she'd never collect now. Forget worries about her reputation. Never again would she have to hire out as a shadden.

Smiling, she lowered the spiddard.

Here was a near-miss of another sort—and one for which she might be grateful for the rest of her life.

If what the Limb had given Breks could reverse the always-fatal effects of a rancer sting, surely it could work the same wonder on other wounds, sicknesses and injuries.

With such a secret Shar Stakeen would have the means to gain wealth and power to match that of any king or Sanctor in the Six Kingdoms. Who would not pay dearly for this extraordinary secret of healing?

She rose from her crouch, about to go down to find out what it was the mottle had given him, and where she could find more—before she killed them all.

No...not yet.

She had to think this through.

That earlier missed shot with a spiddard was one thing—and lucky she had missed. But there could be no failure with this second chance. What had Tranch once said to her?

There will be times when killing, or the threat of it, will prove less effective in helping you achieve your goals than other methods, and I do not solely mean your powers of persuasion as a woman. The instinct for alternatives cannot be taught and can elude otherwise proven shaddens. Experience is never an excuse for inflexibility...

Surely this one of those times, and too important to risk the possibility that the Limb had not yet divulged the secret to the graylock or even Breks. And if he *had*, there was the chance none of the three could be forced to give her the answers she needed. She couldn't as yet know the mettle of Breks' companions. She had a good idea of his. Now, with Amala dead—the piece she might have successfully played—he might be beyond persuasion by any means.

It seemed obvious from the look of him that he didn't care if he lived or died now.

Amala Damarr was no skinny waif yet he had gathered her up in his arms and carried her over to the pool while the other two watched. He might have been staggering within, but outwardly Stakeen saw none of it—only the straight back, the woman's lolling head, the dangling arms and legs. That he could do this now was only more wondrous proof of the miracle the Limb gave him.

Shar Stakeen couldn't take her eyes off him.

And so she wouldn't.

A plan formed quickly.

She'd find out soon enough, but she didn't think Breks and the mottle, anyway, would return whence they'd come. She put herself in his place. What, after all, was there in Draica for him to return *to*, never mind the old Limb? Sooner or later Havaarl Damarr would learn of his presence there—without the daughter—and even Breks couldn't escape death again.

They had journeyed here with the old mottle for a reason beyond merely helping the Timberlimbs, and he would likely want to see that through, to finish what they'd begun, for her sake. Whatever that purpose was, it would take him deeper into the wilderness. The secret to his healing had to be *somewhere* in the Rough Bounds. It made sense. Other substances, including slash and nod, had their source in the Bounds.

So she'd follow, as closely as she had the Wardens, until he led her to what she wanted. Or the three might lead her to others who knew of it, who might be more amenable to persuasion or force, whichever. Then she'd have to kill anyone who might be tempted to keep what had to be hers, and hers alone.

That included Falca Breks. It occurred to her now that he might well come to his senses after he finished this sentimental farewell to his woman and start thinking the same thing she was. He was a cutpurse, a reiver, a Catchall gutterkin who'd been working the streets of Draica long before he'd met Havaarl Damarr's precious daughter, who carried her basting mat into the wilderness.

How long would it take for him to ask the Limb where there was more salvation—to sell this time? A day? A week? If he didn't know already.

There he was, holding her by the pool, rocking her, yet for all Shar Stakeen knew it could have been as much a performance—for his own benefit or the others' for some reason—as the one that presumably first lured Amala Damarr into his grasp. Stakeen knew the masks of men; indeed she did.

Finally, he laid her down at the edge, wrapped the rope-like strands of moss around three flat rocks again and again, and tied off the ends at her belt. Stakeen couldn't see him kiss her one last time, but he must have. Why else would he be bending low over her face?

He slid her over the edge.

Stakeen heard no splash. Nor could they hear her silent clapping for the fine performance, convincingly done—and almost enough to make her believe the ditchlicker might have had his heart behind a kiss the young woman could not feel, and words she could not hear.

The others walked slowly over to embrace him, and they stood there for a time, until Breks gave a nod. The Timberlimb stayed with him, holding the graylock's hobbler while he went over to get the panniers and slingsacks. Then he stopped by the dead Wardens Breks had killed, and rejoined the others with a pair of longshank daggers. Breks belted both, and it was only then that Stakeen remembered one of the Hoster brothers had his falcata.

They slowly walked around the near side of the pool and down, taking the same direction the Wardens and the plump strutterman had. Stakeen left her hiding place. When she finished retrieving her darts, she led her horse back to the trail, and found two others the survivors hadn't taken. She took from the panniers what food they had. With what remained of her own she wouldn't have to worry about hunting for a few days. If nothing else she could butcher the horse for meat to cook. She wasn't worried about Breks and the others outpacing her; they were on foot. Curious, that. Why didn't they take horses to follow the Wardens?

She stopped by the pool, half-expecting to see Amala Damarr's weighted body in the depths, and oddly disappointed she didn't. She broke the mirrored surface of the water to wash her hands and cup water to drink.

Don't worry, Amala, she thought. *I'll take good care of him for as long as I have to, and not an hour more.*

She'd come a long way to kill Falca Breks and now—she felt like laughing out loud—her only mission was to make sure nothing happened to him until she'd gotten what she wanted. Still, she lingered by the pool, going over again what she'd seen, because she was about to end the life she knew for the promise of a much better one. So, careful now…

Had it been some trick of sunlight prismed by cascading water?

No, she'd seen Breks' eyes change. In the time it once took Tranch to crop her black tresses, those eyes changed from—what had Havaarl Damarr said they were?

Blue.

From blue to the gold of Amala Damarr's cropped hair.

Shar Stakeen needed a name for what the Timberlimb had given the strappy Draican, to bring him back so quickly from near-death. It didn't take her long to think of one.

Golden-Eyes.

BOOK TWO:

THE ROUGH BOUNDS

Chapter Twenty:

BEASTS

TWICE ON THE trail Falca stopped to wait for them to catch up. Not the third time.

Impatient with their slower pace he took off at a run, fearing the groods would escape. Ossa would want to help him kill them, but the Wardens' horses would smell his 'snare-taint, alert them, and they'd escape. A running man would be able to overtake horses moving slowly in the perpetual twilight of the forest floor.

He ignored the shouts for him to wait up. Soon, the pleas faded. He was alone again, running as if he had the paving bricks of Draica under his pounding feet, and not a gloomy, undulating trail crisscrossed with roots that should have repeatedly tripped by now.

He'd considered returning to Bastia, killing Lambrey Tallon and this Maldan Hoster there after they returned from fighting the Myrcians. But they might not survive; he'd be waiting for dead men to return. And letting Myrcians kill the two wasn't the same as doing it himself. He had the advantage of surprise either way—they thought he was dead—but pursuing them immediately was better.

Falca didn't care who killed the four groods at the falls, only that Tallon and Hoster weren't among them. There might be other trails, but this one led directly to the river, which ran north to south before curling east. Ossa believed the surviving Wardens had no need to risk crossing it, not when they wanted to catch up to the main Warden army moving into the Bounds south of the river, where the Myrcians had evidently last been seen.

But surely they would stop by the river for the night to let the Allarch's son tend to the wound Amala had given him.

Why…why hadn't she fled instead?

He ran hard, brushing aside branches of scrawny trees starved for sunlight by the forest canopy. This was a Warden trail, marked by blazes of royal red—here on one kelvasta, there on another—and the occasional Timberlimb skull staked through the eye sockets into the fissured bark.

He smelled more than the dank, earthy musk of the forest understory: a tinge of lemon. Gurrus said that came from the very oldest kelvastas that you could thump like melons in the spring after they'd had their fill of winter rains, and get the same sound.

His world shrunk to that scent, the pounding of his footfalls, his huffing breaths—and the memories that always caught up to him, no matter how hard he ran…

He'd been with Amala at the settlement house when he first heard Gurrus say the word. His mind was elsewhere but he caught the word he hadn't heard before, and asked her: "What's a…kushla?" She smiled, a little embarrassed it seemed to him. "Em, I suppose I am. It's what some call me here. It means sun-thicket." Her hair had been long then. "It's this," she said, and flicked a few strands of it, as if she was brushing away a fly…

It was so much more than that, yet to her the name meant only the color of her hair.

Falca wanted to see a sun-thicket now, but those breaks in the canopy were above, not down here.

He gashed the back of his hand on a snag of a fallen branch. Without stopping he scooped up a skein of flessok and wiped away the blood. There seemed to be a lot of flessok on the trail. Had the Wardens pulled some down as they passed?

When he paused not long after to drink from a stream that crossed the trail, he noticed the gash had closed to a pink seam.

He ran on.

FALCA SLACKENED HIS pace as darkness seeped into the forest of giant trees, but ahead there seemed to be a lifting of the deep gloom around him.

Was the river beyond the rise in the trail?

He further slowed to a walk. Before he reached the crest he stopped to listen for voices beyond, heard nothing, not even the chittering and whistles of birds.

There were no trees directly ahead, though he could see in the distance the tops of others glinting with the colors of sunset.

He waited longer, through what could only be a lull in their preparations for the coming night, thinking ahead to his own: more waiting, until all were asleep around a fire except for the sentry. He'd likely be closer to the forest, from where any danger would come. He hoped Maldan Hoster would take the first watch: he'd be attentive to little else save his own misery.

Circle around the camp, then; come up from the river, both longshanks out—one for the sentry, one for the first to awake. He didn't care which he killed first—Tallon or Hoster—as long as both saw his eyes before he slit their throats.

He wasn't worried about the fourth, this Lannid—Maldan's brother?—the one he remembered as being reluctant to hurt Amala.

Perhaps he'd spare him. Let him ride away with a message for the father, should he be so lucky to survive to deliver it: Falca Breks would be only too happy to cull more fruit from his tree if Culldred had any better.

He still heard nothing, crept ahead, wiping sweat from his eyes.

There they were, the horses, drinking at the river's edge, some distance to the north.

But there were seven not the four, and they had twitching mandibles, not tails.

Wild augors.

Falca glanced to the south as far as a bend in the river, saw no one else on the shore. No Wardens. No horses.

He got up slowly, not caring if the beasts sensed his presence. The larger male did, and for a moment Falca thought he'd charge. Strangely, the male herded away the females instead, past oddly misshapen hummocks.

Those could only be the fallen remains of a Limb bridge.

Boughbreaks was directly across the river. Though Gurrus knew the Wardens had destroyed the bridge long ago, he wanted to cross here: the quickest way to the northern Road and east to the Isle.

Many groods had once been here.

They weren't the ones Falka was hunting now.

He walked through the sedge and bracken down to the river strand for water to drink. There was another reason for his thirst, besides the running. Gurrus said the effects of krael would last for up to a day and give him a constant thirst—at least it did for Kelvoi. So it hadn't left him yet: the krael Gurrus had let Ossa think was poison because he couldn't risk that a dying Ossa would take the krael for himself if he knew what it was.

He moved on down the strand, imagining what had happened here years before. The groods would have massed on the banks of the river, shooting fire arrows shot high up into the middle of the bridge filled with Limbs shooting down at them with their own bows to prevent a crossing, retreating only as the burning bridge gave way. There were other hillocks on the opposite side where the planks and flessok cables of the bridge had been swept clear of the river by the swollen spring currents.

Gurrus said Boughbreaks once boasted forty villages in as many mother-trees, extending well beyond the shore. And of the three thousand Kelvoi who lived in communal hovens sheltered by the canopy, only a few had escaped to the east and north. Gurrus had been among those captured. His brother was killed.

Wardens never climbed the trees to attack the villages; they didn't have to. They had only to burn or cut down a handful of trees because Kelvoi villages of whatever size were linked together. It might take the Wardens a week to finally topple a mother-tree, or days to let it burn, but only a few falling kelvastas were enough to seal the fate of the entire settlement.

Falca couldn't see a charred or fallen mother-tree, but he knew they were there, deeper in the forest beyond the river where the sheen of dusk had faded from the water.

The Kelvoi who once lived here were either dead or scattered. Falca might have fisted some Tokanekes—Gurrus' and Frikko's clan—for their scrape money in the time before he met Amala. He didn't know and hadn't cared then who they were, or from where they'd come, or how they'd managed to survive: they were mottles, one way to ensure his survival on the streets. He didn't think about the homes they once had; all he saw were their shacks and makeshift stalls where he rousted them to steal their pitiful earnings selling scrape or rife or baubles like the broken swan's-wing brooch he'd taken from Amala before he gave her to the pool.

He'd known her for only a year.

Gebroan seemed like so long ago. It wasn't. So many times since then, whenever he held something in his hands—it didn't matter what—he would take its measure against what he'd held in his hand in Gebroan at the end: the crystal mace that contained her essence, the soul that Saphrax had lifted from her with the same mace. He doubted he would ever again look forward to anything else with the same excitement and hope that had filled every hour of the journey back to Draica to replenish the empty husk of her with what he carried in his hands, as she had earlier replenished him.

He'd also carried something else with him from Gebroan: the promise he'd made to Frikko. Amala wanted to come with him; she took only a moment to say she'd join him in going to the Rough Bounds, for whatever good they could do there.

And now she was dead.

He kept walking by the river, through the waist-high reeds that choked an eroded bank higher here than where the trail ended. He told himself the groods might have gone on a ways, too—because of the augors?—before stopping for the night. If they had it would take but a moment to drop to his belly before they saw him, and wait…before closing in for the kill, like any other beast in the night.

He heard nothing ahead, saw nothing except a floka above another bend in the river, on its way back to its nest, the day's last straggler, with nothing in its talons to show for the hunt.

He would.

They *were* out there. But now it was necessary to let them know *he* was here, hunting *them*.

It was dark by the time he made a torch of the driest flessok he could find in the forest verge, and wrapped it thickly around the end of a driftwood branch. He stuck the torch into the highest point of the soft river bank, and lit the torch with the sulphered flix he had in a waterproof vial Boket had given him.

While he waited for them to come, he took out one of his longshanks and cut his arm; not deeply, but enough to draw blood he smeared over his arms.

That will bring them, he thought.

He smeared more on his lips, tasted only the usual metallic taint. So maybe the krael was dissipating within him, his eyes fading back to what they once were—as he surely would without Amala.

It crossed his mind to do more, take the longshank and plunge it into his belly—what Laineth had done with Ossa's help. Hadn't Amala wanted him to stab her belly, the night before they left, to show him the remarkable properties of the kinnet?

Don't worry. I won't spoil myself for the children I'll bear for you someday…

He squeezed his eyes shut.

If only she'd been wearing it.

He remembered that Gurrus had dropped something when he unwrapped the kinnet that first night at the Laughing Lout, and hurriedly put it away again.

The krael.

Of what had he been so fearful? He said krael had saved him, too, when he was younger. A poisonous kitterit bit him; the consequence of his clumsy first attempt at the ritual of milking the kolk of a floka's back-claw. The ritual was required for all would-be mehkas who alone supplied the immobilizing kolk in which Tokaneke soldiers dipped their arrow points. His father let him suffer by way of punishment for his inattentiveness—he hadn't seen the kitterit feeding underneath the dead floka—but if Gurrus had not been the son of an elder mehka, his father would have let him die.

Falca knew they were watching. In this place they always were—Ossa's constant reminder—even if you couldn't see them, or sense their presence.

They were out there.

They had been at the falls.

It won't be long now, he thought.

It wasn't.

He heard the clicking first and unsheathed the second longshank, got to his feet. He stepped to the side of the still-burning torch. Before, he wouldn't have been able to distinguish the faint clicking—or even hear it—from all the other sounds of the night. Was that also the result of the krael?

The river murmured behind him.

The clicking grew louder.

Soon, one pair of eyes appeared in the dark forest, then another. Another pair materialized off to his right, then a fourth to his left. His own golden eyes might have been fading, but these were growing to form a diadem of reddish-yellow eyes: six pairs now.

Flenx.

Groods or flenx—was there a difference here?

There was still time for escape, the river. But even if he knew how to swim he wouldn't have taken that way out, not now; not when they knew he was hunting *them.*

One padded ahead more boldly than the others, close enough now for the torchlight to reveal the glistening spittle seeping from its open mouth. One of its fangs was broken, half the length of the others, but still wicked. It raised a paw to click against the headhorn. This one had to be the leader; the rest were smaller, the size of very large dogs.

"I knew you were here," Falca whispered, and struck the hilts of the longshanks together to mark his own clicking.

Tap-tap-tap...

The palms of his hands were dry.

Tap-tap-tap...

The leader hesitated.

Was it the clicking of the daggers that confused the beast, or that it couldn't sense fear with this particular Two-Legs? Was it the nearby torch? Falca took a step away to encourage an attack. The leader turned its great head around, growling at the others, as if to keep them at bay, wanting to make the kill alone. The flenx was suddenly still. Falca tensed for the leap.

It came in heartbeats, yet slowly...or so it seemed. He deflected the head horn—a short, vicious sideways slap with the base of his palm—and yanked back his hand an instant before the claws of a swiping forepaw could shred it. He buried the dagger in the flenx's neck, ripping down as he struck again with the other dagger. Blood spurted out in a hot stream that splashed against his chest.

The beast writhed on the ground, its keening matching Falca's bellowing. The two nearest flenx circled around the dying leader. Falca didn't retreat from his kill. He darted ahead to claim it. Only one of the flenx came at him. Why was it moving so slowly? He sidestepped the leap and with the same momentum gutted the flenx in the belly with both longshanks. He spun away and back, his grunts cresting to screams before subsiding to panting. He dropped a dagger to throw the ebbing torch at the pair of flenx—one dead, the other dying.

The torch burst back into life as fur sizzled and burned. The gut-ripped flenx howled, tried to get away, but two of the remaining flenx gored it with their horns, slashed with their claws, snapped at legs. The others began feasting on the dead one, two of them snarling at the crouching Falca.

He brushed the back of his hands over his mouth, smearing their blood over his own. He'd been striking the longshanks again, over and over, hadn't realized he'd cut his hand. He didn't care. He'd come here to kill them all and so he would in the blackness. The torch was out, smoldering, the smoke mixing with the stink of charred flesh. He heard them chuffing at the dead ones; ripping, tearing, their bright eyes darting crazily as they fed.

Falca got up, wiped away the slickness from his hands, and moved toward the nearest of them, striking the longshanks against one another. They backed off, growling at him…

A hissing light fell from the night, to land among the feeding flenx, illuminating their bloody claws and fangs and the steel of Falca's longshankers. He turned quickly to see Gurrus holding another flickering torch. Ossa ran by him, holding at length the hobbler, not so much to prevent the flenx from attacking, but to block Falca from them.

Still snarling, the beasts dragged the carcasses back beyond the pale of the torch Ossa had thrown. The graylock kept his boot on the butt of the hobber, angling the blade at them. Despite a roaring in his ears, Falca heard him say: "They have the two; that's enough for 'em."

Falca sank to his knees, releasing the longshanks from shaking hands. He felt the warmth of a nearby torch, shut his brimming eyes and, for a moment as he rocked back and forth, imagined it was Amala at his side and not Gurrus.

Chapter Twenty-One:

TWO-TRUNKS

THEY RESTED AT the bottom of a low hill not far from Clawbark and Dawnbringer, the two mother-trees for the small village of Two-Trunks that Gurrus once called his own.

Dawnbringer had been the larger of the two but was now a charred, crownless column that had opened a hole to the sky, allowing sunlight to reach a few young trees rising above koskava shrubs and kinikinik vines on the gentle slope of the hill.

High above in Clawbark there were still remnants of the village hovens, though the fire that destroyed Dawnbringer had also consumed the Road that had once led north to Boughbreaks and east to the bridge across the river.

Falca sat next to Ossa. Whatever wikkano's thoughts were, at least those big hands of his were busy recovering the keen edge to the shitcatcher's axe he had dulled on flenx horns earlier in the day. Gurrus had told him it was not likely there would be a Road bridge over the river, and so Ossa had said they'd have to make something to cross, a raft he called it. The axe was all they had to cut the necessary branches.

Ossa was lying down, his eyes closed, oblivious to the rasping of the whetstone on the axe. Gurrus had found some teskot, which he crushed to make a balm for his hands, but what he needed was krael. All Gurrus could do was offer hope—no promise—that in the days beyond the river, they might find some in a village. The krael of other mehkas was theirs alone to give; they hoarded it fiercely for the cost to them was great. The Kalaleks of the Isle made sure of that.

"If they won't give it, we take it." Falca had said.

"And die in the attempt, at the hands of our hosts," Gurrus said.

"Then we die."

It was not something Falca might have said if Amala was still with them.

The journey from Boughbreaks had been exhausting, and they still had the river to cross before nightfall. They'd had to force their way through dense thickets of spiny ferns, clotted stands of swingbacks and prickly kolale. Falca and Ossa had led the way, slashing with the axe and hobbler.

Only in a few places did there remain evidence of the hunting path. It was no Warden trail, cleared and marked. All they had had to guide them were the remains, high above, of the Road that had once linked Two-Trunks to Boughbreaks. Bits of hanging flessok cable and dangling sections of planking hummed in the wind like a discarded kalo.

They'd seen no sign of the shitcatchers.

If there had still been a usable Road, the journey to Two-Trunks would have taken them only half the morning, or less without pausing to view the spur of mountains further to the south, the racing station, or the Choosing Place Gurrus had once known so well. But without the Road, the walking and stumbling, the paring and parting of undergrowth took them most of the day.

Gurrus had not wanted to come here from Boughbreaks to live, but his father had said Two-Trunks needed a mehka, since theirs had recently chosen Water for his death. That was his stated reason. Gurrus thought that perhaps his father was sending him away in hopes that the shitcatchers might overlook such a small village with but two mother-trees, only a dozen hovens, and scarcely one hundred people. But there was a third reason, revealed only when his ailing father, Ghatruk, summoned him back to Boughbreaks to be with him for his Choosing, for Ghatruk wanted to end his life. The revelation changed Gurrus' life as much as the ensuing shitcatcher attack on Boughbreaks.

He never went back to Two-Trunks, and hadn't wanted to come back now. It wasn't as if he knew Two-Trunks would be yet another derelict village, though that was a probability, given his years away and the Warden shitcatchers' ceaseless forays in the Bounds west of the river. He had told Falca as much, that most likely there would no one left in the village for him to tell of Freaca's heroism and thus honor her memory. Gurrus had known Freaca well, had once even thought that she had the makings of a Patient One—a mehka—though he'd told her that in confidence, because custom forbid females becoming mehkas.

Even so, Gurrus had thought that after Amala's death, Falca would accept the fact that the best thing to do would be to cross over the river at Boughbreaks and follow the northern Road, which surely the shitcatchers hadn't yet entirely destroyed, or the villages along the way. That was the most direct route to the Isle, the one Gurrus and his father had once used.

But Falca had insisted on going south first, to Two-Trunks. "Does it matter," he said, "if there is no one to hear what happened to her? I made the promise to her, and I intend to keep it, if I have to go there alone."

He'd said it the morning after the flenx attacked him—or was it the other way around? That morning he'd taken the Warden axe and hacked off the head-horns of the two he'd killed. Such a deed could not be wholly explained by the krael; the Sun was gone from his eyes by noon.

Gurrus knew he couldn't argue that Amala would want as quick a journey to the Isle as possible to return the kinnet because she was woven into the promise Falca had made to Freaca. They were one and the same to him now.

Gurrus had wept for Amala that night of the flenx, while Falca slept fitfully, a longshank in his hands, as if he meant to kill in his dreams all that couldn't while he was awake. Ossa stood guard first, and then Gurrus. He took his own mourning as the others slept. Only at night did Kelvoi grieve, when all was quiet save the wind rustling in the keska, swaying the hovens. Only then was it best to mourn those who had taken the unseen Road between this life and the next.

The shafts of sunlight had shifted toward Clawbark.

Gurrus wondered if Falca was aware of the rhythm of his axe-sharpening: a half-dozen strokes, then a pause to look up, as if the rasping sound that had been such a constant wherever they'd been, might summon Amala back. Then he would resume again.

She was the first person not of his kind whom Gurrus had ever trusted. She had taught him to speak her language, Arriostan. He taught her his, though the lessons came more easily for him. The last night at the settlement house she'd said to him: "It must be like the sea."

"What must be like the sea?"

"Living high in the tree canopy—what is your word for that?"

"Keska."

"If there is wind there must always be movement no matter what you're doing, even sleeping. So it must be like the sea."

"I have never been on the sea."

She laughed. "Neither have I."

But she had been on the sea, if not physically. She'd been in the crystal mace Falca brought back from Gebroan. Gurrus had been among those Kelvoi refugees at the vigil outside the gates of her home.

Was it possible that Amala could be here now? At least that part of her that Falca had once carried back from that far land where few trees grew?

Gurrus got up and made his way toward Clawbark through the thickets of kolale. He couldn't see Falca but he heard the rasping, fainter now; and then Ossa coughing, fainter still. And Amala?

Is this your home?

It was.

Can we climb up?

We could. But it is a long way up to the hovens and the kastkays that link them ...and longer still for an old mehka.

Where was your hoven?

Between the males' lodge and the gate to the northern Road.

How is it done, the climbing?

I will show you, kushla.

He did, brushing his hand over the cuts in the edges of the tough, scaly bark of a tree higher than the highest tower he'd seen in Draica and Bastia. He was suddenly glad that Falca had insisted on keeping his promise to come here.

All the Tokanekes who went Below used the cuts as well as rope and sometimes mitts and outerboots, both with tightly stitched augor bristles that held fast to the bark. Gurrus went Below too, though not as often as other males who descended more frequently for that which could not be grown, fashioned, or hunted in the nurturing keska above.

Other clans pegged their village trees instead of making cuts; neither hurt the tree. The neighboring Farolas used mitts and outerboots exclusively.

Clawbark must have been abandoned some time ago yet these cuts seemed newer the farther Gurrus moved to his right. Perhaps it was only a trick of the dappled light in this grove, a play of his memory, or diminishing eyesight, though his eyes seemed as keen as ever.

He walked around the great, flaring base of Clawbark—and into a knotted rope that dangled from high above, so high the base of the accepting kastkay was obscured by the lower reaches of the keska foliage.

The rope looked fairly new and well-made, though not the work of an expert braider of flessok. He saw none of the keota resin used to stiffen and preserve the fibers.

Someone was here, and he was Below—perhaps even watching Gurrus now. Otherwise, the rope would have been pulled up.

He looked around, peering through the undergrowth that thickened and rose to low mounds here and there. They were the heaps of the village middens, the accumulation of garbage and whatever else the people dropped from above to attract game. Hunters would secure their descending ropes to kill smaller scavengers and sometimes augors with their bows from a safe distance up the tree.

When Gurrus glimpsed movement, heard a rustling off to his right, his first instinct was to grab the rope and back away against the tree, hoping that if an attack came he might be able to climb up to a safe enough distance, shout for Falca and Ossa, and hold on long enough until they got here.

Gurrus let go of the rope. An augor would have charged him by now, the hour was too early for flenx, and the shitcatchers had horses he would have heard.

He was about to call out when the Kelvoi hunter appeared, holding on to a 'kinik vine to brake his descent from the midden slope. A dead eloe hung from his belt. He shrugged bristleboots from his shoulder to reveal the Tokaneke clan mark on his flange: the eye within the heart.

Gurrus had seen this one before, somewhere, but couldn't remember his name. He still had his dawnstone earbolls. That marked him as one lucky renegade to have escaped death or capture by Warden shitcatchers.

He opened a fist from his chest—a deferential greeting Gurrus hadn't been given in a long time. "We thought you were dead, Gurrus," he said. "I didn't recognize you at first, but then…you were talking to yourself."

"Was I?"

"You always did," he said, and lifted his eyes to Clawbark. "It was a game for us when we were young, to hide near your hoven and hope you might reveal things we weren't supposed to know yet."

"What did you hear?"

"I never joined in but I had friends who told me."

"It was a useful game for me, now that I recall: saying things that should be heard, but might otherwise not be heeded if I spoke directly. I knew some of those ketters. Perhaps your shyness is why I don't remember your name…"

"It's Styada."

"Ah, yes; now I do." Before he'd gone to Boughbreaks, Freaca had come to him for advice about a handsome young male named Styada, her first lover. Everyone wanted the match, including her father, and so she felt she should too, yet she had doubts that she could not resolve alone.

He asked Styada: "Are there others here?"

"No. I'm…I've taken use of your hoven."

"Such a small one. Still, it served me well, despite the reek of sweethand—my own fault, that. The vice stalked me to a far-away place called Draica, where at least I had a better excuse for it."

"Your possessions are gone, most of them, except for your kairesska."

"I've missed that. So much better than a metal blade. As for the other things… you thought I was dead. It's no matter."

"I'll remove my belongings; I haven't much."

"I won't be staying."

"You're going… on? With those two shitcatchers I saw?"

"Across the river, on something we'll make called a raft, and hope the kriluks won't be roused before we're over. And then we'll be going on much farther to the east. There's something…I have to do. One of these men—they're not shitcatchers, by the way—has promised he'll help me do it.

"With respect…how can you be sure of that?"

"Because the promise was also given to someone he loved, perhaps more than his own life."

"That doesn't sound like a shitcatcher."

"I told you he's not, nor is the other."

"They're all the same."

"Not always. Now tell me, when the shitcatchers destroyed Dawnbringer… were you here?"

Styada shook his head. "We knew they were coming. Twenty of us were sent to ambush them before they got here, so the females, the young, and some of the elders could escape. I alone killed six shitcatchers, but they kept coming and…I was captured, along with seven others who survived. Only two of us chanced an escape, Oket and I, but he was killed in the attempt. I killed two more who came after me, and I…I managed to elude the rest. Dawnbringer was still smoldering when I came back, days later."

"How many escaped?"

"Before they destroyed the bridge? I don't know. But the kriluks took many in the river so…something must have happened there. The bones kept washing up on the shore for days after."

Gurrus was thinking how much he had missed talking in the Tongue of his birth. Even now, conversing in the other was like choosing the kindling that would be most effective in starting a fire, and then the wood to keep it going.

But in either language, an eagerness to impress—or lie—was easily discerned.

Did it matter that Falca would fulfill his promise to Freaca with someone who claimed to have killed eight Wardens without suffering any wound Gurrus could see? That he would bequeath the story and memory of her heroism in a distant land to her boastful lover who probably didn't deserve the honor?

No, perhaps it mattered in a different world, where Cloud Hands might choose which lands below to bless or not, but His seed fell equally on the trees of those who needed the nourishment—and those who did not.

There was a reason why all lived in this world. And despite the answers that others assumed he hoarded in that tiny hoven off the Road, Gurrus still had no more of an understanding of why than did Falca, or Ossa, or even Styada—this once shy, now brave killer of Warden shitcatchers—who was now backing away from the others as they came around the tree: Falca with the sharpened axe; Ossa the hobbler.

There was one who might have the answer now, but she'd left them with only the question for others to ponder; and that, too, was the way of the world.

Chapter Twenty-Two:

STYADA

FALCA EXPECTED NOTHING from this Limb except perhaps more questions about Frikko; some he could answer, others he couldn't. He'd known her only briefly, and neither of them could speak the other's language, but he knew then, as now, that she must have suffered terribly on her way to the place of her death, yet she had endured. She was the most courageous person he'd ever known. He could tell Styada that, and so he did, bringing her home in the only way he could: by telling him, through Gurrus, what her fate had been in a far-off land so unlike this one. Halfway through, he realized that he could have been talking about Amala.

Styada backed away from him, with no words of his own for Gurrus, and kept backing away until he reached the base of the tree, and hurriedly strapped on the strange bristled boots. Such was his haste he lost the stingvine-wrapped eloe. He went up the rope quickly, his hands a blur on the knots, the bristle-boots scarcely touching the bark of the tree.

"Never seen a Limb climb that fast," Ossa said.

"More like fleeing," Falca said.

Gurrus sighed. "Perhaps it was just as well Freaca didn't return."

Falca turned abruptly to the mehka. "How can you say that?"

"Perhaps I should have said that she did not expect to return. She knew how difficult a homecoming would be, shunned not only by males but the elder females as well. She breached a custom. Females were forbidden to go Below, much less far beyond to a distant land by the sea that few free Kelvoi had ever seen, and fewer could imagine. I was fond of her, but had she returned, and had I not been captured by Wardens at Boughbreaks—it doesn't matter now."

Ossa picked up the stagger and hobbler from the ground where they'd earlier left them—a gesture at Gurrus' behest, to allay any fears Styada might have about their intentions.

"Tell us anyway," he said.

"As mehka of the village, I would have been expected to do one of three things: have her cast out, shunned for an entire year, or be put to death."

Falca hefted the axe. "Yet she left. And that one…" He nodded up the tree. "That one took off like he thought we were going to kill him."

"Or take his earbolls," Ossa said. "Lucky he still has them."

"You'd think he would want to know more," Falca said. "Frikko was his mate."

Gurrus shook his head. "Her first lover; not his mate. I remember now that everyone wanted the formal union, however. Freaca confided to me her doubts about him. She was young; she thought something was wrong with her for having them. She may well have been right about Styada."

"You know something?"

"We talked."

"Sounds like he was polishing the shovel," Falca said.

"I am not familiar with that expression."

"Boasting, when there's little cause for it."

"Spicing common meat," Ossa said.

"It would appear that Styada is not all he claims," Gurrus said.

Falca shrugged. "Well, whoever is?"

"None of us here, anyway," Ossa said, and nudged Falca with the hobbler shaft. "We should go. There's a river to cross and no means as yet to do it."

Ossa took the lead, slashing through the undergrowth beyond the hillocks. Falca was last to leave the grove of Two-Trunks, taking one last look at the place where Frikko had once lived.

The rope was gone; pulled up or cut. Why? Couldn't be fear; not with Gurrus' presence. Clearly Styada wanted nothing to do with them. Shame, then? Did he feel he wasn't worthy of Frikko? Or was it indignation at the reminder of how Frikko violated Kelvoi customs? And with that perhaps a sulleness that she'd chosen to abandon him for a purpose that did not involve him.

Maybe he just wanted to be alone with his grief up there, to mourn her privately; or imagine from that height what the sea must look like and wonder, yet again, why she was capable of doing something he never could.

Maybe it was a little bit of all these reasons.

Falca didn't have to imagine the sea, but he'd never been up where sun-thickets were found and always would be. He would gladly have traded the memory of one for an hour in the other.

Gurrus must have come back, mindful of him; when Falca turned to leave, the mehka was watching him. He said nothing, and they moved on to where Ossa waited for them. Together, they followed the remnants of the Road east that once had led from Two-Trunks, through more groves of smaller, flessok-draped trees, to the river the Tokanekes named after the kriluks that lurked in the murky waters.

STYADA SQUATTED BY Gurrus' old hoven, staring off beyond the void where the Road had been. The wind had picked up now, soughing through the leaves, enough to give movement to the kastkai. The only other sound, besides a distant knocking was the *keer-i-lee* of the drippingbirds in the nearby cage.

After capturing the mating pair, he'd spent a long time fashioning the cage, whittling the crossing splines with Gurrus' kairesska, and braiding flessok to bind it all together: a thing of beauty. But there was no one to marvel at his craftsmanship, or chide him for keeping the drippingbirds, who should be free to mimic the colors and patterns of the wild, not those of a cage, however well-made.

Gurrus' blade was a thing of beauty, too. He'd gotten it from rough-fleshed Hilk traders, who once came down from the mountains beyond the northern fens to barter with the western clans—when there were still enough Kelvoi to make the journey worthwhile.

Styada was a ketter the last time one came to the village. He'd been too scared to approach the Hilk, but he watched Freaca scour her hands on his skin—up to the knees, anyway. The Hilk laughed, giving her something before the village mehka—not Gurrus at that time—pushed her away as a hindrance to business, and chastised her for boldness unseemly for a female.

Styada had his eye on her from then on. He never knew what prize the Hilk had given her. She kept it a secret, never told him though he asked repeatedly. Once, he searched her family's part of the hoven while they were absent one day, found nothing unusual.

He still wondered what that reward for boldness was, but now he couldn't ask the shitcatcher, this…Falca, whether Freaca had the prize with her when she died, because he'd done it again.

Fled.

He felt foolish and angry with himself for cutting the rope, as if that could somehow prevent the past—and his shame—from following him up. He was frightened that he might be losing his mind, alone here where many had once lived, talking to himself like Gurrus always had. But at least the mehka knew someone was listening.

He felt like putting his hands over his ears so he wouldn't hear that *thock... thock, thock* in the distance. He'd heard the sound before of shitcatchers cutting trees. It would be this Falca doing the cutting, with the axe Styada, from his hiding place on the midden, had seen him sharpening. They were making that...raft, to cross the No-Eyes River because there was no longer a Road bridge over it.

They would still die. They would have to use a pole to push the raft across, and the kriluks would sense the movement as well as the raft itself. Years before, hadn't the kriluks sensed the splash and ensuing struggle of his brother in the water after Kekor, overburdened with onax carcasses from Split-Bole, lost his balance and fell into the river? That's what Styada had later told his mother and father.

Styada watched, helpless to do anything, as the kriluks fastened on Kekor first, knowing he was alive, and dragged him under. But that was the only truth of the matter. Kekor hadn't been overly burdened; he and Styada had had an argument and Styada pushed him, causing him to fall.

He now had the urge to step off the kastkai and end his life, but he couldn't bring himself to do it, any more than he could a different time on the same Road bridge, when at least there would have been honor in jumping down and attacking the shitcatchers crammed into high-sided boats. All he saw below were three ways to die: by axe, spear or kriluks.

He wanted to jump. He couldn't, not even when Kokus pleaded with him, then slapped him, and finally cursed him for a coward before he himself jumped. Styada boasted later that he had, and killed more than his share of shitcatchers, trusting to the few Kelvoi survivors to keep his secret. Not all did, and his cowardice became known. He knew his weakness had shamed Freaca, was part of the reason why she left Two-Trunks with other females to get the help she said was needed for the war against the shitcatchers because there were so few males left. That was her calm answer to the elders' outrage.

She was not in Two-Trunks to see him exiled or executed because Gurrus had been captured or killed at Boughbreaks. Styada went to another village and lied about why he came, telling a story much like he told Gurrus. But Styada was found out when others from Two-Trunks came to this village to ask for males to join in the coming defense against the shitcatchers.

They left with no help and refused to take Styada, though he said he would go. He followed them, intent on killing them for their dishonoring him. He never got the chance. Two-Trunks was under attack. Styada later told himself he couldn't have gotten there in time to help; and anyway, what difference could he alone have made?

He had a talent for excuses, and so he kept making them: why bother venturing beyond Two-Trunks—what was left of it, anyway? Going to another village would only mean more lies, and waiting for shitcatchers to come *there,* and destroy that one, too. He was safe here. Surely the shitcatchers would never return to a place they'd already ravaged. This was his home, his refuge, where he would never be tested again, his secret never revealed. How could it be when there was no one around to suspect he had one?

Until now.

He should have removed his earbolls while his eyes were still wide with astonishment at seeing Gurrus and the shitcatchers he called his friends—for how do you survive capture yet keep the prized dawnstone bolls that marked your coming of age as a male?

Just when Styada thought the cutting finished, and the forest returned to the sounds he'd always known, the knocking resumed. The faint *thock*...*thock*... meant that Gurrus was still not far away, and could still do something he hadn't been able to do before because he hadn't been in the village then: order the death Styada deserved for his cowardice. By accepting it now, Styada could salvage his honor. He could have used Gurrus' kairesska to kill himself; or better yet, simply step off the kastkai and plummet to his death. Could there be honor without a witness? That seemed like a question Gurrus might have posed, talking to himself, and giving the answer for loitering ketters to hear.

He felt like he knew the answer, but he couldn't kill himself.

Gurrus would surely do it for him.

Styada's fear now was that the cutting would stop, the raft assembled for the crossing. Whether they survived or not didn't matter. Gurrus would be gone. And with each passing season, alone up here, Styada would lose more and more of his sanity.

He'd cut the rope, but he'd made more, a task that had filled the empty hours of many days. He knotted the rope on a bough over the kastkai and flung the coil over.

The drippingbirds in the cage were silent, as if they knew he was leaving. He sliced through knot after knot with the kairesska, and pulled out the splines of one side. He was surprised they didn't seem to want to leave. He rattled the cage. "You have to, or you will die here. Go…"

The female took off first, then the male. He watched them, his only companions for so long, disappear in the canopy. They reappeared for a moment in a kushla made deeply golden by the lowering sun, and then they were gone.

He didn't bother with the climbing boots. He'd never need them again. But he did need the kairesska and put the thin, shiny stone blade into his mouth instead of his flessok belt, the better to feel the sharp edge that would take the life he no longer wished to live.

Below, he coiled the rope he had cut before and slung it over his shoulder. Flessok was light yet strong when twisted and braided. Maybe Gurrus and the others would at least remember he'd done that well, when they used his rope to bind the raft together.

If they survived the crossing.

The *thock…thock* of the tree cutting stopped.

He hurried.

BY THE TIME Styada got to the river he saw the timbers had been lined up over two thicker cutlings, awaiting only the binding. The men kneeled around a large pile of flessok. The taller, older shitcatcher with the melted patches of red skin on his forehead and cheeks, was cutting lengths of it with a long-bladed knife: Ossa, Gurrus had named him. Falca—he of the black hair and sky-blue eyes—kneeled next to him, clumsily trying to twist and braid the flessok with hands big as the rump of an onax. Styada was surprised that Gurrus wasn't doing much better, though he had already braided a few lengths of rope piled next to him.

Pausing from their work, they watched him approach. He dropped the coil of his rope next to Gurrus', and pointed at the raft. He didn't have to do that; his intent for the rope was obvious. But Styada needed the shitcatchers away, not knowing if they would interfere with what was going to happen.

Still, he was surprised when they thanked him. Ossa pronounced it better: *kehsu.* Falca picked up the gift and they left for the raft with quiet words Styada didn't understand. He and Ossa were like son and father, or comrades—so it seemed to Styada, who stood stiffly, waiting for them to leave. Falca was the quicker. Either he was more eager to put the rope to use, or he was somehow more aware that Styada wanted to be alone with Gurrus.

It was not proper that Styada should stand while a mehka sat, so he sat, and formally presented the kairesska to Gurrus, with the point toward his own heart.

Gurrus took it with thanks, no doubt thinking that Styada was returning what had once been among his most valuable possessions.

Beyond them, in the middle of the river, lay the islet. Among its trees, rocks and scrub there would be the bones of those who had died in the attack on the shitcatchers.

The dead, it was said, could see and hear in ways not known to the living, and Styada listened for their ghostly jeering at his cowardice—now his inability to confess the truth to a mehka. He heard nothing. He wasn't even worth taunting. Would they still be silent, shun him after he joined them in death?

That would be the worst fate of all.

He couldn't look Gurrus in the eye, but this time he jumped—and told the old mehka what truly he had done—and hadn't.

Gurrus held the kairesska before him, turning the broad, shiny blade, as a ketter might delight at a new toy. He said softly: "So, another gift."

"Please…you don't understand. I'm asking you to…"

"I understand what you want me to do. You still believe in what I was, what I would have done before. That person no longer exists."

The kairesska made a singing sound when he threw it into the river, skimming once, twice, before sinking.

"The look of shock on your face tells me you think that a waste." Gurrus said.

"Who am I to judge what I mehka does?"

"I told you: that person died a long time ago."

"It was a beautiful and useful blade," Styada said.

Gurus got up. Styada rose, too—confused, despairing and angry, though he tried to hide that. What was he to do now, back there, without even the kairesska to cut flessok and the paltry sheaves of kikket he was cultivating, or skin more meat for meals he no longer wanted?

"You have done me a favor," Gurrus said.

"A *favor*?"

"I am a mehka of nothing. Perhaps it's just as well, because when Two-Trunks was filled with our kin, I was no more a mehka than I am now."

"But...you were."

"You seem frustrated, perhaps because you came for death and have received only a mehka's riddles," Gurrus said. "But there is no riddle. "I was then a mehka in name only. I, too, lied about something of great importance, long ago, and kept the truth from everyone, including my father, or so I thought." He gestured toward the others. "Even they do not know. The gift you give me is the chance to tell a Tokaneke about something that has shamed me for too long."

And he did.

Styada had heard of the Kalaleks, those mehkas-of-mehkas; and the Isle. But not of a...sacred Tapestry, the Keta, comprised of kinnets, whatever they were. He couldn't decide if he even believed Gurrus or not. After all, mehkas were expected to conjure stories to inform a lesson.

"You tell me this," he said, "because you know the secret will be safe with me...either dead, or still alive and babbling about things others will not believe except as the ravings of one who has..."

"Believe what you must," Gurrus said. "And now those men need my help to lash the rope you've brought. Falca may have eyes in his hands for things soft and hard, but not for knots; and Ossa...he's dying, and would tell you that if you asked."

He began walking away.

"Wait! What am I to do if..."

Gurrus turned suddenly. "*Enough!*" His dark eyes bore into Styada's. "You squeal like an eloe nursling who wants the milk but thinks himself helpless to find it." He pointed to the raft. "*That* will be held together with the fine rope you brought us."

"You would have bound it without mine."

Gurrus brushed by Styada and snatched up a length of the rope he'd made. "With this pitiful skein? You may help us now, and come with us. Or you may leave and go back to what you were. Whichever you choose, I don't believe you came to the river to die."

✲

STYADA'S DECISION MADE it possible to put the hobbler in Ossa's hands instead of a pole for the crossing. Though the graylock said nothing, it was obvious to Falca his hands and wrists were hurting him after the lashing and dragging of the raft. Ossa could rest them better with the hobbler, keeping watch for kriluks. The Limb and Falca could work the poles for a quicker crossing. The longer they were on the water, the greater the chance of kriluks sensing their presence.

Downriver from the islet the current flowed faster than any of them expected. The front end of the raft kept dipping under, the water sloshing around their ankles, panniers, and slingsacks.

Styada gripped his pole too tightly, pushed off far less often than Falca did, and kept glancing at the islet in the middle of the river, as if that was where the danger lay, and not below.

Every grunt, every swipe of his hands to dry sweat reminded Falca that this rickety raft was no corry gliding along the Moat. The water was deeper, and if he lost his balance and fell in, that would be it. By the time Ossa or Styada could extend hobbler or pole the current would swirl him away, splashing meat for the kriluks.

From what Vere and Gurrus first said about the things, they sounded to Falca like the cutlass worms that Mangles' stormbirds had dropped on the ship he'd taken passage on for Gebroan in pursuit of Saphrax.

"I've dealt with pirates' cutlass worms," Ossa said. "These kriluks haven't got the poison, but they make up for that in size and swarm." He'd seen some along the northern reaches of the river, closer to the Great Fens, that were longer than he was tall. Unlike cutlass worms, kriluks had short, flattened legs that allowed them to move fast in the water—or spring from shallows to kill animals drinking at the river's edge. They had no eyes, sensing movement with long, whisker-like tendrils that sprouted from their bulbous heads. The round mouth was filled with a ring of teeth sized to kill fish. Kriluks could also wrap themselves around bigger prey, until the meal-to-be was water-logged and dead, ready to be sucked dry.

"Once, I was crossing over a tree blown down over a river," Ossa said, "and saw a swarm of them attack an augor that had strayed too close to the water. When they were done with it, you could have wrapped the carcass over you like a coachman's mantle."

"The best way to kill them?" Falca asked.

"Get across before they know you're doing it."

They did get across. The raft ground onto a gravel bar considerably down-river from where they wanted, but that was just fine with Falca. If the kriluks were anything like the cutlass worms he remembered from the *Bay of Tyryns,* he was heartily relieved to have missed them.

They tossed their panniers off the raft. Ossa was first off, with the hobbler and axe, splashing through a narrow channel on the other side of the bar; then Gurrus quickly, up to his knees. The pole still in his hands, Falca was stepping off the raft when Styada shrieked behind him.

Kriluks erupted from the water, slithering over the edge of the raft, rocking it. More slid over the bar. Panicked, Styada dropped his pole. Falca shouted at him to run. He didn't move. Three kriluks blocked his way, knobby heads raised, ring-mouths widening to reveal circles of teeth. Long tendrils swayed in the air.

One leaped at Falca; he batted it way with the end of the pole and it twisted back into the water. He looked back to see another rise at Gurrus, but Ossa, short-handing the long hobbler, halved it with a spray of yellow blood, shouting at Falca to get away from the water.

Styada was still within reach of the pole; Falca thrust it toward him. "Hold on! I'll pull you away." The Limb didn't know the words, but surely he'd understand.

He didn't grab it. The raft seethed with kriluks. Two were wrapping themselves around his ankles, then thighs. Styada punched at them, desperate to keep their mouths away. A kriluk arced onto the thick pole, screwing toward Falca. He felt the weight of the thing, and dropped the pole as Styada twisted off the raft, pulled away by a writhing mass of kriluks that had wrapped him up to his waist. He frantically beat the water, tried to pull them off, but they were dragging him to the deeper depths beyond the end of the raft.

Falca drew a longshank, surged into the water. He felt a tightening around his knees, slashed at the kriluk, got free, but not for long. Another came at him; he stabbed into its maw and through the skin behind the head, feeling the grating of teeth as it bit on the blade. He whirled to slash at yet another, saw Ossa and Gurrus behind him, splashing, grunting, killing more of them, Gurrus two-handing the Warden stagger-axe.

Kriluks churned the water around Styada. He was up to his shoulders now, his hands around one, trying to keep it from biting his face. They slid around

Falca's legs. He shrieked at the sucking bites on his thighs, yet still managed to plunge his dagger hand down, slicing, sawing at the kriluks fastened on him.

There were far too many of them, pulling him deeper into the river. He couldn't stay in the water for much longer, yet Styada was too far away for him to reach through the boil of eels.

One reared up at him. He snagged a fistful of tendrils and severed the head with a stroke of the longshank.

To free both hands he put the longshank in his mouth, tasting the oddly sweet blood. The first kriluk he grabbed near the leg-fins pulled free; he flung it behind him. And another. The next was the one he needed.

Styada screamed. Falca kept pulling on the kriluk. His hands kept slipping despite the raspy, banded scales. He kinked the thing to get a better grip, and pulled Styada closer…closer to him through water infested with kriluks who had yet to fasten on flesh.

Over Styada's screaming Falca heard Ossa shouting behind him.

With one last yank he pulled Styada close enough to grab him after he let go of the kriluk, and wrapped his arm around the Limb's neck. The longshank in his other hand now, he sliced at the head of the kriluk he'd used to get to Styada. Falca had him, but he himself couldn't move with the kriluks—two, three of them?—wrapped around his legs, still trying to pull him back. He tried to loosen their grip, hacking at them with the dagger, but fell, still holding onto Styada.

Ossa gripped him under the shoulders, pulling him back; Gurrus helped with Styada and soon they were out of the water. The kriluks' leg-fins slapped against the gravelly strand.

Ossa had his long knife; Falca tossed his own to Gurrus. The mehka began slicing at the two kriluks still fastened on Styada, who had to be screaming in Tongue the same things Falca was yelling: "Get 'em *off*! Get the *stiting* things *off* me!"

He could reach two of the three on him and he squeezed them, straightening out a length of their squirming bodies. Ossa needed eight vicious swipes to cut all three in half, yellow blood spraying everywhere. He shouted at Falca: "Don't try to pull the heads off; you'll rip out your skin. We need fire to get them off."

The raft still teemed with kriluks. Some rose in the shallows, tendrils waving madly, sensing their prey had escaped.

Falca felt like retching but he grabbed the closest of the two nearby poles, and scythed away a few kriluks before shoving the raft away from the strand, far enough for the current to catch it.

"The *slithing* bastards," he said. "They were underneath the raft all along."

He left the strand with the others, the heads and severed ends of the three kriluks bobbing against him as he ran.

THEY SCOURED THE fringes of the forest for firewood and the makings of a poultice Gurrus called klarry. After Ossa seared the kriluk heads off Falca and Styada, Gurrus smeared the rank-smelling klarry into their swollen bites.

They tossed the heads into the roaring fire. At Ossa's insistence they warily collected remnants of kriluks scattered along the strand while Ossa stood guard with his hobbler.

Having little food left in their panniers and sacks, they had to have something to eat. Ossa insisted the kriluks were a delicacy, though one not often enjoyed, of course. Falca, surly with the pain of the bites, was more than a little doubtful—but he was also more than a little hungry.

They cut the kriluks' remains into sections, spitted them over the fire, roasting them long after the skin crackled and blackened.

Falca had three.

Ossa handed Gurrus a piece. "Please pass that along to our friend Styada over there," he said. "You might also let him know that not everything that tries to kill you tastes as good as these."

Gurrus did so, translating in Tongue, and they all watched as Styada had his first taste of kriluk.

They added more wood to the fire as darkness fell. Falca got talking with Ossa about Mangles and Grippa, his lord in piracy around the Ebony Isles, and he found out that Ossa had been owner and captain of a windwhipper plying the trade route between Milatum, Sandsend and Castlecliff in Myrcia, where his wife and daughter once lived.

Falca might have learned how and why the winds had blown him so far off course, but the moment passed when Gurrus came over. Ossa seemed relieved with that, saying he'd stand the first watch. He took his hobbler beyond the pale of the fire, to smoke his pipe.

"Styada and I have been talking," Gurrus said. "He would thank you for what you did."

Falca nodded at the young Limb, who returned the gesture. Then, to Gurrus: "He came with us and I'm glad he did. Four now is better than three—do you see how Ossa's hand shakes with the pipe? Worse than before, though he insists what he did on the river didn't make it so."

"Styada says he owes you his life, and wishes only the chance to repay the debt."

"He'll get his chance—helping us with Ossa. There's no debt beyond that."

"He would say there is—to you."

Falca stared off at Ossa, wondering if the sot he was smoking helped dull his pain. "All right then. I'll show him how he can repay me." He went over to Styada, and when he returned, Gurrus asked: "What was it you gave him, besides your dagger? I could not see anything else."

"The flenx horns. I'm lucky I didn't lose them in the water. Styada didn't know what I was saying, but I think he understands what I want him to do, since I couldn't possibly braid flessok as well as he, or carve out a hole in each horn. I intend to wear them around my neck."

"He understands you do not want to lose them?"

"I'm sure he does, but not why. I haven't the Tongue for that. Maybe he'll help me with that, too. In the meantime, you'll have to tell him."

"Tell him what?"

"Not how I got them—I couldn't care less whether you mention that. But he should know what they mean to me, and why they can't be lost—until I've used them to kill Maldan Hoster and Lambrey Tallon."

Chapter Twenty-Three:

THE RIVER

SHAR STAKEEN KEPT hidden in the bracken, brushing away pestering river flies, watching Breks and the others killing the eels on the far bank. She'd never seen the likes of these things that could swarm and leap out of the water to strike their prey.

And rarely had she seen so foolish an act as Breks' when he waded back into the river to save the shrieking mottle—who had almost discovered her as she went on to the river, thinking he was out of the way, up that tree. If he'd seen her she would have had to kill him.

As it was, she could only hope that Breks wouldn't attempt to do anything else as stupid as saving the life of a worthless mottle, or he wouldn't live long enough for her to get what she needed from him.

Still, he'd done her a favor: alerting her to the presence of the eels. He also might have given her another. Perhaps the current would take the raft, now drifting downriver, to the near shore. She couldn't count on that, yet the alternative —making her own—would take time. She'd have to wait until the following morning, and Breks might take a lead difficult to overcome. Swimming across was not an option, though she was expert.

The raft disappeared from view. She left her hiding place, retrieved the horse she'd hobbled deeper in the forest. When she was sure they couldn't see her, she led the horse along the river bank, concerned now about the deepening twilight.

Then she saw it.

The raft, caught by thick reeds and a stout, drooping tree branch, had lodged on the near bank.

So she could do it now, before night fell.

Thank you very much, Falca, she thought.

She remembered he hadn't used the full length of the pole until the raft was past the middle of the river, which told her that she might be able to keep mounted for the first part of the crossing. She stroked the horse. First Mally, now this one. There was nothing she could do about it.

With her dagger she quickly sliced the rope binding four of the timbers, choosing the skinniest of them to use as a pole, which she lay athwart the remaining ones. She knotted together the lengths of the rope she'd cut to fashion a short lead, tied it off on her saddle pommel, and then to the raft. She piled her panniers on the raft.

It didn't take much effort for her to push it free from its berth.

After she mounted, the horse balked at the river's edge, but she goaded it with a slap and set the dagger in her teeth.

She got almost to mid-river before deciding it was time to abandon the struggling, increasingly reluctant horse. The warm, murky water swirled above her knees. She saw no sign of the eels, but they had to be gathering below. There could be no question of who was to be their prey.

She brought the reins up, swung one dripping leg over and, sitting sideways in the saddle, she pulled the raft closer, and jumped down as lightly as she could in the middle. The raft dipped, the pole almost floated away, but she quickly grabbed it and cut the lead. She was about to start poling, then thought it might be better not to immediately stir the drink as Breks had done all the way across. Plunging movement below had to be part of how the eels sensed their prey.

Stakeen knelt, ready with a dagger, the pole at her feet, extending beyond the ends of the raft. The mare had turned back for the shore…and whinnied in panic.

Eels leaped from the water, slithering up over the saddle, coiling around the horse's neck. The mare shook her head to get them off, but there had to be as many below, trapping her legs, as above.

Stakeen turned away when the horse went under. She let the raft go with the current before she finally got to her feet, to carefully find the balance of the thing. Tipping the raft over here would not do at all.

She began poling—just enough to guide the raft toward the far shore. By the time she reached it, the river appeared calm. But down below the kriluks were feeding. Mindful of what had happened to Breks and the others, she hurried off the raft, backing away, both daggers in her hands, and waited well back from the river's edge until she was sure no eels had followed. Only then did she go back for the panniers and drag the raft ashore.

The immediate area was as good as any for the night and far enough away from Breks to make a fire. She leaned the raft against two smaller trees. The crude shelter was better than nothing for the night. She wasn't worried about the Draican and his companions coming along the river in the morning. They wouldn't have crossed the river only to continue down the other side. They would be heading inland. Exactly where didn't matter so long as they led her to Golden-Eyes.

Using driftwood branches and rope from the raft, she made a trap that hopefully would provide dinner. As part of her shadden training Stakeen had learned to make traps of all kinds, mostly to snare or kill a man or woman, but she'd mastered smaller snares, too. While she was gone her scent hopefully would diminish to the point where an animal's temptation overrode wariness. She baited the trap with some food, and hung both panniers on a branch away from the trap.

She took only the agonette and spiddard with her, in addition to her daggers, and as darkness set in she followed the river bank toward Breks' camp. She glimpsed a fire before she heard faint snatches of conversation—the mottles'—that sounded like hail chattering on a roof. And a rasping.

Fires were a mixed blessing—as hers would be later. They discouraged predators and provided comfort; they also chastened nighteyes, making it difficult to see beyond the pale of the fire.

She crept closer, keeping low, moving toward them from the river through the bracken, careful with her tread. The two Limbs chattered away; she had no idea what they were saying. For all she knew they could be talking about the very thing she wanted to hear.

The rasping sound: Breks sharpening a longshank dagger, the blade gleaming in the firelight. Did he do nothing but hone his weapons? The last time she'd seen him, earlier in the day, he'd been at the Warden's axe taken from the falls, the golden color gone from his eyes.

She couldn't see his tall companion from where she crouched: the graylock with the scarred melts on his forehead and cheeks. Likely he was taking the first watch, closer to the forest—and there he was, moving to another tree, leaning against it now, looking into the darkness of the forest, and then back to the fire and the others, cradling a hobbler in the crook of his left arm, a Banishman's weapon. He was smoking a pipe, the wisps of smoke trailing away.

It soon became apparent this wouldn't be a night of revelations, though she knew that had been unlikely. The Limbs fell silent; Breks ceased his work before adding more wood to the fire. Still, she lingered, long enough to catch the scent of the sot the tall stumper was smoking and then left as silently as she had come.

The trap had caught a small, yellow-eyed animal. It wasn't dead and hissed when she picked it up by the long, red-ringed tail to skewer it. After slicing off the head and gutting the animal, Stakeen pinned the carcass to a tree with her dagger, to let it bleed out while she collected wood for a fire. She washed her hands in the river, thinking that it had to be the scent of the Banisher's sot-smoke that made her believe the animal she'd caught was the same kind her father had once brought back to her as a gift from Milatum.

As she ate she tried to recall the name she'd given it, but she hadn't had the pet for long. Her mother didn't like it and made her get rid of it. But she remembered her father saying the wee thing had escaped its cage during the voyage, scampering along the decks and rigging as nimbly as she always did in the glow of his return, to show him how daring she was. She knew this pleased him as much as it annoyed her mother. She kept hoping he'd take her with him on his next voyage—never mind she was but a girl.

He never did.

She could see him now: striding down the plank of the windwhipper, pipe clenched in his teeth. She would run to greet him, and he'd pull her in tightly with one arm, holding the pipe in his other hand…

There were many men, not just sailors and denizens of the Heap O' Heads quays in Castlecliff, who enjoyed a pipe of sweet-smelling sot. But Stakeen always associated it with her father, who always came back from a voyage with gifts—out of guilt she knew early on, for his long absences—from cities like Milatum and Girvan in Keshkevar; or Sandsend, Karsor's Bay and Thetis in Gebroan; or Tantallon in the Shelter Isles; places she wanted to visit after he told her about them.

She wasn't surprised she'd forgotten the name of that pet he'd brought her. Sometimes she even had to pause to remember her real name, not the one she had to choose to become a shadden. Occasionally during an apprenticeship, the senior cabalists would say the old name to test an acolyte's progress along the desired path, and would punish any who responded to the old name.

Stakeen never failed, because she wanted to forget that her father had named her after his sleek windwhipper, the fastest of any he helmed between Milatum and Castlecliff, but never fast enough to bring him back to her as quickly as she wanted—or lucky enough to avoid the storm that wrecked it on the Flaggy Shore, all hands lost.

But that was many years ago, and she'd long since picked the meat of those bones as cleanly as the newer ones she now tossed into the fire.

MUCH FARTHER DOWN the river that same night, Lannid Hoster couldn't sleep. There were several reasons for his wretched wakefulness, including the eels that had kept battering the sides of the six boats all day long and into the evening. Besides Lannid, there were seven Wardens in the boat; the other five carried forty more. He was, at least, grateful that Maldan and Lambrey Tallon were not in his.

These Wardens comprised the contingent the Allarch had left at the river rendezvous east of the falls to meet the pursuers of Falca Breks and escort them to the east.

The boats were tied off with stakes pounded into the river bank, but Tallon had ordered the men to stay in the boats for the night. Sleeping men in motionless boats would not attract eels. But this area, evidently, was particularly infested with vicious little cut-nose forras, who had the claws to climb over an encampment stake wall.

Well, a motionless boat crowded with sleeping Wardens might not summon eels, but the snorers among the men were a torment to Lannid, who had grown accustomed at Skene to plugging his ears every night in the dormitory.

Still, he might have crossed over given his earlier, exhausting turn as a poleman, if not for his worrying that Hovus and Cambrill—a tenon no less—were going to attempt an escape. What would he do if they did? And would he succumb to the lure of joining them?

All the way from the falls to the river rendezvous and the boats, he'd thought of his own escape. Alone, of course, he never would have made it back to Bastia. With two others, however? Warden veterans, who knew the lesser trails they'd taken to the river?

Lannid wanted no part of this treason—and involuntary exile in this Scaldasaig, to where his father and the rest of the Wardens were heading; some by boat, most by march. Tallon had only told the men half the truth for now: that the Myrcian threat was to be dealt with at Scaldasaig. Wardens followed orders without question, so that's where they'd be going.

Lannid said nothing to the whispered questions and skepticism of a few other Wardens who wondered how the Allarch, much less Comitor Tallon, could know so much of the Myrcians' whereabouts so soon after entering the Bounds.

Hovus and Cambrill were the closest to Lannid in the boat, and though he did not talk much to them, clearly they were the most troubled at the news of a destination of which they'd never heard. Cambrill kept going on about his wife and three young children in Bastia. Who could blame him for fearing he'd never see his family again? Lannid was sure both men would try to slip away—or was it his own desperation?

If they did make the attempt, it would be his duty to alert Tallon. Or was it? He was a son of the Allarch, but no bound Warden. How, he wondered, could you betray with your silence the greater betrayal of your father's?

Stay or go? Exile awaited him whichever he chose.

He knew they were only waiting for him to fall asleep, and so he made his decision, such as it was. Fearing one choice as much as the other, he closed his eyes. They were right next to him, but how could he stop them—so he could plead later—if he was sleeping soundly?

Not long after he heard them slip over the side of the boat, he found the lure to sleep—in imagining the boldness of escaping with them.

In the morning when he woke, stiff and chilled from the mist that shrouded the river, Lannid was disappointed to see that they had returned. The taller Cambrill and red-haired Hovus sat next to each other against the broad trunk of a tree.

But they weren't moving, and as the mist parted around them briefly, Lannid saw their service daggers stuck in the tree by way of their throats. Next to Hovus, another dagger pinned a bloody scrap of cloth to the same tree.

Lambrey Tallon, standing in the front boat, shouted: "Look well, all of you, at these deserters."

They stretched their legs on the shore, their backs to the dead men, and ate a cold meal of grabble and grudge. Lannid hadn't the stomach for food. He didn't care that he'd pay for that later with hunger. He grabbed a pole, said he'd take the first stint, and had the pole in the water before the last man on his boat finished his breakfast.

They pushed away from the bank, silently, except for the splashing dips of the poles.

No one asked who'd killed Hovus and Cambrill. No doubt Tallon knew, but no one dared ask him, and if they had, he wouldn't have told them. At best he might have said: "What does it matter who kills deserters?"

It did to Lannid.

Alone of anyone on the boats, his brother hadn't looked at the dead men. Who would give up a service dagger but Maldan, who had Breks' falcata to replace it? And the cloth was the same green scrap Lannid had cut away from his sleeve, to stanch the flow of blood from the wound Amala Damarr had given him before he killed her.

That cut still had to be painful, and perhaps that was what kept Maldan awake the night before, and so he had heard the men leaving. Perhaps he informed Tallon—gesturing was all he could do—that he was going after the men, and the Comitor let him.

Guesses, that's all they were, and Lannid could be wrong about them, but not the fact that exile did not await him at the end of this expedition, at Scaldasaig.

His exile was already here, in the guise of a bloody cloth pinned to a tree with his brother's own dagger, next to men whose only betrayal was to his father's treason.

Maldan's speech would be slurred, hard to understand for a while longer, until the cut, from ear to mouth, had time to heal. But he'd found another way to deliver a message: *Had you left us, brother, you would have been sitting next to the others, a dagger through your throat.*

Chapter Twenty-Four:

KUSS

THEY LEFT THE river not long after sunrise, following what little remained of the Road. The Wardens' fire that consumed it left blackened sections of scorched trees where flessok cables had once been secured by high boughs or cuts in the bark.

This Road, Gurrus told them, had been one of the southern routes to the east, though he'd never taken it. A northern Road, which led east from Boughbreaks, was the shorter way to the Lake of Shallan, and he'd travelled that but once. Both skirted the vast fens that lay to the west of the Lake and Isle, and were home to the Katakets who had long ago left villages in the trees to build krannogs in the marshes. Whether they did that voluntarily, as the result of defeat in war and subsequent exile, or a storm that had destroyed their hovens and Roads—the legends differed according to the mehka doing the telling—one thing was certain: they were the least respected of all Kelvoi clans.

Ossa had hunted only once in this territory, but he insisted on leading the way, saying his hands were feeling better. Falca was skeptical of that but deferred to his wishes and the fact that his hobbler was proving to be the most effective means to forge a path through dense vegetation. He stayed close behind with the stagger-axe, to help out when more heft was needed to get through.

Ossa suddenly dropped to a knee at a faint, staccato howling that seemed to Falca oddly paired with a closer brushing, ticking sound. The graylock motioned the others to do the same, and pointed at Falca's stagger, the gesture obvious.

Ossa kept his hobbler at a low angle, bracing the butt against a boot, and leaned back to whisper in Falca's ear: "Tuskers. Ahead to our right."

Falca heard more of the brushing and ticking, then a low thumping, a grunting that grew louder. He couldn't see the tuskers ahead through the undergrowth. The light on the forest floor was murky, the mist sifting between the flessok-draped trees. He turned, motioning to Styada to also be ready with the longshank he'd given him to carve the flenx horns, but the Limb already had it out.

Ossa marked the passage of the tuskers with the hobbler point, the long blade moving from right to left, following the fading of the ticking and grunting. He finally nodded, and they all got up. "A brood," he said. "Eight, maybe more."

"That ticking?" Falca asked.

"Their bristles against the trees. They were moving quickly."

"Away from us?"

"Not us," Gurrus said. "Keerkets—snagwolves."

"That howling," Falca said. "Shouldn't we stay here until after they've passed, too?"

Ossa shook his head. "The 'snags probably aren't following; more likely herding,"

"Herding?

"Well, not like a shepherd with dogs; more a signaling to 'snags out there that meat is coming their way."

"'Save some for us', you mean."

"Just so. They're smart. And they don't eat their own weak or wounded, like flenx."

"You'd think the tuskers would catch on after a while."

"They don't have to. They breed fast."

Styada didn't know most of what they were saying, but he'd heard what they had. He pointed up to the remains of the burned Road, as if to tell them there was a place where they wouldn't have to worry about snagwolves herding a brood of tuskers that could have torn them to shreds in the murky light.

Styada was picking up words at a rate that astonished Falca—and Gurrus, too. One of the first he'd learned was "Warden", and he said it now as he gave the crude Limb gesture for "shitcatchers", as if Falca hadn't understood his halting pronunciation or knew who had destroyed the Road they all wished they could have used.

Shafts of sunlight penetrated the canopy above in bold slashes, offering little warmth until later in the morning when the canopy opened more to reveal the ruins of what had once been village of Split-Boles, Gurrus said.

After that, the terrain decayed as it rose with elevation, becoming fractured with notched vales and narrow gorges; gulches filled with boulders; mossy scree and fallen branches; and storm-toppled kelvastas. The debris had to have been accumulating since the time of Roak and Cassena if the size of the fallen giants was any indication. Falca couldn't believe trees as huge as these had such shallow balls of roots.

With so little left of the Road, there was no point in looking up to use it as a marker. The danger was around them and below, in this kuss, as Gurrus called it, that was found in the uplands, where the northern wind blew more fiercely in the winter, not the more sheltered river valleys or lowlands.

Sometimes they had to climb over a fallen tree. When that was not possible they crawled under. Falca shivered at not only the damp, cool exhalations of dark caves and crevasses below. If you slipped and fell, better hope for a crushed skull, a quick end. A broken arm or leg would only delay the inevitable, unless whatever lurked in the depths of the kuss found you first.

If he'd ever wondered why the Limbs built their Roads—especially over such treacherous terrain—he didn't now.

Surely this kuss would have turned away the Wardens. Somewhere up ahead, if they got through this, there would be an intact Road.

A kelvasta now blocked their way, angling sharply down across an abyss into which they didn't dare descend. The tree had been rotting for a long time. Even if they could somehow have get across to reach it, they couldn't trust using fissures in the bark as handholds and footholds, as they had with more recently fallen trees.

They made their way carefully to the side, Falca in the lead so he could use the stagger to hack away branches of the canopy remains, and those of lesser trees this giant smashed as it fell.

On hands and knees when necessary, they worked their way around a steep rocky outcrop, then through a warren of decayed branches that crumbled at the touch. Finally, where the trunk slimmed down, they were able to climb on top of the tree.

And then they saw why they had to not just keep going, but traverse the giant that spanned the abyss. Styada noticed it first: a Road.

There it was, above and beyond the far upturned ball of the kelvasta. Below, in the kuss of the gorge, they hadn't been able to see it until now. Once slung between supporting trees, it now hung down from the lower reaches of branches: a twisted, skewed, falls of a Road. It was hard to judge at this distance, but Falca gave it the height of Erisa's Campanile.

It didn't appear to be burned, not here. Somewhere else? If so, the fire hadn't spread to the trees themselves.

None of them could move sideways very far on the trunk to see for certain if the Road continued, but Falca thought he saw part of it through the dappled foliage. So did Ossa.

A useable Road would mean Wardens hadn't gotten this deep into the Bounds; that there might be villages along the way where surely food would be offered to a mehka—and krael for a companion who needed it.

Falca glanced at Ossa. Was he thinking the same thing?

All they had to do was climb up to the fallen Road.

First, they had to get to it.

Carefully, they began the crossing. Rot slickened the thick bark; Falca scuffed away sheaves of it to get to better footing beneath. He didn't dare look down to see how far the pieces had fallen. Ossa used his hobbler to do the same thing and then, not trusting his balance, as a walking stick. Styada seemed the most confident with this, frequently stopping to make sure of Gurrus' progress. They paused at midpoint, holding on to several sproutling trees that had taken root in the dead parent, and saw now that this risk would be worth it.

The angle of their bridge was such they couldn't see the fallen edge of the Road, but they glimpsed where it continued, disappearing into denser forest.

The trunk was now wide enough for them to walk abreast, but they kept in single file, stepping warily, until they reached the flaring of the base. They crawled up toward the wild, tangled roots of the huge ball, used them to work their way down. Styada and Gurrus were the first to drop down from a safe height, then Ossa and Falca.

They hacked through undergrowth, to the trees where the Road had fallen away—and saw what had been disguised by distance and hope.

The Road hung by only one cable, the other torn away high above. Gurrus and Styada inspected the surviving cable, and though Gurrus said it seemed to be intact with the resin used to stiffen and strengthen the flessok and prevent rot, they all decided the risk here wasn't worth it.

Ossa examined the planks. If there had still been two supporting cables, they would have been knotted at either end and in the middle. "They're set too closely together," he said. "There's nothing to grip or step on to get up to where the Road continues intact, unless we want to cut away the flessok from every other plank."

Falca shook his head. "We'd be at it for days, in mid-air, with only the single cable bearing our weight."

"These S'keels build differently," Gurrus said. "Tokanekes space the planks a little more, so as not to burden the road with water or snow."

"Well, at least we have a Road to follow," Falca said, "until we find a place where we can climb to it."

AS THE AFTERNOON wore on they made better progress along a ridge above the kuss, though the route took them away from the Road above. When they caught sight of it again it seemed to disappear into greater shafts of sunlight that beckoned through the dense forest. They descended from the ridge to follow it again through more kuss that was, Falca sighed thankfully, at least now free of wind-felled trees, except a smaller one that spanned the top of a ravine pestered by roots. When this narrowed they had to walk single file again to go on, but beyond was a brightness so glaring that Falca—accustomed to the gloom of below—had to squint.

A small, half-moon lake spread around the promontory of an escarpment that rose as high as the Road they'd followed, and extended far beyond the reddish shores of the lake itself, in both directions. Thick veins of dawnstone layered the escarpment from top to bottom.

Thirsty, bloodied by scrapes and cuts, they now faced the prospect of having to move along the bottom of the escarpment to find a place where they could climb up. There was no way to do that here. The cliff was fractured along the dawnstone veins but these were varied, and Falca glumly noted the wide expanses where they'd be unable to find fissures for hands and feet. And Ossa, with his hands…

The graylock nudged Falca. "Look at that," he said, pointing at the bridge over the lake. "Taut as a flina's strings—would that we could plant our feet on the frets."

Falca looked but he was thinking about no less a wonder: Ossa's skin was rotting up his arms from his hands, the 'snare poison slowly seeping to his bones, and yet he could still marvel at this bridge over the lake.

He shielded his eyes from the sun. Were there steps—possibly broad pegs—in one of the two supporting trees of the Road they'd been following? These led up to the level of the Road above the lake, and this bridge widened considerably before the Road continued on to disappear into the forest above the escarpment. More cables angled down from trees within to support the platform—if that's what it was.

Gloves off, Ossa was helping himself to the lake water and Falca knelt to do the same. Gurrus had been right about the water in the Bounds. Compared to this, everything else he'd had was piss the morning after.

Gurrus and Styada were talking, looking at them, as if they were shitting in the lake and not drinking from it. Gurrus shrugged. He and Styada turned away, offering a cupful from their hands to one another, and no more.

Falca wiped his mouth with the back of his grimy hand. "What? It tastes better from someone else?"

"It does, which is why it is preferable not to drink directly from the Water. I was saying to Styada that you and Ossa could not know, and who are we to tell our thirsty friends how they must drink from a sacred place."

"Sacred? No wonder it tastes so good," Falca said.

"If I am not mistaken," Gurrus said, "this is a Choosing Place of the Skeels."

THERE WERE MANY places for Kelvoi to die, and more ways than there once were. But if one was lucky, and reached the end of elder years, the blessing that parents murmured to their newly-born would come to fruition: *May you live long enough to Choose.* And when the decision to die was made, a mehka would be the last companion at the Choosing Place. Other farewells would have already been made among the immediate family. The mehka would simply ask: Sky or Water?

If Sky was chosen, either kolk or a potion of herbs known only to the mehka would be given, enough to dull the talon pain of the floka the mehka would summon to take the Chosen away. The potion would bring peace before he or she was consumed, but not before the gift of being carried away in the sky, for this last memory was indeed a gift. The flokas in their nests would eat the dead, but was this not preferable to having no choice and rotting somewhere?

And Water? Was not water the seed of Cloud Hands?

The mehka would assist the Chosen in taking the steps to the edge, but only the Chosen could take the final one to the lake or river below.

The same potion or kolk would dull the terror of drowning. The last thing one would feel was the sensation of returning to the womb, so it was believed…

✻

GURRUS LEFT WHEN he'd finished. Styada followed him. Ossa put his gloves back on hands streaked with blackened flesh. "I knew this was one of their places," he said, "but I couldn't help myself. I didn't think it mattered; I suppose it does."

With his long strides he soon caught up to the others.

Kneeling by the lake's edge Falca watched them walking toward the escarpment. He dipped his palm in the water, imagining it was Amala's hand from which he took one last drink, and wondered what—if they'd been lucky enough to grow old together—she might have chosen. The same choice they'd had to make for her, there by the rocky ledges of the falls? Or Sky? Was there a floka with big enough wings to carry her away?

He felt a sorrow now that he hadn't loved her for a long enough time to be sure about which choice she might have made. He doubted he'd live long enough to be fortunate enough to make a choice. The Fates had already nodded down at him from their Loom Eternal too many times already. If they weren't bored with his existence by now they would be soon, though hopefully not before he'd gotten to the other lake and its Isle and, before that, found krael for Ossa.

He dipped his hand in the water again. How deeply lay the bones of the Kelvoi on the bottom? Only now did he truly understand that Ossa had been going into the Bounds to find his own Choosing Place, and had forsaken that for a last hope…

It was Ossa's shout, and then a summoning wave that hurried Falca over to where he stood alone at the bottom of the escarpment.

Where were Gurrus and Styada?

STYADA WAS THE one who found it, poking into a vertical fissure in the cliff that Gurrus had passed by. The crack in the dawnstone did not close off, but widened and in the darkness he'd stumbled, not expected there to be steps leading up.

Now, as they all gathered by this entrance, Gurrus seemed almost as proud of Styada's bruised forehead as the younger Limb was.

The mehka was certain the Skeels built the passage to mine the dawnstone. They were a central clan of Kelvarra, trading the dawnstone to those of the east and west. Perhaps, too, the passage was part of ceremonies involving the Choosing Place that were unique to them. The Skeels also had the reputation of being one of the least warlike of the Kelvoi clans, so the passage might also have served as a refuge in times of trouble, a place to hide where one could not Above, no matter how lofty the village.

"Whatever it is, or was," Ossa said, "it has steps and we'll see where they go."

"You found it, Styada; you lead," Falca said.

They crept into the dank darkness, with Ossa behind him, then Gurrus. Only Falca did not grasp Vere's hobbler since he had the stagger. Styada kept the hobbler point and blade out in front of him, in case the passageway was something more than it seemed—which Falca thought was very much a possibility. Why was the burr always the in-between, not the beginning or end?

They didn't talk. The only sounds: Ossa's labored breathing and the little splashes they made in water trickling down the worn steps. Falca had been face down in the gutters of Catchall more than once; the smell of this place was all too similar. The tunnel was so narrow his shoulders brushed the sides and in some places narrower still, and he had to turn and take sidesteps. Twice, he sensed a greater space, once to his left and again to his right, farther up—a doorway off the tunnel? Or a shaft leading down? All he knew was that when he thrust out the butt of the axe it didn't hit the wall. These side chambers seemed to be spaced where the steps switch-backed off in the opposite direction.

Styada announced a third chamber higher up. They stopped to rest at the entrance. Within, a shaft of light angled down, illuminating a patch of uneven dawnstone that, compared to its source, seemed to be on fire. Yet even that couldn't reveal the dimensions of the chamber, only the single twisting root that had extended down that shaft in a futile attempt to find nourishment.

The light and the root had to mean they were getting closer to the surface. Falca seized on that to help quell his traps-and-squeezes. He had to consciously slow himself down so he wouldn't knock into Gurrus ahead of him. He had also, at the entrance far below, begun counting steps.

He could neither read nor write, but he'd learned to count the coins he'd reived or hoped to. He was already up to far more than he'd ever had in his kist when they moved on from the last chamber. He'd thought counting the steps might help keep his mind from where he feared it might go, and for a while it did—until he realized that doing so was most useful only if they had to go back down. Still, he persisted, too stubborn to give up what he'd begun.

Yet dark thoughts were never far, lurking behind him, whispering: the Road and the bridge over the lake were intact, which meant that there could be Limbs above, their village near or far; did it matter? And they might have seen the strangers from hiding places at the top of the cliff; seen them enter: two Limbs and two shitcatchers—a sight unusual enough to cause concern and wariness. So they had blocked the exit and even now were hurrying over the bridge, with ropes, to descend once they crossed, and then go to the entrance, to wait for the inevitable return, and kill them as they emerged, one by one, or block the entrance, sealing the four of them inside, entombed forever…

Falca didn't stop counting until the mesh of light appeared, and with it a change in the air. His dark thoughts receded. Even if this hatch was locked in some way, he could use the stagger to chop away a hole big enough for them to squeeze through. What else could the Limbs have used to make it but wood?

The hatch was not barred. One by one they emerged, finding themselves within a structure whose obvious purpose was to protect the mine's entrance from rain, as the grate had prevented animals from venturing below, yet allowed air to seep below.

Squinting, they stepped into the sunlight.

Weeds and vines covered surrounding low hillocks, but dawnstone gleamed here and there: the guts of what had once been taken out. Wooden buckets, some with the shafts of mallets, hand-picks and short breakers sticking out, nestled against a nearby trough of dawnstone.

Ossa tipped over one of the buckets, to a gush of water. "They haven't been at it for a while."

Falca lifted out one of the iron breakers, smearing the rust off the chiseled edge. "They didn't make this."

"No," Gurrus said. "Kelvoi do not work metal; we trade for it, with Hilks from the north. Or used to."

"Hilks?"

"Shredders-of-rope," Gurrus said. "But I never met a Hilk as big as the one I saw you with after your return from Gebroan. His name was Ballast, was it not? He had unusually smooth skin."

"I'm surprised you remember."

"I had reason to; all of us did at the gate of Amala's home."

So we did, Falca thought.

He couldn't have brought Amala back without Ballast's help. He'd left for his home in the High Vales of Helveylyn not long after she met him, to find another female—a greyla—to restore his roughy, the male stoneskin's pride. Only coupling with a female could do that, a fact Amala hadn't quite understood: "If

I ever begin to smooth *your* roughy out too much, kahyeh, you'd better take a shingle to my backside. Promise me?"

Falca dropped the iron breaker into the bucket, a pail for memories too…

They left with Gurrus and Styada taking the lead. Given that the mine showed no sign of recent activity, it didn't seem likely they'd meet any Skeels up ahead. But if they did, better the Limbs were seen first.

They glimpsed the Road, still intact, angling here and there, high above between the trees. These were big enough, but not quite as massive as those of the lowlands. As with most of the Bounds forest, the trunks were devoid of branches until the onset of the canopy.

The afternoon light sifted through breaks in the canopy, but didn't offer much to the forest understory beyond the mimicking of deep twilight or the murkiness of the hour before dawn. Gurrus, walking next to Falca, nudged him. "Look above," he said.

They were underneath a village.

Chapter Twenty-Five:

CLIMBS AND PUZZLES

FALCA HAD THE greater voice of them all, and Gurrus gave him the words in Tongue to loft it. Birds scattered from dense thickets of banepath, then silence returned to the dismal grove of kelvastas. They walked on, deeper into the gloom underneath the village, between the mounds of overgrown middens—more evidence the Skeels here had abandoned their home.

Styada found the central mother-tree. The four of them could have attempted to circle it, arms at length, and still not matched the kelvasta's girth at its base. Put the Colossus of Roak in Draica's harbor alongside and Falca could have stepped from its dawnstone shoulder to this village—one wonder to the other.

Which was greater? It took ninety-six years, hundreds of masons, thousands of laborers, and depleted the treasuries of three kings, so it was said, to build the Colossus. It probably took Skeels a lot less time to build this village and Road, just as high, with only cables made of braided flessok.

And where *was* the rope they'd need to get up to the Road?

Falca felt dismay that they'd have to keep on Below—but also a sneaking relief he wouldn't have to make the climb.

"There's no rope or cuts in the bark," he said.

"Skeels use those," Gurrus said, pointing.

The short spars were hard to see in the gloaming, projecting out from the deep fissures in the bark, some less than a foot long. Falca kept tilting his head back, following the stitching of the stubby spars, until they were indistinguishable from the trunk itself.

He tugged at two of them. They seemed secure enough, but they were only the first two. "Ah, a long way up, that."

"Rigging is all it is," Ossa said. "You were on that windwhipper to Gebroan, were you not?"

"Below, dredging my guts with every other roll of the ship."

"There's something, my friend: no rolling here, below or above."

Unless he fell.

How could he know if he'd take to heights, having spent his life along flat alleyways? Fall from a canal embankment and you wouldn't die—though you'd get plenty sick if you swallowed the fetid water. Maybe he'd instinctively known something about himself when he passed on a boyhood dare to scale the heights of the Colossus at night.

He sighed. There was only one way to find out.

Ossa hefted his hobbler. "'Snares keep low. If there's one in this jiggo, better we rouse it now and kill it, before it drops on one of us as we start to climb." He made a circuit of the tree, poking, knocking at the bark with the hobbler at arm's length to a height well above his own, finally announcing: "We're safe."

Safe? Falca thought. *Only if we keep our feet on the ground.*

There was no way for Ossa to climb up with the hobbler, so it had to be left, along with the panniers, which had no more food in them, anyway. They decided Falca's stagger might be still be useful, so he loosened his belt and slipped it through at his back. The double-headed blade was uncomfortable, but the risk of it cutting him was minimal, and the least of his worries.

He asked Ossa: "Are you going to be all right? This, ah, rigging goes a long way up."

Ossa flexed his gloved hands. "Well, maybe you should climb third, after Sty and Gurrus." He raised one fist over the other, and brought it down. "That way I won't take you with me."

"How about this instead? Buckle your belt around your chest, under your arms, so you can snag it on the spars and rest if you have to. Better you lose your trews than grip."

FALCA HADN'T GONE far up when he realized he shouldn't have taken the axe. It wasn't hindering the rhythm of his climbing—hand to spar, foot to spar, hand again. Nor was it so much the weight but rather an awareness of a...

presence, not unlike the feeling he'd had when he knew that Havaarl Damarr's phaeton was following him. The farther he climbed the more malevolent it seemed. He knew it wasn't the axe itself, but that didn't douse the feeling.

He told himself he was lucky he had the axe instead of his falcata and scabbard which, at his side and hanging down, would surely have been more of a hindrance.

Still, he wished he had it with him instead.

He thought of calling out to Ossa, and letting him know he had to rid himself of the axe and he'd be back up…sure he would. Ossa wasn't far ahead of him, stepping slowly, resting frequently, using the belt and sometimes the crook of an arm draped over a spar. But going down would mean separation from the others. Styada, if not Gurrus, had to be nearing the top by now, though Falca could see neither as Ossa blocked his sight of them.

He had to stay with them.

They'd be up there, at the top, waiting for him, hands reaching for him.

He hadn't thought of Amala in the darkness of the tunnel, on the steps rising through the cliff, but he did so now, clinging to this tree, feeling the wind he hadn't below, and moving now into sunlight that speared through the canopy to mark a blaze on the bark.

It helped to imagine she'd be up there, too, waiting to pull him over to safety, urging him on, or at least that she was watching him from…somewhere else. That suddenly made him climb a little faster, until he was close enough to Ossa to hear his grunts and loud chuffs of breathing with each spar he grabbed. He stopped to rest frequently.

Sweat pooled in Falca's eyebrows, seeping down. He blinked repeatedly, not daring to release a hand and swipe it away. He looked beyond Ossa to Styada, who was waiting for Gurrus, waiting for them all to catch up, as Amala surely would have been.

Unless she was below.

He hadn't risked glancing down, but he did so now, between his legs. There was nothing below, of course. He cursed himself for his addled thoughts that placed her where there was naught but the straight column of the tree—and green, so much green; dark clouds of it, and not a speck from her eyes, looking up at him.

Fear—not dizziness or queasiness—seized him. He stopped climbing, gripped the spars more tightly, pressed his body so closely to the tree he could have licked the bark. He couldn't dispel the whisper in his mind: *Let go... join her below...that's where she is...*

It would take but moments before the ground hurtled up to meet him, the air roaring in his ears before the sudden, final darkness. There would be no choice at the end; there hadn't for Amala. Who was he to think there would be one for him? With every hour of the day came a choice. His was now.

Choose now, before someone does it for you...

Why wait for the inevitable, when he could discover, within the space of heartbeats, if there was another beginning beyond the end, that place where she had gone?

The more desperately he held on to the spars, the weaker his hands seemed to be getting. He looked up.

They were going on without him.

Perhaps that was best, after all.

He closed his eyes. Something seemed to move over his mind as softly as a breeze through a window. His hands relaxed on the spars, and he thought this was the moment when he would let go.

He did.

But from just one spar, to the one above. He reached out for the next, and another—hand to one, feet to another...

He climbed slowly, not looking down or up to mark his progress. Styada, Gurrus and Ossa had pulled up and pushed off from these same steps, and so would he.

That, too, was a choice.

In time he heard their shouts above him, urging him on. When he finally gained the last spar, three pairs of arms reached out for him, and three pulled him over the edge of the landing, but it was a fourth pair that embraced him.

LATER THAT NIGHT they slept in the lodge of the kobol. It wasn't the largest on the central kastkai, but it still had a supply of firewood and a stone brazier to cook the food they found. They also discovered an urn of rotting leaves, moss, and lichen filled with lunelings, enough of which were still alive to light the chamber that had once served the selects of the kobol: the village council. Gurrus had been surprised that Falca didn't know the klumes—lunelings—were yet something else stolen from the Kelvoi, who for obvious reasons, preferred them over fire for illumination.

When Gurrus woke, the glow from the hanging klumes had dimmed, but it was enough to see a pair of striped rodents scrounging at what little food they'd left on the semi-circle of benches surrounding the brazier.

The others still slept, Ossa uncharacteristically quiet. When Gurrus got up to check his breathing, the rodents scurried away past the shallow, fire-proofed pit under the brazier.

Ossa was still alive.

Falca slept fitfully next to him, below the benches. The last thing Gurrus had seen before he slipped over into sleep was Styada working on a flenx horn with Falca's longshank, and both lay at his side as he, too, slept.

For so many years, whether on a captive's hard ground, or his pallet in the settlement house in Draica, Gurrus had often dreamed of returning to the nights Above: to the soft strains of a kalo; the movement of the village itself in the wind; the creaking of branches and rustlings of leaves; the chittering of onax and kirries in the pens that rimmed the communal areas and braziers of the hovens; the hurried breathing and whispers of coupling lovers young and old; and even the talk in the kobol or chieftain's lodge that had always been more gossip than discussion about problems yet to be resolved...

Gurrus should have slept well; he'd been almost as exhausted by the climb as Ossa. Was it the quiet that woke him up? Or the recurring dream he'd had for so many years about the missing piece he'd never found to a puzzle his father once made for him.

In the dream he relived his fury at the loss, and always in the dream his older brother was the culprit who hid the piece to spite him because he was so very good at puzzles. Most likely Gurrus had lost it, and he came to believe the dream would keep returning until he acknowledged that he alone was to blame. For a time he tried to do that, foolishly thinking that a vow made awake could control the conjurings of his mind while he slept.

Always in the dream his brother took the puzzle piece, never to be found, and always afterwards Gurrus' anger was such that even now he could hear its echoes.

He hadn't had the dream in a long time, but it had returned this night to rupture his sleep and remind him that the Kalalek ketheras—the priests who taught mehka acolytes at the Isle—had given him middling marks for the divining of dreams, how they differed from kesslakors, and how anger can corrupt the clarity of a vision.

Gurrus remained restless. Even if he could have fallen back to sleep, he didn't want to return to the dream he'd just left. He wanted more than dreams.

He sensed an imminent kesslakor—or was that merely a result of his sudden need for answers? He decided to leave while the others slept.

The mistiness outside seemed to confirm his instinct. Fog, which nurtured the trees almost as much as rain, was so necessary for kesslakors, and perhaps when it rolled in more thickly, to conceal the stars twinkling through openings in the canopy, he might find his answers.

He walked over the kastkai, past the trunk of the mother-tree, skirting the opening through which they'd entered the village. The mehka's lodge loomed at the edge of the kastkai, directly across from the chieftain's larger one. Gurrus sat in the doorway, waiting to be enveloped by the fog, yet not wanting to go inside, to be tempted to take whatever else the Skeel mehka had left.

He'd already taken something and wondered if that, too, was part of his restlessness that had grown to a sense of foreboding. He'd found sweethand in the lodge, but no krael to give Ossa. Gurrus had told Falca that if there was none to be found in a mehka's lodge, then there would be none elsewhere, but Falca had continued searching all the village hovens, as if he was somehow responsible for Ossa's sickness. Falca's persistence was interrupted only when they went up to the overgrown bough-garden above one hoven to dig up enough crunchy slove to heat and soften on the brazier. Falca couldn't believe a garden could exist where it did.

They needed to eat; Ossa needed krael to live, and sweethand could prove useful in dulling his pain in the meantime. The thefts could be excused; the village was abandoned after all. Yet they were thefts nonetheless, reminding Gurrus of a much greater one, and the excuse he'd once had for it.

The fog grew thicker, masking the lodges beyond and to either side of the mother- tree, until even the faint klume-lit glow of the kobol's was extinguished. All that was left was the dim outline, on the near side of the mother-tree, of the high pyramid of neatly coiled flessok rope, and the large basket to which the rope was attached at the corners. The villagers once used the basket to haul up what they could not on their backs as they climbed. Ossa had remarked on how beautifully and strongly the baskets were made, so unlike the one Gurrus had seen used at Two-Trunks.

Why would the Skeels have left a village that would have been the envy of other clans, whether Tokanekes, Kleskets or Kaikurras? They hadn't been attacked. What could have caused them to abandon it? There had to be a reason. Did it extend beyond this village, to the Isle itself?

Fog soon enveloped all. He felt its cool presence, like the finest cloth brushed over his skin. A kesslakor might or might not come, but without murkiness there could be no peering into the future or the past if what surrounded one was the present. What the ketheras taught him many years ago had since been confirmed. Would it again? And would it be the last time?

He knew better than to speak aloud: *Where are you? Where have you gone?*

Mehkas were called Patient Ones, and if Gurrus had not always been so patient, he was now for this answer. He waited longer, unmoving, his eyes open so as not to corrupt the vision with the landscape of his mind.

When it came he was so startled he almost rose to his feet, because he did not see the kesslakor as he always had before.

He heard it: a rustling…the beat of wings? Something thudded out there and he felt a momentary shuddering beneath him. Or was that his own? The fog swirled, caressing his face and arms. There came a clicking on the wooden planking of the kastkai. Then all was silent.

He scuttled back deeper into the mehka's lodge, but the doorway was little more than a portal from darkness to darkness. Was it merely a sudden gust of wind that shook the kastkai, rustling the canopy foliage, the clicking a small branch the wind skittered across?

I have come for you. It is time.

Who are you?

You, of all, should know who I am. What I am.

I don't.

So, thefts…and now a lie. You summoned me.

You are mistaken.

You did.

No, what you heard was…I was trying only to summon the answer to why this village was abandoned. Perhaps you bring it.

I know only what you know: that they have left, that the answer can only be found farther along the Road, if at all. Perhaps you confuse your fear about their fate with yours. But I did not hear that, only your summons.

I…I am not ready. I haven't yet chosen Sky or Water. This is not the place.

Thefts, lies and now insults—what kind of mehka are you? Has it been so long that you have forgotten what allows a Summons to be heard, seen and felt? You think I am ignorant of the fact that Place does not matter for one like you, as it does others—such as that young one you saved so he could live on as you. Is there more evidence than that for your summoning me now? I have seen him with you, Below, with those others, who know little of Choosing, whom not even I could carry away. How pitiful you are to think yourself safe with them.

I don't believe you are…there.

You have only to come out for that answer.

Gurrus moved back further, his leg brushing the end of a pallet. His hands trembled.

Why would I Choose now, when I have a task…that only I…

The return of the kinnet?

How can you know of that?

Didn't I just tell you? Give the kinnet to this other one; let him finish what you have begun.

He is too young.

Too young? I think not. Or perhaps you have seen something you fear: failure.

I will not fail. The undertaking is too important.

Your doubts stalk you. You have seen the death of your closest companion, the near-death of another, and the third will surely die before you reach your destination, leaving only two who are not sure why they are on this path of yours.

I will not go with you.

So be it. But you cower where you do not belong. As a mehka you once helped others make their choice, yet you fear to make one yourself. Your father summoned me to take him away. You would have been such lighter meat to carry home.

The wind rose again suddenly. Something hit his face and clattered to the floor of the lodge—a small branch. He picked it up and held it out before him, as if he could parry the talons of the floka if it decided to rip apart the lodge and snatch him. He might as well have tried to flail the fog. He threw the branch away, disgusted with himself for believing a floka had been waiting for him outside. They never came at night. But they never left with empty talons if summoned by a mehka's wordless call.

Gurrus tried yet couldn't bring himself to leave the lodge. He lashed himself for his cowardice. What right had he to say what he did to Styada before, when he couldn't move beyond his fear that the floka still waited for him outside.

He could only hope that the morning, and the lifting of the fog, would reveal that he had summoned something else in the kesslakor. That was enough of a lure, finally, for sleep, and maybe this time in his dreams he would find out where he'd lost the last piece of the puzzle that had remained unfinished for so long.

CHAPTER TWENTY-SIX:

THE ROAD

IN THE MORNING they found Gurrus in the mehka's lodge. He said he'd been restless during the night, had gone out, and when the wind rose he thought it better to find his sleep there.

"Good you did," Falca said, kicking at small branches and swatches of flessok that littered the kastkai. The large basket by the portal opening lay on its side in a tangle of rope from the nearby pile.

Styada suggested—now with almost as many words as gestures—that they should take the rope, dividing it into four lengths which they could knot together should they need it to descend at some point along the Road. He coiled the lengths as he made the cuts. His hands were soon sticky and reddened from the keota resin that the Limbs made from a sap milked from certain trees.

"Roak's legs it stinks," Ossa said.

"Ditchbank at low tide," Falca said.

"Stinks?" Styada said, and shrugged after Gurrus' translation. The language lesson wasn't over yet. After a brief whispering session with Gurrus, Styada announced proudly: "It may…stink…to both you…cobs, "but it…strengthens and preserves the flessok."

Falca grinned. "In that case, we'll get used to the stink, won't we, Ossa?"

They filled their 'skins with rainwater from the chieftain's cistern—each lodge had one—and left the kastkai where the Road continued on. The eastern gateway to the village loomed beyond the last hovens flanking the Road, a cage-like barrier with defensive platforms above it and to either side. Not long after passing through, they came to an intersection where other Roads angled off to the north and south, pathways through a web of cables and rope slung from the trees of the forest. Some of the branches drooped down, grazing the sides of the Roads closely enough to touch.

They were Roads without curves, that neither rose with the land nor dipped down. Falca couldn't see very far into the distance because of the fog. Two birds, with brilliant blue tails, hopped nearby, pecking at the bark surface of a Road. The more cautious of the pair flew off, a wriggling lizard in its beak.

Gurrus told Falca the Kelvoi used the thick bark of young-to-middling trees that had not yet developed deep fissures. Sheavers made one long vertical cut and then peeled back the bark, then cut it into thinner sections equal to the width of a Road. Falca spread his arms and with a lean to either direction could have grasped the rail.

Sheavers soaked and pounded the bark flat in the rainy season, and after the next it was dry and usable. Gurrus said that hoisting the long sections was not difficult since the bark was light, though tough. They had but to lean them to height, and with the help of rope cinched in two holes made at one end, they pulled the sections up, tilting them onto the Road.

Two sets of double-hung flessok cable supported the Roads, with another in the middle. All three extended from tree to tree, secured and knotted around shallow notches or sometimes branches, depending on the tree. Sheavers also knotted vertical ropes between the top and bottom cables to help bear the weight; the upper cable also served as the railing. Rope stitched through small holes near both sides secured the bark paving to the lower cable.

Falca toed one of the holes bored in the resin-soaked bark planking to allow rainwater to drain, and used his longshank to gauge the depth of the hole. When he withdrew the blade his thumb marked less than third of the length.

"You look worried," Ossa said. "At least it's thicker than a paving brick."

"Damn right I'm worried. You can't fall to your death through a paving brick."

The Road was not supposed to sway much because of cross cables bound tautly to more trees along the sides and knotted to the lower cable. To test that, Falca shifted his weight left, then right. To his amazement the Road scarcely moved at all. Nor did it ripple much when he jumped.

"That," he said to Gurrus, "is a lot of work, rope and stink. How in Roak's name do they do it?"

"Any length of rope or cable is the result of many strands of flessok bound together," Gurrus said with a smile.

"Falca, I think he just answered your question," Ossa said.

"Not enough he didn't."

It took Gurrus some time because he kept making asides to Styada, who knew the answers, but was eager for the Arriostan words.

Each hoven was responsible for contributing flessok and keota. The amount for each was set by the kobol of elders, depending on the size of the hoven, and there were sufficient rewards and punishments to ensure the quotas were met. There was no huge central vat to make the resin; each hoven had smaller ones. Everyone gathered flessok—the young, old, males and females. In every hoven there were sheavers, braiders and apprentices to make the rope, and milkers to scar the katoka trees to make them bleed sufficiently to produce the sap for the resin.

Complaints about the quotas? The elder selected by the hoven to represent it in the kobol could take grievances to that council for discussion, just as others could bring theirs about the quality of another hoven's workmanship.

"And they're all gone," Falca said. "We're leaving a village with no one in it and taking a Road with no one on it.

Ossa plucked one of the yellow flowers that dotted the Road. He twirled it clumsily in his gloved fingers, then tucked it away as he looked back toward the village.

"Whenever they left, it wasn't recently."

"Two hundred of them; isn't that what you said, Gurrus?" Falca said.

"Possibly more."

The fog, which had given them pause before the crossroads, showed no signs of lifting, though the sky above the cuts through the forest was brighter with haze.

"No bodies, no signs of a plague or battle," Ossa said.

"No shitcatchers," Styada said.

"Well, whatever the reason they left, we won't find the answer here," Falca said, and turned to Gurrus: "Which way?"

"The way they went?"

Falca had a feeling Gurrus knew he wasn't talking about the Skeels who had left a village that shouldn't have been abandoned. "For us," he said.

"There," Gurrus said, and pointed straight ahead, where the Road to the east disappeared into the fog.

✱

THEIR PACE QUICKENED later that morning as the fog burned off. Blades of sunlight scored the Road ahead through breaks in the canopy, and with each one Falca savored the added warmth. The air, though tinged with the smell of keota, had none of the dankness of Below, and carried more birdsong—another reminder of the gloomy silence and chill they would have had to endure if this Road had been destroyed.

By noon they'd passed eight of the chieftain's marks: a red-stained floka talon always carved into the nearest tree where the Road took a sharper angle.

When they stopped to rest, mainly for Ossa's sake, Gurrus told Falca the marks served more of a purpose than gauging distance. A chieftain's status and prestige was, in part, determined by how well his people maintained the Road that lay within his area of responsibility. The village's own stature was reflected in its chieftain's. Whatever conflicts arose were not usually about which chieftain was doing a poor job, but rather two of them vying for more responsibility, not less.

In Draica, Falca had heard of the Limbs' Roads and knew, as everyone did, that the Wardens were destroying them. He'd given scarcely more thought to that than he would taking a stick to a spider's web in his warehouse home in Slidetown.

Now, he felt an exhilaration being up here, where the air was fresher than any he'd ever breathed. Through breaks in the foliage he could see the jagged white peaks of mountains to the south. He thought he glimpsed an Erseiyr flying between two of them, but it was probably only the shimmering of the day that caused him to think a nearby darting insect was the fabled winged creature in the distance.

Gurrus said that at this pace they might soon be seeing the hills beyond which lay the Isle and the Lake of Shallan.

Surely these Kalaleks would offer krael for Ossa. Why would they not reward a man who'd helped ensure the return of the kinnet? And the sooner there, the sooner Falca could make his way back to Bastia, and see to Maldan Hoster and Lambrey Tallon. If a healthy Ossa wanted to go back with him and add a Myrcian's flourish to their deaths, so much the better.

They went on, scuffing trails through white and purple flowers that grew profusely on the Road where the canopy opened more generously. Flessok blown from trees draped thickly as curtains from the rails, an easy enough reach for Ossa to sop the sweat from his face; he didn't seem to be taking the warmth of the day as well as the others.

Twice they had to clear small branches that had snagged on the Road, or were caught in the railing. In the lead for most of the afternoon, Falca could have stepped over the branches, but with Styada's help, he slid them off the road. He could not hear them land, such was the height of the Road above the ground.

As evening beckoned, they came not to a village but a waystation off the road, similar to one they'd passed earlier in the afternoon, where the blue talon marker changed to another chieftain's: a red triskell of snarling forras.

The small kastkai was crammed with coils of flessok cable; pots of resin and sap; a cistern of water with a woven screen to keep out animals, birds and debris; and stacks of little wooden boxes sealed with sap, that Gurrus said were provisions for those working on the Road.

Dozens of bark sections leaned against the kastkai, two to a side. There was a brazier, with the usual fire-proof pan underneath, but no one felt like cooking on it. They opened a few of the boxes and took their meal under the bark roofing that edged the kastkai, sitting with their backs against rolled-up cushions of flessok.

Falca was so hungry he ate three of the smoked lizards, and even added a couple of ticklers he caught. He also had four pieces of barkbread. Neither bark nor bread, it was made from pressed mushrooms the Kelvoi cultivated in canopy gardens—and something else Gurrus said he'd best not mention. The nuts were sweet enough, but Ossa cracked a tooth on one of the shells. He spit the mouthful into his hand and, with a weary shaking of his head, tossed it—broken tooth and all—over his shoulder.

Falca picked a piece lizard skin from his teeth. "Unless the next village is like the first, we should have met someone along the Road today." He eyed Gurrus, who'd eaten little. That wasn't like him.

"It is not the next village I am worrying about."

"Ah, don't borrow trouble, my friend," Ossa said, sucking at the broken tooth. "Didn't we make good progress today? None of that all-fours mizzling down Below. We've food and water and no worries about being eaten. Not up here, not tonight."

Falca gave Ossa a look to acknowledge the valiant effort. For a while Gurrus picked at some barkbread, sipped his water, but said no more.

While there was still enough light, Styada and Falca corded flessok to tighten and bind up all their chasers.

Falca had an idea what Gurrus was worrying about. If the Kelvoi were gone from these parts, what of the Isle and the kinnet's return and that vision he'd had?

Well, there was naught to be done now except thank the Fates for the sweeter air up here, far above kuss and eels, close enough to Suaila and Cassena, so it seemed, to put hands out and cup the moons.

Cobbling leather wouldn't solve the mystery of why they were alone on the Road, but boots worth the walking would help them get closer to an answer at the Lake of Shallan—if that's where it was.

BRUISED CLOUDS BEGAN piling up to the north by late the following morning; by noon they knew a storm would overtake them. The brightness of the day retreated as the dark clouds advanced, and soon all that was left was a deepening gray and a clear scrim of blue sky to the south.

Birds ceased calling, their songs replaced by rustling of leaves and needles in the surrounding canopy. The wind hadn't arisen enough yet to fully seize the Road, but Falca could feel a trembling beneath him. Lightning flashed, ripping celestial cloth, lifting distant darkness for an instant—a spectacle he'd seldom seen in Draica.

Thunder was an equal rarity there, and so this banging on immense, heavenly shields should have made Falca wish for the solidity of Below. There was no place to hide or flee, no escape at this height should lightning ignite the Road, the wind skew or sever it. Yet he reveled in the storm.

Rain began to fall; gently at first, then torrentially—as if some dam above had been suddenly breached. And with that the gusts grew in strength. Falca leaned ahead, rain pelting his face, gripping a rail with one hand as the others were doing ahead of him. Using two would present more of him, like a sail, to the northern wind.

The Road lurched from side to side, but the restraining cables to either side prevented a greater swaying that could have slid them off. Debris blew off the Road, replaced by more torn away from the heaving canopy. Balls and skeins of flessok flew by Falca, some hitting him. He kept a hand near his face to ward off something harder.

Wind keened through the railings and myriad cables, playing the Road like a monumental instrument. There came a cracking close by, louder than lightning: a huge branch fell over both railings. The Road shuddered. Falca tensed, expecting it to give way and send them all plummeting to their deaths.

The Road held.

He ducked under the branch, lending a hand to Ossa. Falca could scarcely hear him: "They built well—shipwrights they were."

The coil of rope Falca still carried across his shoulder soon became heavy, sodden as his clothes, and he was tempted to leave it. But should the road weaken, without quickly sending them down to their deaths, the rope could save them.

Rainwater streamed along the Road's coarse bark hide, pouring through the holes, sheeting off the sides in a continuous waterfall. Without those holes that helped funnel off the water's weight the Road might have collapsed in such a storm as this. Yet it still sagged in places, and though their inclination was to stay close together should one of them need help, they dared not bunch up for fear of burdening the Road too greatly at any one point.

Ossa was closest to Falca, then Gurrus, but at times Styada, ahead of them all, would disappear from sight where the Road another turn. Usually he would wait for them between the trees supporting the end of one section and the beginning of another, and then move on. This time he wasn't waiting. Falca wiped away the rain from his face, peering through the downpour and branches whipping back and forth over the rails.

Styada was nowhere in sight.

We can't have lost him, he thought.

Had he slipped or fallen off, been caught by a sudden gust, taken to his death, his scream masked by the skirling wind?

Then Falca saw him, coming back toward them around another turn ahead, gesturing vigorously, shouting something Falca couldn't have understood even if he could hear it. Gurrus could. He turned, shouting the good news. Falca quickly relayed it to Ossa.

Styada had found another village.

IT WAS ABANDONED, a derelict even larger than the first, given the size of the kastkai and the greater number of causeways leading to hovens almost obscured by rain and the heaving mass of the canopy. The confines of the kastkai trapped swirling debris, so it was hard for them to tell if the village had been abandoned before or after the other: a second mystery now. But all they cared about now was getting out of the storm.

They hurried into the nearest lodge off the Road. Falca, stooping in low after Ossa, latched the door, sloughed off the rope where the others had left theirs. His chasers squelched with water.

The size of the brazier indicated this was the chieftain's lodge. There was plenty of firewood stacked on either side of the doorway. Falca shaved some of the wood for kindling, got the fire going. He roused it more than he should have, but they needed a big one to dry out their boots and the drenched outer clothing they hung over a bench near the brazier.

Ossa held his hands close to the fire, rubbing them where the skin was less blackened. He took out his pipe, packing it with more difficulty than he'd had before. His hand shook as he lit it, and Falca wondered again if the sot somehow helped dull the effects of the 'snare poisoning. Ossa rarely complained but that pain had to be getting worse.

They heated some of the food they'd taken with them from the waystation and ate in silence. Soon the lodge was filled with the scent of sot and the steaming stink of their leathers and clothes. Gurrus alone had not shed any to dry, and as he leaned back to rest on one of the pallets near the fire, Falca could see the reddish edge of the kinnet. It wasn't the color he'd last seen; then he remembered how the kinnet took on the hues of the immediate surroundings—in this case the flames of the brazier.

His hands warmed now, Falca took out his whetstone and began sharpening the stagger axe and longshank. "You must have some Myrcian blood in you," Ossa said. "You fondle the whetstone as lovingly as the Sanctor does his sceptre."

"What's one to do with the other?" Falca said.

"Nothing except the Sanctor's whetstone sceptre has the spurrose at the top."

"Oh, I see. His is the one that's supposed to keep *all* of Myrcia's blades sharp."

"That's the idea, though I doubt the wankspit has ever used the thing himself."

Styada had the other longshank and was busily working on the second flenx horn; he'd already finished its hole and notches, as he had the tightly braided flessok cord he'd proudly shown Falca the day before.

There were many things Falca wished Amala might have seen since the falls, and Styada was among them: keeping his promise, sounding this word or that, and asking what each meant. They'd all come far, yet in some ways Styada had come the farthest. Frikko may have been right about him before, but she would have been proud of him now.

It was going to be a long night, filled with the sound of slapping, knocking branches; the drumming of the rain; the grating and keening of cables as the wind sang through them. Everything moved—the floor, the stitched bark and planking of roof and walls. Still, the lodge leaked less than his home in Draica did in weather much less worse than this—and he said as much to Ossa.

"Tight as the cabin of my ship," Ossa replied.

"What was its name?" Falca asked.

"*Flury*."

"Your daughter's name."

"Yes. I named the one after the other, over the objections of my wife. Bad luck, she thought. But Roh' liked the name of my ship so much she wanted it for our daughter's name should we ever have one."

"Roh'?"

Ossa blew out a sideways puff of blue smoke. "Rohaise. My other wife."

Outside, the storm continued unabated as he began his tale.

Chapter Twenty-Seven:

TRICE AND THEFT

HIS NAME WAS Mott Demoul, not Ossa Vere, and it wasn't as if he didn't have choices back then.

When Yonoss Belerra came discreetly to his father, Mott was offered the pick of one of his two daughters. The first opportunity to see for himself which he preferred came at a fête the Belerra family was hosting at their manse in Allgate, part of the annual Erseiyr Week festivities marking the Myrcian victory over the Skarrian hordes of Gortahork many years before.

He chose Vasia, the taller, prettier of the two. She was too skinny for his tastes and awkward in conversation, but she danced proficiently enough, albeit in the manner of one who had mastered the steps without the music.

So the match was made between the two most prominent seafaring families in Castlecliff. The Demouls were wealthier; the Belerras closely connected to the Sanctor's Fallskeep retinue. The marriage promised to be mutually fruitful.

Mott knew after the consummation—if not before—that he wouldn't be unfurling every scrap of sail to hurry back to his new bride in Castlecliff. His father reminded him privately that he would have to leave "the other one", telling him that the family could afford whatever it would take to purchase a discreet exit. "No one expects the master of a full-press windwhipper to give up his port swallows, not even these pinch-lipped Belerras, but marriage is another matter. There is much at stake here."

Kevret Demoul had been outraged at his son's first marriage two years earlier in Milatum. He was in poor health. Soon enough Mott would be lord of the family's merchant empire. To have his eldest son take a wife—the daughter of a trading-house factor—in distant Keshkevar, was to him folly that bordered on madness. She had contributed nothing to the family coffers so far, and there was no profit in the weeks he spent with her when in Milatum, while both ship and crew idled.

The fact of the marriage was an embarrassment, and Kevret Demoul ordered it to be kept a secret, the woman's name never mentioned. He forbade Mott's brothers from sailing to Milatum to see who he'd married, as if she carried a plague that might infect them, too.

If they had visited, they would have seen their brother 'sittin' high' as Myrcian sailors said about fair winds and a following sea. He was very happy with auburn-haired, gray-eyed Rohaise Loquin, who had a laugh of noon bells even on the few dreary days that marred the envied seasons of southern Keshkevar. She kept a bountiful garden behind the modest dwelling in which she'd grown up, now hers to share with her tall Myrcian husband. It had a veranda that opened out to a view overlooking the harbor of Milatum and two of its fabled bridges that had been there before the arrival of Colza and the first Arriostan settlers.

She was no daughter of a trading house factor, but Mott had to tell his father something he might understand. Better his disgust than the truth, which might have fatally stricken him. Mott had met her on the bridge for which she had inherited from her late father the municipal contract to maintain the extensive gardens that graced both its ends. Given the gardens' terraces, it could be dangerous as well, but Rohaise was nimble and fearless.

She had a way of sweetening feral oikoi and stray dogs, keeping several of varying breeds. Mott counted himself lucky to be among them. It made him feel better that she would at least have the companionship of pets during his absences.

He did not have to marry her but he did.

He might have obeyed his father and paid her off. She would have found that amusing, surely handed the money back to him, telling him with a smile to spend it on port swallows.

If Mott disobeyed his father, he also did not tell Rohaise that he was already married.

Within a year, the Fates at their Loom Eternal finally took notice of him: Vasia became pregnant; Rohaise remained barren. The Fates weren't satisfied with that, for the child he named after his ship grew tall as her parents, yet had the dark complexion and luxurious hair of Rohaise, with all of her confidence, mischievousness and none of Vasia's physical awkwardness. At five years of age, the girl was climbing the rigging of her namesake.

The Fates certainly were enjoying the halving of his heart, but they weren't done with him yet. When Flury was six, the ship she'd always thought of as hers foundered in a storm off the coast of Gebroan.

It was Mott's own fault, for keeping on when he should have heeded the glass and looming weather, and made for the sheltering lee of an island off the Flaggy Shore. But he was known for pressing on, to either his beloved daughter in Castlecliff or his heartsake in Milatum.

He survived along with a few others, saved by wreckers, only to be swept up in a bloody war between the king of Gebroan and an alliance of princes from Thetis and Trigel. Imprisoned for two years, he was later forced into royal service for a long, disastrous campaign against Tarranga Ullmark, an Iron Lord of the Crumples mountains, captured and sent to work in one of Ullmark's mines. He escaped and managed to get back to Sandsend on the coast. Their amusement over, the Fates now left it to him to decide: where to return first—Castlecliff or Milatum—after you've been presumed dead for seven years?

Vasia and Flury were not at the docks to greet him when he got back to Castlecliff: the first hint that the Fates were *still* not done punishing him for his duplicity. Vasia had taken ill and died around the same time the gale broke apart her husband's ship.

And Flury?

Mott found out that one of his wife's sisters—the closest, if reluctant replacement for the mother—had assumed responsibility for Flury. But the girl, difficult when her father wasn't present, became much more so with both of her parents gone, beyond the control of even those the family hired to bear the brunt of her care in the household.

His mother, Beska, was in poor health, but offered to care for her when she heard of the problems with Flury. It was too late. The girl had been sent away by the sister's husband, Caxo, and he refused to say where, not even to Mott upon his return to Castlecliff. But Caxo did tell him that much else was discovered in the course of trying to learn his fate after the shipwreck. "You're no more fit to be the girl's father than you were a husband for Vasia," he said.

They were in the portico of Caxo's manse in Allgate, close by the falls marking the end of the River Roan that flowed underneath the city. His wife and chamberlain were present, but Mott only heard the one, then the other nervously suggest the matter might be pursued another day. He asked Caxo again where he'd sent Flury, and still Caxo refused to divulge the location, even when Mott flicked his dagger up to the man's throat.

Somehow he stoppered his rage. There had to be another reason why Caxo refused to talk with a blade at this neck, and there were other ways to find out what the frog-eyed patroon had done with Flury.

He turned to leave, saw the wife's hand fly to her mouth—which saved his life. He whirled in time to parry her husband's attack, and this time Mott did what he wanted to do moments before.

Even if the witnesses hadn't altered their story to give Caxo more honor in death than he'd ever had in life, Mott's fate was sealed. He'd killed a prominent member of a family close to the Sanctor, and his own could do little more than keep him from the gallows. The price for that reprieve—and later bribes—crippled the fortunes of the Demouls.

The Gardacs imprisoned him in Browall Keep where he was given the Sanctor's mercy of the Spurrose Trice, reserved for those who would otherwise have been scolded until their eyes popped out, then hung and displayed for all to see along Stellate's Way. His cheeks and forehead were branded with the royal Myrcian spurrose, and should he survive the requisite three years imprisonment, he would be released. Yet few given the Sanctor's mercy lasted for long outside. Mobs killed most of those marked with the Trice within hours after they hurried out of the gate of Browall Keep.

Two of Mott's brothers, however, managed sufficient bribes to free him a month after he'd been brought in. At night and with an escort of a dozen handpicked sailors, they took him away to the safety of a ship moored at the quays of Heap o' Heads. The next day he had a choice of disfigurements: keeping the brand of the Trice to the end of his days, or searing it off with acid.

There was no possibility of staying anywhere in Myrcia, or resuming captaincy of a windwhipper. And so came his last choice: north or south. But south was scarcely more of a choice than remaining in Castlecliff. He couldn't go back to Milatum and Rohaise. Though she might forgive him, the edge to their love would never be as keen, with the evidence forever there to remind her of what he'd never told her. Shoals would always be lurking for the rest of their lives; better she believed he died when his ship foundered on the others.

He sailed to Lucidor and Draica, where you could shit on the street, call it the Sanctor's supper, and have a coin tossed your way. A man so fallen, so disfigured as he could be tempted by bloodsnare dens, scrape and rife, so Mott decided he might as well make money at one of them.

To mark the end of one life and the beginning of another, he took the name of a mizzen swale who had died in the wreck of the *Flury*. No longer was he Mott Demoul. He was now Ossa Vere, and he decided to become a bloodsnare hunter in the Rough Bounds. Within a few years he began making a lot of money, most of which he spent on trying to find out what had happened to his daughter.

And he did.

Caxo hadn't told him where he'd sent her because his reputation would have been ruined if he had. The Cassenites were an outlawed cult in Myrcia, much like the Magians, and evidently Caxo had been a secret adherent.

Flury Demoul had been thirteen when she was given to the cult's leader, the Vasper. She had escaped; Mott discovered that much. He never was able to find out where she had gone, or if she was still alive. Now, it was too late…

Long before Ossa finished, Falca had put away the whetstone, and Gurrus had risen to an elbow to listen more closely. Gurrus was now speaking quietly to Styada, relaying the tale to him in Tongue, since he was clearly curious about what the somber graylock was saying.

Ossa knocked the plug from his pipe, a sharp rapping against the top of the stone brazier. He swept the plug into the ebbing fire. Falca reached over to the pile of wood and added more. "We'll search in the morning, storm or not."

They knew he meant the krael. Ossa put a hand on Falca's shoulder. He could feel the shaking. "We'll probably find none; here or at another village ahead," Ossa said. "Wherever the Limbs have gone, it's the last thing they'd leave behind. It's all right. I've done what I could…what I had to do."

"There will be krael at the Isle," Gurrus said. "I promise you that, Ossa."

"That place could be abandoned, too."

"That has…crossed my mind. But it does not matter if this plague of empty villages has infected the Isle and emptied the Road. And if not, neither does it matter if the ketheras there refuse to offer any krael to a man who has done so much to help an undeserving old mehka return."

"What are you talking about?" Falca said.

"I mean it does not matter," Gurrus said. "I know where and how to get krael without them. But Ossa should know first about the Tapestry and its kinnets."

Much of what he went on to say, with asides to Styada in Tongue, Falca had heard before in that room overlooking Sciamachon's Fountain—except for the mention of krael.

The exalted status and power of the Kalaleks, and their arrogance, was based on more than possession of the Tapestry, that single-most important Kelvoi artifact. For krael was found only at the Lake of Shallan the Isle, and the Kalaleks guarded its secrets as carefully as they did its disbursement to the clans' mehkas, whose status was in turn greatly dependent on the krael. The kethera priests demanded much in exchange from the clans, including consignments of females for their pleasure.

"Scarce better than Cassenites," Ossa muttered.

"They favor the most…accommodating clans," Gurrus continued. "Most acceded to the quotas, my father among them. I once did; later I did not, and there were times when I had to beg mehkas from other clans—and not always successfully—for what my people needed. And now I think Ossa should see a part of what I have been talking about."

He took off his shirt.

"That's *it*, around your middle? *That?*"

"Yes."

"I know, Ossa; I thought it a stable blanket when I first saw it." Falca said. "Or sackcloth. It almost cannot be seen against your skin."

"Just so," Gurrus said. "The kinnet take on the hue of whatever is closest to it. Watch." Gurrus took off the kinnet and held it close to the fire. Ossa's eyebrows raised at the sight of the kinnet's sudden brightening.

Gurrus draped it over the brazier. The flames licked around the edges, but did no more. He pulled it off and handed it to Ossa.

"Well, I'll be caulked; not even warm."

"Nor can it be cut or pierced," Falca said. "Gurrus, he may as well see this, too."

The mehka took the kinnet from Ossa, stretched it out tightly between his hands. Falca stabbed at it once with the longshank, then slashed. As before, it felt as if the dagger was grazing along metal. Styada stroked the kinnet, gingerly, as if it might yet burn his hand.

"There's no scratch," Ossa whispered. "Roak's throat, what *is* that made of?"

"That is one thing no one knows," Gurrus said, "not even the Kalaleks I think. Nor how the Tapestry depictions were etched or woven into the fabric, just that they are revealed only when the Tapestry is wet."

"How did you get it?" Ossa asked.

Gurrus said nothing as he wrapped the kinnet around his belly again, folding it to secure it. Then: "I…It has to be returned."

Ossa's eyes asked Falca the question: *Do you know?*

He did, or at least he had always had the suspicion. He thought it likely Gurrus had told Amala. But she'd never revealed anything to him, and she would have—unless she'd promised Gurrus otherwise. He never asked her, not wanting to put her on the spot. It didn't matter. That Gurrus might have stolen it made no difference to him, of all people. But the theft—if that's what it was—clearly troubled the mehka, and undoubtedly for a long time.

Now, it was up to Gurrus to tell Ossa, if ever he would. Gurrus was saying something to Styada, and Falca thought the moment had passed

"I still don't understand what this Tapestry has to do with krael," Ossa said, "besides the fact that both are to be found at the Isle."

"Neither did I," Gurrus said, "until long after I stole the kinnet."

HE'D BEEN IN the last days of his apprenticeship at the Isle, awaiting only his father's arrival to accompany him home. Ghatruk, an esteemed Tokaneke mehka of Boughbreaks, had high expectations for his son. Gurrus was confident he had exceeded them—except for the one mediocre mark in discerning the difference between kesslakors and dreams. Of the original forty apprentices, only half remained, so demanding was the instruction.

The senior kethera tutor who had given him the highest honors—for aptitude—was also the one Gurrus despised.

His name was Kakedu, and little did he know that Gurrus had shown aptitude of another sort in a dalliance with one of the seven 'krael' females allotted every year to Kakedu. Liaisons of any sort and duration were forbidden to acolytes and should Gurrus' have been discovered, he would have been summarily sent home in disgrace. While the affair lasted, Gurrus considered it his greatest achievement at the Isle, marred only by his lover's complaints about the ill-treatment she suffered from Kakedu.

Gurrus was furious when Kakedu sent Keela away, having had his fill of her. He never stopped to think that she might have been more relieved at the end to her abuse than sad about never seeing Gurrus again. He was possibly more enamored of her after her departure because she'd obviously left with their secret intact. He nursed the complaints she'd voiced about Kakedu's treatment of her and, it was rumored, his other females as well.

That Gurrus would even consider retaliating against Kakedu was a result not only of qualities that gave him such promise as a mehka. As often happens with the young, he felt himself far wiser than he was, if only because the weight of years had yet to humble him with consequences of his actions. His reckless but successful interlude with Keela had dulled his sense of what those might be.

Kakedu had gained his high status for two reasons: he was in charge of the offerings to the legendary syllysk—though Gurrus had never seen the tribute or the kraken that supposedly inhabited the Lake of Shallan—and he was also responsible for supervising the Hall of Revelation where the Tapestry was kept.

Gurrus decided to embarrass him by stealing one of the kinnets comprising the Keta, two nights before the ceremony to mark the successful acolytes' ascension to the brotherhood of Kelvoi mehkas. It was the high point of the year, the only time the ketheras allowed anyone to view this most sacred of Kalalek relics. Supposedly the Tapestry hung from a wall opposite the pool where the priests took their ablutions.

He felt confident that if caught entering the Hall he'd think of some explanation to satisfy a kethera. Hadn't he gotten honors in rhetoric? After all, mehkas were supposed to dispense convincing explanations, cogent argument and believable stories.

Making preparations with his usual thoroughness, he gained access to the Hall without being seen—a bold move during the waning hours of a rainy day, but he had no choice: the Hall was bolted shut from within at night. Or at least that was Gurrus' assumption since he first tried the door at night, and otherwise had observed no kethera locking the door from the outside. Presumably, there was a passageway from the Hall itself to the ketheras' domiciles.

Ketheras came and went as he hid, submerged in the dark water of the shallow pool, breathing through hollow reeds, rehearsing in his mind every step he'd take—from pool to Tapestry to door.

Only when night had fallen, and the last of the priests had shuttered the windows, did he emerge. In the dark he randomly picked one of the kinnets, easily detaching it from a bone clip, rolled it up, and hid it under his upper vestment. He unbolted the door and walked away, buoyant and smug that his plan had worked so well.

Later, he told himself that what he had done served a greater purpose: if he could steal a kinnet so easily others could as well, and there would be changes made. But Kakedu wouldn't be around to make them.

Gurrus intended to keep the kinnet only long enough to embarrass him. Then he would leave it by the Hall's door before the ceremony and his subsequent departure with his father who, as it turned out, had arrived early.

He knew there would be an uproar, but he was stunned by its virulence. Ketheras searched everywhere, interrogated everyone though his own questioning was perfunctory: no one suspected the most highly praised and successful of all the acolytes. Armed priests and their auxiliaries from the village across the lake hurried in pursuit of recently departed pilgrims from one of the Fens clans.

Kakedu was not merely reprimanded and stripped of his rank as a senior kethera. He was blinded, his fingers and tongue cut in half. If this was Kakedu's fate, Gurrus' would be death.

He could not bring himself to confess.

There was no ceremony of the Keta.

Frightened, yet clever as always, Gurrus had hid the kinnet among the formal clothing his father meant to wear at the ceremony. Gurrus was correct in believing that no one would think to search the belongings of one who had not been at the Isle when the theft occurred. The first night after he and his father left, Gurrus took the kinnet back while his father slept, hid it under his clothing, around his waist. The next night—again as his father slept—he fashioned a clip to secure it better.

He kept it hidden well in the years that followed in Boughbreaks then Two-Trunks. He never told his father. He became an exemplary mehka, but as the Wardens began encroaching farther into Kelvarra, and the clans became increasingly fractious and weakened, Gurrus came to believe there was a connection between this and his theft of the kinnet. Who else but he was responsible for the bloody reprisals between the clans of the Fens, their allies, and the Kalaleks who blamed them for the theft? The Tapestry was not whole; neither were the Kelvoi.

Ghatruk waned. Gurrus went to Boughbreaks to be with him at his Choosing. Though he loved his father and would miss him, part of Gurrus was relieved his father would never know his son had taken the kinnet.

So he thought.

Ghatruk chose Sky, and would accept nothing to dull the terrible pain of the floka's claws. When Gurrus asked him why, his father replied that he did not deserve the customary Death's-ease.

"I know you took the kinnet," Ghatruk said. "I should have confronted you long ago, and brought you back with it, and turned away from the death you deserved, but I could not bear to do that. I thought that if I sent you to Two-Trunks, your absence here might help me forget about what you had done. It didn't. I made a choice to live with the rot of shame, and now you must make one: if you wish to be stronger than I, you must return the kinnet."

He promised his father he would. He had the kinnet with him at Boughbreaks. He had krael to take with him, so that if something befell him on the way to the Isle, he would not die until he had returned the kinnet. But he did not expect to return.

Before he could leave the Wardens attacked Boughbreaks and captured him. His brother was killed. For months, until he wound up in Draica, he managed to keep the krael hidden—in body crevices, in his mouth as a swollen sore, or under the bandage of a wound that didn't exist. The kinnet was found only once, used as a rag by a Warden to wipe himself, and tossed back to Gurrus.

It was only until much later, at the settlement house, that Gurrus understood why the Kalaleks had punished Kakedu so severely, and burned the villages of those they thought had taken the kinnet.

One day, when no one else was using the communal tub, he wet the kinnet, almost by accident. That single time was enough to know that the kinnet he'd stolen was the one that depicted the source and the making of krael, even if he did not know what the words on its borders meant, and never would.

The Kelvoi had no written language.

Chapter Twenty-Eight:

TRANCH

SHAR STAKEEN HAD stayed by the gateway to the village to give them time to pick their shelter before she did the same. It seemed likely this one, too, was abandoned though the empty gateway—the Limbs' crude version of a watchtower—was no indication of that. Who would be guarding the village in this downpour?

She gave it a while, hearing nothing except the wind, the snapping of ropes, the knocking and creaking of branches, then went ahead. They would be in a hurry to get out of the weather, no doubt taking one of the lodges off the central platform surrounding a tree trunk of monumental girth. This was no roadside inn to make their acquaintance—unless she meant to play her hand now, and that made no sense. What would they take her for, on a night such as this? No, she would recognize the moment when it came.

She found shelter in one of the communal houses at the end of a narrow planked causeway leading off the platform area that was about the same size as the Heart Hill green near where she'd killed Damarr's hirelings.

These dwellings ringed a common, covered area that had a large brazier of stones. But there would be no fire for her; that would be one too many in this abandoned village.

The smoke from Falca Breks' told her soon enough where he was: not far away at all, below the level of this grouping of dwellings. She could see where the smoke—quickly seized and dissipated by the gusting wind—emerged from the top of the lodge. Perhaps it was her imagination, but she thought she could smell the Banishman's sot. Was that his voice she heard or Breks'?

Stakeen was sure they weren't aware they'd been followed. She meant to keep it that way. She had been trained to wake when she wanted to, as the need required. So she would be up before they were, whether the storm blew itself out by dawn or not. And should they search the village for food before moving on, there were plenty of places for her to hide.

She gathered drifts of the long, bearded moss that had blown off the trees and shaped a nest, much as she'd done to keep alive one winter's day long ago, when she'd burrowed deeply within a snow-mounded hayrick in a crofter's field.

The rain drummed ceaselessly, but it couldn't reach her where she lay deep within her refuge. Again, she thought she heard them talking below. The faint conversation reminded her of voices from the past: those of the dreacons hunting her after she escaped from the Cassenite fhold.

Following Breks and the others had been one of the most difficult things she'd ever done. She was drenched, hungry; her clothing and boots near ruin. But she'd endured worse than this, well before the trials of her shadden apprenticeship. And she'd known, long before she had to memorize a shadden's Hundred Recitations, that nothing was ever wasted; a use could be found for anything, including a storm, if you had the strength of mind to recognize such. Hadn't she used the onset of that winter's storm many years ago, to either end her life or save it? At the time she didn't care which, as long as she never saw the Vasper and his dreacons ever again…

She'd taken what food she could, two stolen shawls, and a pair of mittens. She clung to the underside of a provisioner's cart to slip past the dreacon guards huddled by a fire at the gate, cursing the unseasonably cold weather. The provisioner, too, was attentive only to his misery and in a hurry to get home before nightfall when the storm was expected to worsen.

She let go before he got to the nearest village, hoping that the thickly falling snow would mask the path she took through the forest north of the fhold. And maybe it did. But soon—too soon—she saw torches behind her and, more distantly, the flickering of still more to the east. She tried not to panic. The dreacons would not have dogs; the Vasper allowed none in the fhold: they gave him hives and impaired his breathing. Still, she had to do something quickly besides frantically keeping on. Sound carried too well in quiet of the night. The nearer dreacons might hear her huffing or the snapping of a branch hidden underneath the snow.

Given the cold and snow, the copperleaf tree wasn't as easy to climb as the spars and rigging of her father's ship, but she did it. By the time the dreacons paused nearby, the tell-tale clumps of snow she dislodged had a fresh layer on them.

They were so close she feared they could hear her shivering. They stuck their torches in the snow then warmed their hands in the fur of their winter chastelets.

"She will not last in this. We will find her frozen, brother."

"Then that is how we will return her."

"What good would that…"

"Quiet! You forget who you are with. It is not your place to interpret the Vasper's wishes. If he commands her return, so it will be."

"Not if flenx or snagwolves find her first."

"Then we bring her back in shreds and bones for the Vasper to bless and commit to the Lady's Reliquary—or give them to pigs should the auguring displease him."

She survived that night and the next day but would not have the third if the crofter's dogs had not found her in that one hayrick left in the field. The old man was hard of hearing; his wife couldn't keep her gnarled, bony hands off her, as if the fingers were impoverished roots starved for better soil.

Yet the couple seemed kind enough—or so she thought until the second night when she realized they were only treating her well because that was the best way to keep a stray who could easily flee. They thought she was asleep; she heard them talking in what they assumed were low voices that rose with an argument. The wife believed that the Cassenites would provide a better reward than slavers in Virenz for such sweet cream that had yet to sour.

The husband won the argument.

She played along with his lie about taking her to his younger sister who always wanted a child and had better means to care for one.

She said she was grateful.

She said she would never forget the kindness he and his wife had shown.

She had told much better stories in playing off her mother against her father when it suited her.

On the Virenz road made muddy by a warm spell, she watched how the old man worked the cart and horse—and also how he had to stop often to relieve himself. The last time he did so, she waited until he had his worm in his hands, snapped the reins and took off, leaving him cursing, unable to go after her because he wasn't finished yet.

By the time she got to Draica a week later in a chilly rain that passed for winter on the coast, the food the crofter had brought was long gone, the horse and cart bartered for more.

She stole what she could in the safer, affluent neighborhoods, remembering her father telling her of a place on a hillside in Milatum where he always stayed, that had gardens overlooking the harbor—as did these fashionable, hilly districts called Falconwrist, Beckon and Heart Hill.

Becoming bolder and more adept at stealing, she'd wander down to the quays of Catchall and Ditchbank, thinking about how long it would take her to have enough money, if ever, for passage to Milatum, that place her father talked about with such longing in his heart that she knew it had to be beautiful. She'd been very young, but she remembered.

She knew that sooner or later her luck in reiving would end, and while she might find work as a laundress or servant, the pay beyond room and board—if she was lucky—would be a pittance. She'd never get to Milatum.

She had one thing to offer, as she had before. The only difference was that it would be her choice—such as it was.

Falconwrist spread out over a ridge above the canals and squalor of Catchall and Slidetown, but below the higher elevations of Beckon and Heart Hill. She'd seen a manse with a single red turret that faced the royal citadel of Cross Keys Island, and it took only a night watching the phaetons and lesser carriages coming and going for her to know its business. At least from the top rooms there would be a view of the harbor and ships passing the Colossus of Roak, a daily reminder of why she had made her choice.

Within another week she stolen enough—from idling, carelessly attended phaetons and the maze of markets around Erisa's Campanile—to pawn for coin. She begged for more along the concourses of Rhysselia's Garden where the better moods of people made for a better haul. She bought nicer clothes, meadowbride perfume, and a brush for her long, dark hair. One rainy night she bathed in Sciamachon's Fountain before she presented herself at the manse of the red turret.

And it was done.

For the next four years she worked herself up in the trade and by the fifth she was touted as no mere swallow but a courtesan who entertained in the Red Turret, the youngest ever to have that honor. Some said she must have been trained in a hetera's school in Gebroan. She was highly profitable to the spurs—a brother and sister—who ran the house. After six years she'd gained enough status to choose whom she would accommodate. It was time to go.

The spurs would not let her.

But among her clientele were influential and powerful men, two of whom were sympathetic to her desires, perhaps because they were hopeful of some measure of exclusivity. With their assistance she bought her freedom from the spurs.

She set herself up in Beckon with fewer though more generous clients, and soon recouped the cost of her independence. With another year of this—and no spurs' cut to smidge her profit—she would have what she needed to go to Milatum and exchange one business for another: buying a windwhipper and paying men instead to spread the sails and fill the hold with cargo.

One night changed all.

A new client, younger than her usual sticklers, came to her with a recommendation from Lesto Talade. A prominent Tidesback merchant, Talade had helped her buy her escape from the Red Turret. She trusted him as much as she could anyone.

This new stickler—Surket Marr—posted a guard on the second floor landing. When he informed her of his tastes, she insisted on a fee considerably more than what she usually required.

It was an autumn night and, for once, not drizzling. Three lunelings lit her bedchamber. It wasn't until much later that she understood how the intruder could have gained access to her second story rooms through the locked outer door, and gotten so close without a sound.

Marr was an energetic enough rider but without finesse. At first, when he stiffened, grunted and his eyes popped wide, she thought he'd loosed his muck—every man was different in the throes. He dropped his head to her breasts—and she saw the man behind him, one knee on the end of the bed.

Her hand went to the protruding hilt of the large sliverheart she kept between the mattresses near the headboard. The intruder struck again. She knew she had but moments to live.

The killer bent over to grab Marr by the scruff of his hair and haul him off her with his left hand. Marr's cudgie bounced stiffly as he tumbled off the bed. She sprang to her knees, slashing with the sliverheart, deeply slicing the side of the intruder's neck, then back again. She pushed hard off the bed, leaped past him before he could bring his right hand and dagger around. He staggered, tripped over Marr. She plunged the sliverheart into his heart—and again, to make sure he was dead.

It was her final and most profitable night. The assailant and Marr's dead guard yielded little money, but Marr had more than enough to pay for the extra attention he requested. Then there were the rings that had made his clumsy caresses so annoying. He also had a very expensive sword: hilt of gold braid, jeweled pommel. Beautifully detailed marshfang etchings from crossguard to tip may not have added utility to the blade but certainly hinted at royal stature for Surket Marr.

She dragged the three bodies down to the street, cleaned the blood as best she could, and later took a draught that would let her sleep. The next morning the bodies had been stripped of their clothes; by noon the Red Feathers had taken away the corpses; by mid-afternoon she paid a visit to Lesto Talade after selling the sword and rings.

His shock at seeing her was evidence enough that his recommendation of Surket Marr had been only the means to make sure of the end—what better place to assassinate a man than where he is most vulnerable. And, of course, a young woman.

"You are remarkable to have survived the ordeal," he said, and apologized for the arrangement which he claimed had come to him second hand. "The man must have had enemies."

She got what she came for—the knowledge that Talade could never again be trusted.

Had he asked for her services again she would have refused, despite the fact that directly or indirectly he brought her almost half of her income. He didn't ask—and neither did any other of her clients. That night had ruined her trade, the matter easy prey for gossip:

She'd killed the one; no, it was three…

She'd acted on a long-held vexation…

She was someone prone to fits of madness…

What man would risk a night with such a courtesan? She was running out of the money she had saved, slide by slide, night after night.

Only one man came to her, a month later. He said his name was Corro, and though he paid her well, he said it wasn't for a slide. In her experience there were a few such men, but they were never as young or handsome as this one. "What then?" she asked.

"Your time, to talk to someone."

She agreed, but would only meet the person in the daytime, at a sufficiently safe place and it was decided: the Limping Bridge at Rhysselia's Gardens.

The next day she saw Corro accompanied by a woman perhaps twenty years older than she was. Ringlets of dark hair skimmed her ears. Corro moved on as the woman began tossing a few morsels from a pouch to the swans below.

"What is this about?" she said.

The older woman kept feeding the swans, all but ignoring the question. Finally, the woman tucked away the pouch. "I wanted to see the young swallow they say killed one of the best shaddens in Lucidor. Do you know what they are?"

"I've heard of them."

"Did you?"

"Yes."

"How?"

"With the same sliverheart I have with me now."

"I didn't ask you with what; I asked you how. Anyone can hold a blade."

She told the woman what happened. "And I'd be dead now if he had pulled the stickler off by a leg and not his hair."

"So, he got too close before he had to," the woman said. "He assumed you would curl up like any other…quiver would, naked in her bed. Or perhaps he had something else in mind before he killed you. Either way, he was careless and deserved to die."

"That one," she said, nodding toward Corro who was leaning at the end of the bridge, watching them. "Is he a shadden?"

The woman smiled. One of her teeth was a blue jewel. "He's my lover."

"I would have said your son."

"The younger they are the more amenable to training. Such as you. "

"That's not my preference."

"Preference? Is that a luxury you can presently afford?"

"That's none of your business."

"Just so. You have none."

"And how do you know that?"

The woman shrugged. "One has only to listen."

"Who are you? I have your coin but not the reason for it yet."

"Of course you do. There are not many of us—females of our ilk, that is. You have the makings."

"Why would I want to become a shadden?"

"I think you know; we just discussed that. Meet me here in a week to give me your answer."

"What's in this for you?"

"A shadden must replace himself—or herself—when the time has come to leave. Mine is at hand."

A week later Flury Demoul learned that the shadden's name was Tranch. She suggested the name Flury later took: Shar Stakeen.

Tranch said: "Do you like it?"

"Yes—where did it come from?"

"That doesn't matter."

Shar Stakeen found out later that her new name had been Tranch's before she, too, left the one behind as required, to take another.

Chapter Twenty-Nine:

THE BLOODSNARE

THEY LEFT A pool of shade, stepping into dappling sunlight. Falca and Styada knelt closer to the edge of the planking than the others. A yellow bird with black-tipped wings chirped close by—*thurreep*...*thurreep*—and swooped down where the Road should have been.

The storm of the night before had given way to blue sky by mid-morning though farther to the south rain clouds darkened portions of the gleaming, silvered river. The Fens they'd first glimpsed through a break in the canopy appeared now only as the absence of forest toward the northeast, a lighter green tinged with the gray-brown of sunken woodland. The meres of the Fens extended far to the north but Gurrus had said they should pass the southern end by nightfall. He estimated that from there to the Lake of Shallan and the Isle was probably not more than a day's journey.

That was before they knew the Road was gone.

Falca couldn't see where it had been severed from the supporting cables. The break wasn't here; it came at the next pair of huge stanchion trees ahead among all the lesser ones. And while the fallen Road didn't drop off sharply, the twisting slide was steep, ending with wreckage of undulating coils amidst the forest understory, as if a dark, giant serpent had shed its skin.

Had the storm caused the break? Conflict between clans?—in these parts the Tuksoskas and Karkeeks. That was as good an explanation as any for why two villages had been abandoned, their people fleeing to the north to avoid the fighting. Yet that left the question: if there was a war going on, where were the Kelvoi soldiers or refugees who hadn't already fled?

Well, it didn't matter what had brought down the Road. All that mattered was that now it would take them much longer to get to the Isle where—with or without the Kalaleks' consent—they would get the krael Ossa needed. That, and returning the kinnet without Gurrus forfeiting his life.

But Falca was worried that Ossa wouldn't last long enough to *get* to the Isle. Only a day before he hadn't the graveyard cough. He was getting worse. Even if the Road continued beyond the breach, there would be no going Above to speed them along. Once Below they'd have to stay there; Ossa would be too weak to make another climb. Of course, he would insist he could.

Falca got up, tossed away the stick he'd been twirling in his fingers. He shrugged off his coil of flessok rope, gave an end to Styada, hoisted him up. Standing on Falca's shoulders, the Limb made the anchor knot, then jumped nimbly down.

Ossa was easily Styada's equal in making knots, but the mariner reluctantly deferred to the Limb for the important ones joining the ends of the other coils of rope. When he was finished, Falca slid the entire length of rope over the edge of the Road.

They decided the descent should be made one by one since there was no point in risking all four of them at the same time. There was no telling if the rope would be long enough.

"What's a little slide at the tail end of the Road?" Ossa said.

"Gurrus and Sty'll be your cushion," Falca said. "They'll pick the splinters out of your arse."

"They're going first? I'm the bigger one."

"You'll be there for me. I'm going last, if only so none of you can see me shaking like a leaf."

Whether or not Gurrus needed the instruction he asked Styada to show him how to best wrap the rope around his wrists to play it out and take the burden off his hands. Then, with a little wave, the Tokaneke disappeared over the edge.

They waited for the shout—which came surprisingly soon. "He must have flown down," Ossa said, as Gurrus gathered up the slack rope. He gave a nod to Falca, made sure of the kinnet, though if he lost his grip and fell, the kinnet wouldn't save him.

Gurrus took longer than Styada but that was to be expected.

Falca pulled up the rope a little, made a loop into which the graylock stepped and slid it up beneath his arms. Ossa knew what to do: keep it tight as he could, use his weakened hands only to feed out the rope as he descended.

He began coughing again, though not as badly as previous rack-ups.

"If it's worse on the way down just... hold on best you can," Falca said. The words sounded foolish, but what else could he tell him?

"If I can't...I didn't finish what I was telling you last night. It's a fair piece to Milatum...but after you're done with that Allarch's muckleshoot and the other one..."

"We'll be going together," Falca said. "Down there, too."

Ossa backed away toward the precipice and let out enough rope to fall away, slowly...slowly...and then he was gone.

Separately, Styada and Gurrus were not a test of the rope's strength; Ossa was.

There was nothing Falca could do if the rope broke, or if Ossa let go...

"Hold on," he whispered. "Hold on."

The rope stayed taut.

Ossa had made it down.

But Falca heard no shouts, however faint, from any of them that would have signaled his own turn now. Ossa might not have the breath to call up, yet surely Styada would.

When the shout came Falca blew out a sigh of relief and wiped the sweat from his hands, getting ready. Then: another shout, followed by still more—as if they thought he was balking at the descent, seized with fear again, and they were yelling encouragement. Why would they think that? He'd gone up before; why would he hesitate going down?

Something was wrong...

SHAR STAKEEN WASN'T SO far back along the Road that she couldn't see Breks grab the rope, lean out over the abyss—and disappear.

She hurried ahead. There was no chance he would see her, unless she crawled right up to the brink and he looked back up. She had to see the direction they would take once he joined the other three. She couldn't use the rope for this. With his weight it was taut as a spiddard cord ready to fire. But if the Road's end was still strong enough to hold him as he pushed off, it would suffice for her.

She crawled the last few feet on her belly. The shouts were odd. Though faint, they still came to her as jeers, as if those below thought him a fool for going down. What kind of companions did Breks have?

Then she saw the other men, eight of them, tiny figures from this crow's nest height, surrounding the graylock Banisher and the Limbs.

This was no group Breks had expected to meet. For one thing, he couldn't have known beforehand the Road would have fallen at this point, so why would a meeting be arranged here? The men had swords or hobblers—glinting splinters—and several poked at the three.

No wonder they jeered Breks for his foolishness.

She cursed him for worse than that. Who did the ditchie think he was? Of what ship did he think he was captain, to try and save a few of his endangered crew? Who was he trying to impress? His jularky mat-girl was dead.

It wasn't quite disbelief; by now she had a full measure of the man and not just the killing of Wardens or saving that mottle from slithing eels. Still, what sane person would go down to the same fate as the others' when he could have stayed safely above? These other men wouldn't risk a climb up that rope to get him; he'd cut it and send them plunging to their deaths.

If he'd done as he *should* have, she could have concocted a story to explain her presence, and in time get what she needed to know about Golden-Eyes, using whatever means necessary before she killed him. Surely by now he would know. She wouldn't need the old Limb or graylock as a back-up source.

Now, his fate was out of her hands. From this distance she couldn't kill the eight, whoever they were, to fork the strappyjack from his own stewpot.

She reached over to the rope. Still tight; he wasn't down yet. She was tempted to cut the rope, be done with it—and him. It almost seemed as if he knew she was following him. And taunting her. How could a man she'd never spoken to rouse in her such anger and frustration? They were reactions that could kill a shadden if she wasn't careful.

Suddenly, her plan seemed as foolish as Breks' descent. Better to go back, take what she had of Damarr's money, move on to Milatum where, unlike Draica, there would be no consequences of her failure to bring home the daughter.

She calmed herself. It helped to remember, yet again, the reason why she was following the man.

She'd come too far to quit now. If these eight men were intent on killing, they would have already begun with the Banisher and the mottles. So there was a chance they had other plans for them. All she had to do was follow.

Nothing ever wasted?

No, not even Falca Breks' idiocy.

What better way to incur his gratitude—and thus get him to loosen his tongue about Golden-Eyes—than to kill the men who'd captured him? Tonight. Given surprise and darkness the eight posed no problem for a shadden.

The rope slackened. Stakeen saw him walking slowly ahead. Two of the hunters prodded him toward his companions at the point of hobbler and sword. He turned, and for a moment she thought he'd do something to get himself killed—reprising Amala Damarr's stupidity—and depriving her of the best option to get the Golden-Eyes.

Breks went on without incident. Stakeen exhaled her relief, whispering: "That's it, Falca. I'll take care of them soon enough."

She marked the direction they took as they disappeared into the forest. She wasted no time going over, descending hand over hand, using the knots.

The rope extended past the point where the Road curved and twisted out, but not all the way to the ground. They may have gone with this slide, but Stakeen had the spiddard and didn't want to risk damaging it or losing the darts in a tumble. She couldn't use one without the other, later, to kill Breks' captors. The agonette would be good for only one, possibly two.

She came to the rope's end, side-stepped to the edge of the Road, then over the cable railing. She'd made worse jumps. Pushing off with her feet, letting go of the rope, she flexed her knees upon landing close to the flaring trunk of the massive tree, in the shadow of the hanging Road. She was checking to make sure she hadn't lost any spiddard darts…when she heard a sound—like someone sucking in his breath. She spun, grabbing at her dagger.

She saw no one lurking by the tree…

A writhing brown mass the size of a saddle fell on her, as if someone had dropped a thick, heavy blanket, sodden with piss, over her head.

Day turned to night.

Stakeen blindly stumbled back. A tentacle rasped across her mouth, scouring her lips, stifling her screams. She gagged at the stench, the sucking pressure. More tentacles tightened around her arms, preventing her from fully drawing her dagger. She managed to get her other hand free but couldn't grip a tentacle to tear the thing off her; its oily flesh was too slippery.

A bloodsnare.

Something sharp pierced her shoulder, more of a sting than bite. She couldn't see where she was; her only hope was to smash into the tree—she still had to be near it—and crush the 'snare.

The impact loosened the tentacle around her dagger hand. She yanked the blade out and stabbed. A staccato squealing came as discordant notes—the popping of flina strings. She slashed wildly at it, felt hot splashes of blood. As the tentacles drooped away from her she knocked the bloodsnare off, and with a quick thrust of the dagger pinned it to the tree from which it had sprung.

She sank to her knees, her breathing ragged, not willing to retrieve her dagger before the bloodsnare was dead. The bulbous, protective hoods of those black eyes quivered. One tentacle snaked toward the beak that had blood on its prong—her blood. The 'snare's yellow ooze dripped into the tree's furrows past five listless tentacles. When the sixth fell, she rose and removed her dagger and wiped it off with a handful of salal she ripped from the ground.

Stakeen had never been in a bloodsnare den, but she'd heard of the aulosts the ghorgens played on their living instruments, and how repeated matings would eventually take the ghorgen consort's life.

She didn't think the poison would kill her but had no idea how quickly and badly the poison would sicken her.

She didn't have to wait long.

Her shoulder was already sore. She began to feel a tingling in her hands and feet...and the swelling of her face.

She couldn't stay here in the open, easy prey for the denizens of the night to come; she wouldn't live to see the morning. There was no possibility of climbing back up to the Road where she would be safe while the sickness lasted. She couldn't take a deep breath. The tingling in her extremities seemed to be adding weight. She felt like she was going to vomit, then did. When she raised her head she saw the hump in the fallen Road.

Stakeen staggered toward it, so dizzy the Road appeared to be moving. The hummock wasn't far, yet the effort exhausted her. The Road lay draped over a boulder, creating a little cave, and she crawled in as far as she could, already imagining the red eyes of flenx peering at her, clicking their head-horns with their claws, swiping at her, while other flenx on the roof of bark tried to rip it away to get at her...

She mustered the effort to stick the dagger in the ground between her and the opening, curled up in the darkness of her damp refuge, and began to shiver uncontrollably.

Chapter Thirty:

CULLDRED'S BOOK

PICTUS SELASSA, one of my Red Hands, informed me this evening after our stakewall had been completed that we should be arriving at Scaldasaig within two days. So this will be the last use of the folding table I have written on for this, my ninth foray into the Rough Bounds.

My gillie Fidlech has carried it strapped on his back without complaint for every one. No doubt his private cursing of the burden ceased after the fourth, when the burlbright veneer took the lash of a mottle stingvine that also shattered a hanging vial of ink and halved a long pouch of quills. If not for my portable table, Fiddy's back would have been scarred for life.

He will be toting it again for me soon enough for the coming campaigns into the heartlands of the south, though he shouldn't expect to be so lucky again. Stingvines are one thing; Myrcian steel and diadems another. In the meantime, I am looking forward to a proper escribore on which to record my legacy. If Furka Vat's carpenters are not capable of making a fine one for me at Scaldasaig then all has been a lie.

The Red Hands did well fulfilling my previous orders to blaze a trail for us to follow as close to the river as possible, marking the route with cairns. The reasons for this are obvious: a source of water for 4,000 men and one less approach to defend at night since mottles never attack from the river.

By themselves the Sixteen could not have cleared the route for the four prossars. For that we have used teams of augors that had been penned at the castlet I had constructed earlier, at a hidden location by the river, two days' march from Bastia, in anticipation of the final campaign into the Bounds for Wardens our child-king and his regents still believe are the King's Own.

Not only have the augors been the means to trample a path for all of us to follow east; they have also provided our meat. They are almost gone, but with only a day or so more, and the worst of the terrain behind us, that presents no problem. The Red Hands most recently returned from Scaldasaig informed me that, true to her word, Heresa had Vat build the two castlets and barracks for us. The few hundred Wardens already there have stockpiled provisions to last us all for a few weeks. After that we shall get what we need when I take the prossars for the first campaign into the south.

I expected the mottles would attack us at some point, though it came earlier than I anticipated, and at dawn—not later in the day as they usually do, to try to take advantage of fatigue and the lack of a stake wall. They came at dawn, toward the rear of our lengthened encampment, against the Second and Third, which killed most of the Limbs as they leaped down from netting flung over the wall.

The slaughter was over by the time the Red Hands and I got there. Some of the men were already prising out the dawnstone earbolls they often later carve into dice or three-star gaming pieces. I'd previously given strict orders against pursuit in the event of an ambush, and so there was none.

We burned our dead—only six—by the river, so that they would not be scavenged. We did not count the mottle dead, but our men must have thrown at least a hundred over the stake wall to get them at a more satisfactory distance from the subsequent breakfast fires.

That night I summoned the basileii of the prossars—Urien Crovie, Elcuin Siburon, Straggus Vott and Aldrach Aarl—and told them each to bring a mottle earboll. When they arrived I asked them to imagine the face of my writing table as a blank map of the Six Kingdoms, and to place an earboll to mark the location of the capital cities of three: Castlecliff, Draica and Milatum; and also Arzardys, the Myrcian city closest to the Vales of Semetros in northern Keshkevar.

There was, of course, considerable empty space between the earbolls and into that vacancy I placed my own marker, an earboll I took from the first mottle I ever killed—a good luck charm I have long kept, its dawnstone swirls polished to a sheen by my fingers.

I pointed to my marker. "That," I said, "is where we are going: a place called Scaldasaig. There is no Myrcian incursion, but I have no hesitation in promising you many Myrcies to kill before long."

As augors keened at their stakes, and insects eddied about the campfires, and men rolled their earboll dice or tended to their weapons and equipment, I told the basileii of my purpose—now theirs as well: nothing less than the founding of a Seventh Kingdom.

And the bone in the throat of the central kingdoms of Myrcia and Keshkevar?

The fortress of Scaldasaig.

It lies very near a bend in the river we have followed. The river continues on past cataracts deep within a gorge through the mountains and eventually into the heartland of Myrcia. From our base at Scaldasaig we shall control that river. Protected by the Bounds to the north, east and west, and the mountains to the south, it will be difficult for our enemies to bring armies to bear upon us—whether from Lucidor, central Myrcia and its eastern province of Riian, or northern Keshkevar.

I promised the basileii the harvests of fertile fields awaiting our Warden scythe, the subjugation of cities at the Kingdoms' core, and a way of life better than what we left in Bastia. If they had regrets I asked them only to remember the dishonor accorded Wardens by the treachery of Cross Keys after the last war, in which Wardens were the saviors of the kingdom but at a terrible cost; and how Wardens were forbidden to wear their black helms. All our brethren had done then after the war was assert a loyalty to Lucidor—and not scheming politicians who did none of the fighting.

Yet even after that emasculation Cross Keys still feared the few surviving Wardens and exiled them to a far eastern province, to watch over rabble in the Banishlands and cleanse the Bounds. Which they did. Some of us had fathers who were Wardens then. That time has passed, but it shall not be forgotten. If Wardens are to be forever exiled, I told the basileii, let us take exile in dreams of the rewards of magnificent conquests.

There were nods at all of this, as I knew there would be—as well as concerns, especially from Urien Crovie. "Allarch, you see the center but…is that not merely the bull's-eye for the kingdoms that could surround us; in turn or allied with others?"

"What I see, Urien, is the spider near the center of the web."

It was understandable that these men, who have so little faith in walls, would see the potential of a trap in Scaldasaig and not a base from which to unleash our power. I am aware as they of the limitations of a stronghold, however formidable. So that was why, I told them, that we shall build beacon towers—to be designed by Lannid, though I didn't tell them this—within three days march of Scaldasaig. There will always be a rotation of the prossars, with no more than three campaigning elsewhere, and at least one stationed at or near Scaldasaig.

Given this ring of beacon towers we shall always have warning of an enemy's approach. The home prossar will serve as a mobile force—this drew smiles from Siburon and Vott—to harry the enemy, disabling siege machines en route or those built on site, or at the very least minimizing their use. If attacked, this prossar would not give battle but would elude pursuit, drawing the enemy away; that in itself would serve to blunt the effects of any siege. Eventually, however, our conquests would be the best defense for Scaldasaig.

Crovie persisted with his worries. "I am all for conquests, Allarch…yet with an army of but four prossars?"

"Four, Urien, then six, then ten…the answer should be obvious: the Myrcian breadbasket north and south of the River Roan, and Coit Celidon in Riian, and the Vales of Semetros are filled with more than just women, granaries and gold.

"We shall have our pick of men who will prefer a better fate than execution. There will be plenty of men with axes to grind about their distant and indifferent masters in Castlecliff and Milatum. Do not forget that the people along the Roan thrice rebelled against the Cascade Throne, and Riian has ever been tenuous for Sanctors. We will be halving the power of Myrcia, splitting it in two with our own.

"Furthermore, I doubt that the House of Keshkev will prove to be any more agreeable to the people of northern Keshkevar than the House of Attallissia it replaced. So we shall let these men grind staggers and skurrs instead, and train them to be as bound as any true Warden.

"And do not forget Lucidor, where there are fathers and grandfathers who were Wardens once. If every other one of them has passed along his bitterness to sons and grandsons, we shall have more men once we have returned to Bastia and taken it, our new banners replacing the old, and seen to the women and families some of us have left behind. Some may stay with the garrison; some may go to Scaldasaig. That shall be our colony and must be seeded from everywhere.

"But in the meantime, we shall announce our presence in Gorgeback. I anticipate and welcome the ensuing outraged response from the more imposing citadel at Arzardys. Let the Myrcians track us back to Scaldasaig; let them weaken themselves in a futile attempt at crushing us there, because while four prossars could not take Arzardys before, after that three will do so easily; at least that is the estimation of my agents in the vicinity. After Arzardys, we shall have the iron and smiths to give us back our helms."

There was a delay in our progress the next day, after the basileii spoke to their respective prossars, as per my instructions. I anticipated as many as one hundred men might react to the news in a way unacceptable for bound Wardens, but only thirty proved troublesome, all from the First.

They were brought to me at the van and given the Bloodwing, so that all their brethren could bear witness to their disloyalty, see their chests cut open, their ribs and lungs pulled out. All the mutineers had died well before our entire force had passed.

Aldrach Aarl, basileus of the First, was one of them though he took no direct part in this minor insurrection. Whether or not he betrayed me with a lack of persuasiveness or enthusiasm in what he told his men, I cannot say. I was not with him back there; I did not hear what he said.

What I did hear all too clearly the night before was his silence. He alone of the four said not a word, offered nothing, and it was this that concerned me more than Urien Crovie's nettlesome comments. That Aldrach Aarl was commander of the afflicted prossar, and thus bore responsibility for its behavior, was a convenient excuse for his punishment, though not a necessary one.

Comitor Yakiv Fidore has assumed temporary command of the First until we get to Scaldasaig.

It was an unfortunate episode yet worth the pause. In their own way, Aldrach Aarl and the others have served me better than any others might in campaigns to come, their Bloodwings a reminder of believing our supposed treason worse than the earlier betrayal of Warden honor and sacrifice by a dead king's Regents who fled Cross Keys to safety in Lucidor's darkest hour, and returned to claim a victory they had done nothing to achieve.

Chapter Thirty-One:

CAGES

LOP HELD THE girl so the men below could see her over the thorns draped over the top of the crude ramparts.

"The Fens shall have an heir!" he shouted, then whispered to the girl: "At least for tonight." And loudly again: "She's promised me a son!"

He'd already told the men, but showing her now was part of the celebration of the evening feast to come though she would not be present. This was their only chance to see their Gavilor's young woman, the only female among the fifty-odd men—fenners they called themselves. Lop never allowed her to leave his hall on the little hill that crowned one end of his islet kingdom, a smear of land rising from black water.

Wherever the men were below—on the rickety parapet surrounding the krannog; by the firepit or gates; stringing up fish, wags and springers on the drying racks; or idling among the huts—they hooted and whistled, clashing swords, hobblers and staves.

Lop was especially pleased to notice other men too, at the far end of the causeway, an earthen scar that linked the krannog to the deadwoods: the hunters he'd sent out in the morning to find something suitable for the feast. Lop was sick of fish and springers. He wanted meat for the meal his men didn't know would be his last here.

He let the girl down. She had a comely height, but still came up short—to the end of his beard that still had a few bits of breakfast in it.

"If the fenners canna spread yer sticks themselves," he said, "they don't care if ye was to broach a hart with wings come the nine, so long as they get tha splitear I promised 'em tonight.

"But make no mistake, tha show was as much fer you as them down 'ere. One last reminder how lucky ye were I was the one what found ye that night, not them. And don't forget tha groods." He cocked his massive head to the southeast. "But none, there or here, will ever have ye."

"They'll come after," the girl said.

"Nat drunk, nat wi' tha shorn moons tonight, and nat after I hole tha three boats before we take the fourth to cross the mere to the south."

They left the ramparts and went inside his dwelling. Lop called it his Great Hall, but it was little more than a pigs' wallow of three rooms, and he knew it. For the first week of her captivity he kept her locked in the smallest of the rooms until he deemed the precaution no longer necessary. Still, he only allowed her a wooden spoon with which to eat. When he slept he kept his own blade stuck high on a rafter.

He wasn't worried she'd use his gavilor. The club was so heavy she could scarcely lift it, though her arms were surprisingly strong for someone so young.

He told her to go finish preparing the rest of the food they would need for at least the first few days. Everything else he was going to take was by the door: the gavilor, his sack of money—some of it swag from those last few fists in Stagfall before he escaped over the mountains into the Bounds. He inherited the prized pieces of gold from his predecessor here, Tavrar by name, whom he'd killed in a challenge.

Lop didn't know where the Skarrian shingle-lip got all the money. Some said he'd nicked the royal payroll for the Myrcian garrison at Skenfrith, but that wouldn't explain the bigger eclats, lucras and splendents. Wherever Tavrar had gotten it, the cache was his now. Five men had tried to challenge him for it; he'd dumped their bodies in the fens for the marshfangs, the blackened blood on his gavilor the only remaining evidence they'd ever existed.

Lop wasn't going to leave that gavilor behind, because one day he'd gild it and have licklogs kiss it as they knelt before him in a proper hall that wasn't fouled with the stench of peat smoke, or mice that burrowed into what passed for bread here.

Even now the girl had just found a squeaker, picked it up by the tail she'd halved cutting through the loaf, and tossed it into the hearth, followed by the scrap of tail and lastly the ravaged portions of the bread, saving only what the mouse hadn't eaten through yet. She'd didn't shriek as another quiver might have. He was curious why she hadn't seen the gnawed hole before she began cutting.

Well, it didn't matter if there'd be less bread for the journey.

She wouldn't be needing any.

Pity he couldn't take her with him. She was a purlie gretel, slim, with the mane of black hair and those mismatched eyes she said were a family quirk.

Sure, there could be money made by spurring her, or selling her outright in the bigger towns of eastern Myrcia or Riian—but he didn't need what she'd bring him; he had that sack full of money. And anyway, getting to where he had to go would be difficult enough even without a quiver to watch over. She might be compliant and uncomplaining, but she'd still be a burden.

If he couldn't take her with him, however, he wasn't going to let the fenners have her. She was, and would always be his—the Gavilor's—and no one else's. Sparing her the fate he'd mentioned had nothing to do with it.

He wanted two more things from her before he killed her—and getting those might have proved irksome if she'd known the truth before. The first? He always had her groom his beard with a tusker bristle brush: one hundred or two hundred strokes, depending on his mood. Afterwards, he always satisfied himself with her.

So it would be this last time. And now was better than later. It would take only a few moments to choke the life out of her, his blunt thumbs pressing hard on a throat once adorned with the gold chain of the sunstone pendant he took from her the night he got her. The pendant was now at the bottom of the sack, along with the rings and torcs from the men who'd been with her at the river's edge.

After she'd fetched the brush, she stood before him as sat on the trestle chair.

"How many this time?"

"Three hundred."

After all, today was a special occasion.

In truth, he took more pleasure in her grooming him than spreading her firm thighs. He always required her to keep her eyes closed. She could use the brush without looking, and though she couldn't harm him with either brush or hands, his throat was close to her.

This time he asked her to open her eyes. He wondered if it had been true, and she was carrying his child, would it have a mongrel's pair like these? In this light, the blue one seemed more gray.

"That's enough," he said, and she closed her eyes. "G'head wi' the brush." He closed his own eyes, sure of her, and thought how much he'd miss this, and how long a time it might be until he paid someone else to do it.

Nahhh, he couldn't take her. He had to leave before it was too late.

He'd lied to the fenners about the groods never being able to successfully attack here. Mottle villages were easily enough destroyed: break the Roads and that was that. But the Fens? Take a step off the causeway and a man could exhaust himself trying to get out of the swamp before the marshfangs came. And why would the Wardies go to much greater efforts to build what was necessary to reach the krannog in force? The prize wasn't worth it. Anyway, the groods had theirs.

Indeed they did.

Which, of course, was why he was leaving.

Lop knew the Warden scuts well, as only a Banishlands stumper could. He'd only wanted to keep a little of his business and not give over the stiting, pay-up-or-else traff they began taking. After he killed two of them in a bust-up near Flune's rig, there'd been no choice for him except to run to Myrcia. After he'd worn out his welcome in three cities along the Roan there was no place else to go but across the mountains again and into the Bounds.

The groods were close; only a matter of time before they found this place. They couldn't know, until after they came, that there was nothing here. They'd cull a few fenners, kill the rest.

Lop had no intention of being around when that happened.

He would be leaving with regret—not much but a little. And that included what she was doing right now, the gentle tugging and stroking of his beard, brushing it as he'd instructed her.

To be sure, the krannog was a miserable shit-step. But it had been his for over a year now, as king of the fenners. There were a few who'd been here since Tavrar came across it, and told the story of how the Skarrian found it. Looking only for a refuge for himself and his gold, he discovered the causeway that began in the deadwoods and followed it, curious about the smoke drifting over the meres.

The krannog was burned, charred Limbs everywhere; it was plain enough there had been a battle here between clans. The fire smoldered for months after because of the peat beneath, but Tavrar made himself at home nonetheless. Who would follow him into such a place?

There were about thirty fenners when Lop arrived but more came, choosing as he did the Bounds over a gibbet or scolding, for at least the Bounds came with a dice roll.

Tavrar built crude gates, a palisade and a low mound where he had placed his hut, distinguished only by the totem of a peculiar and massive root he brought back from the deadwoods. Tavrar fancied that it bore a resemblance to the Gavilor, the hereditary warhammer of Skarrian kings. In the huts the fenners laughed: a root was only a root no matter the size.

Lop didn't sneer, however.

The first thing he did after killing Tavrar in a challenge was to shape the root to his liking, for balance and heft, and he soon never went among the men without it. If some of them grumbled that the trunk-armed Banishlands stumper now required them to call him Gavilor instead of Lop, their complaints faded when he began production of splitear, a drink made from the mashed bulbs of a reed that grew in profusion on hummocks in the Fens.

There were fens, too, bordering the northern Banishlands where his father came from, and he passed along to his son the secret for making this particularly potent version of scorchbelly.

Lop himself led raids to capture more Limbs, to haul the fill for the Gavilor's Rise. Tavrar's low mound wouldn't do for the new king of the fens. The mottles cut and hauled the most useable of the deadwoods to improve the palisade. Lop added a drawbridge, rivaling the best of the Banishlands' rigs, to the end of the causeway. After the Limbs were worked to death their bodies were added to the mix. The contribution wasn't much, but every little bit helped…

"That's two hundred, Gavilor," the girl said.

"Whaddid I say? Three hundred. Keep going."

He was pleased she called him by his proper title; she hadn't always and had paid the price. He was going to miss that, too.

But his reign here had to end. For years there'd been only a couple hundred groods in that fortress below the bluffs, near where the river curled south. With the recent arrivals there had to be twenty times that many. Lop doubted anyone of authority in Myrcia, east or west, knew that Lucidor had sent the King's Own Wardens—all of them it seemed—so far to the east.

Whatever plan Cross Keys had hatched it was big, no doubt about that. And while the krannog was but a fly in the drink, it would be plucked out, a mere annoyance, but squashed nonetheless. Lop had to leave before that happened. He'd have plenty of time before he reached the border to figure out a way to use his knowledge of the Wardens' presence to his advantage, yet live to enjoy the reward. Who else but the Myrcian provincial governor in Gorgeback or Skenfrith should hear what he had to say about what the Wardens had done? The Myrcies wouldn't believe it; they'd demand proof.

So who better to guide Myrcian Garda scouts back than a Warden-hating stumper from the Banishlands? He'd have to get his reward upfront, however, because his usefulness would only last until they saw what shouldn't be there in the wilderness of the Rough Bounds…

The girl heard what Lop did, ceased her brushing, opened her eyes.

Someone was shouting for him from below the Rise. A second shout followed the first as he went to the door, frowning, annoyed at the interruption. They knew he would not be making his appearance until after sunset. He hefted his gavilor before unbarring the door, and strode out to the entrance between the thorn-topped wall.

Lop allowed his men to summon him by title, though he required them to remain at the bottom of the eight steps of the Rise, hands empty.

Bicket was already halfway up the steps. He'd always had the shaky left hand, yet he seemed to be more twitchy than usual. His grin stretched from one ear to where his other once was. If it had been anyone other than Bicket, Lop would have claffed him from one end of the krannog to the other.

"Get offa the Rise," Lop shouted. "This better be more'n about the feast-meat."

Bicket scurried down a few steps, then turned with a swipe at his nose. "Which I b-b-brung b-back m-more'n that, Gav'lor."

"What're ye tippin'?"

"I got someone f-fer ye, oh yes I do."

"And who mighty be?"

"The 'snare hunter what killed Boney."

Lop's haunchy hand tightened on the gavilor. He hadn't been with his brother and Bicket when they encountered a 'snare hunter coming out of the Bounds by Slit's rig, and tried to steal his catch. Only Bicket had escaped.

"Yer sure it's him?" Lop said.

"Yerra, I'm sure. Got the same m-marks, yes he do. I w-wuz the one w-what said doona kill 'em—he's w-with another and two L-limbs. Figgered ye'd w-wanna see to things yerself, thass w-what I said. P-put 'em all in the Cage, I said."

"Awright, go back and make sure nothing happens 'fore I get to 'em."

"Doona take too long, b-beggin' yer p-pardon. It's what he's sick, the hunter, an' I thought he m-might p-peel off 'fore I b-brung'm b-back fer ye." The tick-tongue knuckled his brow and left.

Lop went back inside. He wanted that last slide with the girl before killing her, so the rut would have to wait until after he dealt with the 'snare hunter who killed his brother. He told her to get into her room and prepare herself. "I won't be long," he said. At the door he paused, pulling on the beard she'd softened with the brushing.

Naahh, the gretel'd be safe where she was. He wouldn't be long; he'd left her alone before. She wasn't going anywhere. There was no place for her to go.

He hurried down his Rise to go take care of the last bit of business from his old life, before he began a new one in a few hours.

THE MEN GAVE way for him as he approached the ketch with his gavilor. Bicket pushed away a few fenners taunting the captives, so he could display his catch.

"Thass him, Gav'lor, see? L-like I told ye. Dint get no name, b-buts him, tha face. Th'other one's f-from Draica, soey says."

The 'snare hunter sat against the rear of the pen, coughing, flicking away bloody spittle with a raw, black-scabbed hand. Whatever their purpose this deep in the Bounds when Bicket, Loso and the others caught them, the two mottles and the Draican clearly wanted nothing to do with the graylock. The mottles huddled together at one front corner of the cage; the black-haired man squatted in the other.

"Awright," Lop said. "Bickie, you and Loso take tha graylock out and bring'm to the pit. We'll do the others later. Clear away!"

At one time Lop had stuffed as many as ten mottles in the ketch, his supply for the krannog work. A thick iron pin served as a lock for the gatehatch; that and a guard or two was enough to keep the occasional prisoner in. The hatchway was low enough so that even Bicket and Loso—both none too tall—had to stoop to enter. The hunter—obviously 'snare-sick and resigned to his fate—gave Bicket no problem, but said he couldn't stand. Loso, nicked hangar-sword in hand, stayed near the opened hatch, eyeing the Draican.

"Drag'm out if you have to," Lop yelled and turned to leave, followed by his men who whooped, clashed swords, sloshed splitear from wooden tankards, well on their way to being soused.

He whirled at the shriek from Bicket, saw the Draican lunge at Loso, a feint to lure Loso into committing a strike. The Draican pull up short, the hangar missing him by inches. One of the mottles hurled himself into Loso from behind, buckling him at the knees; the other grabbed the dagger from the startled Bicket.

The Draican was on Loso now—the edge of a hand chopping down hard his throat. It took only moments for Lop and the nearest men to get back, but by then the Draican had a fist snarled in Loso's greasy hair, a knee at his back, and the hangar at his neck, using him to block the entrance to the ketch.

The Draican breathed heavily. "Who wants to try?" He smashed the fenner's head into the ground.

Loso's eyes were rolling white, but he wasn't dead yet. The men looked at Lop, as if they expected him to charge into the pen on all-fours. Its small size denied the hulking Lop any room to skull the Draican with his gavilor.

"*Bicket?!*" Lop roared.

"He...he dunned m-my blade," Bicket croaked, despite the dagger a Limb pressed against his throat.

The hunter's laughter ended with coughing.

The Draican tapped Loso's head with the sword. "Is he worth it? Or the other one? You'll lose more trying to get in. So why not you and I, by that pit, to settle it?"

"Ye doona want that," Lop said.

"Your butterman bragged about you all the way here, you and that pricked-out root in your hand. Your men don't seem to think you'd have anything to lose."

Lop's beard hid the full flush in his face. Never mind he'd have to crawl in, he was tempted to grab a sword from the nearest fenner—Roko—and rush the ketch and kill this scut who didn't seem to realize *he* was the one in a cage. Fenners hooted and yelled their encouragement to teach the cob a lesson and skull the other.

"Get'm, Gav'lor! He wants a challenge!"

"You never lost one!"

"Make it six!

Lop's thoughts came quickly: there was no reason to risk anything now; and as for the graylock, wouldn't Boney prefer—by way of vengeance—the slower death of 'snare poisoning than the mercy of a quick kill?

He was sure he could take the Draica in a challenge, but he might not be as easy as the others. Lop had seen him change hands with Loso's sword, and suspected the Draican was defted right and left—always tricky, that. He was also very quick for a strapper, though he hadn't Lop's size, couldn't match his strength. And the scut was canny, supposedly cowering in one corner of the ketch with the mottles in the other, to give the impression none of them cared about the graylock: a perfectly timed ruse—with mottles, no less.

Lop could tell the man's confidence wasn't faked, and he was persistent in using the one pick he had for this lock. If Lop had planned to stay, he'd have to kill the Draican, of course…but he wasn't.

Lop thought of his own fakery with the display of the girl to announce his coming heir. Maybe his successor was already here. He decided he didn't care if the Draican survived to take his place. Why should he? He'd be long gone by the morning.

He said: "Naah, I think not. Yer not worth the sweat. Ye have yer hangar, but it won't do y'any good, except killing the two in there. They're dead to me. Ye'll be begging fer food and water soon enough."

He picked out four of the nearest men to guard the cage for the night, reassuring them they'd get their share of splitear, and chose four more to relieve them at dawn. One of them, Squinch, was pointing away at the Rise with his sword: "Uh, Gav'lor…"

He turned from Bicket's mewling and the clotted gasps coming from Loso's crushed throat—and saw the girl dragging his sack of gold from the Hall, stopping when she reached the open gateway to the wall. At the edge of the steps leading down from his Rise she tried to lift up the sack, but it was too heavy. She dropped it and began scooping handfuls of Lop's treasure, flinging out gold eclats, lucras and splendents beyond the steps, as she would seed to a fallow field.

Chapter Thirty-Two:

THE SUNSTONE PENDANT

THE SIGHT OF the girl stunned Falca as much as the showering coin. She hurled fistfuls, pausing only to shout: "He was going to leave! And take all of *this* with him! Tonight, while you were drunk!"

"*She lies*!" Lop roared, jabbing the massive gavilor at the girl. No one moved toward the Rise, except for Lop. He flinched at a spray of coins, batting them away as if he was swiping at pestering insects. He whirled to face the fenners. 'Stay back, alla ye! She *lies*, I say!"

"Who's ta say?" someone shouted.

"Who cares? Proof's in tha gold," yelled another.

Lop cut off the first man to break, smashing the gavilor into his face so hard teeth flew out like so much yellow corn. A second man rushed forward, then a third, then more. Lop skulled one man as he darted away with a few coins; another grabbed more behind his back, only to lose them when a fenner hinged his hand at the wrist with a sword strike.

Lop struck here, struck there, but couldn't cosh everyone scrabbling for the gold. The girl kept flinging these bright scraps for the dogs she'd loosed. They scrambled for the treasure, snatching what they could, ducking blows, parrying hangars with ringing clashes, staves with resounding cracks.

The four guards Lop had left by the ketch abandoned their posts with nary a glance back. Bicket had a use now; Falca and Styada shoved him over Loso and out of the pen.

They went out, too, but not far. Falca had his eye on the low hill, the thorn-topped wall. Gurrus motioned to the gate. It was still barred but the way was clear. "No," Falca said. There was no boon there, escaping at Ossa's pace. What they needed before they fled was here—and it wasn't what these fenners were killing each other to get.

The girl brushed back her long, raven hair and heaved the diminished sack as she would a pail of slops. She may have been aiming for Lop, but hit Bicket square in the head as he scuttled along on his hands, stuffing coins into his mouth since he had no pockets. The sack's landing purged more coins. Bicket had no time to retrieve them. He raced away, spitting what he had in his mouth into the sack, heading for the gate, bent low from the weight of loot, a dead man's hangar now cradled in his arms.

Seeing him, Lop charged through an obstructing ruck of brawling men, smashing left and right with his gavilor.

Falca could hear the chinking of the sack as Bicket ran past. The tick-tongue had to drop the sack and hangar to unbar the gate but by that time others, including Lop, were closing on him. Bicket grabbed the sword and slashed across the face of the nearest fenner, but the next cleaved his shoulder, yanking him away from the sack—only to have another contest the sack just before Lop arrived. He swung his gavilor, cracking one man's knee, another's skull—and hurried toward the gate.

The dozen men who'd left the melee swarmed him there. Lop towered above them all, bellowing his rage. With one hand, he swung the gavilor down on this arm, that head, pulped the face of another fenner—and ran through the gate.

It was a wonder to Falca that any man went after him, yet many did.

Now was their chance.

There were no men near the cage, but about ten were fighting by a second, smaller gate not far from the steps leading up to the hillock, where the girl had flung Lop's gold.

Ossa wavered on his feet. Falca quickly belted his sword, took an arm over his shoulder to help the graylock walk, gripping him at his elbow and not the scabbed, blackened hand.

Gurrus had Bicket's dagger, Styada some fenner's sword. They hurried around the firepit, passing by the dead, the dismembered, the gut-stabbed. One wounded fenner was ransacking the body of another for coins the man might have stashed before he died.

When they reached the gate at the top of the hill Ossa took a knee to catch his breath. Gurrus and Styada stayed with him, guarding the entryway. Falca went ahead to try the door to Lop's ramshackle dwelling.

The girl had barred it, no doubt expecting the worst after what she'd done.

Pounding on it would only frighten her more

Falca darted to the side of a window no wider than his fist and shouted: "It's all right. He's gone. The others are gone or dead or will be soon."

Could she even hear him? He didn't dare show himself fully. Lop wouldn't have left her alone in there with any weapon, but she might have found something to jab through the slit window.

"*Listen* to me! We're only four—two Limbs and our sick friend; my name is Falca Breks. We were in that cage; we'll not harm you in yours. You saved our lives. We need food and water, then we leave."

He heard no movement within. Had she killed herself rather than endure the other fate? He didn't know what else to say that might allay the girl's fears—if she was still alive.

The hill was high enough for Falca to see, over the thorns, the departure of two dugout boats. Were there more? A lone fenner in each one poled frantically away.

They'd killed to get the gold, coin by coin, and all they cared about was escaping with it. What good would it do them in the Fens? What they were taking wasn't treasure spilled in Catchall, where at least it could be spent. Where did the fools think they could go with it *here*? It was a question Falca might not have asked a year ago. He knew them; he'd once been like them.

He got the tick-tongue's dagger from Gurrus.

"We should go," the mehka said, pointing below.

Two fenners stumbled back in through the gate, one bent over, holding his stomach, another the stump of a hand gushing blood. They staggered off toward one of the huts lining the lee of the palisade. Five—no, six—more were eyeing the hill and their odds against two Limbs and two men, one of whom couldn't hold a sword. Falca knew they must have liked their chances for getting Lop's woman, the only treasure left now to take.

He tossed the dagger through the window, hearing it clatter on the floor within. If she was alive she'd know what it would mean to have the blade.

Ossa's voice rasped from a spate of coughing. "Falca…better we leave now." He was showing Styada how to wield the sword with two hands, though he couldn't grip it himself.

The door opened.

Falca didn't hesitate going in; the young woman wouldn't have opened if she meant to greet him with a dagger-thrust. She had the blade, but stood away, by another window, holding in her other bloody hand stems of thorns that could have ripped the eyes of an attacker.

She couldn't have been more than twenty years old.

Falca said: "All we need is food and water, then…"

"You can't have this," she said, and tapped the sunstone pendant nestled between her breasts, but Falca hadn't been staring at that. He'd never seen mismatched eyes: light blue and dark gray. "I knew it was in there, the sack," she said. "He thought it'd be safe when he left."

Falca shook his head. "We don't want it."

"I won't let you have it."

"I said we don't want it."

"It was mine before."

"It still is."

Falca asked her name.

"It's…Raleva."

"Where's your home?"

"East of Stagfall…by the Roan."

"My friend outside, he's from Myrcia, too. Where we're going is far from there, but you can come with us, if you want."

"He said the same thing…I knew he was going to kill me…after."

"It's all right now. But we have to leave quickly—do you know how many boats they have, beyond that postern gate?"

"Four, I think."

"That leaves two for us—if they're still there," Falca said. "I'm going outside now. Two Limbs will be coming in to get what we need—will you help them?"

She nodded.

Falca and Ossa kept watch by the gateway after Gurrus and Styada went in.

There were six fenners by the pit, eyeing the hill, clearly waiting for Falca and the others to go—and leave the girl to them. One man grinned, flicked a finger from his forehead, as if to thank Falca in advance for the gift.

She had been right about the boats. He could see two now, pulled halfway clear of the water—and the bodies of fenners killed trying to take them. One man lay draped over the side of the nearer boat; two more crumpled by the bow of the other.

Closer: a dying fenner was crawling toward the steps, but Falca wasn't worried about him.

Gurrus came out with three 'skins of water, draped by their straps across his chest. Styada carried a stitched leather sack, bulging at the bottom. "Not… much," he said, "but it is enough for…few days…"

Raleva handed Falca a small butt of water, but he passed it on to Ossa before he gulped his fill.

Falca went down first, sword at the ready, then Gurrus and Raleva close to Ossa, helping him with the steps. Styada, both hands on his sword, came last. The six fenners dispersed around the pit, three to a side. Falca whispered back to the others: "Let 'em think we're going to the main gate; we're for the boats beyond the postern."

At the bottom of the steps the dying fenner—his beard as black as Lop's was red—asked Falca to kill him. He managed a roll to his side, revealing more than his mortal wound and blood-soaked dirt: four gold coins he'd lain upon to hide.

"Tay'm fer tha mercy, beggin' ye. Tha' hangar or the mottle's."

"I'll do it," Raleva said, "if you tell me which hut is Stribor's."

The fenner weakly raised his arm, pointed. "Tha end'un."

"What's there?" Falca said.

"Lop gave my bow to someone named Stribor."

Before Falca could stop her, she was off at a run toward the row of huts crowding the palisade next to the cage.

The fenners saw the chance to cull their prize. Two carried staves, one a longshank; the rest swords.

Falca snatched up the gold coins.

"You missed these," he shouted, and threw them away from the hut from which Raleva had not yet emerged. The men saw the skittering gold and broke off to root among the bodies for them.

Falca bolted for the hut. Ossa, Gurrus and Styada followed him instead of making for the postern gate. Ossa wound up closest to the nearest fenner, who snatched a coin from a wounded man at the same time Ossa picked up a staff from the ground, grimacing in pain from the mere grip of it.

Raleva rushed from the hut with her bow and quiver. The fenners had gotten their gold. Five of them—the sixth skulked away at the sight of her nocking an arrow—were spreading out now, trying to move behind Falca and the others, to prevent her from shooting.

She picked off the lead, a shot that split the difference in distance between Styada and Ossa. She couldn't shoot again in that direction since two more fenners were moving toward him now. She had a clear shot at another pair coming toward her, to Falca's right. He caught the nearest at the knees, a glancing strike that slowed him enough to give her time to take the second man down. He stumbled, bowing his head toward the arrow in his gut, and fell. The other limped away.

Gurrus darted in front of Ossa to protect him, taking a slashing blow at his belly. The impact lifted him off his feet, twisting him away from Ossa. The mehka would have died if he hadn't been wearing the kinnet. Styada howled, charging past him, but the fenner parried his clumsy two-handed swing, only to take Ossa's staff at the side of his head. Ossa lost the staff with the blow, but by then Falca was on the man, stabbing him in the groin. He screamed, rolled away. The last one took off, backing away with his hangar until he tripped over a corpse, scrambled to his feet again, whining: "Lop wadn't 'ere…the gretel wuzzours."

Raleva had another arrow ready, but swung the bow away from him toward the steps of Lop's hill. The dying fenner was on his side, wavering on an elbow. Falca could see there were only three arrows in the quiver she'd slung over her shoulder. "Save it," he said. "I'll do it."

She let fly the shaft. The man's head jerked and he slumped to his back, the arrow angling from his chest.

Falca and Raleva were the last through the postern. No one followed. He could see five men on the hill, no doubt hoping there was still something of value they could find in the hall. Two more were running up the steps.

Marsh birds rose from the boats. They hadn't finished with the burly fenner's eyes yet, and cawed their complaint as Falca pulled the dead man off while Styada and Raleva steadied the boat. Ossa couldn't use his hands to slide the boat free of the muck but with Gurrus' help shouldered it loose.

The boats were Karkeek progues, Gurrus said, or at least that's what Falca thought he heard; the mehka was wheezing badly from the blow he'd taken. They seemed to have been hollowed with fire, and were hewed to shape from a single log, flaring out toward the water-line for stability. A pole lay askew in each boat.

Falca and Ossa took one progue; Gurrus, Styada and Raleva the second, with the younger Limb doing the poling. Standing near the progue's stern, Falca was unsteady at first, but soon found his balance. The boat rippled through the black water, parting the shoulder-high reeds. He gave his back to where he thought the sun had gone down—all that he knew about the direction they should be going.

Insects buzzed, springers resumed their blurting croaks after the boats glided on. Birds chirped and warbled their last calls of the day. A circling floka swooped down, vanishing behind a tussock of roots and vegetation rising above the reeds, then reappeared with its squirming prey: a small red-banded marshfang. Gripped at the neck by the floka's talons, and unable to use its teeth or claws, the screeching marshfang twisted to get free—but not for long. The floka flew off with its limp prey in the direction the progues were taking.

All was quiet now except for the splashes Falca and Styada made with the poles, the brushing of reeds alongside the boats—and Raleva, who began to weep softly after she fitted an arrow to the bow that lay across her knees.

Chapter Thirty-Three:

THE KINNET

SHAR STAKEEN WOKE to daylight, still sick from the bloodsnare poisoning. The sharp needling pain in her hands and feet was gone, replaced by an overall aching and dizziness that caused her to retch.

She remembered now that Breks had been captured by—was it eight men? There were others taken with him…that graylock Banisher. He was in danger. She couldn't stay here until the 'snare sickness was completely gone. She had no idea how long she'd been in this little cave formed by the collapsing Road. A day? Two days? So it might already be too late to try to save Breks. She remembered why. And that got her moving.

She crawled out, taking her two daggers with her, and stumbled off in the direction Breks' captors had taken. She found a path—at least it seemed like one. After a while she felt better, enough to keep on at a run…and then stopped, as if she'd run into a wall that wasn't there.

In her delirium and haste, she'd forgotten to take the spiddard and agonette. Never mind the pannier with Havaarl Damarr's gold and everything else in it; without those weapons she stood little chance of killing eight men. Two daggers wouldn't be enough.

Sickness be damned; shaddens did not make such mistakes.

She had no choice except going back to get everything.

She didn't get far.

There were only two of them, heads poking above a rotting log alongside the path, close enough to spit at. They were as shocked to see her as she was them. The one with the top-knotted yellow hair shouted back over his shoulder: "Plodie! Ne're mine Lop fer now. We foun' a quiv!"

Stakeen threw both daggers, stuck both men as they clambered over the log. One fell ahead, the other behind.

She ran.

A stump snag gashed her left thigh, a branch ripped her spring cape. She lost the heel to her right boot. By the time she stumbled out of the forest verge her face and arms were streaked with blood from the scratches and cuts of bushwhacking through the undergrowth.

Mist steamed off the river.

The hunters were not far behind. Over her breathing she could hear grunts, shouts, the crackling of branches.

She thought the dizziness had gone, but it returned to plague her balance, make her feel like throwing up again. She couldn't swim across the river. It was too wide here. And not with those eels; she wouldn't make it halfway.

But downriver there was a rocky, sparsely wooded islet—maybe closer than she thought. A refuge. She'd have to swim fast.

She ran down the gravelly strand.

Hopefully the hunters would try to cross, too. Given their numbers and the likely clumsiness of their swimming, maybe the eels would do her work for her. If the men didn't pursue her across, she could wait until darkness and go back over and kill them as they slept. And then return to the fallen Road for her spiddard, agonette, and gold—and hope that Breks, if she could find him, wasn't dead...

Two hunters emerged from the forest, then three more who were not so exhausted they couldn't leer at seeing her trapped. Between them the five carried three short swords, a broken shaft hobbler and a stave.

The islet was no longer an option.

She backed up, already seeing in her mind how she'd disarm two of them—and then break for the forest if she couldn't finish it here with weapons she took from them. It was obvious the hunters were much more tired than she was—her shadden's training hadn't deserted her in that regard. All she'd need was time to get back to the Road. Her spiddard and agonette would do the rest.

But they didn't move toward her now. They were hesitating, scowling at something beyond, up river.

"Wharr they doin' here?"

"We gotta go."

One of them waggled a finger at her. "C'mon, dozy. Ye don't want alla them Wardies; we're only five."

Stakeen didn't look back. She had her eye on the only hunter who wasn't drifting back now toward the forest verge.

Another shouted back at this one: "Plodie! Y'aint got tha time—groods can have tha quiv."

"Not fer what she done to Linket and Wishbone they won't," he said, more to Stakeen than the one who yelled. "A bloody poose's what they'll get."

He charged her. She scooped up gravel into his face, skewing his strike. His sword spit sparks on the strand, narrowly missing her gashed leg. She spun away, dizziness flaring again. The shoreline seemed to heave up, and with it the Wardens jumping from the boats at the river's edge.

She stumbled and rolled into a middling boulder by the water's edge. The hunter's sword rasped down the edge, cutting deeply into her leg above her right knee. She rolled away. The hunter hesitated, cursed—and fled.

Stakeen rose and fell back against the boulder, blood from her wound seeping through her fingers.

Soon, someone shouted close by: "Never mind those scuts; just bring the woman to my boat—and get something to bind her leg."

She turned to see who'd said it: the Warden officer she'd narrowly missed with the spiddard shot. He grinned at her, revealing the blue gums she hadn't noticed before at the waterfall where Amala Damarr had died.

BY NOON OSSA could no longer walk by himself.

The pain was worse, no longer pinpricks in his hands. The cold fire in his legs and arms now flared in his belly. It wouldn't have mattered if the land had been flatter like that past the Fens, and less difficult than this hilly terrain. They still would have had to help him—Falca on his right, the young woman on his left. He could feel the knot of their clasped hands behind his back at his belt, keeping him up.

He couldn't think of her name. Maybe it was the splintering headache that was just as bad whether he kept his eyes open or shut. How could he have forgotten her name in so short a time, in the day—more than that?—since the night on the mere.

He should have been able remember her name; he remembered everything else about what she'd told them the first night after the fens, by the head of the lake he'd hoped was the one, but wasn't: something about going after the man who'd raped and killed her mother.

"I'll find him for you," he said to her, again and again. She didn't seem to know what he was mumbling about so he kept trying to say it more clearly, until Falca whispered: *don't talk...save your strength...just keep on, it's not far.* And Gurrus telling him the same thing as he walked ahead with the Limb—Styada; that was his name—saying it was just beyond the end of this lake.

Yet that didn't make any sense...until he remembered Gurrus saying before that there were three lakes and the biggest had the island in the middle of it, but it wasn't really a lake because there was a passage north to the sea. Ossa wished he hadn't heard that because it somehow made him think of Rohaise and the passage he should have made back to her, to tell her he was sorry, so very sorry...

Why were they going to this lake? He tried to think of the reason. Had the pain in his head seared that away, too, along with the girl's name? How could he forget something so important?

He was thirsty again though still wet from the last time Falca and the young woman had given him water. He had to have more or he would burn up. Did they hear him ask for more water?

They must have. She and Falca soon let him collapse into water, immersing him in an embrace so soothing he wanted it to take him away. Falca wouldn't let that happen, would only let him drink and pulled him back, saying he *had* to keep going. If Falca said that it must be necessary. He trusted Falca—a Draican no less—like the son he'd never had.

But there were others he'd trusted, too: Boket...Vessa. And Laineth.

The triumph of recalling the names got him going, and there was a moment shortly after they went on by the lake that he thought he could walk without help.

Then the cold fire came back; he stumbled and fell, slipping their grasp, and this time he didn't think he could get up again.

They were all around him now. Falca was talking to Gurrus about the... kinnet.

The kinnet. *That's* why they were going to this island in the middle of a lake that wasn't a lake. Falca was telling him now that he had to open his eyes, and look at the kinnet because what was on it would make him better if he could only keep going, and even Styada joined in to promise him it wasn't far.

He opened his eyes. Dizziness overwhelmed him. He threw up, saw the blood in it, but Falca didn't back away…kept telling him to keep his eyes open—*look, you have to look*—and he did…and saw Gurrus appear next to the young woman who held the other end of the dripping kinnet so he could see.

It was no bigger than a flag or scrap of sail shredded by the wreck of the *Flury*. The lake-blue color of the kinnet began to dissolve, replaced by others so bright they hurt his eyes. He looked away at Falca for an explanation yet Falca was staring at this transformation too, whispering something Ossa couldn't hear. The young woman's blue and gray eyes were wide, and so he forced his slitted, weighted eyes wider.

"Here is what will heal you," Gurrus said. "The trees have it, and they are thick down to the water of Shallan. We have to get there and take the krael as it is shown on this. Do you see?"

He saw at one end of the kinnet only a single tree wrapped by vines that snaked underneath, spreading out to form a lower border…and depictions of sea waves and beasts… and under that words like nothing he'd ever seen before…and more of the words at the top border between what had to be Erseiyrs at the corners.

And in between a giant of a man was taking something from the tree, his right hand reaching high over the vines, his other hand below. In the next panel he was offering what he'd taken—krael?—to the prostrate figure of a woman surrounded by others clearly saddened by her condition. Ossa wanted to believe that the woman was…Laineth…or Flury.

She alone had no color; all else was brilliant on the kinnet—the words and sea in blue, a lighter blue than the lake, the color of Falca's eyes; the Erseiyr a dark red; the kraken purple; the vines and trees in shades of green; the giant and the woman's attendants in hues of dark flesh, their clothing shimmering in silvers and golds; and in the giant's right hand something russet; in his left something yellow…

Ossa blinked. Was this some trick of the eye? His sickness? He thought he saw the giant close his right fist in the next panel, and from that descended a rust-red stream that poured into a chalice held by one of the attendants, who passed it to another, who gave it to the dying woman.

Then the giant flung the yellow below, to be taken on the barbed tongues of the beasts…

Ossa was sure there had been five of them before, but now he saw only four.

Whiteness faded from the woman. She rose and the upraised hands of her consorts seemed to summon one of the Erseiyrs—or had the giant transformed into that creature? He couldn't tell; the kinnet was fading now, as if a vast wing had passed over, shadowing all, and the last thing he saw, as he rose too, was that wing enfolding her and taking her away.

Falca and the girl were staring at Gurrus in such a way that Ossa knew this hadn't been his sickness or a trick of the eye. With Styada's help Gurrus folded the kinnet lengthwise, wrapped it around himself, tucked in a fold, not bothering to hide it under his clothing. He said to the young woman: "You must always remember seeing only a poorly dyed cloth taken from a line."

She and Falca stayed close to him through the last of the afternoon. He saw another lake to the south, the smallest of the three of Shallan, but his eyesight blurred more frequently as the forest began to thin with a rising of the land.

They had to help him again as the rocky slope grew steeper, the woodland diminishing further.

Every step hurt, but he felt the pain not so much in his feet and legs as his belly and chest.

Distantly, he heard Gurrus telling Styada that the krael trees grew much more thickly along the shore, some rising to the height of the bluff that overlooked the lake, so you could see where they were free of the vines that snarled and infested the lower portions of their trunks. Those vines formed an almost impenetrable barrier, broken only by the switch-backed path the Kalaleks maintained to link the shore to the rim road they patrolled during summer months.

Ossa didn't have the breath to ask Gurrus why, but Falca did: the krael was most likely culled from the trees in the summer. That was the only explanation for why no one was allowed to journey to the Isle in that season.

They stopped by a split boulder, from whose crevice a sapling rose.

Ossa couldn't go on.

He tried but couldn't make his legs work any longer. His friends couldn't move his legs for him.

Falca: "We'll help him up."

Gurrus: "The Kalaleks might see us all up there. Here is better."

Falca: "We bring it to him, then."

Ossa had forgotten what that was—again; yet it seemed so strange he could recall Gurrus saying he'd never approached Shallan from this direction, only from the Road to the north that ended near the bluff and the path down to the shore…and that the view of the Isle rising from the lake that led to the sea, the verdant swathe of encircling forest, the mountains farther to the east, was the most beautiful he'd ever seen…

Krael.

That's what Falca meant.

A forest of krael trees: what would save him.

Ossa wanted to glimpse them, just one, as he had on the kinnet, but he couldn't make it far enough.

All he could see before his heavy lids closed were the mountains Gurrus said rose beyond the Isle—and two flokas teasing each other high above where he imagined the trees would be in that lush ring around the shore of the Lake of Shallan.

Ossa had told himself after the wreck of the *Flury* that there had been no way to avoid the storm that day long ago. That hadn't been true then. It was now.

He lay down. The release from his burden felt so good he wondered why he'd tried so hard to keep on all this way. Because of what he'd promised Laineth? He never expected, from all that had happened before in his life, to have the choice to merely lie down and make an end of it. He wondered if he'd even be conscious of the moment when it came.

The young woman was the closest of them all to him, and this time she understood the question Ossa kept asking.

"It's Raleva," she said. Then, to Falca and Gurrus and Styada: "We have to hurry."

Ossa tried to tell her that knowing her name again was enough to take with him; that the other thing didn't matter now. But he couldn't get the words out, and he fell away.

BOOK THREE:

THE LAKE OF SHALLAN

Chapter Thirty-Four:

CINNAMON AND ELIXITH

OSSA WAS STILL breathing in shallow rasps when Falca and Gurrus left, scrambling up the thinly wooded slope toward the Kalaleks' rim road. The quicker they could get up there the sooner they'd smell the tell-tale cinnamon and elixith. If Ossa could last another hour or two, they'd have the krael for him.

That night on the fens Gurrus had told Falca something he'd never mentioned before: how Amala had once asked him what he thought of this Breks fellow. He'd urged her to be careful with the man, given his reputation, but that at least he carried the scent of something that reminded Gurrus of a place he'd known years before. To that Amala had laughed. "You lived in an abandoned spice warehouse, too?" Only later did he learn the names for the scents: cinnamon tinged with elixith.

Falca was already thinking beyond getting krael for Ossa. He had to convince Gurrus that all he had to do was leave the kinnet on that bridge he said was formed of the skeleton of a kraken, or syllysk, as the Kalalek priests called it. If left at night, the kinnet would be found by the ketheras in the morning—and the Tapestry would be whole again. The promise to his father didn't require him to cross that bridge with it, never to return.

Falca was first to the rim road.

He should have been able to smell the forest below and not just the stink of his own sweat. The wind should have carried the scent.

Had Gurrus led them to the wrong place? Had he forgotten where it was after all these years? After all, he'd come to the Isle only once, and that time from the north.

He was about to ask him when Gurrus bolted ahead. After all this, the old mehka still had his legs. By the time Falca reached him Gurrus had already turned back, to slump down against the nearest of the spindly trees impoverished by the stony soil of this precipice.

Somewhere above, the Fates at their Loom Eternal were laughing as they'd never laughed before.

"*No*...by the throat of Roak, no..." Falca whispered.

It didn't matter now if Ossa managed to hang on to his life for two more hours or days.

They'd never get the krael.

There was no need to worry about Kalalek priests on the track behind them, or anywhere else on this bluff overlooking the Lake of Shallan and the Isle.

Falca put a hand on Gurrus' shoulder, felt the trembling.

Gurrus ducked his head away but not quickly enough. In Draica, Falca had given cause for many Limbs to weep, but he'd never seen one cry until now.

His hand fell away as Gurrus got up, and said: "It is just as well Ossa...and Amala...will never see this."

What was worse—seeing that it had all been in vain, or believing salvation was at hand yet being unable to reach it? Falca dug his teeth deeply into his lip. What was down there shouldn't be there.

He felt too numb for anger.

The wind, brisk enough to sift through his long hair, carried the faint raps of hammering, woodcutting, shouts of laughter and the wailing of many Timberlimbs, but no scent of cinnamon and elixith—only the smoke of cooking fires, the stench of thousands of Wardens encamped in two stockades and Timberlimbs held captive in a third.

Green and black pennons fluttered above the corner towers of the timbered Warden castlets and the rows of barracks within. The three stockades rose close by the shore; behind them countless stumps were all that remained of the forest that once had encircled the lake from shore to bluff, interrupted only by a lesser vale to the west, where Falca glimpsed a group of about fifty Wardens heading north on a road toward the lake.

Some of the stumps were already overgrown, clotted with yellow-flowering vines. The wasteland appeared as an undulating blanket, golden in the dusk with grasses and weeds that had grown since the forest had been cut down.

They'd used it all except for stacks of timbers piled high along the shoreline between the lake and the Warden castlet nearest the Limbs' stockade. All of it was gone to build the stockade walls and barracks, and those of the workers closer to the road; or turned into scores of wagons and massive, wheeled sleds that transported blocks of quarried stone; or cut for scaffolding and flooring; for beams, hoardings and gates; for the fires of blacksmiths and mortar-makers; for the planking of the bridge that stretched across the southern end of the lake to the Isle from an unfinished barbican on the near shore.

Many boats supported that bridge, but it had to be temporary, to be replaced by a causeway of stone, some of which was still on sleds left at the end of the road. Falca saw pens for augors and drays, but the Limb slaves had to have done most of the hauling of stone from a quarry, taking it across the bridge to build the castle that rose from the Isle Gurrus had left long ago with secrets of the Kalalek priests and the shame of his theft.

He was at Falca's side now, shaking his head. "There is nothing to be done for Ossa…or all those Kelvoi."

"We'll have to find a place to bury him."

"I would summon a floka if one could take a man of his size."

"Stones over him, then."

"We can gather them with the kinnet. It is but a blanket after all—we should go, while there still is enough light."

"Soon."

"Falca…what more is there to see? What once was there is no longer. It was a dream after all, not a kesslakor—I was never good at knowing the difference." He turned by the wind-skewed tree where he'd slumped.

Falca watched Gurrus descend and wondered whether the mehka would be summoning a floka for himself tomorrow. He had come all this way prepared to die at the Kalaleks' hands for what he'd done, but what now? What was left for him? Going with Styada to find one of the Kelvoi clans that had fled to the northern reaches of the Bounds, there to live out his life knowing he'd failed in his promise to his father, his vision a falsehood. What could Falca say to counter a belief that what was down there was a consequence of what he'd done?

He looked back toward the lake.

Whatever Culldred Hoster intended, he seemed to have brought all of his Wardens to make it happen. The Allarch's ambition had to have been many years in the planning. The castle was proof enough of that: a fortress that rivaled the size of Cross Keys.

Here, in the middle of nowhere, was Lambrey Tallon's destination.

Falca had no doubt that Maldan Hoster would be with his father.

He'd wanted so badly to see the life fade from the eyes of the one who had killed Amala, even if it was the last thing he himself ever saw.

The last of the light had not yet faded from the mountain crags to the east, or the tops of the towers, gatehouse and keep that ringed walls still being whitewashed from scaffolding hanging from the parapets. The keep at the northern end loomed massively, rising from a narrowing of the inner ward—the highest point on the Isle. Beyond, an awe stretched away into the distance—to the ocean beyond the Bounds?

Two southern towers dominated a long rocky spur jutting out like a crooked finger toward the bridge. Falca counted eight more along the walls of the castle that followed the contours of the Isle. It had the rough shape of an arrowhead, with the bridge like the arrow's shaft at the bottom. The eastern edge rose higher than the western, and higher still at the northern tip of the arrow where the great keep was. Along that eastern side the rocky slope fell away steeply from the base of the wall and towers.

A turreted gatehouse at the end of a wall separating the inner and outer wards fronted an inlet guarded by flanking towers. This must have been where the Limb bridge spanning the lake had ended at the Isle. The ruins of the bridge appeared as white flecks on the deepening blue of the water.

Surrounded by water too deep to fill in, the walls couldn't be undermined. The western and southern sides of the fortress might tempt besiegers more than the east, but those flanks were also much farther from the shore. The great keep at the northern faced the awe and was on the highest ground of all.

Siege machines would be useless; the distance to the Isle was too far. The massive rocks needed to batter those walls would splash uselessly into the lake.

He figured only a hundred men would be needed to hold this castle; 20,000 couldn't take it.

Those hundred Wardens inside would have wells for water and stocks of food. There seemed to be plenty of room within the walls to grow what they needed when those ran out. Falca could see portions of green rectangles of gardens in the larger outer ward. Were they the last vestige of the meadow where Gurrus said the priests sometimes took the mehka acolytes for their lessons on better days? And that inlet…Falca couldn't see a dock but there had to be one. So the castle could be supplied that way.

This castle could never be taken by force or its hundred defenders starved out. And surely Culldred would loose the rest of the Wardens to attack besiegers outside; at the very least cutting their lines of supply. It's what Falca would do if he was the Allarch.

For whatever the reason, however he'd done it, the Warden Allarch had claimed the Kalaleks' Isle and built a stronghold that would soon be the envy of monarchs throughout the Six Kingdoms.

Falca was about to go back down…when he noticed something that seemed worth a better look if he could get it. He hurried back to the Kalalek track, kept going north until he could see between the Limbs' stockade and the adjacent Warden castlet. Sentries, tiny at this distance, guarded the gates to both enclosures.

Was it a shading of the diminishing light, or were trees rising above and beyond the corner watcher tower of the castlet nearest the Limbs' prison?

Trees.

He was sure of it now—yet trees nothing like the giants he'd come to know, that had thick, straight trunks mostly clear of branches below the canopy. These seemed shapeless, with little difference between trunk and foliage. Was that the result of the vines Gurrus said infested the forest?

The trees were on the larger of two islets not far from the shore, though the distance was probably greater than it looked from this vantage point. A rocky outcrop partially hid some of the trees. The smaller islet was barren.

He realized he hadn't seen them before because the wind had been stronger, snapping out the Warden flag on the tower. The castlet and that tower were almost at the edge of the lake, so the islets had been hidden. And he'd been transfixed by the sight of this impregnable fortress, the devastation of the forest of krael trees.

Why hadn't these last trees been felled, too? The answer seemed obvious: why bother with the few trees on that second islet beyond the first? They weren't worth the effort when there had been more than enough on the shore.

Krael trees?

There was only one way to find out.

Falca couldn't waste precious time going back down to tell Gurrus. Once he was down on the shore, two would be more easily noticed than one. He'd taken a dagger with him to cut away vines, though not a sword; Gurrus had said that if they encountered Kalaleks on the track all would be lost anyway, and that remained the case with Wardens below.

The track led around the bluff to the path from the Road Gurrus and his father had taken long ago, and then down to the shore and the ruined bridge of kraken bones. Falca had seen the scar of that path meandering through the field of stumps.

Cassena and Suaila were on the rise, their ribbons as yet faint upon the lake. Only a few evening stars were out. The rest appeared as fallen constellations: in the castlet torches and camp fires below; in the lanterns strung along the bridge, and the distant pinpoints of torch light at the castle's gates, wall-walks and towers.

The track wound along the bluff, a gray trail obscured here and there by dark knolls and thickets of bushes. Falca wanted to run but dared not. A twisted ankle, a wrenched knee, could mean Ossa's death—if he wasn't dead already.

"Not yet, old man," Falca whispered, "not yet."

HE LOOKED DOWN at the lake to see where the old bridge ended at the shoreline. Despite the darkness, the broken stitching of the bridge gleamed white, bright as the sheen of the moon ribbons that flanked it. Thanks to the Sisters, he found the pathway down, its presence more fully revealed by the absence of stumps. He missed the gulch where the path had been eroded by rains, and fell hard. Luckily, he only scraped his hands, bruised an elbow. He took it more carefully after that.

There had been a landing of some sort, now overgrown. Something scuttled out behind the far end, startling him. It hissed and scurried away. He took a deep breath, went on.

The forest had once reached the edge of the lake's bank, and as he walked quickly along the shoreline he pushed away decaying roots. Where the bank sloughed away he waded through the shallows as silently as he could to avoid splashing. The wind had picked up enough for whispers of lapping water.

Falca couldn't see much above the bank at this point, but he knew he was near the stockade of Limbs. There had to be thousands of them crammed into a huge pen not much bigger than Lop's krannog, the stench so bad he had to breathe through his mouth.

He crept close enough to the stockade to hear moaning, whimpering, scufflings, a piercing cry—and moved on. Then: a creak of stiff leather. Someone cleared his throat and spat.

Falca knelt behind the bank, looked over, then peeked around a stump.

Two Wardens.

"…Scaldy's done, so why're they still here, s'all I'm sayin'. All the bitch needs is a few every day for'r pet, which she oughter have better things to do, being…"

"Watch yer mouth."

"Who's ta hear? *Them*? All I'm sayin' is I'm sick of the stink and…"

"It *ain't* done, you dolt. Leaseways the bridge and barty, and then there's the work by the river which ain't even…"

"I know that! All I'm sayin' is we don't need so many of 'em here."

"Get used to it. There'll be a ketch for 'em there too. Word is that us'n the First'll be quartered by the river when it's done."

"Roak's balls."

"Yah, but when it's done, we'll be the ones to put the torch to it when we don't need the mottles no longer."

"I 'spose that makes sense—how else you get rid of that many? But where'd you hear it?

"The talk was Blue-gums—careful! It's got hands out."

"They keep tryin' to climb up."

"It's what they do, ya snotwipe. Crack 'em back! Why else're we out here?"

Ahead, Falca could see the corner of the castlet close—too close—to the shore. The islets were dark humps in the lake, faintly silhouetted by the distant light of the castle and bridge—and farther out than he'd thought.

Since he couldn't swim he needed something to help him float, and saw nothing around big enough. Then he remembered the piles of timber. He hadn't passed them so they must be ahead…and closer to the castlet and that tower.

He moved on, keeping low.

Torches flanked the guards at the gate. A couple of groods were filling a cart with wood from a huge pile of timber. The *thunk-thunk* of the loading ceased abruptly with a curse as some of the pieces tumbled off.

Falca kept an eye on the patrolling guards who were now by the low entrance to the Limb stockade, talking to the sentries.

When the Wardens at the pile were finally done with their loading they each took a rail to pull the creaking cart. The castlet guards opened the gate for them.

The pile of wood lay between the lake-side corners of the Limb stockade and the castlet's guard tower. This was not that high, yet the sentry within—Falca could discern the paleness of his hands on the timbered embrasure—would be certain to see him carrying a large piece of wood from the pile to the water if he happened to look in that direction.

Falca waited until those hands disappeared, then slid around the stump and crawled to the woodpile, now shielding him from the guard tower. If a shout came, the alarm would end it all here.

Moments passed.

The sentry hadn't seen him, but his presence near the stockade had roused Limbs on that side. Falca couldn't understand what they were saying; he didn't have to. Dozens of arms poked through narrow gaps in the palisade, reaching for him, voices pleading for…food? Water? A weapon? Everything he couldn't give them now. All they sensed was that he wasn't a Warden.

The commotion flared loudly enough to attract the attention of not only the guards stationed by the castlet gate but also the tower's sentry. One of the castlet guards was joined by another with a torch—from the stockade?—and they went over to check out the disturbance. Falca pressed himself against the pile of wood. His hands slid over a cut branch he could use for a weapon.

If the Wardens came around they'd find him, and if they did there was but one thing to do: take this branch and bolt for the stockade entrance. There might be time to unbar the gate and free some Limbs, maybe snatch a stagger in the confusion and keep the gate open. Not all the Limbs might escape before the alarm brought reinforcements from the castlet, but enough would. He couldn't be among them. More likely he'd be dead; either way he wouldn't let Wardens pursue him back to Gurrus and the others.

The groods were on the other side, cursing and shouting at their captives, pounding at the timbers with the flat of their staggers to the cries of Limbs who hadn't jerked back their arms quickly enough. The flickering, bobbing torch stayed on the other side of the pile though the light spilled over, revealing motes of insects in the air. The Wardens were looking for breaches in the stockade, high and low. Finding none they left, their steps and grumbling receding. The torch light faded.

The logs had all been shorn of branches, sawed to varying sizes, some longer than Falca was tall, some shorter. A few of the thicker ones had been split lengthwise. No longer needed for construction, this was now firewood for the castlets. The timber had to have been taken from the forest, but Falca smelled nothing of Gurrus' promised scents, perhaps because the wood had not been recently cut. Still, shouldn't there have been some faint residue left? Had Gurrus been wrong about this, his memory corroded by all the years since he'd been here?

Falca carefully pulled back a log that seemed big enough to keep him afloat, yet wouldn't be too heavy to carry to the lake. Still hidden, he lowered the near end, gauging the heft of it, then carried it to the edge of the pile, pausing only to look up at the castlet tower. He didn't see the sentry now but that meant nothing for the crucial moments ahead. All it would take was a step or two, then a sideways glance.

There seemed to be nothing between him and the water that might trip him, cause him to lose the log with a thud that could be heard. He took a deep breath and went for it, carrying the log so his back faced the tower. He was almost to the water when his right foot slipped on flat stone. He staggered to one side before regaining his balance. Had he been carrying the log on his shoulder instead of at waist level he might have dropped it.

He waded into water so cold it caught his breath…and went on, deeper and deeper until the shoreline fell away from his feet. He draped his left arm over the log at its midpoint, paddling with his other hand. At first he didn't seem to be making any progress, even with vigorous kicking. Yet slowly he made his way toward the nearer, barren islet. Its jagged outcrops soon shielded him from view of the tower.

In this cold water the effort of advancing both the log and his own sodden weight soon began to sap his strength, numbing his body more quickly than he expected. He had to quell the fear of slipping away and drowning. It didn't help to realize that if the wooded islet had been farther away he would not have made it.

The log bumped against rock. He slid his hands toward the blessed end of it, careful not to let go. There'd be no way back if the log drifted off. With one hand on a branch nub of the log, the other clawing at rock, he crawled ahead and swung around to sit in front of the log's end and pulled back. The log caught—not enough. He lifted it a bit, pulled again, then scrunched back, got to his knees and hauled one last time to get the log far enough out of the water so it wouldn't float away.

He was exhausted, chilled and soaked.

But the air carried the scent of cinnamon and elixith.

✵

THE TREES HAD somehow found purchase in a wide crevice that calved the islet almost in half save for a rocky promontory facing the shore. Falca slipped on a moss-covered rock, fell into a foul manger of rotting leaves and brambles that raked his face and hands. He got up, gingerly yanking thorny tendrils snarled in his hair, thinking that the gloves he'd once worn in Draica would have served him well in this place.

The nearest tree loomed overhead, branches and foliage blotting out stars, scarring one of the Sister moons. The trunk twisted away from the Isle toward the shore; the leaves of yellow-flowering vines snaked around, constricting it in thick, spiraling lacing. Nearer the base of the tree the vines were big around as his arm. Higher, where they thinned and tapered off, there seemed to be no flowers.

The smell of cinnamon and elixith was more pungent now. Did the flowering vines release the scent? He brushed his hand over the leaves—a soft rustling—then skimmed some off with the dagger, exposing bulging twists, some overlapping others.

He needed a sure way to climb up, or he'd slip and fall. He couldn't pull the vines away from the tree so he used the dagger as a lever. Now, he could yank them out far enough to get his hand under and around the vines, to use as a crude rope when he couldn't grab a branch.

He tried a few to see if they would hold his weight.

They did.

He made his way up, mouthing the dagger until he needed it to loosen a vine. According to what he'd seen on the kinnet, the krael would be found above the vines, which began to get smaller, the leaves thinner and scarcer. His handholds became easier to fashion—and also more tenuous.

If he kept going he would risk falling away with nothing to grip except the living rope he'd ripped from the tree. He had no choice. So far he'd felt nothing unusual, none of the hard scaling that might be the krael. But he thought he could see it, ever so faintly above: a russet discoloration on the trunk, a splotchy lightening between the withered white leaves of vines.

So that was it: traps-and-squeezes.

The tree suffered from that, too.

If not stopped, the vines would eventually wrap the tree in a living, suffocating web.

So the tree was producing the krael, killing the higher vines, anyway, before they could entirely cover the host.

No vines, no krael.

Falca wasn't close enough yet; he had to keep climbing, take the risk that the krael he'd come for might kill him, too.

He almost plummeted when a vine pulled away in his hand. He quickly grabbed another and this one held fast. He could see the krael more clearly now, the ochre scaling just beyond his reach, encircling the trunk. The white leaves crumbled away when his wrist brushed them, fluttering down like snowflakes.

He needed one hand to get the krael and drop it into the soggy pouch at his belt, but he also needed the dagger.

He stretched, took another step, pushing up from the vine where his right foot was wedged. He felt it giving way. He had to get the krael now…and took the dagger from his mouth with his right hand. With his knuckles he felt the lapping scales, and slipped the dagger point underneath, prising a chunk off, trapping it with his thumb. Lifting up the flap with his wrist, he dropped the krael into the pouch.

He lost another piece to this awkward process, hearing it rustle through the vine leaves as it fell. But he got more—until his foothold gave way. He slid down, his only hope now the vine he still gripped with his left hand. If that pulled away…

It did.

Dropping the knife he grabbed another vine he'd loosened on his way up, clawing with his fingers.

This one held. His foot caught another, at a knot where it had grown over a thicker vine, and that stopped him.

On his way down he fought the urge to hurry now that he had the krael. Eagerness to get back could cause a misstep and while that might not be fatal to him, it would be for Ossa. The krael could slide out from his safekeep, never to be recovered in the crevice and undergrowth below. Falca might never survive a second climb up this tree or one of the others to get more. He'd been lucky. The High Fates had either not been paying attention or they'd been in a generous mood.

He was just as careful getting back to the log. He took off the pouch, and clamped down hard on it with his teeth. There was no other place for it, unless he wanted to have the lake water make a soup of the krael. The safekeep hung from his mouth like the bird Harro Scapp's dog retrieved that day on the Moat.

He pushed the log in the water, draped his left arm over, used his right hand to paddle as he kicked ahead. The bottom of the pouch rested on the log, but he kept it tightly in his mouth. He was a dog; he'd always been a dog, and this was one bird he wasn't going to lose in the water.

As he passed by the smaller islet he saw the two groods, silhouetted by torches, back at work piling more timbers into the cart. He steered the log away from them, heading to a point farther up the shoreline, kept looking at the stockade for Wardens patrolling the perimeter. He still hadn't seen them by the time he reached the bank, water sluicing off him, a pitiful water-logged beast rising from the lake—what had Gurrus called the other? He couldn't remember.

He dropped the pouch from his aching mouth, felt his teeth marks in the leather as he put it back on his sodden belt. His chasers squelched. His legs were too tired for a run as yet, but that was just as well.

To his left, at a distance, the stockade was silent. Sentries appeared. He ducked down behind the nearest stump. Waiting for them to turn the corner and move away, he thought about later hiding behind the stumps and ambushing two groods making their rounds, and taking one of their ruerains, hooded mantlets and staggers. However ill-fitting, the disguise would only have to last long enough to overcome the guards at the stockade entrance, open it, toss staggers to the Limbs. Many would choose to flee, but enough would stay to fight the Wardens. Without weapons it would be slaughter, but a few Limbs might escape, to tell the story of this night. That would have to be enough.

Maybe Ossa could help him, if he got back in time.

Raleva would have to find her own way back home—a dangerous journey without companions. Still, a young woman of such skill with a bow wouldn't be easy prey.

And if Ossa was already dead? Falca would have to go it alone. He wasn't going to turn his back on all these Timberlimbs more than once.

He'd come to the Bounds with Amala to help them and that time had come. He had krael for Ossa, and maybe the Fates at their Loom Eternal might *still* have been in a generous enough mood to keep him alive until Falca got back to give it to him.

Amala was gone, but in a way she'd be with him when he freed the Limbs in that stockade. And then, if he lived, he had to figure out a way to get close enough Maldan Hoster and Tallon to kill them.

As he walked quickly along the shore, the moon ribbons on the lake seemed the closest he'd ever get to that field his father told him about.

Where tha ribbons a' tha full moons cross a field on a cloudless night, with the Silver Trail in the southern sky, there ye'll find riches, boy...and look sharp because there's but a single night o' the year it happens...

Well, the night was cloudless, the lake could have been a vast field, and the Silver Trail was there in the southern sky.

Suddenly, he thought of a way to get within the walls of the castle, perhaps close enough to kill either Tallon or Maldan Hoster, if not both; and keep the promise he'd made to himself—and Amala—every night since the falls.

He fingered the flenx horn.

But that was only part of it.

There was other treasure besides the riches his father promised he'd find if he looked sharp, something far beyond Falca's wildest dreams when he was stealing fruit from Poash and money from Timberlimb scrapemongers.

Gurrus might call it a fanciful dream, not a vision. He might say he couldn't possibly do what was necessary. Still, he was a mehka, whose life and been shadowed by a single theft a long time ago. And the one to come—if they could do it—would surely make Gurrus believe that he'd been destined to steal the kinnet all along.

Chapter Thirty-Five:

RALEVA

FEIGNING SLEEP, Raleva had heard them leave at dawn, felt the hand on her shoulder—Falca's or Ossa's, she couldn't tell—but there was no rousing to it. She was sitting up now, staring up the slope to the bluff, wondering how they could see the track with the mist rising so thickly off the lake below.

Gurrus said the night before that no mehka had ever attempted a feat of such magnitude, and if he was to try it would be best to leave at dawn and wait as close to the pen of Kelvoi as possible. In all that was discussed of Falca's plan on the bluff, after Ossa felt well enough to go up and see the castle for himself, there'd been no talk of her joining them. She couldn't look at him, not with those eyes, when he told her he was sorry they could not go with her, but there was nothing to be done about it. She'd been relieved because she was afraid of his eyes that seemed feral as a beast's in the dark.

Gurrus may have sensed her fear when he reminded her again that the eyes came with the healing and would not last. That brought her a wave of shame that crested later with Ossa's fatherly embrace, and his thanking her for all she'd done helping him get to this place—which she knew without a doubt would kill him before those golden eyes faded.

She didn't know why she pretended to be asleep when they left. Was it the habit of pretense she'd found necessary with Lop? That had been a matter of survival, but with these men? From what was she hiding? Saying farewell to companions who'd saved her life, who would be dead by nightfall? Or Ossa's golden eyes?

The night before they'd lit a small fire behind a boulder, and she'd busied herself fletching the last of the arrows she'd made as they talked about Falca's plan. Occasionally she glanced furtively at Ossa, still astonished at his transformation: the scars were gone from his forehead and cheeks; the blackened, festering hands clear. It was like seeing a different man. Her father had scars, the most prominent a sickle shape on his right forearm. It seemed strange to her that she never knew how he'd gotten it, yet she knew how Ossa had gotten his.

Maybe she'd pretended to be asleep for another reason, the way she'd once faked being sick so she would not have to leave the loft she shared with her brother, Beclan, when her mother's sister arrived for the yearly visit with her brood. Raleva was expected to entertain cousins she detested, who always teased her about her mismatched eyes. Was it so simple as merely not wanting to do something she did not want to do? Because if she'd gotten up with her friends she might have been tempted to go with them.

No, it couldn't be that. Falca and Ossa—and Gurrus, too—didn't expect her to stay and wouldn't have let her even if she wanted to join them down there.

What she wanted was to go home.

And she had to get herself up now and…go.

She went over yet again what she had to do: walk south to the river, find a safe place for the night, then head west until she came to the ford. No, best to head west a bit before going to the river. She'd seen the boats that supported the bridge to the Isle and castle—Falca said he'd heard groods call it…Scaldy-something—and they had to have come from somewhere, bringing in Wardens and supplies over time.

Falca estimated 4,000 of them down there, so likely the Wardens' road to the river ended with some outpost, a waystation for the route to the quarry that should be avoided at all costs. She could find the ford again. She, Bofor and the others had marked it, so they could find it again. They did the same for the trail that led to the pass south through the mountains. From there it was only six days to the Roan.

Raleva got up, and saw that they hadn't taken the waterskins and the leather sack they'd taken from Lop's hall—evidence they didn't expect to be back. But she didn't remember anyone leaving the sack by her bow and quiver. The 'skins were mostly empty. Well, she could fill one or two in the lake where Gurrus immersed the kinnet. When she opened the sack she found that they'd left more than what little remained of the food.

The flat chunk of russet krael fit into the palm of her hand. Falca must have slipped it in while she'd been sleeping: a farewell gift should she need it on her way back home. Now she knew why Gurrus had made the point of reminding her—as if she hadn't seen herself—of how finely the krael had to be worked to mix with water so nothing would lodge in the throat, and how Gurrus and Falca said the krael must be kept a secret, for her own safety.

She lifted out the other thing Falca had left. No, not left—given to her. He knew she'd find it.

She'd seen him take it out to hold, once before his sharpening of blades and once after. A habit twice-seen could be called a ritual. She knew the name of Falca's woman, that the Wardens had killed her not long after she, Falca, Ossa and Gurrus had entered the Bounds.

She sank back down, numbed by the gifts. Why the swan's-wing brooch? The answer was obvious: he'd rather she have it than some Warden who looted his body after the killing, and tossed away a common, worthless bauble, so paltry compared to the sunstone pendant her mother had given her that terrible day, telling her not to cry because *they* might hear her. Raleva did anyway, stuffing fingers in her mouth and biting hard…

Dawn now; twilight then—was there so much difference in the shadows they cast?

THE KESHKAN BRIGANDS came that terrible day at twilight, but it was found out later that only seven of the eighteen were Keshkan, the rest Myrcians from Riian. There was time only for Larella Barra to hush and hurry her thirteen year-old daughter and ten year-old son to the springhouse built into a low hill opposite the Barras' stead, and tell them to hide in the lower level at the rear of the cellar, beneath the trap door where it was cold enough to keep blocks of river ice year round. The last thing her mother did before leaving to help her husband was give Raleva the pendant. She knew what would likely happen to her, for outside there was only her husband, Lodan, and three of his stead-men to fight the eighteen.

Peeking through a crack in the low springhouse door, Raleva saw how her father tried to draw them away and he did—but not all of them. Five stayed by the stead, including one who had only a thumb and forefinger on his left hand. He hit her mother's head twice with the swing her father had made the year before, to knock the fight from her. He raped her. Then he cut her throat.

They took time ransacking the stead. They killed the wounded, including two of their own, and dragged all the dead to her home, then set it afire. They never did search the springhouse before riding off.

It took Raleva and Beclan three days to get back to Ketys, where her grandparents lived, though the food she took from the springhouse lasted only two. She and her brother could have gotten there sooner, but after passing the charred remains of two other steads—the Votadins' and Dariems'—she was too fearful of stopping at any other to ask for help.

Her grandfather Lukan and grandmother Rui summoned their two other sons and forty other steaders to join them in tracking down the raiders. Her famous grandfather could have gathered twenty times that number if there had been time for that.

They caught up to the outlaws at Dirlbridge, near Castle Rising, killing all—except for the one missing the fingers on his left hand. Before he died, the renegades' leader divulged his name: Semett Crute. Said he'd had a falling out with the man after the raid. Crute was last seen heading north toward the mountains and presumably the sanctuary of the Rough Bounds.

They didn't pursue him. They were far from their steads, their harvests were nigh. Some of the men were wounded, including her grandfather. Seven had been killed.

The resolution wasn't enough for Raleva. She remained haunted by the terror of that day and her helplessness. She wished she'd never looked through that crack in the springhouse door. She always wore her mother's pendant, a wedding gift from her father, and dreamed of someday going after Semett Crute. Knowing how slimmer the chances became with each passing year of finding the man still alive, she was impatient with hers.

Her grandparents cared for her and Beclan at their home bordering the long lake with the ruins of a manor on a bell-shaped island.

She asked her grandmother, who was still fond of hunting with her bow in the forests, to teach her how to use it. Rui agreed. But only when Raleva learned that patience was the better part of the aim did she become proficient; as good if not better than her grandmother. It was a variation of that lesson that may have helped her survive the nightmare of the krannog.

She shared her dream with her brother, whom she loved dearly. Yet she knew it would be up to her. Beclan was a sweet, delicate boy, fond of sketching. He was also prone to fits of uncontrollable shivering, especially in the summer.

Though Raleva's dream ebbed at times as her years became crowded, she never let it go—not even when the handsome young man, whom her friends thought was such a good match, asked her to marry him. Her assent came with a condition.

Bofor Critting, son of the wealthiest landowner between Stagfall and Ketys, knew what it was and quickly—too quickly as it turned out—agreed to go with her to the Rough Bounds; he and four of his more restless, adventurous friends. She left without telling her grandparents, but why should she? She was almost twenty, a woman now who could make her own decisions.

At a crossroads village south of the pass through The Reeks, Bofor got drunk and would have made a greater fool of himself with the daughter of the innkeeper had his friends not interceded. Raleva was furious with him and went on alone the next morning. Bofor and his friends caught up to her. She hadn't known it before but his charms extended to contrition and apology.

Three weeks later, he and his four friends were dead, and Lop was pushing her up the steps with his gavilor to the byre he called his manor.

RALEVA WANTED SO much to go home now to her brother and grandparents. Lukan and Rui were the kind of people you could talk to and know that as soon as you left they wouldn't be dishing out what you'd confided on someone else's plate.

They wouldn't waste time reminding her what a terrible way it had been to find out that Bofor wouldn't have made a good husband; that she'd been foolish to think she could find—in the vastness of the Bounds, with youths as young as she—the man who raped and murdered her mother, and kill him. Nor would they try to lessen the responsibility she felt for Bofor's death and those of his friends. The vow of vengeance had been hers, not theirs.

What was done was done, they would say. All you could do was move on—with a heavier load, yes. But hopefully that would help you choose a better direction to take.

Her grandfather once told her there was a choice that was the most crucial a man or woman could make, but one that was often overlooked or ignored among all the others on the shelf.

"Some make the choice early in life," he said, "some later; some without realizing they'd done so, and some never at all."

"I'm not good at riddles, Granda," she said.

He wouldn't tell her, nor would her grandmother. All Granda Lukie said was something about an answer always being better if you thought of it yourself.

She walked up to the bluff wanting to see in the early morning light what she couldn't the night before. It was hopeless, of course; that certainty hadn't changed for them and all those Timberlimbs down there in the stockade, a ketch Ossa called it. How could it not be hopeless, with all those thousands of Wardens so close by—and that castle?

She'd never seen Falls Keep in Castlecliff, but Ossa said the fortress on the Isle was easily its rival. Falca's plan seemed as foolish as…going off to hunt for Semett Crute in the wilderness of the Rough Bounds.

Yet…but for this height and the scabbed land girdling the lake, this place was not so different than where she'd spent much of her life. There were mountains in the distance. And hadn't she always imagined more than ruins on the isle of that lake by her grandparents' home?

She saw him below, a lone figure on the road leading from the south and the river. The sun had barely risen over the mountains. The mist off the lake wreathed much of the castle and shore, so it was hard to tell at this distance… but she knew it was Falca below, carrying, as he'd said, no weapon except for the hidden flenx horns around his neck. He hadn't told her why he had them but Gurrus had, their first night away from the fens.

Who else but Falca would be approaching the lake and the unfinished bridge to the castle? Not a Warden; not a quarryman, carpenter or mason early on the rise.

She hadn't believed him when he said: "It's just fisting groods this time, not Limbs; that's all."

She remembered Ossa shaking his head, rubbing his forehead, as if unsure the scars were gone.

"That's all? Falca, you may as well try to steal the Sanctor's Azure Tower, or your Cross Keys in Draica."

"True enough. But if 20,000 men couldn't take that place, what chance would you give Culldred's 4000? Better one to close the door before pissing in the pot. I'll need a little help, though."

Raleva hurried down to gather wood for a fire. She'd need this…flessok and she hoped she'd have time to collect enough. At least she had the arrows: fifteen without fletching, the points shaved and hardened with flame, yet the shafts were straight enough. They wouldn't be very accurate; she'd made them for use with small game. But they'd have range enough, and with the broad target she had in mind accuracy wouldn't be necessary. She would cut off the point and make a slit to snare the flessok.

In addition to the arrows she had left from the krannog, she'd given much more time making seven better ones, with fletching cut from feathers of a lake fowl she shot for dinner one night. She'd culled and fashioned the arrowheads from shaling stones along the shore, then tightly bound both heads and fletching with coarse thread she pulled from the frayed hem of her sark.

She made these arrows for the bigger game she expected to encounter on her way home—and there would certainly be enough of that when she went down to join Ossa, Gurrus and Styada after she used the cruder shafts.

She'd use them all even if Gurrus wasn't successful. She hadn't known it when her grandmother gave her the bow, but this was what all those seven years of instruction had been for. Her only regret now was that she would never be able to tell her grandparents that she'd solved the riddle. Then again, that wasn't something you'd boast about or display; a prize won at a fair. And maybe that was something they hadn't told her, either.

All that mattered was that she'd know it.

Chapter Thirty-Six:

HERESA'S BANNERS

SITTING STRAIGHT-backed on the padded window ledge, Heresa Hoster watched the five Cruthin women. They were stitching the last design on the banners, pausing occasionally to mask a yawn or exchange covert glances about the faint, persistent moans coming from a nearby room, and no doubt wondering why the Lady Heresa kept a vigil here and not there.

Perhaps they were also wondering why she had summoned them again from their village to the north along the awe to embroider such an unusual addition to the banners they thought they'd finished two weeks before in the great hall below.

Heresa didn't care they'd had to make the journey for only a few hours' work. They were lucky she was paying them anything at all.

She'd been surprised at the quality of the work, considering who they were—wives and daughters of farmers and fishermen exiled to a remote land where only mottles lived. But to make sure their renderings were consistent for this final detail, she'd placed her most precious possession on a low stand, over a square of pressed black linen.

Circina, the youngest and prettiest of the women, had proven to be the most skilled with needle and thread, and so Heresa had given her the largest flag to work on. Unlike the others, Circina didn't have to keep glancing at the stand. It was as if a single look had been enough for her fingers to obey the image in her mind.

That large banner, three times the size of the other four, would remain at Scaldasaig. The prossars would take the rest within a fortnight when they marched south into Myrcia for the campaign that would replenish the Hoster coffers, and quiet any grumbling among the men about tardy pay and few women.

More banners would eventually be needed, but five would suffice for now: one each for the thousand-man prossars, and the biggest to fly above the eight-sided keep the master-mason, Furka Vat, insisted on calling a turris in the Gebroanan fashion.

This chamber on the floor directly below its battlements was supposed to have been Cossum's. Heresa had chosen it for the nearness to her own, if not her husband's, so she could easily visit him and talk—how she'd missed that over the last five years; and for the two windows that lured the best of the morning light. The chamber also had the best views of the lake, awe and mountains. The rooms for Maldan and Lannid were smaller, each having only one window that looked out to the inner ward and the castle itself.

Heresa couldn't take her eyes off Circina's graceful hands.

She'd thought, briefly, to sew the banners herself. Hadn't she overseen everything else here in her husband's absence? But the years had leached the suppleness from her fingers, if not the memory of the touch she'd once had for the needle.

Her older sister had ridiculed, then ruined her first efforts at sewing, deliberately spilling red wine on the chemise of whisp, and giving the silk evening shawl to the cat to shred. Her mother, far from punishing Lalla, forbade Heresa the budding avocation as unseemly for one of her station, who could ill-afford an eccentric display of common work. "Your bosom and violet eyes may well be bait for a suitor, 'Resa, but the thinness of your smile and sour demeanor are not. Look to your sister as your model if you would dream of curtains of spun glass for your home."

And Heresa did just that one night while her sister slept, managing to pierce both of Lalla's full lips with a needle as she woke up screaming.

If only her mother were here now, to see the banners her younger daughter had personally designed if not stitched. Would she be aghast at the budding avocation of treason the banners represented and consider that unseemly for one of her station? Or would she smile approvingly at the common work of betrayal?

The banners, of course, were not colorful bunting to be displayed on special occasions. Something had to replace the royal standard of Lucidor and its marshfang crest. After all, she and Culldred, soon to be marked as traitors if not already, couldn't very well keep displaying the pride of Cross Keys.

Heresa chose fields of light blue, green, and dark blue. Against each, respectively: a majestic great-winged bird the disgusting mottles called a floka; the Wardens' black stagger; and the lake-beast—what Heresa thought it looked like, anyway—that was now penned in the inlet below a southeast tower she'd just named after Cossum.

Culldred had approved the design, devices and colors shortly after his arrival. The choice of green was for the Wardens, of course, and also for the Bounds and fertile provinces of central Myrcia and northern Keshkevar that would in time be the breadbasket of the Hosters' Seventh Kingdom. The dark blue represented the seas, northern and southern, that would be hers as well—if she lived long enough. The light blue was the color of the sky, arching over all.

Culldred quibbled with her choice of the lake-beast, but grudgingly gave his nod after she told him its fierceness had caused the deaths of five men during the capture, never mind those all the Limbs sacrificed to lure it to the pen. He liked the floka most of all. She'd gotten a real one for him as a welcoming gift.

Before his arrival she'd sent Wardens and a few Cruthin men out capture a fledging. Not all the men returned. Some of those who did were now of little use even in the kitchens, garden and orchards.

Years before, when Culldred would return from a campaign in the Bounds—back when he wasn't obsessed with his scribbling, when he would at least occasionally come to her chamber without her having to ask—he would speak with amazement at the flokas he'd seen: graceful in flight, intelligent, powerful.

Well, he had one now, in a specially constructed aviary: a useful pet indeed for Heresa to suggest to his medicant the reason for his sudden sickness, since Kubelai could think of no other.

Oh, it was terrible…terrible. But what could she have done when the Allarch insisted on feeding the bird himself, and had gotten gashed by the talons—or had the fledgling beaked him? Who could have known the creature he so admired carried such a mysterious disease?

A difficult bird, to be sure, but a Cruthin hawker had assured Heresa it would eventually take to training, giving her confidence in her idea that perhaps more flokas could be captured and used in various ways for later campaigns.

She was even more pleased with her other pet. How very fitting for her to have such a thing that had never been wholly seen, yet could thus be deliciously imagined; a creature that lurked below, as powerful in its element as flokas were in theirs…

Heresa got up stiffly—wincing, pursing her lips—and made a slow circuit around the women to check their progress. Her hand lingered only on Circina's shoulder. Satisfied the seamstresses were well along, she didn't bother to ask if they needed the tiny model any longer; certainly Circina didn't. Heresa wanted it back in her hand.

Back at the window, the heft of it only made her wish Cossum was with her now, looking out at the lake; or perhaps outside on the bordering allure, the wind gently rustling his green and black checkered cape. She thought she could hear the water lapping against the turris' batter a hundred feet below, but that was only her imagination, of course.

She glanced at the women. By now Cossum might already have basted Circina, slaking her on the very banner she'd stitched so well; basted them all except for the toothless old one, whose wrinkles marred the neck markings the Cruthin favored.

If there had been any doubt about what she had to do about her husband it vanished with the news of Cossum's death. That was Culldred's fault, and she had to summon all her skill to feign grief as she sat by his bedside in those first hours after he was stricken, reading over the last entries of the book she'd found hidden away in his campaign chest.

She'd taken great pleasure in confirming what she'd suspected: Culldred planned to replace her now that she'd served her purpose here. And pride that she'd played her part so well via the gliffed messages carried back by the Red Hands.

And there was satisfaction that he wouldn't be siring any more offspring with a younger woman now. Of course, she wouldn't be delivering any, either; she was past her time for that. Still, she worried. Now that Cossum was gone, from whose seed would her grandchildren come? Who would inherit her dreams? Whores and captives aside, there would likely be few takers for Maldan and Lannid, for different reasons.

What woman would have the patience for Lannid's clumsiness, or tolerate the books that were his true passion?

Maldan's wound would heal to scar, but still remain more disfigurement than titillation for some daughter of a subjugated Myrcian or Keshkan lord, who would forever cringe with embarrassment at his slurred speech.

Heresa once had hopes for Bovik, though even back in Bastia she'd suspected he preferred the company of soldiers beyond the kinship of a campaign; a suspicion Culldred shared, as the book revealed.

Still, one way or another, it would be up to Maldan and Lannid.

Cossum, the one she wanted most to share her dream, would see none of it. And it had been hers, as much as her husband's, though he arrived to take possession of it as if he'd been the one, not her, who had endured five years of constant attention to Scaldasaig's progress: living in drafty temporary quarters; suffering the noise and filth of construction and the stink of the mottle slaves; settling disputes; insisting on changes; and avoiding the leers of Furka Vat and the sight of the wen he constantly rubbed, as if he was trying to conjure magic from an amulet.

Ten years ago a small detachment of Wardens, lost in the Bounds, discovered the lake and isle, with its meadow and rocky eastern slopes that rose to a prominence adorned only by a scattering of buildings so unlike the usual mottle villages high in the trees.

Upon their return, Culldred didn't immediately see the possibilities, though he should have, coming from a line of Wardens that went back generations, the last a disgraced Allarch. Never mind he was the bastard son, sold in a squealer's basket by his mother to the small edificia at Crinnan, in the foothills of Mt. Scaldasaig, with only his dead father's stolen sceptre to mark his Warden provenance and fetch a better price.

But Heresa saw the potential of that discovery of the mottles' isle.

She saw something much grander than the match her sister made by marrying into a family with close connections to one of the same scheming Regents who had deposed—by way of a shadden—their own father, seneschal to Extarr, the late and unloved king of Lucidor.

Heresa's dear mother—who seemed to schedule the family outrage over her husband's assassination as she might a tutor for her daughters' lessons—had once told her to look to her sister as an example.

And so she had, after seeing how useful betrayal could be.

Convincing her new husband, soon to be stationed in Bastia, was the easiest part; that and helping him advance, step by step, toward the Allarch's sceptre they both craved.

The money came from few sources at first, then many: the surly trades, including blackmail; sale of Limb skins; payoffs in markets for dawnstone and young swallows—many of them for the Vasper, who was particularly fond of dark hair; skimming of proceeds from various royal mines south of Bastia; the doubling of traffs in the Banishlands. Disguising Wardens as brigands to rob royal tax stages had been lucrative until Cross Keys added more guards. Lastly, there was the sale of the lake island, galley and estate, among several others which Culldred had claimed by default from the owners, citing charges of collusion with Myrcian agents—a well that never seemed to run dry.

By the time of Heresa's 'disappearance'—someone Culldred could trust had to be at this isle—Warden procurers had discreetly hired over one hundred skilled artisans from Slacere, Nostoy, Virenz and Draica, of course, as well as Castlecliff in Myrcia. The man the Hosters chose to design and build Scaldasaig, a master-mason and architect named Furka Vat, found a hundred more quarriers, stone-masons, mortar-makers, carpenters and smiths. Culldred knew where to find enough Limbs for the laboring and hauling.

Vat was either Keshkan, Gebroanan or Skarrian by birth; no one knew for certain. Whatever the murkiness of his past, it was known he had designed and built the fortifications at the terminus of the great aqueduct at Sandsend, and Bucca Crag castle overlooking the straits west of the Shelter Isles, as well as the Anaktora citadel in Attallissia, whose rebel lords had held out against a Keshkev siege for over a year until treachery alone proved their undoing.

Vat had also picked the losing side in a border dispute between Gebroan and Keshkevar. He fled to Castlecliff where, for reasons he had never fully explained, he had to abruptly leave for Draica. His seeming eagerness in accepting the challenges of building Scaldasaig had given the Hosters the impression that another departure was imminent: the man, a genius in building formidable castles, was running out of kingdoms and patrons to hire him. Yet brilliant he was, and the Hosters were pleased to get his talents for a price much less than they expected.

Culldred had been ecstatic with the results. "The little man has saved his best for last. You've done well, Heresa." He said it almost affectionately, the fool, as if she'd done what she had out of any wellspring of love. Though he shared his general plans for Scaldasaig, he kept other plans as hidden as she did hers. They made a pair all right, so much alike—which, of course, extended to sharing the same conclusion: that the other was no longer necessary for the dream of a Seventh Kingdom.

All that remained was to finish the causeway, barbican and the whitewashing of the walls. The mottles would be kept here until the work was done. Then, all but a thousand would be killed, those being needed as future feed for her kraken pet, and to work on the river stronghold which Lannid could take to completion as well as the beacon towers. Vat already had prepared the plans. That bastion controlling the river would be the first line of defense against any attack from the south and west.

After the master-mason was dead and their previous payments to him taken back, Lannid could design another fortress built to the north, where the Cruthin had their village and crude hall made from timbers of the two ships that had brought them and their offensive beliefs from the coast of Riian years ago to exile on a remote shore.

And the precious gold that had been necessary for years now to purchase grain, livestock, ale for the men here, saplings for the orchard—and seamstresses—would be taken back, the Cruthins' disgusting idols smashed for rubble to fill in the fortress walls. Heresa would give the men a choice of death or soldiering; and Circina, at least, a choice none of the other women there could have. Heresa took care of her pets.

Scaldasaig, sited amidst the still mostly untapped wealth of the Bounds, would remain the first-cut jewel in the seventh crown. Eventually, Heresa would order a much-expanded Warden army to take Milatum in Keshkevar, thus adding access to the southern ocean as well as the northern, cutting the Six Kingdoms in two. From there, with forces ten—twenty—times what they had now, they could turn to the east and west under many more of these banners…"Patra Heresa?"

Heresa turned from the window. "Finished?"

Circina nodded for all of the women.

"Excellent," Heresa said, and thought of something else she had to decide upon soon. *Patra* would no longer suffice; *Sanctress* was much better. "Place the banners here where I was sitting so I may see them; then you may go. The steward has your due and will take you to the boat. You have men from the village waiting on the shore to escort you back?"

Circina nodded.

They filed by her, each holding a folded banner with the corner turned up so Heresa could inspect the work. The old woman's was the worst but she thanked her anyway; after all, the crone's sister had been very useful in fulfilling the private request Heresa had made earlier about obtaining certain poisons.

Circina was the last in line. To her alone Heresa nodded, whispering: "Yours pleases me most." She held the ring against what the young woman had done: a perfectly embroidered eye, the blue just as Heresa remembered, within the gold and emeralds of a ring.

"That…if I may ask, patra…"

"Of course, child."

"The ring…whose is it?"

"It was my son's…the dearest of my sons," she said. "Now he will be able to see all that I once wished him to see—from the keep here or wherever our soldiers take our cause." She clasped her hand, gently she thought, on Circina's shoulder, then brushed the back of her fingers against the thick dark curls of the young woman's hair. Heresa let the gesture linger too long, felt the flinching. She quickly drew away and Circina took that as a dismissal.

Heresa watched her at the door, smoothing her hair, wiping at her shoulder as if nursing a bruise, brushing away bird droppings. Or perhaps one of the Cruthin escorts was her lover, and she was only arranging herself for when she would soon see him, and gossip about the Lady who had insisted she and the others thoroughly wash their hands before embroidering eyes on banners.

Heresa sighed: such a pity, whatever it was. Such a simple gesture to decide Circina's fate when Wardens came to claim their miserable village for its men, women and Hoster gold paid to them for five years of services.

Certainly there would be even better seamstresses in Myrcia to fashion more banners and eyes for Cossum to bear witness to the dream he would never see. Perhaps she might attempt a lesser pennon, if she could find a healing balm for her hands.

She summoned Tolo and Fystos, her servants for this floor.

"Yesh, pa'Resha?" Tolo said, knuckling his brow.

"Are your hands clean?—show me, both of you."

They did.

"Good. Take these below, then," she said, pointing at the stacked banners. "All but the largest one. I shall personally deliver them to the castlets—a good thing, don't you agree, for the men to see their…Lady among them, and on horseback no less?"

Tolo nodded.

Heresa had become quite comfortable in the saddle over the past five years. "But first I must tend to my husband."

"Yesh, pa'Resha." He gave her another knuckle. "He wash ashkin orroo… bu' I int wanner 'rupoo ashz oo ishruked me."

"I know, I could hear him. You're considerate, dear Tolo, but he seems to have quieted now, which I fear could be a worsening."

The two servants followed her, each carrying two of the banners.

No, she didn't need Culldred for what was to come. Had Sephasia needed a husband to bring to a successful conclusion the war against stoneskin rebels, and the later annexation to Lucidor of an entire Helveylyn province west of Lake Verdul?

The basileii in the camps would respect her desire to inform them personally of the shocking news about Culldred. The meeting with the basileii scheduled for this afternoon in the hall would have to be postponed, but they'd understand her need to get back to her husband's side. The fount of their loyalty necessitated a show of her devotion to the Allarch. But she had to gauge their loyalty and if that was in the least suspect, she'd replace those basileii with men who owed their promotion to her, such as Lambrey Tallon. Once he'd successfully concluded the matter of Furka Vat, she would give him the gold cingulet of a basileus, with the understanding that he'd have to either share or get rid of his foundling whore. That would show an even hand to the rest of the Sixteen. It behooved her to have them in tow.

Women would be scarce for a while yet; when there wasn't enough to go around, morale could suffer—and that included her own. Tallon's woman was young, comely and tall. Heresa could abide one of the three, but not all.

Her thoughts returned to Circina. She supposed she could rise above the slight and be merciful to her. There was, behind her, clomping evidence of the loyalty and devotion that could result from mercy.

Dear Tolo…

Hadn't he long since grown accustomed to the wooden foot she'd had made to replace the one with which he was born? She couldn't order half a tongue and an ear to replace what he'd lost, of course, but he made do. All in all, those last two prunings were a merciful punishment for his indiscretion. She could have had him killed.

Dear loyal Tolo…

He'd been with her these five years now, and going on two now since his punishment. Only she could understand what he was saying. Then again, she was the only one who needed to.

✵

CULLDRED'S BEDCLOTHES WERE soaked with sweat. He shivered and twitched despite the draught Kubelai had given him to ease him into a moaning sleep.

The medicant took Heresa aside at the foot of the bed by the west window kept open for the cooling air. Maldan stood on one side of the bed, gently itching at the raw scar on his face; Lannid on the other, bending over, whispering something to his father.

"I don't know what else can be done for him, my Lady," Kubelai said. "I've given him a dose that helps reduce the severity of the wracks, but the potency is such it would kill him if given too frequently. Without it he convulses, claws at his belly, chest and neck, and tears away the dressings for the wounds. There is blood in his bile—this truly confounds me."

"As it does me. Yesterday he boasted to me about the block of causeway stone he lifted to urge the workers on; a warning he said, lest they find their heads over another one."

"That is our Allarch—the strength of two men. But I fear it will be some time before he lifts another, if ever.

"I know you have done all you can," Heresa cooed, "with such limited means brought from so far." She bit her lip, rather too hard for the effect. "Just make him as comfortable as possible. I will be back by noon, if not sooner. The basileii have to be informed, and I wish an escort of my sons. There is no point in having them linger here, seeing their father as he is, especially when the draught wears away. Now, I'd like a moment with him…please."

Maldan and Lannid waited by the door with Kubelai as she bent over her husband to stroke his feverish, sweating forehead, feeling the ridge of an old scar that somehow made his head seem less massive than it was. She nestled her hand in one of his limp, stubby fingers, staying at his side long enough to have counted the coarse black hairs that sprouted at the end of his great knob of a nose.

Then, certain this last tenderness was being observed, she kissed her husband on the lips, causing him to stir. She stroked his bristly cheek one last time, sighed loudly, and walked to the door. Neither Kubelai—his back to her now—nor her sons as they turned for the antechamber, saw her wipe her lips on one sleeve, her sweaty hand on the other.

Chapter Thirty-Seven:

FALCA'S WALK

FALCA NEVER HAD to use the story he'd concocted to explain his presence on the road leading to the castle's bridge: bloodsnare hunter, captured by outlaws, escaped—*and could you spare a little food?*

Most of the tradesmen had already left their timbered barracks flanking the road to begin the morning's work. On scaffolding lacing the half-finished towers of the shore-side barbican, masons checked the set of the previous day's courses of stone. One yawned as he inspected the ropes of the pulley and tackle hoists that would lift more material for this day's efforts. Surrounded by stacks of pails, mortar-makers mixed their slurry in troughs.

He passed by blacksmiths stoking the fires of two forges. Carpenters sharpened adzes, saws and chisels, though one sat smoking his pipe on the edge of the partially framed drawbridge that had yet to be fitted to the barbican.

Not far away, Wardens escorted a long line of Limbs toward the site, passing between dozens of wagons, wheeled sleds, stacks of timber and quarried stone that had yet to be dressed. The Limbs were not bound, nor could they be for the coming work, but there were enough groods, their staggers and flouts at the ready, to make sure they kept on without trouble. Two Limbs fell away down the line. Several Wardens hauled them off toward one of the wagons and there, listless but still alive, they were roped and left—for what further purpose Falca could only guess, but it couldn't be rest or reprieve.

He knew Gurrus, Styada and Ossa had to be watching this too, though they'd probably lost sight of him by now. Was Gurrus worrying about all the

Limbs being taken away from the lake before it was time? Neither Falca nor the others had realized that some of the captives would be sent to the quarry, wherever that was. Would there be enough for the reive?

Wherever the three were watching, they could not see all the tools the Limbs could use later as weapons—here or in the castle itself: carpenters' axes, saws and augers; blacksmiths' hammers; stone-cutters' mallets, saws and chisels; quarriers' pickaxes and bars; even mortar-maker's hoes and the shovels Limbs used to fill baskets with rubble.

Many of these leaned against wagons and scaffolding, tools as yet unclaimed by tardy workers. Falca considered pilfering one, if only because it would feel good to have something in his hand, and to appear like he was one of the workers. The urge for pretense was strong. He decided against it: why would a man seeking an audience with the Warden Allarch be carrying a shovel, hammer or hoe?

No groods guarded the bridge landing. That would not be the case at the gateway to the castle itself across the lake. He fell in behind two wagons pulled by drays, the *clop-clop* of hooves echoing hollowly on the abraded timbers. One wagon was presumably filled with lime for whitewashing; the accompanying men rested long-handled bristle brushes over their shoulders. The other wagon carried firewood.

Supported by pontoons of boats, the bridge closely matched the adjacent course of what Falca guessed would be a stone causeway linking barbican to the castle's gate. But work on the stone piers that would support the low arches had only just begun past the squared-off rear of the barbican.

He walked on, keeping close to the last of the men behind the second wagon. He wanted to believe the unsteadiness in his legs was the movement of this worn yet sturdy floating bridge. The sensation was not unlike walking the Road.

The idea had been his; now he had to get inside to kill Culldred Hoster, thus depriving the Wardens of their Allarch and, with luck, Maldan Hoster. He wasn't counting on any more to kill Lambrey Tallon—two out of three would have to do.

Where the father would be, so would the son, especially to hear Falca's offer. The rest would be up to Gurrus and the Timberlimbs—and their willingness to fight.

He hoped that when the moment came he'd have his falcata again in his hands. Falca wanted a throw of the dice with it again, that's all. Heartbeats would do for the killing of Culldred, and a few more for the cutting of the cord of flessok around his neck and skewering Maldan Hoster's eyes with the flenx horns. But after that...if he was still alive? What of the castle itself?

Gaining control of the gatehouse was crucial to prevent Wardens in the castlets from crossing over the lake to help their brethren. Could one man do that? Should he somehow be able to escape after killing the Allarch he might be able to force his way into the gatehouse. But control it?

Falca felt confident he could at least stir the hornet's nest, and once inside hope that opportunities might arise that he couldn't have foreseen on the outside—if he lived long enough to seize them.

Still, if there was any certainty at all to this long walk across the water, it was that he'd be more useful inside than out, where he'd be just one more man against thousands of Wardens, as opposed to, what?—a hundred groods inside? The Limbs wouldn't need him to tell them what to do, where to go. They'd built the fucking place. They wouldn't need his encouragement to kill shitcatchers.

Inside or out, it was all an end: cut around the bone anyway you wanted, but that still wouldn't give you more meat.

Were the Fates bickering now about whether to let a crouchalley from Draica take Culldred Hoster and one more son with him?

Falca was almost at the midpoint of the bridge that had to be at least four times longer than the height of the tree he'd climbed. One of the men ahead of him poked a companion, pointing to the right. The man laughed, rubbing his belly. Falca saw nothing but a long craggy islet that curled closely around a tower spanning the entrance to a narrow inlet between.

The first wagon had almost reached the wooden dock whose length extended from where the stone causeway would eventually connect to the gatehouse, but for the time being accommodated the end of the pontoon bridge. The drawbridge was lowered, taut chains angling down from massive drum towers flanking a sally-port scarcely wide enough for two wagons to pass.

The towers loomed sixty feet high or more, Falca guessed. Halfway down, over the sally's arched entrance, six jutting corbels supported a short thick brow of battlements and the machicolations that were the bane of besiegers. Behind an embrasure a sentry idly watched the wagons approaching, then disappeared from view behind a merlon.

Falca looked to the walls in either direction from the gatetowers. Sharp spikes of finials topped the merlons. Vertical slits of arrow-loops were spaced at regular intervals along the walls. He saw no sentries. Their absence could be explained by the lack of any perceived threat—as if anything could threaten this citadel. The siting alone on an isle far from shore was enough to discourage any attack.

And that would be the key to the reive.

Falca put himself in Culldred's place: why keep more than a hundred or so Wardens to garrison a fortress like this? Stash the rest of the men away, to bite the arse of an army weary of a march to wilderness and foolish enough to attempt a siege; or send them elsewhere to feed from a larger trough—not the ravaging of Timberlimb villages. No need for more slaves now. All the shine needed to pay for this castle wouldn't be found hidden in Kelvoi hovens.

The royals of Cross Keys had gotten very ambitious. The King's Own Wardens now had a base here to strike into the Myrcian heartland, a very expensive base. No wonder Lambrey Tallon had wanted to know the whereabouts of the sacks of gold in Cossum Hoster's boat.

But something still didn't add up.

Where *was* the Myrcian force that necessitated Culldred taking all the Wardens into the Bounds to confront? Either the Allarch had declined a battle, leaving Bastia and eastern Lucidor to their fates…or the Myrcian threat was a phantom.

So that's it, he thought.

Cross Keys had nothing to do with this.

The Warden Allarch's ambition was all his. He'd seen a pocket to pick and what a pocket it was! Culldred was nothing more than a thief, as Falca had been on the streets of Draica, snatching a patroon's safekeep one day, a wealthy lady's pulsing leechstone necklace the next. All that differed was the magnitude of the reive: Cullded was going to steal territory, and lots of it.

And who better to help a thief than another who would bring something that could make it happen sooner rather than later? Culldred would listen all right, and hopefully Maldan, too, at his side, listening closely enough to give Falca the moment he needed to kill them both.

A Warden tenon, rubbing the shaved back of his head with his flout, stood talking with two other bored-looking groods at a corner of the dock, letting the wagons pass without waving them on.

Falca could keep on with the workers through the sally and into the outer ward, but then what? Better to state his business now rather than later, when he might meet suspicion about why he hadn't already done so.

As the second wagon made the turn toward the drawbridge, he said: "A request, tenon."

Annoyed at the interruption the officer furrowed his brow. "What?"

"I've come to see the Allarch."

The tenon stepped ahead, taking a moment to assess Falca's empty hands first, then the unkempt beard, the wild hair, the ripped tunic and flayed chasers. "You want to see the Allarch," he said slowly.

"Or his son Maldan."

"Is *that* all? Why not the Lady Heresa as well? Or bees in the hives, birds in the dovecote? I'd let you have your audience with shit in the stables if I saw a rake and bucket," he said. The nearby groods laughed.

The tenon dismissed Falca with a jerk of his officer's flout. "Get out of here."

Falca didn't move. "Tell either one that Falca Breks has something both will very much want to see."

The nearest grood reached over his shoulder and drew his stagger, took a step toward Falca. "Shall I kill him, tenon?"

Falca ignored the grood, his black-shaft axe, and kept his eyes on the Warden officer, knowing the tenon had to be wondering now whether there was something more to the persistence of this fool. Falca splayed his empty hands. "All I ask is for someone to give the message. If neither will see me, kill me then. Do that now and the Allarch will add your bodies to mine."

That flushed the tenon's broad face. He drew his skurr, tucked the tip under Falca's chin.

"H'aint worth the walk," muttered the other grood. "Doan care whatty says."

"Shut up, Yovol," the tenon said. Falca felt sword edge now, as if the Warden was deciding where to begin shaving his beard. "Who are you?"

"I told you. Falca Breks."

"You're none of 'em—cutter, layer, banger. You haven't the hands. I see naught in 'em to peddle to the Allarch or his son."

"You've seen his wound; a nasty cut, that. I can make it disappear."

The tenon lifted the point of his sword, raising Falca's chin. "If you're a mage I see only a very unsuccessful one."

Falca shrugged. "Why would I lie only to make certain of my death?"

At that moment, he heard a rumbling behind him and turned to see a horse-drawn wagon and driver approaching on the bridge, filled with a half-dozen Limbs roped to the strakes. He stepped away to let the wagon pass.

The tenon sheathed his sword.

"Shivvy, take him through and tell Retkin and Snetter to escort him on to the keep. If the Allarch won't see him, throw him over the wall." The tenon smiled. "But hurry back—I want to know if he's healed his broken neck."

WITH A GROOD ahead and one behind, Falca took the first of the steps curling up and outside the massive eight-sided keep. These ended at the level of the second floor. Even at the first of the keep's four stories, the elevation was such that Falca, looking back to his left, could see the tops of the towers, even those of the far gatehouse drums. He paused too long. The grood behind pushed him roughly ahead.

On the way from the outer to the narrowing inner ward, Falca had made his counts carefully so he wouldn't seem too curious about the castle, but he did pause to ask its name—twice—pretending he hadn't heard it the first time. He didn't care what the name was, but the moment gave him the opportunity to steal more glances.

He didn't mark those working in the long garden, or by the livestock sheds, both set back from the outer ward's east and west walls. They weren't Wardens, wouldn't figure into what hopefully was to come. But he saw perhaps ten groods coming and going from the barracks on either side of the gatehouse and two more guarding a pen not so much bigger than the one at the krannog, and set close by the entrance to a corner tower. The one by the islet?

Four more Wardens tended horses by the stables. About fifteen were exercising in the training yard, and more still in what seemed like an armory near the wall separating the wards. He observed maybe a dozen groods on the parapets.

A peaceful day in Scaldasaig.

With any luck it wouldn't be for long.

There would be more Wardens he couldn't see in the towers, barracks and gatehouses—the nearer one giving access to the inner ward and, he guessed, the fortified inlet he'd seen before from the heights above the lake.

He had counted more than men, carefully noting the three iron-sheathed cullies and two thick doors for the main gatehouse sally, and one each for the second. In the inner ward he saw a hawker trying to put a hood and jesses on a caged young floka. Below and away to his left, a lone figure looked up at him, hoe in hand, from the herb garden. On a lower terrace, a netted man or woman walked between the hives of bees. On another, someone emerged from the dovecote carrying two limp pigeons.

Falca paused again halfway up the keep's stairway which hugged the first flank beyond that facing the yard—the left flank, so right-handed attackers would be hampered by the near wall, unlike defenders. The hawker had yet to subdue the caged floka. Falca wished he was superstitious so he could believe that a hopeful sign.

To the right of the inner gatehouse, inlet and quay, unseen men in the two towers flanking the entrance to the cove winched back a chain—a faint rasping—to presumably let a boat pass through to the lake.

The grood behind pushed him ahead over the last of the steps. "Too late for second thoughts, scut."

Their footfalls sounded hollowly on a deadfall that could be slid back into the wall. One guard stood by the door that faced the straight edge of the western flank of the keep. A second grood sentry turned from a parapet embrasure. "What ya got there, Snetter?" he said.

"Tenon Kereni said to bring him. Wants to see th'Allarch, an' if he don't, this one's over the wall; thass th'orders."

"Word ain't out yet, but th'Allarch's taken ill. What I hear, it's bad. This scut could be Roak himself but he ain't seeing no one."

Snetter smiled. "What I wanted to hear. Rettie?"

"Naught staggies, now," the sentry said.

"Jus' gimme a hand with'm, Freggo. You think I want a mess to clean? Didn' I jus' tell you Kereni said to toss'm over tha wall."

Snetter had his arm now, Rettie the other but Falca wasn't going to wait for the sentry to lay on. A stomped boot, a knee to one stick's groin, the heel of a hand to the chin of another—he'd been in as tight an alley as this before—well, almost. Maybe he could get past them, through that door and last long enough to find Maldan.

They had him turned around toward the nearest embrasure, and through it he glimpsed that boat on the lake before he looked down for the boot smash. He had his hands up by his neck, as if fearful for his last moment—but he was feeling for the flessok cord that held the flenx horns…

"What's going on here?" shouted a voice behind them, by the door.

Falca felt the grips slacken enough to let him turn partially around as his captors were doing, and with that came a familiar sound: his falcata sliding from the scabbard. The woman who now appeared directly behind Maldan Hoster wore a gold-trimmed black mantle and flared wimple that matched the violet color of her eyes. Culldred's wife?

Maldan strode forward toward the Wardens, then stopped short, as if they brandished weapons and not hasty salutes; offered menace and not apologies for alarming the Lady. A second man was at her side. The brother.

"What is it, Maldy?" the woman said.

He pointed, unable or unwilling to speak, his mouth a ruined bird's hole.

Amala had missed the right eye by the width of two fingers, but she'd caught part of his lips, wormed with stitch-marks now, that would never wholly meet again.

Maldan still couldn't find his voice.

"Who *is* this one?" the Lady Hoster demanded.

"He killed Cossum, mother," the brother said. "His name is Falca Breks."

Falca seized his chance. "I've come to heal your son's wound."

Chapter Thirty-Eight:

HOSTER HALL

WARDENS SURROUNDED FALCA as they led him into into the great hall, past staircases flanking the thick, iron-strapped door. Above and to his right a columned pentice, adorned with an elaborately carved frieze, ran the length of the cavernous chamber. Below this gallery a dozen long benches and tables were stored against the interior wall. A servant paused to gape at Falca before going back into the kitchens with the gossip. The largest of the three hooded hearths—the only one crackling with fire—was set in the wall behind a dais.

Culldred's wife took the steps up to the dais, breaking a shaft of morning light that slanted into the hall from arched, quillons windows. She sat in the bigger of two nest-wing chairs, and gestured to the servants carrying bundles. "Put them beside me—there's a good Tolo." The servant did so, knuckling his brow.

Falca's guards stopped him well away from the dais, one of them whispering before forcing him down: "On your knees b'fore the Lady. Yer not the salt at this table."

He glanced back at the door. Two more groods were coming in now, obeying the woman's earlier summons outside. Maldan Hoster stood off to his right, a hand on the hilt of the sheathed falcata, his brother next to him.

With Culldred on his sickbed somewhere, the chance for killing him was gone. Maldan then? Falca would have a stagger in his back before he could reach him.

He had to play this on, get to a demonstration of the krael that would provide time for events to unfold outside the castle—and for the moments of distraction he needed to kill Maldan. The man had the build of a Catchall canal-heave, yet that could mean he lacked quickness. Falca wasn't worried about the brother.

The woman had something in her fingers he couldn't quite see. A ring? With her blade of a beak and wattled chin she seemed like a plump-breasted hen glaring at him for the theft of her eggs.

"You're sure it's him, the both of you?" she said in a nasally voice. "It's one thing to summarily execute an imposter, and quite another to savor the death of your brother's murderer."

"We're sure, mother," Lannid said. His brother shoved him aside, burbling something Falca took pleasure in not understanding. The younger Hoster seemed unperturbed by the physical vehemence. "I think what Maldan is trying to say is that what pains him more than his wound is that I must speak for him."

"Lannid, this is no time for jousting with your brother. I know what he said and it wasn't that. However Cossie's murderer cheated death, all that matters now is that he pay for it. Perhaps the deadfall outside, where we can drop his severed quarters, so his blood will only sully the rocks below. Or…hmmm… perhaps my pet. Lalla hasn't been fed yet this morning—don't roll your eyes at me, Lannid. Why bother keeping one if it's not named? My sister would be honored to have such a dear, monstrous thing named after her."

Maldan spit out more incoherence, but Lannid seemed to understand what he was saying.

"Beast or deadfall, yes indeed. But for what he did to you? His *woman* did that. *He* was dying from that bite of your pet."

"I doubt she could have done that," the Lady Hoster said. "A bladesman like your brother?"

"I was there, mother."

"So you were, and I'm sure you were very brave. But enough of this squabbling; Lalla gets him. I'm sure your father would agree that a demonstration of her appetite will prove useful. Two or three mottles should be enough to encourage—what's his name again?"

"Breks. Falca Breks," Lannid said. "Evidently he once knew Lambrey Tallon in Draica but their friendship has…lapsed."

"A pity then that Comitor Tallon isn't available to assist me here, but he has responsibilities elsewhere at the moment. So it's up to me to encourage this murderer to divulge the location of what he stole from our Cossum in Bastia, in exchange for a quicker and tidier end. There's the trade you seek, Breks, and it pains me to offer that much."

Falca scratched his beard where his scar had been. "I thought it'd be obvious I came here to trade for something else."

A grood cuffed him. "Address Her Ladyship Heresa properly."

"Your trembling will be obvious enough," Heresa said, "when you see Lalla being fed."

"I don't expect to. Why would I…"

A blow to the back of his head knocked him to his hands, toward Maldan, and for a moment Falca thought to keep going…toward the falcata. But Lannid was in the way, eyeing him. "Before he answers for Cossum, I think we should let him finish telling us why a murderer would willingly come to his own execution."

Heresa rubbed the ring, rolling it over in her hands. Then: "Perhaps there's some sense in that—if he's brief." She pointed a finger at Falca. "I believe my son asked you a question."

"Which I'm only too happy to answer, my…Lady. I should be dead. The reason why I'm not is in here." He patted the pouch. "I have the means to make what I stole in Bastia mere drops in the bucket."

"My son's death has no price."

"Surely there's one to heal the Allarch since his tide ebbs. Or a price to allow Maldan the pleasure of speaking for himself, with lips as pretty as they once were. I believe I promised you that outside."

He couldn't see if this hard Hoster turd had drawn the falcata at that last jab; Lannid was still in the way.

"You boast of what's in a peasant's pouch?" Heresa said.

"Why would I risk my life with empty boasts?" Falca patted his safekeep again. "With your permission."

Heresa gave it, as if brushing away a pestering fly.

Falca put a piece of krael on the floor before him.

"*That?* You tout dark ginger. Rust from an iron grate."

Falca shook his head. "The Timberlimbs call it krael. A companion gave it to me not long ago."

"My husband has spent many years in the Rough Bounds. Never has he mentioned anything close to your claim."

"Nor would the Limbs want shitcatchers—excuse the coarseness, my Lady—to know its secret. I stand here as proof that it heals the effects of poison, sickness of all kinds and severity, and wounds of the flesh—though it cannot restore life once that is gone. I've come to believe that it may even prolong life."

"There must be a thousand common peddlers across the Six Kingdoms at this very moment who are promising the same for water they just drew from a well. But supposing this…krael is as you say. We have thousands of mottles across the lake to tell us; we don't need you."

"Only a very few—Timberlimb priests—know where more of it can be obtained."

"Yet somehow *you* know. And your source is conveniently dead, of course."

Falca nodded. "As is my other companion who helped me get the information from him."

"You've taken your thieving and murdering beyond the alleys and streets of Draica—my husband mentioned your thoroughly despicable past."

"It's a pleasure to be in the presence of one who appreciates thoroughness, my Lady. This castle, too, is nothing if not…thoroughly built."

Falca expected to be cuffed again, but evidently the groods couldn't decide if he'd insulted or complimented Her Ladyship.

Lannid came over to examine the krael. "So," he said, hefting it, "you come here, wishing to do a pus-heart's business with us after my brother killed Amala Damarr. I find that hard to believe."

"As I do your acquaintance with her. She never mentioned you."

"I knew her twin brother."

"Then you might also know his death was part of the reason why we had to leave Draica so…quickly; the pair of us and an old Limb."

"How lucky for her to die by the sword—how ironic it was yours—and not betrayal."

Falca shrugged. "Once a ditchie, always a ditchie. Still, we'll never know. If it wasn't for your brother I'd have remained as ignorant of the Limb's secret as you."

Falca caught the krael Lannid tossed with disgust, and put it back in his safekeep.

"And I," Heresa said, "find it equally hard to believe that you would offer the fount of this supposed secret to us, something that could have made you alone a very wealthy man."

"I could have done that, yes. But alone it would have taken time. You can understand the impatience for reward for one such as me, used to fisting mottles for a coin here, a coin there. I much prefer a quicker path to reward. You and the Allarch—and 4,000 Wardens I'm guessing—could make that possible."

"There was such a path in Bastia."

"Yes, that. Well, it's still there, close to the city. I'm sure the conquest of Bastia has crossed your husband's mind. With what I'm offering the Allarch, that could be accomplished sooner rather than later. But until such time, best I keep the exact whereabouts of that boatload of gold to myself."

Lannid said: "He shits here as well as he did in Draica—excuse me mother."

"All I ask is the chance to give you proof of what I have to offer—a demonstration. Surely you'd want that before we discuss the details of our partnership—what do you say, Maldan? In the time it once took me to hone that falcata you have now, you'll be smiling as clearly as I remember at the ledges below the waterfall."

Maldan drew the blade, and might have ended it there but for Heresa's sharp command: "No, you can have his eyes and tongue later—especially his tongue."

Maldan stood down, reluctantly, spewing out mishmash before sheathing the falcata.

"Of course it's poison, Maldy," Heresa said. Then, to Falca: "We're done here. A few days in chains above Lalla's pen, listening to the screams of mottles as they're lowered into the water should convince you to tell us about the gold for which you murdered my dearest son. Perhaps we'll let you go if you do, to wander without your eyes and that tongue; perhaps back to Draica to beg on the streets if you're lucky to get there."

"You can cripple me, my Lady, but not the pleasure in knowing I'd given you the wrong location for the gold, six sacks of it, each as fat as a sow. But to get it you need me in Bastia, with my parts still where they belong."

Heresa nodded at Falca's guards, who hauled him to his feet.

"All that's needed to prove my claim," he said, as slowly as he could, "is what Maldan so wishes to do: cut my face as his was. I'll take the krael myself—with enough left over to cure your husband's sickness."

"Get him out of my sight," she said. "The Armorer's tower will do."

Falca didn't expect a heavy dice roll from Lannid, who moved quickly to block the Wardens from hauling him away. "Mother…wait. What do we have to lose? If there's any chance to help father…"

"Don't be a fool. Breks only wants to spare himself a worse fate."

"Perhaps so, and he deserves it. But if that's your reluctance, I'll cut myself for the proof…or Maldan can slice his face. If Breks is not…"

"Of course he's lying."

"I…I don't understand your objection. Why would he come here with lies that would ensure his death? But if he *is* lying then all we've lost is gold that can be replaced in time. That and a greater spectacle of his death is…isn't that a price well worth paying for the possibility of having father sitting beside you?"

Falca kept his mouth shut. Nothing else he could say would help now. The son had made the case as well as it could be.

The Lady Heresa sat motionless in the chair, staring at the ring, turning it over and over in her fingers, ignoring Maldan's garbling and the guards who waited upon her word, their hands locked on Falca's arms. He felt the skurr of another at his back.

"Very well," Heresa said. She sighed, as if finally convinced of the necessity of putting a beloved old dog out of his misery. "A demonstration. But not him; not you, Lannid; and not Maldan." She salvaged a smile. "I have someone else in mind to taste his poison."

Chapter Thirty-Nine:

THE SQUINT

FURKA VAT DECIDED to stay at the squint a while longer. He'd hoped to gain more useful, possibly lucrative information from the scheduled convocation of basileii in the hall below to take with him, but that meeting had evidently been postponed due to the Allarch's sudden illness.

Vat's curiosity with what he'd heard in the hall below wasn't something he could sell as he might detailed plans for an imminent campaign by the Warden prossars. Yet it might prove an entertaining diversion, and there was time to pass before he escaped come nightfall, when sentries walking the allures could not see his two boats or hear his six men at the muffled oars. Those six, masons all, waited for him now far below. They'd been with him since Anaktora and he trusted them if only because he paid them very well.

He wondered how far Lambrey Tallon, the Hosters' favorite hound, had taken the search: certainly past the inner ward to the larger outer; perhaps even beyond the lake, thinking Vat had already fled. The master-mason was going to miss his spyglass which he used to monitor the progress of construction, past and present, from a central vantage point. But the spyglass had been necessary for the ruse, to lead the hound astray. No matter how thoroughly Tallon searched with his men, he'd never find the one who had built Scaldasaig—or his gold.

It had happened before: patrons running out of money, refusing to pay him, or deciding his death was a more desirable way to settle accounts. Vat knew the Hosters well enough by now, at least the Lady Heresa with those violet eyes and pillows for breasts, to be certain they would not have paid him the last of his due, even if the strapper below had not stolen a treasure hoard from them in Bastia, and had now foolishly come to them with such a preposterous offer.

No matter. Vat would get his due, and more…much more. Even if the Hosters had paid him in full, he would be paid again by someone else, because he always added more than walls, towers and gatehouses to the fortresses he designed and built: cleverly disguised passageways, hidden squints, tunnels and posterns—secrets only he knew about.

Elsewhere, at various times, Vat had been paid to inform a provincial lord, a king and a Sanctor—through a third party of course—about how one of his superbly designed castles, held by a rival or rebel, could be taken. For one fortress, Bucca Crag, he'd been paid three times, because he never divulged all of the secrets to any one patron.

Scaldasaig was his crowning achievement, both for what could be seen—and what couldn't. The siting alone made it nigh impossible to breach. But who would ever blame the Six Kingdoms' preeminent master-mason for the design and construction of an impregnable fortress that falls by treachery?

Because of its size, siting and the obvious political aims of the Hosters, Vat had built into Scaldasaig more secrets than usual, and had been richly rewarded, though not always in ways immediately profitable.

Hidden behind one squint, he knew that Tallon's woman never shut her eyes as he energetically basted her in the tower chamber where he kept her; and that she had curious tattoos on the soles of her feet Blue-gums hadn't noticed—at least during the single time Vat had observed them rutting—though the man certainly had noticed the pair displayed above the globes of her rump. She deserved better than a man with such a thick pelt of hair on his back.

And hidden behind other squints Vat knew that the surly, disfigured Hoster brother preferred his right hand to quickly pleasure himself; and his bookish, more patient sibling the left. Vat knew that one of Culldred's last healthy acts was greasing his cudgie between his wife's voluminous parcels but little else, which begged the question of how he'd managed to sire four sons, including the one this Falca Breks had evidently murdered.

He'd also learned of their intent to kill him before the last work was done on Scaldasaig, primarily because they did not want his talents procured by anyone else in the Six Kingdoms. The money, or lack of it, was only the secondary reason. In this very squint he'd listened—marveling again at his own genius for designing a hall that carried sound so well—to Culldred, his basileii, and the

Red Hands discussing general plans for future campaigns, two days before the Allarch took sick.

So which monarch—from any of the Six Kindoms save Helveylyn, perhaps—would pay him the most for information not only about these plans, but also for the way in which Scaldasaig could be taken without the folly and extraordinary expense of a siege that had little chance of succeeding? There were four ways this could be done, including his own escape route tonight: one for each successor tenant. Thus, he'd be paid four times for the same unassailable fortress.

Scaldasaig was his best work yet—until he topped it with his own: a citadel that would be truly unassailable because he would never auction its secrets. Secrets there would be, of course; he was incapable of designing without them.

But there would be no false wall in his fortress, as there was in the turris cellar of this one. The wall, hiding access to useful tunnels, could only be discovered by close measures. And who would have the rule and eye? Pantry maids and servants?

There would be no false bottom of a pentice floor overlooking his great hall, a hidden market for someone to lie on his belly and choose the wares to resell later; no one behind a carefully concealed opening in a dawnstone frieze that ran the length of the pentice gallery and depicted the triumph of an Allarch's Wardens in battle.

Furka Vat had personally sculpted the frieze and ensured the silence of the lesser masons who had installed the twenty facing blocks of dawnstone while Heresa Hoster was absent from the turris. Access to this particular squint and the others on the floor above was gained through a low, undetectable pivot door behind the southeastern stairwell, part of a network of passageways that began below the inner ward.

He had to crawl to this vantage point, but he was small of stature, with delicate hands that belied his trade. Those hands and his grossly outsized ears and eyes had once cursed his youth, but he counted all as blessings now. To that he added the absence of rats. They would infest this space soon enough, but presently there were none—at least he heard no skiffling and chittering, nothing to distract him from the view of the woman being led into Hoster Hall.

IT TOOK ALL of Shar Stakeen's self-control to mask her shock at seeing Falca Breks.

The effort came with a sudden pause and parting lips which might have caused him to wonder why a woman he'd never seen before should seem so surprised—but a Warden pushed her from behind, not caring if she stumbled. She limped ahead with a more severe hitch, and hoped that would be cover enough.

She remembered the Hoster brothers, of course. The Lady Heresa she'd met only briefly upon her arrival in Scaldasaig, and a somber meeting it was, given the news of her son's death. Heresa seemed scarcely to notice the ruin of Maldan's face. Tallon had hurried Stakeen off to his chambers in one of the gatehouse bartizans opposite the keep.

Stakeen eyed them, one by one, especially Breks. She was seeing in her mind his being led away by those outlaws. She'd thought that would be the end of him, and with it her dream.

Yet here he was, in the last place imaginable for the killer of Cossum Hoster, standing before a table with a bowl, cup and pouch upon it, with Warden guards close behind him. He looked away from her now, toward Maldan, then to Heresa, then back to the disfigured son.

Heresa beckoned her forward with a flick of two fingers. Stakeen limped a few steps away from the Wardens.

"So far to come with a wound, my dear," Heresa said. "My sincerest apologies, and also on behalf of Comitor Tallon. It's one thing for a mere soldier to force himself upon an injured swallow, but the most esteemed of my husband's Red Hands?" She ticked her tongue. "Of course, your wound is the reason why I've summoned you—the upper leg is it?

"Now, this man to your right would heal it with what's in that bowl on the table. We've been discussing the matter of…before and after, shall we say. He insists what he's peddling is remarkably beneficial. I am skeptical."

Stakeen glanced at the table, bit her lip, not so much for the effect of a woman about to die, but to keep herself from smiling. She wasn't in the least skeptical. Breks would surely have anticipated that someone else besides his intended target would taste for poison.

It could only be the Golden-Eyes.

The others may have seen resignation in her deep sigh, the shutting of her eyes, but that was only profound relief that she had not tried to escape on her way here. Nothing good could have come from a summons by the Allarch's wife, especially with Lambrey Tallon absent. Still, she hadn't known the intent. And while she could have killed her Warden escorts—all they saw was a limping quiver and not a shadden—what about after? She could have made it out of the keep, but across the ward, with a dozen sentries on the parapets marking her slow escape to nowhere?

No, she'd known instinctively to wait for better odds, just as she had before with Tallon. In the meantime, a woman like her would remain a prize most men would be loathe to kill or discard, and thus they could be manipulated like Tallon, who she knew was smitten with her—and not just because the slides came without complaint or protest from a woman who'd stitched her own wound. The necessary smiles, resurrected from the past, came easily. Without a doubt he'd enjoyed few better than her…

A guard poked her. "The Lady Heresa has asked you twice to show it."

"She seems to have found modesty," Heresa murmured. "Lannid, assist her." Before he could do so, Stakeen lifted high the hem of the duvelin—some servant girl's—that Tallon had found for her to wear. She bunched the front of it at her waist, with the thought that if the strutterman knew what she'd done to him before, he'd be doing more than blushing.

"It's…there," he said, in a way that made it obvious he'd never seen much else of a woman. He seemed relieved when she dropped the curtain.

Heresa motioned to Breks. "Get on with it."

As Stakeen watched him pour half of the watery mixture from the bowl into the cup, she understood how he'd gotten in here and stayed alive. Who wouldn't at least *listen* to a man who should be dead, who claimed to have something so miraculous and potentially lucrative?

Whatever else he'd told them, he could have only one intent. The fact that Maldan Hoster had almost killed him was only part of it. The brute had killed his woman. Stakeen had seen Breks sentimentally cutting a lock of her hair as a keepsake. Why else was he here if not for vengeance, and for that he'd need only the briefest of distractions.

She wasn't going to let him have it.

If *he* didn't care to live much longer, *she* did—until she got the secret of Golden-Eyes.

At Heresa's command, Stakeen's guards grabbed her arms, expecting resistance from someone brought here to drink poison. One gripped a fistful of her hair, ready to ease the delivery.

"Get your hands off me," she said. "I'll take it myself."

"As she wishes," Heresa said, and pursed her thin lips with a smile. "It's just as well Comitor Tallon isn't here so he cannot see how willing you are, my dear, to take poison meant for my son. I'm sure he'll eventually find another stray for his kennel."

Stakeen closed her hands around the cup Breks extended and thought, too late, to add a tremble to her fingers. She nodded, which seemed to puzzle him, but he couldn't know it was only fleeting admiration of his audacity—worthy of a shadden—that was nonetheless wasted on the uselessness of avenging the death of his woman.

He asked her name.

"Shar Stakeen," she said, and drank it all at once, the liquid more bitter than sweet, and almost hot enough to scald her tongue. How could that be? He hadn't heated it.

Her heart began to pound hard, then harder. She became disoriented and fell away to the faint clatter of something—the dropping cup? Someone caught her—Breks?

She felt the currents of her own blood—how could *that* be?—and a sudden pressure in her eyes, as if someone was gouging thumbs into them…and a tingling and tightening in her leg. She heard the sound of moaning, knew it was hers over a galloping heart…

They were talking somewhere far away though she knew they were close, and she wanted to tell the bitch Heresa she wasn't dying, but she couldn't speak. She wanted to get up; she couldn't.

Soon, her heart calmed, the roaring in her ears lessened. She heard, distantly, a woman's voice telling someone to put a sword to her misery. For a moment Stakeen thought it was Tranch, not Heresa. Then Breks said: "No, she isn't dying; you'll see the eyes soon…"

She opened them. And it was as if she had thrown a dagger at the Allarch's wife, stopping her at the edge of the dais. Heresa lurched back to her chair but did not sit.

Shar Stakeen got up slowly. The Wardens guarding Breks shrank back. She raised her duvelin again, to peer at the wonder of the fading scratch and stitches where once the cut had been.

"She's fit to dance," Breks said. "The cup's yours to fill now, Maldan, so you can take a turn with her. Show her your smile while you're at it. Why not sing to her? You can sing, can't you?"

Maldan snatched the cup from his brother, who'd plucked it from the floor, and tossed it to Breks. Still shocked and mute, Heresa nonetheless nodded at Breks' guards, and they let him return to the table. He poured the remaining contents of the bowl into the cup, extending it as he had for Stakeen, a lure for Maldan.

His other hand was at his throat. Stakeen knew, without a doubt, he had something hidden—a sliverheart? She stepped in front of Maldan before he got close. "I'll give it to you," she said. "From one who can dance, to another who will sing again."

Breks hesitated—the flicker of a frown—but let her take the cup. What else could he do? She mouthed the words: *I'm saving your life…*

She doubted he understood, and wouldn't until much later when she killed him after getting what she had to have.

Maldan drained the cup greedily, spilling some of the contents. Stakeen could have caught him when he sagged, as could his brother who was almost as close. But all Lannid did was pick up the cup Maldan had dropped.

Heresa hurried down from the dais. Stakeen stepped away to let her kneel by her son. Her excitement was apparent enough, but there was something else Stakeen sensed. A shadow of dismay? Or was it only the shaking of her head in disbelief at the effects of Golden-Eyes?

Stakeen could have easily killed them both. She could have stepped aside to let Breks make a rush with his hidden sliverheart. A glance at him told her the fool would do it: two swiping cuts with the sliverheart across their necks. Mother and son deserved that fate.

She stayed where she was so Breks couldn't do it, not without shoving her out of the way. She wasn't going to budge.

Heresa caressed her son's face, and rose, motioning to the guards to help Maldan to his feet. She walked slowly back to her chair on the dais. Maldan massaged his healed lips, staring at Stakeen. He touched his eyes, looked at his fingers, expecting to see—what?—golden residue? *This one*, Stakeen thought, *is a man most content with a mirror*. For some reason she doubted that Falca Breks ever much looked into one, and he had more reason to do so.

"You," Heresa said to Breks. "How long will it last, the eyes?"

"A day, maybe less."

"And your price? For the knowledge of where more of this…krael can be had?"

Stakeen liked her name for it much better.

Breks had his eyes on Maldan, or was it the falcata? Was he, even now, assessing the chance she'd never let him have? Or was he trying to think of an answer to a question he never thought he'd live long enough to hear?

"Well?" Heresa said.

He turned back to her. "Milatum."

She laughed. "*Milatum*? You, a crouchalley from Draica would have... *Milatum*?"

Maldan sneered. "Why not Suaila and Cassena? The Sisters cannot be reached either, but at least you've seen them."

"Have you seen Milatum?" Breks replied. "Yet here we are, much closer to reaching that city than we were in Bastia."

He's making this up as he goes along, Stakeen thought. *He never expected to get this far.*

Milatum? It was absurd.

Where had Breks poached the same dream for which she saved her coins at the Red Turret? Even Castlecliff paled in comparison to the city her father had always spoken of so longingly.

Heresa shook her head, still amused. "And what makes you think far Milatum is in our power to give you?"

Stakeen never got the chance to hear his answer.

FURKA VAT WATCHED the rats below scurry in all directions.

Maldan Hoster bolted toward the door, joining the two Wardens who had burst into the hall with the alarm. Two more closed around Heresa as she ordered the other three and a servant to take Breks and the woman down to the cellar and guard them while the garrison crushed the attack. Lannid Hoster took the pouch of krael; Vat thought he heard him say that his father needed it now.

Only after the three Wardens hustled the pair away at the point of their skurrs, did the master-mason leave the squint, crawling along the passageway. As much as he wished to witness this challenge to five years of his life, it could be fatal to do so, however short-lived the assault. And not because Tallon and his men might spot him outside.

No, it was the risk of being carried away by one of the flokas that evidently were dropping mottles into the yards, onto parapets and towers. Vat doubted even these huge birds could bear the weight of a Warden in ruerain armor, but a man not all that much bigger than a mottle? Let them hook their talons in Wardens, and devour *them* shred by shred.

Furka Vat had his own prize now to carry away. Poor Heresa: she couldn't have picked a better refuge for him to do so. He had bait to offer Breks—the certainty of escape, for surely he knew Heresa Hoster would at least attempt to torture him for his wondrous secret. But coming from a stranger in a dark cellar illuminated only by lunelings? Was that bait enough for a man who came willingly into Scaldasaig? Would he leave as willingly?

Vat had additional means of persuasion: three of his six men should be enough for Breks. And the woman? They would take her, too; possibly use her later to force Breks' cooperation. He doubted the Draican could be moved by force or fear. Whether it was greed or something else, coming here to do business with the mother and father of a son he'd murdered was not the mark of a cowardly licklog, however addled the man's brains were. Milatum, indeed!

Still, one could never gauge a man until he was tested. Vat had seen supposedly brave soldiers crumble like chalk before the hammer. One thing was certain: he could never plumb that line if Falca Breks remained in Scaldasaig.

He came to the end of the passageway, slid over the edge, his tiny feet touching the steps of the vertical well, and hurried down past the pivot door.

However long it took, by honey or hammer, Vat intended to get from Breks the secret which would make the selling of others, at Scaldasaig or elsewhere, a beggar's cup to lords, kings, the Myrcian Sanctor and any number of ambitious usurpers—never mind wealthy patroons and merchants.

What had Breks said? *Mere drops in the bucket...*

Vat smiled. Were there buckets enough in the Six Kingdoms to fill with gold to be paid for the means to live a longer life without fear of sickness or wounds, plagues or poison?

CHAPTER FORTY:

THE WAY OUT

A TEMPEST OF black wings churned the lake water white. Ossa could feel the spray in his face though he was well away on the slope above the shoreline. The krael trees on the islet swayed as flokas passed, carrying Limbs to the castle, and again as they returned to the stockade for more.

In skeins and serried lines that seemed to stitch together the sky itself, the flokas kept coming, from all directions now—and not only from the mountains to the east where Ossa had first seen them, before Raleva's fire arrows arced from the bluff to the castlet roofs. She was at his side now, her hair tangled in the wind, protecting Gurrus, too, as he kept on with the wordless summoning. Ossa had a stagger in his belt and a sword, both honed by Falca; she but a half-dozen arrows for her bow.

Gurrus huddled by the stump where he'd begun the summoning above the stockade, his eyes shut, his clothes rustling with the floka-wind at the place he'd chosen halfway up from the shore. He hadn't been clutching Styada's shoulder when he began, but he was now, as if together they made the spades of the anchor. Styada, his eyes shut, too, kept his arm curled around Gurrus' waist.

Thousands of Limbs wailed in the stockade. Burning augors keened, horses brayed, men screamed, shields clashed as Wardens raised them over their heads for protection against the beaks and talons of attacking flokas.

The smoky, turbulent air seethed with dirt, cinders, chunks of flesh, bits of ruerain armor and pieces of masonry. The shattered shaft of a Warden's pilar flew by. A measuring cord snagged on a nearby stump; a mason's square skipped over another. Hair swirling around her face, fouling her vision, Raleva didn't see the Warden shield kiting toward her. Ossa did. He lunged to take it at his back, and luckily not on an edge of the dagger-like blades at the bottom.

She shouted her thanks; close as she was, he couldn't hear it. He picked up the rectangular shield—blood smeared the four interlocking-fists insignia on the front—and rammed it down into the earth: meager protection for them all yet better than they had before.

Raleva put down her bow, gestured to Ossa—a chopping motion. He gathered her wild hair in a sheaf, cut it off at the shoulders. He had the odd thought to pocket the harvest before he gave it to the wind.

Even at this distance he could feel the heat from the castlets, smell the stink of the blaze and roasting flesh. The Wardens who had tried to extinguish Raleva's fire-arrows had been swept off the roofs by waves of screeching flokas wheeling around the shore, their wings acting as bellows to fan the flames.

Warden bowmen had killed dozens of flokas but whether dead or dying the great birds hurtled down, crushing the archers. Hundreds of groods must have perished by now in the pyres, but thousands more had escaped, cramming the shoreline, sheltering under their shields.

By the shore-side of the Limb stockade, where the flokas had to come in lower, Wardens hurled their pilars—iron-shanked javelins with a flaring hand-grip mid-point in the wooden shaft. Most pierced wings, or missed, but one struck a floka in the neck as it took off with a Limb holding on above the closed talons.

The Limb let go before the floka plummeted into a turtle of Wardens, impaled on the pilars bristling up between the raised shields. The gruesome tent of wings and shields collapsed. A few groods crawled out from under, scrambled up to run toward the protection of another turtle. A floka, returning from the castle, swooped down after them. One escaped; two stumbled, dropping staggers and skurrs as the floka flew on to the top of the stockade.

The two Wardens didn't elude their fate, though Ossa couldn't see the slashing talons. A floka didn't have to quickly kill. If its out-sized backclaw didn't decapitate or disembowel a victim, there was a poison that quickly stunned. The effect could last for hours. Ossa once witnessed a floka attack the biggest augor he'd ever seen, circle high and descend again to feast on the immobilized beast while it was still alive.

Surprisingly, the Limb hadn't been killed by the fall. He'd crawled to a stricken Warden twice his size, yet now helpless as a new-born. He stabbed the Warden with his own sword, then the other, and collapsed, his final token of victory a thrown pilar that narrowly missed him.

A burning corner tower of the nearest castlet crashed, taking with it an adjoining section of the wall. Wardens scattered in the shower of flame and cinders, but some began hauling fiery skeletal timbers toward the shore-side of the Limbs' stockade, using their staggers to lever or hook the pieces. Other Wardens protected them with raised shields and pilars. Flokas harried them in the open, snapping off javelins, ripping away shields, but the Wardens gained the wall and there was little more the flokas could do.

Dozens more circled above the huge pen. When the stockade began to burn, they wouldn't be able to descend and carry away more Limbs. They may have taken a hundred to the castle; Ossa guessed that wouldn't be enough. What had quickened the castlet fires would do the same here. The stockade would become a furnace, incinerating thousands of Limbs within.

Wardens hauled a dead floka toward the fire. They scuttled under its wings as those above attacked, and emerged as they flew on. The feathers quickly caught fire. More groods came around the corner of the pen, the closest any had come to Ossa and the others. He counted five, shields and pilars aloft. The flokas weren't attacking them, perhaps sensing that their wing-wind would only accelerate the fire now burning on the other side of the pen.

Raleva shouted close into Ossa's ear: "There's more behind them. They're bringing the fire around."

He took the stagger out from his belt, gave her the sword. "We have to leave Gurrus. Put this by Styada." He wrenched the shield from the ground. When Raleva returned he pulled her close. "Take the two at the rear; I have the first two. Stay behind me until we're close and step away."

She nodded. He grazed the ends of her hair. A thought came and went quickly: that she'd survive, to grow it back in full someday, for herself—and maybe a young man worthy of her, whom the Fates placed in her path.

The groods would not suspect that the man approaching with a Warden shield and stagger was not one of them—until it was too late.

They didn't; not until Raleva shot the first, then another as Ossa closed on his two. They lowered their shields but had no time to swing pilars around. He struck at their legs with the stagger-axe, feeling bone: disabling wounds. No time to finish them off—there was the fifth who had his stagger out now and delivered a blow so hard to the shield it split the wood by the boss—and stuck.

Ossa dropped the shield, swung the stagger, cleaving the Warden's left shoulder at the neck. He wrenched free the double-headed axe to a gush of blood, and turned to see another Warden twist against the palisade, his belly pinned by an arrow. Limbs wrenched his head back. He'd been carrying the burning timber with his ruerain.

Limbs had snared the other hauler, too, holding him, through gaps in the palisade, by leg and neck. He broke free—and into the blade of Ossa's stagger that caught him in the chest.

One of the wounded Wardens hobbled away; Ossa finished him off, Raleva another with a shot to the groin. They used pilars to lever the timber away from the pen, quickly gathered as many weapons as they could cradle in their arms, and hurried around corner of the stockade.

They began chopping at the slimmest of these split krael logs, Ossa with one stagger, Raleva with hers.

Thunk...thunk...thunk...

His chest burned, his hands trembled, his fingers became more numb with each biting stroke. Limbs shouted within, pounding on the timbers, the din so loud Ossa could hardly hear himself grunting with each swing of the axe. He couldn't tell if the smoke he smelled was from the castlet or the pen burning on the other side.

The first log gave way. He and Raleva wrenched it off and began chopping on the next. Chips of wood flew, pecking at his face and hands.

Thunk...thunk...thunk...

GURRUS SWAYED WITH the powerful, rhythmic beat of her wings, willing himself to hold on for a little longer. The floka was aware of his weakness and so had flared her talons to give him a place to stand, if precariously, his elbows hooked around her legs. She'd broken off attacking the shitcatchers to come for him. Blood smeared her three front talons and the larger back claw.

The summoning had exhausted him. He knew when the floka came for him that he hadn't the strength to reach the Isle though he told Styada otherwise—one last lie in service to the promise he'd given his father. If not for the lie Styada would not have left him, and someone had to reach the Isle to return the kinnet.

Gurrus wanted a few more moments, to see as his far-distant ancestors had seen, before they left the sky and eyries, before their talons became hands. That legend had always been passed on, yet only now did he truly believe it. He took scant comfort that his kesslakor had been at least partially true and not wholly a common dream.

Smoke rose above the flames of the shitcatchers' encampments and the pen where they kept the Kelvoi slaves. The drifting smoke carried the stench of Wardens, augors and horses, but little of charring Kelvoi flesh.

They were almost out of the pen. Gurrus wished that he could call now to Ossa and Raleva as he had called the flokas, to thank them. He had no doubt they'd freed many Kelovi.

Some of them were fleeing toward the path and bluff; most were not. They surged along the far side of the burning encampments and around toward the end of the bridge, converging at the side and rear of many—too many—shitcatchers who were fighting more Kelvoi at the bridge. It did not surprise Gurrus that his brethren knew to go there. That is where he, too, would have gone to die if he had escaped from the pen.

The kesslakor was only partially true because the Kelvoi were losing. He'd envisioned a victory. Flokas were still carrying Kelvoi to the castle, and many were continuing to attack the soldiers: diving, swooping, snagging shields to allow others to slash with talons.

But there were too many shitcatchers to overcome. Unless a Warden was stunned by the kolk in a floka's backclaw, five Kelvoi might die to overcome a single shitcatcher so a sixth could gain his sword or axe. Gurrus hoped a few might live and escape, to carry back to the hovens in the north the tale of this day.

He and Styada were among the last to be carried toward the Isle. Styada was almost there now; Gurrus could see the glint of the sword Ossa had left him. He had eagerly taken that; less so the kinnet Gurrus insisted he wear. He hoped it would keep Styada safe long enough to find Falca—if he was still alive—and die at his side.

He remembered how his father would admonish him for his yearnings for more; his inability to be satisfied, the ease with which he was able to get what he wanted but should not have desired—all of it behavior unseemly for the son of a mehka. And surely now he would not approve.

Choose one, Gurrus; Sky or Water. No one has ever chosen both…

But he already had made one choice; now he would have the other.

He felt himself slipping, yet there were the talons keeping him from falling away. He could not thank all those who had answered his summons, but he did with this one, Sreekree.

Pass on my gratitude to those who survive and a lament for those who do not.

I will. Do you wish the Death's-ease?

No. Save your kolk for another of them below.

Now he would find out if the other part of the legend was true: that the most worthy of Kelvoi would return as flokas, to what they once were. He allowed himself the briefest fancy that the one carrying him was Amala, whose friendship would have shocked all and banished him from his own people; who knew it was time now…who curled her talons to let him return to her, wing to wing, and so his hands slid down over them and closed on air.

FALCA WAS THINKING how the woman's eyes looked like those of the flenx that night after Amala's death; about the musty smell of lunelings in this darkened cellar; and being unable to do a cramming thing to help the Limbs…and then came a faint, prolonged squeaking, followed by a rustling, a quick tapping.

The sounds hadn't come from the top of the stairs and the floor-hatch the groods had shut behind them earlier. No, the sound seemed to have come from deeper in the cellar. Foraging rats? The soft rasping of lunelings squirming in their earthen beds somewhere close by in this storeroom?

The woman, Shar Stakeen, moved past him by the stairway and leaned over. He felt her breath on his cheek, the cupping hand. "Just in case it isn't a scullery maid hiding down here."

She slipped away, but not far. The gleam of her eyes returned, lower now, the only brightness in the dark.

She wants to hide, so be it, Falca thought.

He stepped ahead, so that whoever it was wouldn't be able to see those eyes. He waited long enough to think that maybe the sound had been the skittering of rats after all…until he heard a metallic tink and harsh breathing, as if some-one had made a climb.

The corner of a storeroom blushed with the glow of lunelings, revealing a man scarcely bigger than a large Limb, with out-sized ears and sunken eyes. Dead lunelings coiled around his hands, the tail ends secured by his thumbs. He wore a triangular pendant—a tiny mason's level—from the top of which hung a sparkling red jewel.

The bunched luneling light was more than enough for Falca to see the men behind, three of them, in plain leather caps, one a hawk's bill. They came forward at a nod from the wee man: a trio well-sized for persuasion, two of them flanking Falca. Between them they hefted a stonecutter's pick-axe, a prising bar and carpenter's adze.

The little man said: "I'm here to get you out."

"With help I see. And you are…?"

"Furka Vat. I'm the one who built this place—where's the woman?"

There was no reason to involve her. Falca pointed up. "The Wardens kept her."

Vat rubbed at a wen on his cheek the size of the jewel. "A pity. Where better than down here to fully appreciate those remarkable eyes."

So that's it, he thought. *The krael.* He said: "I'm curious—how did you hear what went on above, in the hall? Surely you weren't eavesdropping in the kitchens like the other householders."

"Never mind that. First, let's get you out, and then we can talk about what healed the woman and brightened her eyes."

"I'm missing the difference—you or Heresa Hoster."

"Oh, but there is one: to me, and certainly to the man who murdered her son—she'll never forget that. Now, shall we go?"

Falca quickly considered his choices. Down here, with three groods guarding the hatch, he wasn't going to be able to be of much help to the Limbs above. But this Vat obviously had another way out. And if there was one there might be another—and a chance to take it. He couldn't do that if he made a move now and they coshed him. He might be able to take one, but not all of them.

"Very well," Falca said. "As you say, we'll talk later."

Two of the men prodded Falca from behind. The third man stayed close behind. Vat led the way, the luneling glow casting shadows on the walls.

They trudged deeper into the cellar.

Falca never heard Shar Stakeen come up from behind—and neither did the deek bringing up the rear. She must have yanked him back by the neck. In quick succession: a grunt, the clattering of dropped iron, the cracking of a head on the floor.

Falca shouldered his other escort into the near wall with such force the man huffed his breath. The crowbar clanged, sparking against stone. Falca yanked it free from his grasp, and dropped as the third man's adze struck the wall above his head. Grit sprayed the back of Falca's head. He swung the bar low and hard, cracking bone, before this one could recover for a second strike. He scrambled to his feet, stepping over the groaning deek, breathing hard.

All was blackness. Vat had fled. Falca hurried after him, keeping the bar in front, a blind man's stick tapping floor to wall and across to the other. If he got to the entrance, wherever it was, all was lost.

Stakeen was behind him, whispering urgently. Twice he echoed the calls, giving a shout the third time—never mind the groods now—for ahead was the faintest light that faded quickly from a doorway. The bar chattered along the wall, then fell away to emptiness. Knowing Vat had no weapon, Falca rushed through the doorway.

The dim light in the room illuminated only ceiling-high cases of bottles set against the far wall. Vat frantically shed lunelings from his hands in the open space between one case along the wall and another angling out into this wine cellar. Brighter light shone beyond a low wooden door.

Falca bolted toward him, lunging with the crowbar, preventing him from closing the door at the last moment. He fell heavily but held on to the bar as Vat, on the other side, tried to shove it out, then yank it free when he realized he was pushing against Falca's weight. Cursing, he gave it up. Falca scrambled to his feet, ducked through with the bar—and knocked over a pail of squirming lunelings on the small landing. The bucket clattered down the narrow circular stairwell lit by more lunes hanging from hooks set in the rough-hewn walls.

Stakeen backed in, crouching as he had, pulling on a looped rope fixed to the squeaking outer casement—what they'd heard before. She slammed the low door. "No bolt on this—but what's to keep out if no one knows it's here?"

She was breathing as if she'd been out for an evening stroll.

Who *was* this woman?

"By the way," she said, "thanks for telling Vat the Wardens had me—it helped."

"Helped? You could have stayed hidden. I'm the one—never mind; let's get out of here. The groods above must have heard the ruck down here."

Falca took the lead down the steps. The passage was so narrow the rough stone walls bruised his shoulders. Only lunelings spitted on the walls kept his traps-and-squeezes at bay.

They hurried as fast as they dared, given the steepness of the descent. Falca's prising bar banged here and there against the walls. Twice, he almost slipped on the lunes spilled from the bucket he'd kicked off the landing above.

The stairwell ended at another landing smaller than the first. There was the pail, improbably upright, as if someone had left it at the opening of the tunnel that beckoned with lunelight, unlike the second tunnel here.

Stakeen entered the lit tunnel, but not far; Falca the other. He tapped the bar on the floor ahead, shivering with the chill of this black maw, remembering what Heresa Hoster had threatened. This tunnel seemed more like a lair for her pet beast than passage. But hadn't she also hinted at a watery pen for the thing?

Back at the landing he asked Stakeen if she'd heard anything.

"Nothing, but it slopes down. There's probably a hidden postern somewhere in the rock below the walls. You?"

He shook his head. "It's level, as far as I went. The little bastard wouldn't have taken that one. He and his men wouldn't have come through the dark, to take us back through it."

She headed for the lit tunnel.

Falca caught her arm "Not that way. He could have more men down there, wherever it leads."

"It leads to our escape."

"Go if you want—if you can swim as well as you…"

"That? Any woman who grew up with four older brothers who treated me like a fifth could have done the same—so you'd rather deal with a hundred Wardens above than Furka Vat and a few more of his henchies?"

"I have friends up there who need help."

She smiled. "I assume you're not talking about the bitch and her brood. Well, why not? I'd like the chance to hear why flokas would carry Limbs to battle, and why your price for these eyes was something that could never be given."

"And I'd like to hear a few things from you, too," Falca said, "but I doubt either of us will ever get a chance for answers. Let's go."

In the tunnel, Falca felt like he was being swallowed up. As the dim light receded behind the woman, his traps-and-squeezes returned. He used the bar to make sure there were, in fact, two sides to the passage; that it wasn't a ledge cut into the rock, with nothing on the other side. He crouched lower than he had to, so he could skid the bar along the floor and make sure there wasn't a trap along the way—and not covered like the deadfall beyond the top of the steps leading into the great hall.

The bar rasped and chittered in the blackness of this…throat, for that's what it seemed like to Falca. In places he had to turn to get his shoulders past the sides of it, and each time he saw the woman's eyes before he went on. Her hand never left his belt; without that constant touch he would not have known she was there. Or was it only his louder breathing that masked hers?

He wanted to move more quickly, to reach the end of this tunnel, to see if the wonder of Gurrus' summoning of flokas would be enough—and then do what he could to help. There was only one place that mattered: the gateway to Scaldasaig.

The only hope was to lower the cullies, and shut the gates to prevent thousands of groods from pouring into Scaldasaig from the bridge. If this tunnel led anywhere close to the small pen where those Limbs were kept, he and Stakeen could free them. There'd been no more than ten in there—a pittance. But if enough of the Limbs carried to the castle by the flokas were still alive, they might be able to overwhelm the Wardens at the drum towers and salleyport.

They went in deeper and deeper. Falca saw no glint of an end, breathed no better air, heard no sound of lake water lapping by the opening of a postern. His greatest fear was that the tunnel would lead outside the walls. His escape would mean the abandonment of Gurrus, Styada, Ossa and all the Limb captives—and helplessly watching thousands of Wardens stream across the bridge.

He could see it now, a vision he glimpsed for a moment, as if daylight had pierced this tomb-like passage. It dissolved, suddenly painful: a rock sticking out from the wall jabbed his shoulder.

The vision returned with the darkness. Falca realized it had only been interrupted, and the end of it so startled him he thought he had to be dreaming… dreaming all of this back in that darkened room of the inn by Sciamachon's Fountain, with Gurrus and Amala. They hadn't even begun their journey; she was still with him…

"Falca? Are you all right? We can always go back, take the other way."

"No."

The voice wasn't Amala's, and what he'd seen wasn't a dream but what he'd once scorned as such. What had Gurrus called it? Falca could hear him now giving him the answer.

Kesslakor…

What else could it be when you were awake, moving, and capable of feeling a rock jab your shoulder? Where else did fear, hope and voices mingle but in the darkness necessary for a vision?

The chances of success were slim, but it was worth the try, beginning wherever the light might finally meet them. It could work…it might work.

"What might work?" Shar Stakeen said,

He hadn't realized he'd spoken aloud.

"A way out," he said, quickening his pace so much her hand left his belt.

"We're doing that."

He turned and met those golden eyes, as feral as his had been. "No, not for us."

Chapter Forty-One:

HUMS AND CLAWS

BEFORE LEAVING TO join the killing-feast on the turris ramparts the three Wardens ordered Tolo Glessar to stay on the floor-hatch that led down to the cellar. One of them, the optio said: "The Lady said yer not fit for the fight above, but she thinks you're a heavy enough sack of potatoes to keep that poxy pair below until it's over."

Tolo did as he was told but grabbed a knife from the sculllery just in case. He stopped tapping it on his wooden foot when he heard the sounds below. He first thought the Draican was fucking the woman and stayed where he was, sitting against the wall, his legs thick as joists over the hatch-handle. He didn't care if the Draican had a go down there in the dark; so much the better if he was basting Lambrey Tallon's quiver.

All seemed quiet now so he assumed they were done.

Then he heard the moaning. He got up.

The sounds, though faint, weren't a woman's. What had the flenxy-eyed woman done to the Draican, this Falca Breks? Tolo figured there'd be no harm in checking it out. The pair wouldn't be trying to lure him down, hoping to overcome him and escape. Why would Breks want to escape so soon after he'd arrived? Tallon's woman might, but surely she realized there was no way to get out of Scaldasaig.

He speared a luneling from the kitchen bucket with the knife, opened the hatch and clumped down the steps. There was enough light for him to see the boots of one man lying not far away from the stairs, the arms of another beyond—and his broken neck.

Tolo recognized him as one of Furka Vat's lead masons, Lofel Zahar. Had he and the other dead man taken refuge from the fighting above? But there'd been no one in the cellar when the Wardens shoved Breks and Tallon's woman down there, leastways by the stairs.

Tolo frowned, scratched the nub of his left ear. Breks and the woman had to have killed them. Why? There was no place to go, and they wouldn't have left a carpenter's adze—there it was again: the groaning; fainter and deeper in. The Draican? The woman this time?

He took the adze, trudged ahead, keeping the lune stuck on the point of the kitchen knife, and stopped when he heard a creaking ahead off to his right, coming from the wine and cider room. He waited, listening. The groaning stopped. He went on. The luneling slipped off the knife, and when he stooped to put it back on, he saw the smeared trail of blood.

There was no one else in the low-ceilinged room except for a man who hadn't quite made it through an opening by the carcase of bottles that should have been flush against the far wall.

Tolo put the adze down, rolled over the body: no answers from this one. But as he pulled the carcase open more and lodged the dead man against it, he realized he didn't need answers. He might be slow afoot, with half his hearing; he might sound like he was talking through mouthful of food, but he wasn't stupid.

Beyond the low portal where he squatted, holding the lunelinged knife, there was a landing and circular stairs leading down. This could only be Furka Vat's doing, and he'd bet his good right foot that the Hosters didn't know anything about this this hole in the wall.

No wonder Tallon hadn't found the master-mason. The Draican and Bluegum's woman couldn't have known about this. The men wouldn't have acted without Vat's bidding so that probably meant the runt was with them when they came for the pair. There could only be one reason why Vat wanted the man, but how had he known about the Draican's krael that healed the woman and Maldan? Scaldasaig's snidgy little architect hadn't been in Hoster Hall.

It seemed Breks had more of an edge to him than clever words. Those had been pleasurable enough for Tolo to hear, more often than not coming at Heresa's expense, but this was something else again. His respect ticked up for the man—and the woman, too. The Draican couldn't have taken all three of Vat's men by himself.

And Furka Vat couldn't have managed Breks and the woman without his henchies. So that meant Breks and the woman had escaped, whether Vat was with them or not.

Tolo gave no thought of pursuit. If the bitch preferred him as he was, why bother with a slow, clumping chase, risk a scuff down there with the strappy-jack and his new friend who, without weapons, had coshed Vat's men?

As for the prospect of his own escape, he might as well be one of the flokas bringing mottles into Scaldasaig for slaughter. Wherever those stairs led, the passage had to go to water and boats hidden under some rocky overhang below the walls. How else to leave the Isle? But he couldn't swim, and it wasn't likely there'd be a boat left for him after the others had taken theirs.

Even if there was one, where would he go, the likes of him? Back to the streets of Bastia, to beg or hand-wrestle for his meals and drink? He wouldn't survive the trek back, anyway.

There was only one place he *wanted* to go, and for a moment in the hall, standing under the pentice with the other knucklers, he'd thought he might be able to get there: by volunteering to take the cup. But he hadn't stepped forward, made the gesture, never mind the words which only Heresa would have understood and likely ignored.

All he could do now was go up and tell the bitch what he'd found. She might order him killed for what she would think his fault, which was no more his doing than the other that had cost him an ear, and half his tongue—all for the crime of not knocking on her door loudly enough to tell her the dinner was cooling on the table in the hall below. Maybe he shouldn't have entered her chambers, but if she hadn't been at the rut with one of the Red Hands she would have heard him outside.

Kill him she might, yet that would at least be an escape from the shame he felt in being afraid of her—he who had never lost a match in the pits with any opponent, not even augors or the stoneskin that one time.

Short of killing him, what else could she do? Take the other ear, the last of his tongue? Just as she and Culldred had taken most of his pit-shine.

Yet he could take something from *her* now by telling her that *all* of them were gone: Breks, the woman and Vat. And with them the chance to pry the secret of those golden eyes so wasted on her bitten turd of a son. Tolo didn't care to puzzle things out further: such as why Breks would still want to escape if the master-mason hadn't been successful in capturing him. Something else was going on. But for Tolo, all that mattered was that Heresa wouldn't get what she wanted.

One of his few pleasures was to clump up to the turris battlements at night, done with his fetches and knuckling for the day, to gaze upon the ribbons of the moons upon the water, and think that the winnings they'd taken from him—their price for culling him from the hulks—might at least have gone for the last course of stone Furka Vat added to the keep, and so give him that much more to see or imagine in the distance.

He wasn't supposed to go up there, but he chose his moments to match the more tolerant sentries who thought him harmless. At first he bought his time by hand-wrestling a bored guard or two in an embrasure. Soon, they didn't bother with a challenge, for he never lost. He once had a voice, too, as resonant as his arms and legs were powerful, and he knew how to tell a story, but all the sentries heard up there was his humming.

Tolo left the room with its secret passageway, his wooden foot slipping on the trail of blood. He caught his balance though the luneling slipped off the knife. No matter, he could find his way back to the stairs. He'd fetched much from down here before, but nothing to compare to what he was bringing back up now.

He remembered a favorite ditty, "Kegs of Eggs", and began humming as he stepped around the two dead men. He wished Heresa was here now, forced to listen. Oh, she wouldn't remember it, though she once heard him singing it at a minstrel fest at the Lake Meleke villa. This was shortly before her well-crafted disappearance, and the long journey to a destination that could not be revealed; a trip that would later cost him his foot in an attack by a pack of forras. If they hadn't been close to Scaldasaig, Lambrey Tallon would have left him to die. The wankspit had been at the fest also. He, along with Tolo had been handpicked as Heresa's personal bodyguard, as if the Red Hands weren't enough.

Tallon had glared at him for his boisterous singing, but it was Heresa who shut him up: "We're paying them to sing, not you."

Halfway up the stairs, Tolo changed his mind about where Furka Vat might have used his pit-shine, that tiny portion of the money the Hosters needed to build Scaldasaig. He imagined now that his paltry contribution was the secret door in the cellar and the passage down, the way to freedom for the Draican and the woman—Tallon's no longer. And perhaps Furka Vat, too, with all the gold the Allarch and his Lady would never get back. He knew about that. He might have only one ear but that didn't mean he couldn't listen. Being thought of as a mere sack of potatoes had its advantages.

MALDAN HOSTER DUCKED out from underneath the wing of a dead floka hanging over a rear turret of the Drums. He wiped the blood off the falcata onto the black feathers. He hadn't killed the floka; it had been shot by two bowmen Kereni ordered up to the battlements of the Drums. The blood was from a mottle who had tried to flee, the last of the dozen the flokas dropped here at the gateway to Scaldasaig.

The falcata was a wonder, better than a stagger or skurr, and with it Maldan had killed five of the mottles himself. His father, who by now had the Eyes, too, would be proud of him. Yet heads of mottles or floka feathers weren't enough, nor the word of Uviah and Guldur, the only other men left alive on the Drums, to confirm his prowess. Anyone could yank out a feather the length an arm from a dead floka; Maldan wanted more to boast about in the years to come, when songs were sung in the halls about this day.

He'd kept his back mated to a merlon and let the mottles come to him instead of exposing himself in the open as the others had done so they could hurl their pilars. He ducked and sidestepped each time a floka dove at him, the backclaws raking the stone behind him as the great bird flew over.

Except for Guldur and Uviah, other Wardens hadn't been so lucky. Without shields they had naught but pilars to keep the flokas at bay. Once those were gone—thrown or cracked like twigs by talons—they had only skurrs and staggers, neither much good against swiftly moving creatures with wings whose breadth could span the width of Hoster Hall.

One by one Wardens fell to backclaws; a gash was all it took on the arm or shoulder, a slice that ripped open a ruerain. Had the wound been from any other common edge they could have fought on. They stumbled and fell, stunned to helplessness by that poisoned backclaw, and the mottles swarmed over them for the kill.

He could have saved some, but with Kereni among the first to fall, he couldn't risk it; he had to assume command here. He'd made the right decision, easily killing mottles who attacked him, and now the flokas seemed leery of dropping more. Two dead ones lay on the far drum tower, their wings covering much of it and many of the dead, Warden and mottle alike. Closer, a wounded floka stretched over the pitched center roof, shuddering, head lolling, the beak opening and closing as slowly as its red-rimmed eyes, the talons making feeble efforts to claw out the pilar in its neck.

Cossum had his namesake tower, as did Bovik. The Drums would be named after him now. Maldan was certain his father would see to that, for who else had the initiative to signal the Wardens to abandon Cossum's and Bovik's at the southeast corner, and toss the entry bars so the mottles couldn't defend the towers later?

No one else but him had seen what had to be done. The Drums were the key, to be protected at all costs, the sally kept open for the arrival of the shore-side prossars. The other towers didn't matter.

There had been ten Wardens each at Cossum's and Bovik's and Maldan had counted fifteen arriving below. He glimpsed perhaps twenty mottles on the battlements of Cossum's, shrieking with triumph, stabbing the air with the trowels and hoes and saws abandoned by the workers around the barbican: mere animals with tools.

There could be no doubt he'd saved Scaldasaig. Between the massive towers of the Drums, in the sally with its gates and cullies, the flokas couldn't get at the twenty-odd Wardens who were keeping the entryway clear for reinforcements that would be coming soon. And without flokas the Limbs would be so much butchered meat in the sally.

He watched a lone floka circling directly above, waiting for him to move away from the shelter of the turret, perhaps so it could swoop down to its wounded mate. They seemed to fly in pairs, and they were clever, these monstrous ravens. Somehow, they'd known to drop the mottles onto the towers and parapets where there had been few sentries posted for a morning that began so uneventfully. Maldan had no doubt this one would come down for the kill, sensing it was useless to bring more mottles if he was still alive.

He ignored Uviah's and Guldur's shouting, went into the cave made by the floka's body, stepped over the mottle's and quickly took the steps up—not down. The tower was *his*; he was loathe to leave it.

At the top a bowman lay crumpled at a corner embrasure, his bloody body fissured from crotch to neck, his bow snapped in half. Maldan pulled him away, wanting this vantage point, which had the best view of the bridge and shore.

The castlets and Limb stockade were ablaze. Most of the flokas were attacking the massed prossars on the shore now, but the huge birds were only delaying the inevitable. There were too many Wardens, shields aloft, hurling pilars, pressing forward, their discipline magnificent even at this distance as they reformed their turtles, stepping over the dead and stunned to keep on despite the barrage of flokas hurtling down upon the shields.

He had a mind to go down and lead a sortie over the bridge, to smash into the rear of the Limbs and hasten the moment when the prossars broke through the mottles holding out a the far end of the bridge. No, that time would be coming soon enough—where *was* that floka?

He swiped at his eyes with the back of a bloody hand, eyes that felt wet, as if he'd been weeping, yet the wetness seemed only to heighten his vision.

There…there it was: wheeling around now; beginning a dive, the wings motionless, beating no longer.

My floka, he thought…

It was as much his as the fledgling his mother captured as a gift for his father.

He knew what would happen when the surge of wind came, the moment before the kill. He'd seen it below. He braced himself, gripping the hilt of the falcata, the perfect weapon—heavy, but long and superbly balanced—to take his prize. Maldan had to give the Draican bastard this: he kept the blade sharp.

Maldan felt the gust, kept his eyes on those talons and backclaw, timing the descent. Wait a heartbeat too long and the floka would slash him.

He stepped quickly to his right and struck.

The falcata sliced through the wrist-thick leg above the talons.

His prize thumped against a merlon as he lunged ahead before the floka could split his skull with its beak. He backed against the wall, ready again with the falcata, but the floka took off, screeching, trailing a stream of purple blood.

Maldan retrieved his totem, and noticed a plump sac on the scaly leg above the backclaw which had a tiny channel, a hole just behind the tip. He smiled as he hooked the claw into his ruerain belt.

Here was his song and boast, and the insignia that would fill the space between the four-square fists of his honorary battleshield. But it was much more than that. The sac had to contain the poxy liquid that channeled into a floka's backclaw, and was forced out and into the victim.

Before the day was over he would cut out as many of those sacs as he could from dead flokas. No one else had to know why he was doing it. With this blessing smeared on the falcata, he could become a legend unequaled in the long history of the Wardens.

He was about to begin his culling of the sacs from the dead flokas below when he saw two figures running between the grove of fruit trees and the small quay at the end of the castle's southeast inner mere. The floka he'd wounded passed over them, and at first Maldan thought the pair were Cruthin scum trying to find refuge from the battle.

They came closer.

He couldn't believe his eyes.

Breks.

How had he escaped—and with Lambrey Tallon's woman? He could see her eyes even in the glare of sunlight. They seemed to be heading for the mottles' pen, a shed built against the wall just beyond Cossum's Tower. Breks carried a…prising bar? Where had he gotten that? The tall quiver had no weapon he could discern.

There were about ten mottles in the holding-pen. A Warden guard lay motionless nearby, slashed by a floka, no doubt. Was Breks going to free the mottles there, to help him escape through the sally? It wouldn't be enough. There were at least as many Wardens within the sally where flokas couldn't reach, and as many or more in the winch rooms above the cullies.

However Breks and the woman had escaped, they were clearly trying to flee from the attack. Yet it seemed very odd. A crouchalley he was but no craven lickspigot, not having brazenly sauntered into Scaldasaig with his pouch of krael and Cossum's blood on his hands, to demand an audience with the Allarch.

Maldan hurried down from the turret, trying to puzzle it out. Why would Breks want to escape *now*? Mother had laughingly indulged his ludicrous price—Milatum. If anything, the arrogant ditchlicker should have wanted to stay safely guarded in the turris, hoping the attack would fail. Limbs and flokas couldn't give him what he supposedly wanted.

Maldan peered through an embrasure.

Breks unbarred the pen's hatch. Mottles stumbled out, some bolting for the gates but the Draican wasn't joining them. He was waving at the remaining mottles to follow him in the opposite direction, toward Cossum's tower. For a moment Maldan's unease faded. If the scut thought that a better route for escape, he would be in for a surprise. He couldn't know that there were no boats in the outer mere, and all the mottles he'd taken to help raise the cully of Cossum's tower there would be useless. He and the woman would be trapped and…

Maldan suddenly realized he was staring at the answer: Cossum's lowered cully.

Breks wasn't trying to escape.

The Limbs and flokas couldn't give him Milatum, but he'd hoped they could give him what he *really* wanted.

Scaldasaig.

With the secret of krael to sell for mercenaries, and a recovered Shofet's hoard, he'd have all he'd need to keep it. Maldan remembered his mother's threats in the hall. Had she given this guttering reiver the idea how he might steal it?

There it was: he wasn't trying to get *out.*

He was going to try to keep thousands of Wardens from getting *in*—and there was only one way to do that now.

It was impossible. It couldn't work. Breks was a ditchlicker only too willing to place himself on the block, but how could he be certain?

Maldan calmed himself. The Draican wouldn't have the time, or the muscle to do it, not even with the woman to help him.

He shouted for Guldur and Uviah. They'd be more than enough to help him handle a man wielding only a prising bar. Breks would be in for a surprise, because what he'd seen wouldn't be what he needed.

Maldan hoped the Hole was big enough to stuff him down in one piece; after all, he was no mottle. But if not, Maldan had his falcata to pare him down.

Lalla wouldn't care how the meat came to her.

Chapter Forty-Two:

ABOVE AND BELOW

FALCA COULDN'T REMEMBER the word for 'friend' in Tongue, much less all those needed to explain to the Limbs why he needed their help. Freeing them from this small pen would have to be enough. Five followed but they scattered as soon as they saw where he was leading them. He couldn't blame them for not wanting to go into that tower from which no Limb ever returned. The beast's watery lair was somewhere below the tower. The pen was its pantry.

There was no time to go after the Limbs; that would only confirm their fear—which at least told him that the tower had to be the one with the lowered cully he'd seen from the bridge. He and Stakeen would shortly find out if only the two of them had the muscle to winch up the portcullis meant to guard the water passage through that tower.

They reached the base of the stairs leading up to the allure: the wallwalk which browed the front of the massive square tower. They were halfway up, Stakeen matching him step for step at his side, when something glanced off her head.

It was a hand, severed at the wrist, and not a Limb's.

She kicked the curled fingers away. "Can't they see we're not Wardens?"

"They only see we want to get in."

Falca ducked the leg—shorn below the knee, boot still on—that followed. He saw but two Limbs above, crowding an embrasure: one held Warden's stagger, the other an equally bloody mortar-maker's hoe. The Limbs taunted them: *'K'selo! K'selo!'*

Falca knew what the word meant since it had been directed at him often enough on the streets of Draica: *Up yours!*

A head came down next, shaved and numeraled at the back in Warden fashion but minus the eyes. It bumped and rolled all the way down the steps, pinwheeling blood, thumping into two timbers, reminding Falca of something he'd tried hard to forget: Amala, an empty, butchering her own dog with scissors. The dog's name was Shindy.

Shindyvarrek. Storm friend.

"*Varrek! Shindyvarrek!*" he shouted at the Limbs, four of them now crowding the embrasure, one with a Warden's broken pilar. Falca shouted the words again, thumping his chest and Stakeen's shoulder for good measure. He didn't wait for a response. Telling the Limbs that friends approached might not cover the bet, but they had to go on up.

He had only the prising bar, Stakeen the two common knives she'd taken from the table over the hole-stone they pushed off the ground floor of an eastern tower to get out of the infernally long tunnel. She had a third tucked in her belt, taken from a workman who'd made the mistake of trying to fight alongside two Wardens that flokas slashed and stunned before they could reach the safety of the orchard in the outer ward.

At least the Limbs hadn't barred the door farther down the landing. The door must have been left open by retreating Wardens. From the numbers Falca had seen crossing the outer ward, there couldn't have been many in the tower when the attack began. No wonder they'd fled.

If any Limbs had come down for an ambush at the entry they'd be off to the right, not behind the half-opened door. "*Varrek…varrek*," Falca yelled, and waited a moment. Stakeen had a knife in each hand. Falca sidestepped in, keeping his back to the door, the bar ready in his hands. She followed quickly.

The large chamber was empty, speared by meager light from arrow loops. Grated windows on opposite walls no doubt overlooked the course of the water-passage below. To Falca's right, near the corner, more stairs led up and down. He glimpsed another stairwell in a far corner of the chamber.

A fire still crackled in a hearth, a blackened haunch of meat hanging from a spit. Trenchers, bowls and cups littered the trestle table, its benches askew. The attack had interrupted the noon meal. However many groods had been killed or wounded above, some must have fled; the wooden bars to the door were missing. Had the Wardens thrown them outside so the Limbs couldn't barricade their prize?

Two rows of murderholes lined the center of the room's floor, including a bigger, grated opening in the middle. That had to be where the Limbs from the pen were dropped to the lake-kraken in the passage below. And that, Falca guessed, had to lead to another body of water which in turn led through a similar entry tower like this one, then on into the inner mere they'd run past in the outer ward. How else to keep trapped the syllysk?

The windlass drum at the west wall was set high enough for the spokes to clear, but not by much. The drum wasn't as wide as the top edge of the portcullis itself, which rose just above the level of the floor. At either end, chains led up to heavy pulleys fixed to a stout beam of the ceiling, then down again to wrap around the circular drum. There wasn't much chain there, not yet. There would be when they raised the cully.

Falca quickly set the iron ratchet spar, chose his spoke, Stakeen another. They began pushing at the spokes, one after another. The cully rose slightly from the floor, with the *click...click...click* of the ratchet.

He was closer to the window and saw in the distance flokas swooping and diving through the swirling smoke of the fires, harrying the thousands of Wardens at the shore-side of the bridge. The clashing of shields, the screams of Wardens and Limbs, the screeching of the flokas all merged into a roar of battle that had to be the source of his sudden burr: some of the Wardens had broken through the Limbs by the barbican.

The chains tightened.

Click...click...click...

Yet that wasn't it.

Falca had sensed something wasn't right as soon as he came into this chamber. It wasn't fear that they might not be able to raise the portcullis in time, and loose the syllysk before the Wardens swarmed across the bridge. Nor was it the likelihood the thing would just swim away. The only hope they had—a slim one—was that the beast would smash into the bridge of anchored boats.

Click...click...

No, it was the prod of having forgotten...overlooked something crucial, something he shouldn't have. Something was wrong.

"Why are you stopping?" Stakeen said.

"It's too easy."

He looked up to the pulleys on the beam and realized what the burr was. He cursed.

"For Roak's sake, Falca; what's the matter?"

"The damned cully stops at the water-line!"

"Of course it does."

"No, no…We're raising a cully meant to block a small ship, *not* what's underneath. There must be something else below to cage the beast. We're in the *wrong* place."

Light from the arrow loop between the nearest stairwell and the door flashed quickly—three times—followed by a muffled shout.

Wardens.

RUSHING THROUGH THE doorway first, from greater to lesser light, Maldan caught only the movement by the stairwell on the far side of the chamber. He knew it was them by their height, not mottles down from the parapets. Uviah and Guldur began to give chase; Maldan called the men back.

"Let them trap themselves. There's no way across below. They need this side of the passage, not the other. I'm going down to cut the haul-rope anyway. Both of you stay; I want no surprises up here. Understood?"

The scavs nodded.

"One more thing. When they realize their mistake they'll come back up. They may be foolish enough to attack you here, but if they don't, let them go."

Uviah scratched the scar where one eyebrow had been. "Let 'em go, Tenon?"

"You think they'll escape, with the prossars soon coming across the bridge? I need the man either dead or out of this tower."

"What about the mottles up 'ere?" Guldur said, pointing.

"Never mind them; they'll stay close to their fucking birds."

Maldan hurried down the stairs, pleased with his altered plan—yet more proof of his ability to adapt to the situation—a quality his father had always thought he lacked.

It was a pity about the Hole, but you couldn't drop someone to the beast who was already down there. And the woman? One thing was certain: Lambrey Tallon may have found her by the river, but *he* would be the last to baste her. A Golden-Eyes basting, the two of them: another song for the hall. If his father's favorite Red Hand didn't like it, there was always the edge of the falcata dipped in the honey of a floka's backclaw to calm him down.

FALCA STOOD WITH his back against the wall, ready to shatter the legs of the first Warden coming down. He hoped it would be Maldan Hoster. Stakeen, knives out, was on the other side of the stairwell end. At the far end of the passage, the lowered cully gridded light that fell on dark, placid water and part of the other stairwell and walkway.

Through the arched portal nearer to them, Falca glimpsed the outer mere and a section of the castle wall where it narrowed between two towers. The groods should have already come down by this stairwell or the others. Hoster may not have guessed their intent, but he'd be eager to kill them.

"Can't wait any longer," Falca said, and moved quickly toward the gate that spanned the gloomier middle of the passage. It had to be at least twenty feet wide, and rose almost to the level of the flanking walkways. A thick beam capped the top. Angled pikes protruded from the near face of the gate's mesh, which wasn't as closely set as the cully's. Presumably there were more spikes below the water to discourage the syllysk.

He saw no windlass fixed to the stone abutment beyond the gate, nor coil of rope, and he cursed himself for a fool—twice now. He should have looked first for rope attached to the gate, but his thoughts had been of the expected pursuit, ambushing the three, and then going to get the Limbs to help him and Stakeen open the gate.

"There it is, over there…the rope," Falca said.

"They knew that," Stakeen said. "We're on the wrong side."

"I'm going across."

"On the *gate*? It's too dangerous, we should…"

"It has to get over *here* for the pull. We'll need help. You'll have to go up and get the Limbs, as many…"

"The other stairwell is the only way."

Falca shook his head. "It's what they want us to do."

"So we kill them."

"With a bar and knives?"

"Better odds than your crossing on the gate. You fall in… the bitch's pet is in the water somewhere."

"There's no time for this. Get the Limbs! I'll walk the rope back if it's too heavy for the throw."

"Falca…"

"*Do* it, Shar. *Now!*"

He already had the bar at the level, feeling for the balance of it. He had the crazy notion that he might have to first fend her off from stopping him. She turned away abruptly. He saw her golden eyes again at the stairwell, and then she was gone.

Falca stepped out onto the top of the gate, bit his lip at the unforgiving width—maybe a foot, if that. He shuffled, leery of moving quicker, but soon found that short steps worked better, as did gently cradling the bar, not gripping tightly. He kept his eyes down to make sure of his next steps, told himself that if he lost his balance he must fall to the left of the gate; the other side was the pen and somewhere the syllysk lurked between the gate and the far end of the outer mere. It looked like the beast had tried to escape before—some of the stout, angling spikes, thick as his arm, had been snapped off.

He couldn't resist the temptation to look ahead, see how far he had to go…

The golden eyes so startled him he almost fell. He righted himself at a crouch, lowering the bar. The abutment to the left of the gate's end blocked his view of Maldan Hoster, but then he saw him sheathing the falcata, the eyes vanishing as he turned to the wall. Falca knew instantly he would have spurned the sword only for something much longer.

He was halfway across, couldn't swing the bar or parry, not with such a narrow base. Back or ahead? The only difference was that retreat would only delay the inevitable.

He stepped ahead quickly as he dared. Maldan had a gaff, with pointed end and frowned hook. Whether it was the shock of seeing that, or the slick beam, Falca's left foot slipped off. He scissored his body to the right, shifting the bar as Hoster swung the gaff. The bar took most of the blow, yet it was delivered so ferociously that the flat of the hook still hit him below the knee, scything him off the gate.

He splashed into the water on his back, let the bar go, flailing with his arms, sensing he'd fallen on the cully side of the gate, but not far. Before he went down again, he saw Maldan on the abutment projecting out behind the end of the gate.

If he surfaced there Hoster would impale him with the gaff, or split his skull. He fought panic, managed to keep his mouth closed, and kicked with all his strength, clawing under the water, its coldness already leaching his strength.

His hands found an edge of the gate. He needed air desperately. Then a powerful urge overrode that: a screaming inner voice—*NO, NOT HERE…*

He kept kicking, pulling himself through a wide opening. As he surfaced on the safe side, gasping his breaths into a slimy beam, his hand on a spike, he didn't know if it was the distant shouting behind him that he'd heard somehow, or his own instinct urging him to go where Maldan Hoster would not expect him to: beyond the protection of the gate and back *into* the syllysk's pen.

Hoster had ceased slapping, spearing the water with the gaff on the other side of the gate, but the beast might be on its way, or even now rising from the depths of the passage. Falca had to get out of the water—quickly—and the gate was the only ladder he had. Hoster was close—still on the abutment?—taunting Shar Stakeen: "He's gone! He's drowned!"

If she hadn't seen him before she surely did now as he pushed off from the crotch of the spike, water sluicing off, his feet scrabbling in the grid, his hands at the top of the gate where it met the walkway.

Hoster saw him, would have gutted him had he stood, but he rolled away, stopped by the coil of rope. The Warden thrust with the gaff. Falca leaped from the abutment, the wicked point missing him by inches. The hook caught in the rope; he seized the shaft. Hoster let it go, drawing the falcata, and quickly stepped past the lethal end of the gaff.

Instead of retreating to give himself time to reverse the gaff, Falca surprised him by lunging at his legs. Hoster tripped back over the coil of rope, losing the falcata which rasped over the walkway stone.

Draped upon the coil of rope, Falca held on to the Warden's boots as he tried to twist away, kick out. He got one leg free; Falca grabbed the other boot at the ankle, his hands a vise. He rolled off the rope, held on, and rose to his knees, a turning capstan now, forcing the brute over the edge of the walkway.

Hoster clawed at the corner of the abutment. Had Falca left to get the falcata, the man might have succeeded in climbing out. Falca ripped the flenx horns from his neck, and stabbed the back of the Warden's hand, then the other so hard he felt the jarring of the stone beneath.

Screams reverberated in the cavern of the passage. Maldan Hoster fell back into the water, his eyes coins of gold, and only then did Falca remember he'd promised himself the eyes of Amala's killer.

The hands would have to do.

MALDAN CLUNG TO the gate by elbow and wrist, screaming for Uviah and Guldur as Breks threw the thinner, weighted rope over the passage. He twisted in the water to see the woman catch it on the rebound from the wall and begin pulling, helped by five or six mottles.

The hawser dipped, rose and dipped again on the other side of the gate. He had only to swim through the gate to grab the rope and stop the hauling, but he couldn't force himself to do that. The beast was coming. Breks had already summoned it. Mother said Lalla was attracted by movement in the water which was why she'd insisted the mottles be dropped alive from the Hole above.

Maldan wanted to do it. Breks had done it. But there was no one here to later sing a song of how he'd given his life to keep the gate closed, and even if he did swim through he couldn't grip the rope, not with his ruined hands. He might be able to climb up onto the gate or walkway, but after? How could he fight with useless hands? Breks had the gaff and falcata.

On the other side, a Limb had found the second gaff used to hook or stab mottles back to where they belonged in the passageway. He'd enjoyed watching the futility of some who tried to escape from Lalla by swimming through to the safe lee of the gate.

He couldn't just cling to the gate as it opened; that would only bring him to the far side where the mottles would shred him to pieces with the gaff if the beast didn't get him first.

Breks was at the stairwell, waiting in ambush for Uviah and Guldur. Maldan screamed for them anyway. Through a square in the gate he saw the rope slithering past him, skipping away: The woman and her pack of Limbs were pulling it down the walkway for a better hauling angle, past the stairwell, into the glare of the portal to the outer mere.

He felt the tug of the gate as it began to creak open with a rippling of water. There was only one hope—swimming to the cully. Shed the weight of boots, ruerain, scabbard? No time, and he hadn't the hands to do it. But he could swim. He was strong in the water, better than any of his brothers.

He pushed off, immediately feeling the burden of boots and armor, but kept kicking, churning the water. His hands no longer throbbed with pain; he could cup them. That fueled his hope and diminished his fear of what was behind him. He could do it, reach the bottom of the cully and…

…then climb up high so the beast couldn't get him…and wait until it passed under and swam away around the spur of land, surely…and then he could make his way along the cully, back to the shore under the walls to the landing by the Drums…and join the last of the men coming over the bridge and hunt Breks down…and Breks would be the one trapped, not him.

He thought he heard a sharp scream. The ambush at the stairs? He kept stroking, powerfully, aware he was into the grid of light shimmering on the black water. He was almost there…

One hand smashed against a broad point of the portcullis, but the pain and his exhaustion was nothing compared to his exultation. The cully was higher than it should be, but he might be able to reach the nearest horizontal bar. He looked back, blinking the water from his eyes.

The gate was almost open now.

He felt the pressure of water surging toward him. Waves of water sloshed over the rim of the walkways; the gate thudded against stone. Pushed ahead on the rushing tide the floka's claw—his totem—tumbled toward him.

The onrushing tide lifted him. Frantically, he grabbed for a higher iron bar, pulled himself up. His left boot snagged on a point. He lodged a knee, pushed up. Water pressed him against the cully, roiling underneath him, the grid still parceling out daylight and a prisoner's view of the bridge packed with thousands of men.

Much closer, his saw his hands were clear of the stab wounds, but this fleeting wonder—his last—came with a terrible wrenching below, and his final thought was that this wonder wouldn't be enough.

KNEELING BY THE stairway beside the bodies of the two Wardens he killed, Falca heard the joyous whooping of Limbs and golden-eyed Shar Stakeen shouting to him across the passage. Did those eyes have something to do with convincing enough of them to come down?

Water sluiced back over the edge of the walkways, the only evidence now of the syllysk's passing, a *shusshing* that reminded him of the rivulets that trickled into the pool below the falls where Amala died.

Shar shouted something else but it was lost in the echoing jubilation of the Limbs. He was too tired to yell back. He got to his feet, gestured up. She nodded. He stepped over the bodies, the falcata once more in his hand, to go up and see if this would be all for naught.

Falca hoped the image of Maldan Hoster's death would last him a lifetime—though that probably could be counted in hours. He had paused to watch Maldan Hoster climbing higher on the cully until he realized he'd lost his body at the waist, and dropped between the spiny ridges of the syllysk, slipping away into the water as the beast sunk back into the depths of the passage.

✵

SHE HAD NO name for the Isle, nor did she remember her mother had birthed her there long ago. She only knew it was the place she had to go to deliver her brood, where she could feed her young and protect them from the male who had seeded her and might yet return to devour them. She knew that until she led them out, her instinctual duty done, they would be safe from the only other predator she feared, who came from above yet could hunt below. That had been the fate of her mother far away, but she did not know that and could not know the name given to that creature by all who dwelled on land, whether they revered the creatures as gods or not: the Erseiyrs.

Nothing had hindered her passage from the lake and down to the entrance of the channel that led to the cavern. Nothing blocked her way when she left four times to feed in the deep waters of the lake and awe that led to the ocean beyond, and so bring back sustenance to her young. She was aware of the puny creatures inhabiting the Isle, but the passage remained open—until she came back to the Isle the fifth and last time.

The way down to the cavern was blocked and barbed and she could hear her young, helpless and hungry. In her rage she rammed the obstacle repeatedly, to no avail: the way was crooked and she could not gather sufficient momentum to destroy it, as she could the food-bearers that moved on the surface of deeper waters.

She lost one of her eyes to the barbs, but stayed close until she knew that a youngling had died, and so would she if she did not eat. But she could not leave for the deeper water to hunt. That way out, too, was blocked and barbed now. She did not starve. The puny creatures gave her food and she took it, but she could not bring it to her two remaining younglings.

She was trapped.

The second of her offspring died.

The last had now fallen silent, replaced by a sound so painful to her that she thrashed her body, scored her underbelly and sides along the rock to rid herself of the pain, but it persisted. She swam toward the source of her agony, away from the barbs that had taken the eye, to end her life on the others so she would not have to endure the torment any longer, and that of her brood's silence.

But these barbs were gone now, the passage clear and she kept on, rising to take the last food of this place. The source of the sound lay directly ahead, like those she'd heard mingling with the wailings of her young before they died, yet much louder and more painful than the sounds of the creatures that fed her and sometimes watched her.

This was a shoal of those sounds; the water teemed with them, barbs that seemed to pierce her everywhere and nowhere. She sensed she was not bleeding. Never before had she felt such pain. They were attacking her with the sounds, these creatures who had trapped her, prevented her from nurturing her young.

She was trapped no longer. She sensed there was nothing between her and them. She reveled in the deeper water, the distance and thus the means to gather her strength to destroy them. Her rage returned, further blunting her pain as she swam quickly toward the source of her agony: a reef teeming with puny creatures upon the water.

LAMBREY TALLON GRIPPED the shortened reins, his knuckles taut and white. The others with him remained in their saddles, too stunned to dismount from the lathered horses they'd ridden hard up the river road that morning, Red Hands all: Vopel, Giff, Gaimar, Scibar, and the optio Feccan, Tallon's second-in-command.

They'd pulled up abreast, across the crest of the road where it dipped down toward the lakeshore from the cut in the bluff. No one said a word. The fleeing workmen they'd passed on the way had said there'd been an attack, and they'd seen smoke drifting over the bluff, but this…*this* was beyond curses.

If they'd been sixty and not six, Tallon would have given them the order they did not want to hear but would have obeyed without question. They might have killed ten times their number of mottles down there before they died, but that would not have saved the encircled remnants of the First, nor the Allarch, nor the castle he boasted would be in his own lifetime the bone in the throat of the Six Kingdoms.

No doubt Culldred would rather be dead than know he'd played the fool for Furka Vat, sending the six after a wagon-load of chests that were empty, not filled with the money the Allarch wanted back. And dead he probably was.

The success of Vat's ruse had saved their lives, but Lambrey Tallon was not thinking about that now. If the High Fates—those sons-of-bitches—hadn't had their amusement for the day, they'd have made sure the wee bastard hadn't yet escaped from Scaldasaig, his cleverness and skill at hiding trumped by this unforeseen attack, his paychests useless ransom to save his life because mottles had no use for gold.

The hope for that was fleeting. The earlier search had been thorough. Vat had escaped, however he'd done it. There would be no escape for all the Wardens down there. Culldred's sons were no loss and neither was Heresa, whom he had never quite trusted after he rebuffed her overtures the last time he was at Scaldasaig.

And Shar Stakeen?

He'd never know now if, as he suspected, her talents in bed were matched by the lies she told him about who she was, and how she'd come to be in the Bounds. For two days it hadn't mattered. Would it ever have?

The nickering horses stamped and snorted their unease at the screeching of flokas quilting the skies and shore. The incessant *keeraw*...*keeraw*...cut through the turbulence of screams and wails of dying men and Limbs, the clanging of metal, the clashing and knocking of shields. Scores of flokas were attacking the rear echelon of the Wardens—the First prossar by the wavering flenx standard—who were hemmed in by the lake on one side and thousands of encircling mottles on the shore, making their stand by the half-finished barbican. The First was his—or would have been—given Aldrach Aarl's Bloodwing, and Culldred's promise of a basileus' gold cingulet.

There was nothing he could do to help them.

He pulled out from his belt the spyglass taken from the runty deek, now dead, whom Furka Vat had chosen to ride from the gates in his stead, no doubt hooded, with the well-known glass at his eye to complete the disguise.

The floating bridge was gone, save for the severed ends. Wreckage littered the water: smashed boats and planking; thousands of shields and bodies tossed by waves churned up by the flokas above. They swooped, dove, wheeled around to dive again at survivors clinging to the few boats still intact or to makeshift rafts of shields. All the others caught in the crossing—and burdened by ruerains, sodden boots and gambesons—had drowned.

Wardens crammed the landing at the end of the bridge. There was nowhere for them to go. The outer cully had been lowered, and with each pass flokas, a dozen of them at the Drums alone, thinned their ranks. Mottles on the ramparts and flanking wall-walks added to the toll, hurling captured pilars and staggers, and shoving off dead Wardens through the embrasures. Still more flokas carried Limbs across the water to Scaldasaig. Tallon knew they'd keep bringing more until every man in the garrison was dead.

Only one thing could have destroyed the temporary pontoon bridge. With the spyglass Tallon caught the wake of the beast before it disappeared beyond the rocky finger of land that jutted out south of the towers named after the Allarch's dead sons. Those few mottles at the top of Cossum's tower couldn't have opened the gate below. No, somehow the lake-kraken—Heresa's pet—had done it. Gored by the gate spikes, *somehow* it had gotten through—at the very moment thousands of Wardens were charging over the long bridge.

And then Lambrey Tallon saw her with those mottles, the glass bringing clarity to what had been distant figures a moment before: Shar Stakeen at an embrasure. And next to her…

Lambrey Tallon blinked, lowered the spyglass.

It couldn't be…had to be his eyes…the smoke…a trick of the lens that made her eyes like jewels in the sun…and the man beside her had to be…could *only* be someone else—a Cruthin hireling with the falcata Maldan had taken from the dying Breks at the falls so far from here.

He looked again, and saw the face of the man whose betrayal long ago had sent him to a River Rhys prison hulk, whose agonizing death at the falls had given Lambrey Tallon the greatest pleasure he'd ever known.

Yet here he was, pointing away, and now his hand was on her arm, and she was nodding—the woman who brought Tallon to a basting sweat only two days before.

"Comitor?"

The voice—Feccan's beside him—came distantly. He had the urge to give the optio the glass, and…what? Order him to see something else than what was there on Cossum's tower?

"Nothing, Feccie. It's…nothing." Saying anything else would mean an explanation he could not give, and the certainty of the men talking later about a man who should be dead but wasn't. Falca Breks' resurrection now prompted another: Tallon's loathing for a man he thought was gone forever, his revenge so sweetly sated.

The comitor could say nothing; if he did they would only marvel later, whispering behind his back, about how Falca Breks unleashed the beast. Who else could have done it? Shar Stakeen must have helped him; she was at his side. And somehow the man willed the kraken to smash into the bridge. If he could cheat death he could do that.

And still more whispers: of how Breks escaped death at the falls and here yet *again*…impossibly here…to kill the rest of the Hosters…and be *rewarded* with the most formidable castle in the Six Kingdoms *and* one quiver to replace the other.

Leaving me, he thought, *with a spyglass, beggar's change in my pocket and the hope of selling six swords to some petty southern noble, when I once would surely have commanded the army of a Seventh Kingdom.*

Lambrey Tallon bent Furka Vat's spyglass in half, cracking the lens, and hurled it away. He jerked his reins, spurred his mount to a gallop, leaving the others to catch up, follow him south and wonder at whom he was screaming: "The least you can do now, you *sons-of-bitches,* is give me a ford to cross the fucking river."

Chapter Forty-Three:

MERCIES

MOVEMENT ROUSED STYADA: a floka was carrying him to his death. Then he realized what he'd heard was Falca's breathing, not the beating of wings; the pain not from talons but his wounds.

He remembered lying on the top of the tower, wondering if the shitcatcher next to him would die before he did and hearing the shout from below: *Varrek! Varrek!* Falca's voice. Yet only a tall female with shining eyes came up, gesturing her need to have the Kelvoi go below with her.

The others, mostly Skeels, refused. He got to his knees, picked up the bloody sword Ossa had left for him, rose unsteadily to his feet. He screamed at them, shaming them to go down with the female. She had to be with Falca; she would not have come up without him if he didn't need help.

The Skeels obeyed him. Earlier, they'd been astonished when a shitcatcher tried to stab him in the belly with a spear. The force of the thrust hurled Styada back against the stone wall. A second stab should have impaled him.

The kinnet saved him. Styada charged the equally astonished shitcatcher. He couldn't remember now how he'd gotten his other wounds, only that he'd bloodied the sword and collapsed near the kneeling shitcatcher who clutched his groin, hands brimming red…

Now, he heard Falca saying words he didn't know—*gatehouse…cully…keep*—then familiar oaths sweetened with surprise and relief it seemed. Styada felt himself lowered and pulled into darkness, coolness: the place where his breaths would cease? But Falca lifted him again, carried him through the darkness that soon brightened, bringing back warmth and a different sound to Falca's breathing…and something else—not what Styada heard, but what he didn't: the clicking of the flenx horns around Falca's neck.

They were gone.

Styada's pain couldn't overwhelm the pride he felt in making the holes in the bone for the flessok cord he braided so tightly. He didn't think he'd get the chance to find out where Falca used the horns.

He did hear fatigue in Falca's breathing and wanted to tell him to let him down; that he'd come farther than he ever thought possible. He couldn't form the words.

Falca kept on.

It didn't matter where his friend was taking him, for at the end there would be Gurrus and Freaca. He had returned the kinnet to the Isle, which had in turn given him something he never dreamed he'd ever find.

UNABLE TO MOVE, Lannid Hoster lay on his side close enough to his father to touch him. He could hear flokas screeching, scraping talons on stone, which had to be the death throes of others, not the one that had brought about this teasing harbinger of death that let him breathe, let tears fall, but do little more, not even move his tongue.

He couldn't turn his head to see anything beyond what lay directly in front of him: four Wardens, dead or immobilized as he was. Blood pooled about his right hand. He watched the stream, thinking, in spite of everything, that Furka Vat's masons had carelessly measured the level of the flooring on the keep's battlements.

Lannid didn't know if the blood was his own, his father's, or the dead mottle straddling his legs. He felt no pain from his wound, but it couldn't have been severe. The floka had grazed him on the arm with its backclaw, screeching in agony at the pilar a dying Warden had plunged into its belly.

When he'd come up with Tolo, his father was already dead. The eyes, so briefly golden, darkened now beyond amber, stared off in one direction, his body faced another: a floka's beak or talons had all almost completely decapitated him.

At least his father hadn't seen his pitiful efforts to get to him, flailing away with Stesso Kubelai's sword at the attacking flokas, to no more effect than batting at apples in a tree.

The Limbs were all dead or dying then, but the flokas hadn't flown off yet. The few remaining Wardens fought on as Lannid kept screaming, unsuccessfully, at Tolo to take the pouch of krael, go back down and escape.

More flokas would surely be coming, dropping more Limbs. More mottles would be coming up from the yards. If he couldn't move, could not even feel the pain of his gashed arm, perhaps he would feel nothing when they killed him. He had no regrets about coming back up, nor did he want to lie to himself and believe he did it because of his father. Lannid despised what his father had done. At least now he would never wonder if he would have had the courage to walk away from it.

No, he went back up from the cellar because there was no place else to go.

But there had been…

He knew now why his mother had left his father's chambers so abruptly, had not stayed to witness the miracle of the krael Falca Breks had brought. Lannid had gone to find her, because her name was the first word Culldred had spoken after he regained consciousness. She was in Cossum's room, with Tolo. She said he had discovered a hiding place, through which Breks and the woman—and Furka Vat—had evidently escaped. She wanted him to come with her and Tolo and quickly. Yet surely there was time to tell his father about this. It seemed odd to Lannid that she didn't want her son to do that, saying the Allarch would want them to go while they could. "None of us could persuade your brave father to leave the fight and abandon his duty; not I, not you or Stesso, and certainly not Tolo."

She was right.

His golden-eyed father had his voice back, and the whispers of Stesso Kubelai at his ear as well. He clenched the sword that had been placed at the foot of the bed in anticipation of his death, the point facing out, for Wardens believed there were as many enemies to be vanquished in death as in life.

"Go with your mother and Tolo," Culldred said. "Look out for her; you can do that. I could not bear it if anything were to happen to her, especially now. I cannot spare the men; you and Tolo must keep her safe. She and I will have much to talk about when this is over." He smiled in the strangest way, as if there would, in fact, be little to discuss.

Below in the cellar, Tolo refused to follow Lannid and Heresa through that low, secret portal. Lannid didn't understand. "Why won't you come? We'll be safe there."

Tolo garbled his words but the head-shaking was an obvious enough refusal. Heresa would have none of it. "Nonsense. You can still row a boat if there's one to be had."

That had seemed strangest of all to Lannid: why the need to take a boat? They'd be safe in this secret place.

Tolo didn't move, kept rubbing the stump of his ear—that punishment, along with a halved tongue, for his raping of a Cruthin woman, a favorite of his mother's. When Lannid had heard of what he'd done, he could not believe it. Tolo?

"I should have asked you before," Lannid said to him. "Did you do it? Did you rape that woman?"

Tolo shook his head.

Heresa sighed. "Lannid, this isn't the time for what's past. He's paid his due; I've forgiven him. We..."

"He says he didn't do it."

"What do you *think* he'd say? He wants to stay and die, let him."

But Lannid persisted with Tolo. "You were punished for something else, then?"

The servant nodded, pointing at Heresa, then at his own eyes, and lastly made a circle of his thumb and forefinger, poking another through it.

She slapped the hand away. "How *dare* you! Who do you think you are, you stupid cripple." She pulled at Lannid. "He...we *must* go now."

Lannid turned to face his mother. He'd thought she'd taken the pouch of krael for safekeeping, but now that seemed to have another purpose. Why had she seemed so reluctant to see if the krael could save his father, after it had been obvious it wasn't poison?

"Was it you...what happened to father?"

"Lannid, not *now*! We'll talk of this..."

"That's what father said. You weren't with him in the room after; you couldn't bear to see me give the krael to him. That's why you want to leave...he suspects it was *your* poison, not a floka's."

He snatched the pouch from her and pushed her away. After closing the door, then the casement, he looked for something to wedge it so she couldn't escape. He realized there was no need of that, or wondering how she could be capable of poisoning her husband, or asking her why she'd done it, because he heard no wailing or pounding or screaming as an innocent person might have done. Even now she was capable of silence. That seemed proof enough, all the answer he needed as he followed Tolo, crunching on shards of broken bottles underfoot, back the way they'd come.

Neither did he need an answer for why Stesso Kubelai accosted them in the hall, shoving aside fleeing Cruthin householders, swatting the last of them with the flat of his father's deathbed sword to get to Lannid and Tolo more quickly. He'd shed his green vestments. Lannid thought the medicant should have been on the battlements with the Allarch. His skill with a blade had always seemed to exceed that of his ministrations to the Hoster family.

Kubelai blocked Lannid's way, ignoring Tolo, saying the Allarch had sent him down to guard Lannid and his mother in the cellar. But he wanted to know if the Lady Heresa had the krael, not why they'd left her.

"My mother has it," Lannid said, instantly wishing he'd looked Kublai in the eyes, to give heft to the lie.

"Lannid, this…matter lies within the province of a medicant such as I, entrusted with the well-being of many, including your family. Surely you understand that."

"I said she has it."

"Or perhaps you took it from her?" He tapped the sword point on Lannid's chest.

Tolo punched away the sword and was on Kubelai, another fist separating the medicant's hand from hilt. As Lannid picked up the sword, Tolo swept the man's legs from under him and quickly locked them in a scissoring hold. Kubelai ceased his shrieking long enough to draw a hidden shortshrift dagger and struck twice—a shallow stab at Tolo's shoulder—then punched his head, a blow that would have dazed any other man.

Kubelai screamed as Tolo broke first the right leg, then the left: *crack…crack*. His cut hand seeping blood, Tolo got out from under, pushing away the useless legs as if they were sagging gates to a pasture.

Halfway up the stairwell leading to the battlement Lannid turned to wait for him. Tolo was saying something Lannid couldn't understand. Stesso Kubelai's screams below reverberated over the clumping of Tolo's wooden foot on the stone steps, and soon the screeching of the flokas masked that as they continued up. Lannid saw an arm reaching inside to the landing above. A shadow darkened the stairwell, then passed. The arm remained, not moving, the fingers curled, as if waiting to accept Lannid's sword, so he could flee back down, go back to where he belonged…

Now, Lannid opened his eyes at voices—Limbs', four of them, with Falca Breks by the turret and stairwell. They stepped over the bodies of Wardens near the doorway, ducking under the wing of a dead floka, Breks moving more quickly than the mottles though he was twice the size of the biggest. He looked around hurriedly, as if he had yet to make his escape and not much time to do it.

Why had he abandoned his escape with Tallon's woman, much less come up here? He wouldn't have known down there in the landing of the tunnel that Scaldasaig might yet be his for the taking. And where *was* the woman?

Lannid couldn't move his head to follow Breks, but he was clearly looking for something. When he glimpsed him again the Draican was staring at him—or was it his father close by? Lannid knew now what the ditchlicker was seeking. He had the crooked sword—the falcata; that meant Maldan was dead, and Lannid wouldn't have time now to sift through the years to find something about his brother to mourn before Breks killed him, too.

He sensed Breks close now, could hear his breathing and the clacking talk of the mottles. He tensed, waiting for the stab or cut across the throat, but the Draican put aside the falcata as he kneeled. Lannid could scarcely feel the hands on him, rolling him this way and that. When Breks stood, closing a big hand around the pouch, Lannid thought it would happen now; Breks had the sword in his hand and had to know he was still alive because Lannid had closed his eyes, wondering what he would feel, if anything.

It didn't happen.

He opened his eyes again. Breks saw that too, motioned to the Limbs, and left, stepping over the bodies as quickly as he'd come.

This had to be only a brief reprieve. Lannid was sure Breks would be back up to take his time killing the last son of Culldred Hoster.

He realized now it was all of a piece. Breks was part of this attack. Some Limb had given him krael at the falls where Maldan killed Amala. So Breks had followed them all. And once Breks saw the destination, he meant to have it.

She was the reason.

They took her from him and so he would take what was theirs: Scaldasaig. All this because of Amala Damarr. He'd been wrong about Breks. He had the urge to laugh now but nothing came out but a hiss of breath through a mouth locked open.

Lannid once wrote secret verse about her that he would never have dared to show her even if he'd been successful in saving her life and bringing her back to Draica. Yet Falca Breks had somehow marshaled the help of more Limbs, and they in turn the flokas, to help him take, in her name, a fortress built to defy a royal army.

He wished he could speak if only to ask him, before he died, if all this was worth her life. It wouldn't have been for Lannid.

He had only one portion of the sky to look at as he waited for his death. More flokas circled. Close by, the wing of a dead one hung over merlons and embrasures, a second by the cistern where he'd last seen Tolo.

The servant was now crawling out from under that wing, into Lannid's field of vision. Tolo knelt, clasping with his good hand the bloody shoulder into which Kubelai had plunged the dagger. The straps of his wooden foot had been shorn. Tolo pulled the useless thing off the stump of his ankle, tossed it away and rose, canting to one side as he lurched toward Lannid.

TOLO LIFTED HIM up in his arms.

He couldn't fathom why the Draican hadn't killed Lannid. The man had been in a hurry, but it would have taken only a moment to cut the throat of Culldred's last son.

Whatever the reason, it offered the flimsiest of hopes: that Breks might part with a piece of krael—not for himself but for Lannid, who was no soldier, who wasn't like the rest of them. And the plague of it all? How do you gesture for a reprieve, ask for mercy from someone who wouldn't understand what you're saying? What a joke it was that only Heresa could understand his mush-mouth utterances.

Maybe he should have taken the krael from Lannid, but it was too late for that now, and the Draican might not even be in the hall. There might not be any more of the krael left in the pouch, anyway. At the worst, Breks would kill them both. Still, there was a chance.

Tolo almost dropped Lannid in the stairwell, had to shove him hard against the wall to get under him again to recover his balance, such as it was. Without the wooden foot he was short-legged; that threw everything off. Each step sent splinters of pain up his legs, into his hips, and lower back. Compared to that the shoulder and hand were nothing.

He heard Limbs beyond the last of the steps down. Their clacketing speech seemed to have an excited lilt. He prepared himself for the worst: if there were only Limbs in the hall, ransacking the kitchens for food, he and Lannid would be dead very soon.

The echoing shouts ceased after he turned the corner of the stairwell. They stared at him now: the dozen mottles gathered around the dais, including one who was sitting on Heresa's chair. The Draican's hand went to the hilt of the falcata at his belt. He stepped away from the dais, where another Limb sat.

Lannid's head lolled and bobbed with Tolo's lopsided gait. A few Limbs resumed shouting, brandishing swords and pilars but Breks, among them now, shook his head, put a hand on a Limb's dagger, lowering it. He walked over to Tolo, whispered: "Not here, you'll have to go farther with him."

Farther? He couldn't carry Lannid farther, had to let him down. The Draican surprised him with help. Together they lifted him back up, each taking an arm over a shoulder. That made it possible for Tolo to go on. Breks called back to the Limb on the dais, who rose to his feet, surrounded by the other mottles: "Take them above; you know what has to be done. Can you do that, Sty?"

The Limb nodded, said a few words to the others. They followed him—some reluctantly, eyeing Tolo, as if denied their due.

He asked Breks where they were going, forgetting that to everyone else except Heresa his words were incomprehensible, though they were always so clear to Tolo. Breks remained silent as they left the hall, ascending the staircase that led to the rooms above, between the hall and battlements. The Draican took most of Lannid's weight on the steps. Near the top, Breks said to Lannid: "You're not going die; the floka's Claw should only last through the night."

The room Heresa had prepared for Cossum was the closest off the landing, and so that was the one they entered, jostling by the table where the Cruthin women had sewed the banners. They put Lannid down on the ledge, brushing aside an open book with strange words on the pages. He was trying to say something yet all that came out was a soft wheeze. Tolo hobbled over to the canopied bed which, like all the furniture made by Vat's carpenters, had a faint smell of cinnamon and something else—Tolo could never figure out what.

He collapsed on the bed, thinking of the thin pallet in his closet-like room in the narrow hallway linking this room to Heresa's chambers. Blood from his split stump smeared the fine coverlet of the bed—which somehow made the pain easier to bear.

He thanked Breks for his life and Lannid's. This time Breks seemed to know what he was saying, and nodded.

Tolo thought he'd quickly leave, not wanting to linger here and possibly risk the Limbs wondering where his loyalty lay. And the Draican was lord of Scaldasaig now; there was much for him to oversee, including the fires that would consume the dead.

The man didn't leave. He walked over to the table in the center of the room and picked up a goose-neck ewer of water Tolo had filled for the Cruthin seamstresses. He'd never cleared the cups after the women's departure.

Breks gestured toward Lannid with the ewer: "There's enough here, but you'll have to wait to drink; otherwise you'd drown on a cup of water."

Tolo recognized the pouch of krael Breks took from a pocket and emptied on the table. He crushed a piece with his fingers, kneading it to a powder and slid that from his palm into the cup, filling it with water from the ewer. Swirling the cup, he walked over to Tolo, who took it with both hands, tears coursing down his cheeks.

Chapter Forty-Four:

THE EMBRASURE

Far below Scaldasaig, Heresa Hoster leaned against a rocky outcrop, consoling herself with the thought that at least her tomb was one vast enough for echoes and surely unmatched by any Sanctress' or queen's in the history of the Six Kingdoms.

It didn't seem likely, however, that she'd live to add the singular boast about walking away from such a tomb.

The lunelings she'd taken from spits along the tunnel walls were fading. Soon there would be only that distant scrim of daylight and its tapering reflection upon the reddish water. Even if she knew how, it seemed too far to swim to that low, jagged opening to the lake.

The waters of the cavern cast an ochre hue on the nearest rocks and crags. She'd have to climb up and over them, but even if she could do that, what was the point besides breathing better air at the opening? The passage narrowed at the end and she'd still have to cross it. And if she managed to do that without drowning, she'd have to make her way along the base of the castle wall, and in places the wall rose straight up from the water. Either way she went outside there was only one way to get off the Isle—the bridge—and the mottles or those flokas would kill her. Or Wardens would take her back to Culldred, a fate not worth the rescue.

There had been another tunnel, but she'd taken the one that went down—a foolish choice in hindsight, considering her hope for escape by boat. Her plan had been to somehow get to the Cruthin village up the awe, throw herself at their mercy, though she'd rather die than barter Cossum's ring for her life.

She should have realized that even if there had been another boat after Vat, Breks and the woman had taken theirs, it would have been set adrift or scuttled. And there it was, half-submerged at the end of a mooring rope wrapped around a post wedged in a crevice of shelving rock.

Her only choice was to go back up, take the other tunnel, see where it led. The lunelings might fade out before she reached the end of the high path she'd taken down here, and in the blackness she'd likely veer off and fall to her death; the path led over a narrow ridge. Still, that quick end was better than slowly dying here.

When she saw the luneling light above on the path she thought for a moment that Lannid had changed his mind, come to his senses. With his skill at making things he could repair the boat while she repaired the lie about her innocence.

But then she saw the Eyes, closer now, beyond the pale of the lunes.

Culldred.

It was too late to throw away the lunelings now; he'd seen them. Wherever she hid, he'd find her. More lies wouldn't work, not any longer. The Scourge of the Bounds, the hammer she'd used to forge her dream didn't have as nimble a mind as he believed, but give him a task and he'd finish it—two reasons why she'd picked him to marry, though he thought he'd chosen her. And his task now could only be to kill her for the poisoning.

She did not intend, however, to meet her end mewling and pleading.

She called out, the words echoing: "It seems we were paying Vat for more than we thought. He could at least have left a boat for the money. There's no way out."

A woman's voice startled Heresa. "I didn't come for that."

Shar Stakeen didn't approach directly. She moved around her, and Heresa turned with her own light as the young woman stabbed the darkness with spitted lunes in one hand, a sword in the other.

"Who else do you think is hiding down here?" Heresa said. "Maldan or Wardens would have killed you already. My servant? Lannid? You would have heard an idiot's shuffling or a soft, ungrateful son's complaints about the chill down here."

"Where is it—the pouch of krael?"

"That? Does someone up there need it? Please tell me Breks is dying—finally."

"Do you have it or not?"

"Do you see it on me, or anywhere close by?" Heresa said. "But if I did have it, I'd throw it into the water and let him die."

"Oh, he's alive and well, still very much a means to an end—which happens to be mine now, not yours. He's searching above for the krael. I thought he'd appreciate my coming down here to see if you had it."

"Well, well—it seems I have someone to share this darkness with after all."

"Thank your medicant," Stakeen said. "He kept begging us for a cup of the krael, though he wasn't sure if you had it or your son."

"Begged?"

"Screaming. Your servant broke his knees. An impressive feat. You've misused the man's talents. I imagine by now the Limbs have killed your medicant and tossed him over the parapets—toss the lunelings, too, if you would."

"How much more darkness do you need to kill me?"

Stakeen didn't wait. She halved the dangling lunes with her sword and only then did Heresa drop the remnants.

As the woman flicked the pieces into the water, she said: "Why would I want to kill you quickly and deprive you of the time to think about what Falca has done to your family? Lannid should be dead by now. Maldan? Falca didn't actually kill him, but he loosed your pet which did the rest before it demolished the bridge—with most of your Wardens on it.

"His friends—those mottles and their flokas—finished off those who didn't drown. He's taken everything from you and now he has Scaldasaig. You should have killed him in the hall when you had the chance; I'm very grateful you didn't."

"For what?" Heresa said. "The opportunity to spread your legs for him instead of Lambrey Tallon?"

Stakeen smiled. "It's occurred to me that might help to get from him what he never would have told you."

Heresa Hoster, of all people, could sense opportunity, whether it was a despised sleeping sister, a man like her husband—or Falca Breks, who thought he'd won. And now here was opportunity with the woman who'd helped him.

She called out as Stakeen was leaving. "Well done, my dear. I couldn't do better myself. If you were my daughter I would be *so* proud of you—a comforting thought for the time I have left. But has it also occurred to you that your strappy-jack could be one of those men who are more useful in death than in life?"

Stakeen turned, her eyes glistening. "And by that you mean?"

"Only that you haven't thought of everything. Who do you think paid for such a magnificent lid to my coffin down here? There are two chests of gold remaining for the work Furka Vat never completed. They may as well be yours: my bequest to the daughter I so desperately wanted. You are, you know."

"Where are the chests?"

"Hidden above where you'd never find them. Two chests of gold are very little, of course, compared to what this krael would bring you, wherever the source is. But it's more than enough to tide you over until you can bring enough of it to market, shall we say; to those buyers wealthy enough to meet your price. What, would you heal innkeepers' brats and wives along the way for food and lodging? You would never get to where you must be. If a mother can't get there, it's only natural she'd want it for a daughter."

Heresa knew she had the golden-eyed bitch who would have walked away, leaving her to dwell on the wreckage of what Breks had done to her. "Yes, you could try to get it from me now. You would fail. What more have I to lose? You could kill me here, but I'd rather you do it above, where I might have one last look at what your Falca took from me—after you've brought me the proof he's dead. I'd prefer his head, so I could spit in his vacant eyes, but a hand and his tongue will do, and the falcata. Once I have the proof, I'll show you where the cache is."

Shar Stakeen left without another word. As Heresa watched her ascending the path by luneling light, she weighed the odds that the woman would do it—and thought that likely.

The woman had been with Breks all the while up there, perhaps even making sure he came to no harm. Hadn't Heresa—playing the fiercely protective wife—kept a close watch on her husband when she could? The Red Hands bodyguard had been her idea as much as his.

Whoever Shar Stakeen was, she seemed as expert with purpose as well as a sword. Heresa could do nothing now about whether the woman got the secret of the krael from him. But she couldn't know there were no chests of gold; it wasn't likely Lambrey Tallon had told her about his mission to recover money paid to Furka Vat.

At least Heresa would have the pleasure—besides the bloody parceling of Falca Breks—of knowing that she'd deceived Lambrey's whore about the other. Together those were worth a hundred torches to brighten the darkness down here.

✻

From the keep's battlements Falca watched the floka carry Styada away over the water. Scores of others, dead Limbs dangling from talons, flew off to the north and east, but he didn't think feasting in eyries had been the reason why so many flokas answered Gurrus' summoning.

Falca silently urged Styada to hold on until his floka brought him to the shore, though he knew Styada would not let go, not now, not as Gurrus had done.

He'd told Falca this particular floka—a female—was the one that had carried Gurrus, yet how could Styada have known that? Still, while a dozen others took away dead Limbs from the keep, one had kept circling above while Styada and the rest of the Limbs slid dead Wardens—including Culldred—over the embrasures along the southern ramparts, to be collected later for the pyres.

And still that floka circled after the Limbs went down, the only witness to Falca's and Styada's embrace and farewell. Then she came down for him.

Falca didn't want to take the kinnet but Styada insisted. Having been returned to the Isle, it had to stay. Tomorrow they would search the keep for the Tapestry; where else would it be? Until then, Styada said he was needed across the lake. There would be more pyres there to burn the dead shitcatchers and the giving of dead Kelvoi to the lake waters. There were not enough flokas to carry all the dead away for Sky, and someone had to go the islet to get krael for the wounded.

Styada said he would look for Ossa and Raleva. Falca feared the worst. The last Styada had seen of them—as the flokas took him and Gurrus away—they had been set upon by Wardens close to the fire that engulfed the stockade. Falca could only hope that the krael Ossa had taken before might heal a wound, and that Raleva still had the piece he'd given her for the journey home she'd never taken.

She was a brave young woman. What happened here had been no more her fight than Frikko's in Gebroan.

Or Shar Stakeen's.

At least he could ask her now, if not Raleva, why she stayed to help him. He couldn't have done it without her. And where was she? He wasn't concerned she'd encountered trouble below, searching for the pouch of krael she believed Heresa might have taken, not knowing he'd found it with Lannid.

There was no one left in the keep to give a woman of her abilities trouble. Still, she should have returned by now. The thought had crossed his mind earlier that she might have discovered an extra boat down there that Vat had abandoned in his haste to escape, and left. But he'd seen no boat nearby on the lake, only a distant speck that may have been Furka Vat's.

No, more likely she was as tired as he was, and was resting somewhere.

Lannid Hoster would probably rouse to hatred in the morning. Ossa had once told him of the effect of the Claw and its duration, so for most of the night, anyway, Falca could safely sleep—if that was even possible after such a day. Perhaps he should have slid Lannid off to his death like the few stunned Wardens who had not already bled to death from Claw slashes, or killed outright by Limbs who had neither the means nor the desire to keep these men captive.

Now, it was up to Lannid to decide whether the mercy lasted longer than a night. If Falca had to kill him in the morning, then so be it.

And Tolo?

Falca had rarely seen the likes of that one. To carry a man of Lannid's size would have been difficult for someone with two feet under him, much less one. By now he had his pairs back—ears and feet—and his tongue. He deserved the krael. Tolo had the opportunity to take the pouch for himself but didn't, and instead broke the legs of the man who would have.

Falca supposed he'd done it, too, for the brother who had long begged on Furrow Street, whom he should have done more to help while he was still alive, if only to more frequently add shine to the cup he held between the stumps of his wrists. But even if Ferrex wasn't dead, with Falca back in Draica to restore his hands, he doubted whether his brother would take the krael, much less return to Scaldasaig with him.

He could hear Ferrex saying: *And where would I beg, brother? What use is your bigger cup if there's no one around to fill it with a pity here, a pity there? No, I have my own corner; enjoy yours—you who thieved so much more than me yet avoided the consequences. You must like dispensing this…krael like you're a Sanctor, a king of the Bounds, to the deserving of your flock…*

He tucked the kinnet into his belt. Such a king to take boots, breeches and gamby from a similarly-sized dead grood for the journey south, to replace his sodden, tattered clothes and rotting chasers—unless he could find a better fit in Culldred's chambers in this keep, or those of his sons.

But why stop there? He could take whatever he wanted from this place. If Scaldasaig wasn't his now, whose was it? He wished Amala and Gurrus were with him now, to share in his victory that no king or Sanctor could have achieved unless he brought an army to besiege the fortress for a year, and perhaps not even then.

Had the return of the kinnet and the fulfillment of his promise to Frikko been worth the lives of Amala, and Gurrus, and Ossa and Raleva and thousands of Limbs?

Not if the victory proved fleeting. Once he left, who would keep Scaldasaig out of the hands of others who would surely seize it? Who would prevent others from doing to the Limbs what the Wardens had done? Once the shores of Lake Shallan were again verdant with krael trees, how long would it be before the Wardens' successors discovered what those trees contained?

Was it up to him to see that wouldn't happen? What *more* could he do? Hadn't he done enough? He wanted Amala at his side more than anything else. He could bestow krael upon the deserving. He had his falcata again. But there was no bringing her back.

She wasn't here.

There was only Shar Stakeen.

SHE DRAGGED BACK Furka Vat's two henchies to join the third and propped all three against the closed carcase. She had no intention of going back down. The weight of the bodies would keep Heresa where she belonged once she realized she'd never spit in the lifeless eyes of Falca Breks.

In the time it had taken Stakeen to leave Heresa's cavernous tomb, she'd decided that the woman was lying about the cache of gold. And even if she wasn't, Falca might prove more useful *alive* than dead.

She couldn't pin down the moment when she began to doubt the necessity of killing him after she got what she wanted. Perhaps that was only the realization that she could always kill him later if she chose.

They had worked well together this day.

His boldness in coming here, his bravado in the hall, the smooth, conniving words, paled in comparison to what he did afterwards in the watery pen of the beast. She would never forget that. The man had a gift for adapting to situations as they arose, how he saw—as Tranch once put it—*where the light was behind the shadows.*

You could teach skill with weapons, prepare as best you could for inevitable obstacles; you could never imagine all beforehand. It was how you reacted to the unforeseen that often decided whether you lived or died.

She tossed away the lunelings when she reached the stairwell.

Such a man as she'd seen this day could be useful later, someone whose competence she could trust. With a man like that at her side, she could reach her dream that much quicker, for he was a man who followed through. He could have turned around at the waterfall after Amala Damarr's death. Yet he'd kept on through the Bounds, to come here and kill Maldan Hoster to avenge that death. Against all odds, he'd done that; very soon he would be doing much more.

And such devotion to that woman. Stakeen couldn't help but wonder: if it had been her instead of Amala Damarr would he have done the same? The indulgent, childish thought persisted through the kitchens and into the hall.

Well, a lover's devotion and a desire for revenge could go only so far. There was some other reason why he and Amala had left Draica, and it couldn't merely be the reason the father supposed. There was something else that kept Falca going and whatever it was he hadn't abandoned it. Now he had his reward—and so would she. He wouldn't have had his triumph without her.

If Amala Damarr had been in that cellar with him, Falca never would have gotten out, and none of the rest would have come to pass.

She decided to look for him first on the battlements. Where else would he be reveling in his—in *their*—triumph? Where else would the new Lord of Scaldasaig await his true Lady? It was time for what she had come so far to get, enduring all those days tracking him, crossing that river of deadly eels, almost dying from the bloodsnare, losing the gold the father had given her for the return of his daughter…*and* enduring the pelt of hair on Lambrey Tallon's back.

When the moment came, it would be no more than meeting a stickler at an appointed hour at the Red Turret. It was astounding what some of them had told her afterwards, how talkative they could be. Early on she'd learned the lesson: the older ones paid her as much for talk and companionship as the slide. So she listened, though all she wanted to do was show them the door and wash for the next.

This wouldn't be the same. The stakes were much, much higher than the passing of a splendent or lucra from a stickler's hand to hers. Here was one time she would encourage talk afterwards, even if she had to stroke a pelt thicker than Tallon's to coax him. And she would listen, as eagerly as she once did to the stories her father brought home with him from Milatum along with the gifts that were her reward for his being absent in her life for too long.

✵

STAKEEN STOPPED TEN feet away from him, partially hidden by a bristling pile of Warden weapons. Seemingly lost in thought, he didn't sense her presence behind him. She had her sword; his falcata and scabbard was propped against an embrasure. In one hand he had a scrap of cloth, which puzzled her; she hadn't seen him with it before. Some totem from a dead Warden?

She toyed with the moment. How easily she could kill him, get the hand that Havaarl Damarr had wanted almost as much as the return of his daughter. She saw in her mind the spot in the air where she'd sever hand from wrist after he turned suddenly, tossing the cloth, grabbing the falcata. She was still a shadden. But the daughter was dead, and the man she'd come so far to kill would indeed be worth more alive than dead.

"Falca?"

He surprised her: he wasn't startled at all, didn't whirl around as he reached for his weapon. It was as if he'd heard her, known she was behind him all along. His smile seemed different. He replaced the falcata on the embrasure with that odd cloth and when she joined him there, his hand lingered at her waist.

"Where are they all?" she asked, very much aware of his touch. She couldn't remember the Limb's name; then it came to her: "And Styada?"

"Gone. They're all gone…or dead."

"So is she."

He nodded. Was that for Amala, or did he know she meant Heresa?

"Some are healing," he said.

"Healing?"

Instead of answering he brushed fingers gently over her eyes. "They're fading back. By morning the gold will be gone."

"I'd like to see them before they do; there must be a mirror in one of the rooms below, perhaps Heresa's or Culldred's." She smiled. This was proving easier than she thought.

"No, not yet."

She knew then it would be here…and why not? Why not where they could see their reward in all its immensity, from the highest point on the Isle…*their* Isle now.

She felt his kiss in her delta.

His hand was still at her waist, more firmly now, as if to make sure she wouldn't break away and leave him. How did he know that's exactly what she needed now?

He unfolded the cloth slowly and draped it, fold by fold, over the edge of the embrasure.

"What's that?" she whispered.

"For now a blanket."

Her eyes never left his as she began to unbuckle her belt, but he brushed aside her hands and she let him do it himself. A long time ago there had been men who paid extra for the pleasure of undressing her though they never knew it. Neither would he.

She turned away from him, giving herself to the narrow openness of the embrasure. This cloth was like nothing she'd ever felt, but it would be much better than rough stone scouring her. She heard the *clink* of his belt buckle, felt the brush of his breeches against her and then the warmth of his flesh on hers. She wished her hair was longer to catch the breeze, so she could tell him what she liked for him to do with her tresses, but in time that would happen. She smelled drifting smoke and glimpsed the last of the flokas passing high in the distance over those islets she'd seen from the tower.

She was overflowing, impatient for him. "Falca...please..."

Even as she said it she felt him parting her with his hand, and she reached around to put hers over his, to spread herself wider. Her fingers came away slick and wet. She bit on them as he entered her, and winced—it had been a long time; too long.

He sensed that, took his time to reach his length. And when he slowly began to move inside her he brought her hands behind her, just as she liked.

But then, lowering himself over her, driving more deeply into her, he kissed them.

That came as a shock to her. No one had ever kissed her hands before.

She closed her eyes. It didn't matter if he was thinking of Amala Damarr.

The next time he wouldn't be.

Chapter Forty-Five:

AMALA'S KEEP

FALCA FOUND THE jeweled, silver mirror in Heresa Hoster's chambers below the battlements. Shar Stakeen had her look but said nothing about the fading eyes, only that never again would she keep her hair so short.

They nestled together on the bed, her head on his chest. She was not used to the softness of pillows. Falca said he wasn't either, so Heresa's remained untouched. The room had the scent of cinnamon and something else: "What is it, do you think?" she asked him, stroking his hard belly.

"Elixith."

"Now how do you know that?"

He told her about the spice warehouse in Draica—if not the sisters with whom he'd once shared it—but not much more because she fell asleep soon.

He wasn't accustomed to the bed either, not after the nights on the cabin roof of Harro Scapp's corry; the swaying floors of Limb hovens; the thin pallet he shared with Amala in the tiny room overlooking Sciamachon's fountain, where she placed the kinnet over her belly, telling him to stab her there and not to worry because the kinnet would protect her womb for the children they would have someday…

Shar Stakeen's breathing was the softness here. He found himself listening for it because he could scarcely hear it. On the verge of crossing over himself, he thought he would sleep well into the morning he was so tired.

He didn't.

Night had fallen when he awoke, restless, and far from a return to sleep. Shar stirred but didn't awaken when he left the bed. He got dressed, padded out to the allure that girded the keep under the overhanging brow of the battlements.

He'd left the kinnet there; that was only part of his burr. He could always get it later. The wind blew lightly, scarcely ruffling the moon ribbons upon the lake. The kinnet would not be blown off, and there was no one left to take something that looked like a stable blanket.

Was it the sighing of the wind, or Amala, visiting him where he wished she was now, sighing over his betrayal?

A stable blanket, kahyeh? Surely by now you know it's not a blanket. Betrayal? Is that your burr, why you're restless? You can't fuck my memory for the rest of your life. But did you have to use the kinnet for her cushion? Were you trying to pierce it after all?

He had only one answer for her.

The burr was a dream, kushla; you weren't in it. I couldn't find you in that bedside cup I had when I was young. Maybe that's because I never told you about it. Now, I wish I had.

He hadn't before, because whatever hopes his mother and father had poured into that cup, night after night in the squalid tenement by the Corry Roads, vanished in their absence, replaced by years of doing whatever was necessary to stay alive: scheming, killing, fleeing, thieving; and making sure others, like Lambrey Tallon, would not in turn steal what he'd stolen; and fisting Limbs for scrape money by day, counting the pittance of coins by night.

Then, the only dream that seemed possible was stealing enough to leave Draica before the inevitability of a messy death—not greatness—around the corner of an alley; before being taken in chains to a prison hulk along the River Rhys or the royal mines at Clure.

The dream was this: the victory of the day before had been in that cup all along.

Why did it bother him?

What better dream could there be? What greater accomplishment than the taking of a fortress built to defy a king's army, yet one that had fallen to *him*: a ditchlicking gutterkin from the quays of Catchall. The idea had been his, had it not? Why should he not claim the reward—as well as the woman who had crucially helped him?

Shar Stakeen had been in his dream, all right. How could she not have been after such a slaking?

He dreamed, too, of his own men on the ramparts of Scaldasaig; men like him, who had no home, no place else to go. He could not block the alleys of

Draica, but he could the tunnels of Scaldasaig, to make sure others could not surprise him in his fortress.

His golden banners snapped in the wind from the keep and towers; banners depicting that common cup of dreams; and underneath the cup the falcata, that legendary Gebroanan sword after which his father named him; and flanking that on the banner were great-winged flokas.

And around the lakeshore the krael trees once again reached the height of the bluffs, the trees seeded from the islet, as was a grove within Scaldasaig. He would live to see the trees as Gurrus had when he was young, for krael also slowed the years. Hadn't that happened with Sovay, the daughter of Laineth, Ossa's barrow-mate; the blind girl adopted by Boket and Vessa?

He would not be foolish about the krael, which could heal all but the worst wounds—such as plucked out eyes and heads unhinged from necks.

But he would see the shore verdant again—then burn the trees after the krael was harvested, and his Scaldasaig storerooms filled with it, protected by walls so no one could steal it from him. He alone would set the price as high as he wanted. Everyone in the Six Kingdoms who could afford that price would pay it gladly.

He once hoarded his shine for passage far beyond Draica, to fabled Milatum, but he could in time hire and lead an army to seize it. His fanciful request of Heresa Hoster in the hall was in his dream much less fanciful than he'd thought.

And the Timberlimbs? He would let them come to see the Tapestry here. He would let them have their villages and Roads and dispense to their mehkas the alms of krael—but only enough to keep them from another summoning of flokas to harry and kill wealthy pilgrims journeying to Scaldasaig, if not take back the Isle that once had been theirs.

At the end of the dream Shar Stakeen told him the keep should be named, because it overlooked all that was theirs now. A name came to him at once. She did not think much of his choice. *She's not with you now, Falca. And if she had been, she couldn't have done what I did for you.*

HE SMELLED THE stench of the pyres from within the castle, one in each ward. There were others on the shore, as well as smaller fires where celebrating Limbs feasted on roasted horses and augors. The tiny specks of torches on the islets meant that Styada was true to his word about getting krael for the wounded.

He heard a rustling behind him: Shar Stakeen, her eyes ambering, in a coverlet wrapped around her shoulders.

"I was going to wake you," she said. "Restless?"

"A dream woke me, nothing more."

She smiled. "The vaunty lord of Scaldasaig has trouble conquering sleep?"

"I always have—so it's Myrcia, then?"

"Myrcia?"

"Where you're from, your home."

"It once was. How did you know? I don't remember telling you."

"You didn't. It was a guess. The only people I've heard ever use the word 'vaunty' were from Myrcia—you're a fair piece away from there, as one of them liked to say."

"For many years now."

"What of your family; those brothers?"

"Falca…do you truly want to know?"

"We have all night; neither of us seems able to sleep."

She'd lost them all, she said. Her father came back from a sea voyage, on a plagued ship quarantined off the quays of Heap O' Heads in Castlecliff. He had two of her brothers on the windwhipper. Her mother broke the quarantine, so desperate was she to see her husband and sons. She was not allowed to return. All of them died within a week.

"The other two?" Falca asked.

"Soldiers in the Garda…"

One was killed in a skirmish along the Gebroanan border; the other contracted the fetters while posted at the garrison in Skenfrith and died of the disease. She became obsessed with what happened to her family, determined to apprentice to a healer somewhere beyond Myrcia. She sold the family manse and left for Draica, where she met a man named Surket Marr and followed him to Bastia, so smitten was she.

Not long after he abandoned her, she met an elderly healer woman, Tranch by name, who had long sought a capable younger woman to take her place, someone willing to accompany her two sons into the Bounds to collect herbs and plants for potions and poultices.

On the third trip they encountered Wardens—and Lambrey Tallon—who killed the brothers and took her to Scaldasaig…

Shar Stakeen told the story quickly, as if eager to be done with it, as well she might; after all, Falca had lost his family, too.

"I understand now why you took the krael so readily in the hall," he said. "I didn't at the time."

She shrugged. "What was there to lose? Either it was the wondrous thing you claimed, or I'd be dead of the poison and with my family. It *is* a wonder—you know that better than I. But tell me, have you thought about what it could… mean…for you? There's no limit to what it could bring you here…or us."

He suddenly wondered when she'd begun to think about what it could mean. In the hall? The tunnel, when she decided to help him? Or on the embrasure, looking out over the lake? He had the strangest feeling that he was back in Draica, in an alley, sensing someone waiting for him around the corner.

She touched his arm. "You look like I said something wrong; I'm sorry if I have. But is it so presumptuous to be curious about something that saved your life and healed my own trifling wound? All I meant is that it could save so many others."

Falca shook his head.

"You don't think it would?"

"I've a hunch you're going to ask me where there's more—I don't know. The one who did—his name was Gurrus—never trusted me enough to tell me, and now he's dead."

"But he saved your life with it."

"Only because he knew someone else didn't want me to die, my…a woman Maldan killed soon after. I kept asking Gurrus where he got the krael; he never would say. He knew the secret would be too tempting for a crouchalley who made part of his living fisting Limbs of the money they made selling scrape by the canals of Draica. I thought he might change his mind if I helped him destroy the Wardens here…if we were successful in bringing back the kinnet to the Isle. But it's too late to ask him now."

"Yours was a remarkable performance in the hall, and I only heard the last of it. Milatum was especially entertaining."

"She asked and I said the first thing that came to my mind—I've always wanted to go to there and now I will."

"You're…leaving?"

"Yes."

The coverlet had slipped off a shoulder; she drew it up tighter. "When would that be?"

"Soon. There's something yet for Styada and I to do here."

"Well, that…at least you have the pouch of krael to take with you."

"There's none left," he lied. "I gave away the last of it to Tolo."

"You gave it to…Heresa's servant?"

Falca nodded. "You sound shocked—he needed it more than I."

Shar Stakeen took a few moments, as if weighing that need. She smiled. "And why not? A fine gesture, though a pity some of it had to be wasted on Maldan and Culldred. The strutterman was so eager to heal his father. That didn't…"

"Strutterman?"

"Oh, I meant to say Lannid. The other's a poke of Maldan's I heard upon my arrival here; brothers can say cruel things to each other, that I know. But the krael—I suppose I *am* disappointed I can't bring a piece of it back to show Tranch. She wouldn't believe me unless she took it herself to heal her withered leg."

She gave Falca's hand a chaste squeeze and left, but at the door she turned. "The *kinnet*?"

"What we used for a blanket is a revered relic of the Limbs that was once stolen from here long ago and had to be returned."

"A revered relic? It will always be a blanket to me, Falca."

Did she smile again or was it a shadow cast by moonlight in the doorway?

His quick lies surprised him, as did his lack of an offer for her to accompany him and Raleva south to Myrcia. Where else would she be going now? Was his sudden wariness just about the krael? The dream he had? Or the fact that she was a woman who'd demonstrated extraordinarily lethal skills? And never mind her softer ones.

Had it all been about the krael for her? She was right about one thing: it could save so many—but only those who could afford the miracle. Wars would be fought over krael if it got into the wrong hands. The victor would keep it for himself to sell, and only the wealthiest in the Six Kingdoms would benefit; everyone else would sicken and die as they always had; go without that ear, foot, tongue or scarred face. The only ones who would keep their years instead of the inevitable consequences of them would be those who least deserved the reprieve.

There it was again: his thinking like a king, a Sanctor, or even some kind of god. But if so, then anyone could be a god who lived in the world as it was.

He would never forget the hour with her at the embrasure, his sudden desire for her. That hour had seemed fated to happen, as if he had no choice in the matter—or her. The inevitability hadn't bothered him before. It did now.

She made him uneasy, want to look behind. And that was the puzzling part: that's where she'd been for most of a day he'd never forget, either.

Another room would be best for the remainder of the night. He was about to go find one when he saw the torches approaching the keep. Curious, he went farther along the allure to have a closer look.

STAKEEN HEARD THE faint yet distinct shouts as she sat on the bed, weighing the choice of forcing the matter now or waking him later with a dagger at his throat.

So those are their names, she thought.

Ossa had to be the sot-smoking graylock. And this Raleva? Stakeen wondered if Falca had basted the woman, whoever she was, as thoroughly as he had her. She waited for him to rush in, exultant that his companions were still alive, but he must have taken another way down from the allure.

She had no doubt he'd been lying. He didn't know, of course, that she'd been at the falls to see Amala Damarr die before he was given the krael. She was glad he'd lied to her. Relieved, in fact. That lie was as potent as krael to heal her sickness, and it *had* been a sickness; she didn't realize how sick she was until the lie.

And he was as sick as she.

The man who would walk away from both krael and Scaldasaig was neither spotted nor withered, but he was surely diseased. Give it all up? For what? More alleys and petty thefts in Milatum?

Yet her own foolishness—her sickness—rivaled his. She felt the prickling of fear now, after the fact, as if she'd survived a fall that should have killed her. Where had she gotten the idea that he might willingly share this secret of krael with her; stay with her, share the same dreams she had for Scaldasaig; be Sanctor to her Sanctress, or whatever they chose to call themselves, their bond never to be sundered or abandoned; a bond sealed not only by the riches and power they would accrue from the krael but something more?

No, *that* made her sickness worse than his.

She should have known herself better. Why had she ever forgotten that she could rely on no one but herself and hadn't for a long time?

Breks was gutter-born and bred; that's what he would always be. The reprieve of his lie let her return to what she was, who she was. Her earlier fear now seemed like a...relic, a possession of someone else she suspected of following

Falca Breks for other reasons besides the secret of Golden-Eyes, all the way from the falls where Amala Damarr had so stupidly died when she didn't have to.

It had been a close thing.

That someone else had been *her*.

She'd gone out to the allure to bring him back because she thought the moment had come and—she had to admit it—because she wanted him again. And that, too, marked her fear; she saw that so clearly now.

There was a means to deal with that: what she had once planned on doing, or so she'd thought at the time. She had to kill him after she got what she wanted, and not because a Draican patroon was paying her to do it: she had to. She didn't know how to be anything else than what she was. She couldn't let Falca Breks go afterwards. He would always be out there, somewhere—and if he was she'd never be safe.

It would be a pity in one regard. But after she became wealthy from the krael, she could have all the men she wanted to summon at her whim, and certainly among them there would be a few who could please her as much as he had with that...crystal slaking she'd felt so deeply within her; a slow, shattering of... *crystal.* There was no other word for it.

She dressed quickly, sheathed her dagger, took her sword. She decided against hiding the falcata. No sense in risking his suspicions if he came back up here, though that was unlikely. She left the room more quietly than she'd entered, a shadden once more. She had to get one more thing before she got the other.

Stakeen felt confident he would tell her. She had more options now than a blade at his throat. He would not want to see his friends die so soon after their return. Or perhaps they knew about the krael, the graylock especially, since he'd been with him at the falls. One of them would break and tell her even if all knew she'd kill them after. She knew from both experience and a shadden's Hundred Recitations that a person almost always clung to the hope he would not die—right up to the moment he did.

Should all else fail she had a last resort—and there it was, exactly where he'd left it on the embrasure.

The blanket.

She considered the obvious connection between this...kinnet and Styada, whom Falca had been so desperate to save. Why? Maybe Falca hadn't been lying and Styada alone knew where the krael was. At the very least the kinnet would ensure her success in getting what she wanted—the precious kinnet in return for the krael. She wasn't worried about Styada and his Limbs overwhelming her. The exchange could be handled in a way to minimize that risk.

She folded the kinnet so that it would better hide under her duvelin.

The wind carried the last of the smoke and stench from the embering pyres in the courtyards of Scaldasaig. The ribbons of Suaila and Cassena brightened the lake. This height made no difference, of course, but it still seemed to bring the moons somehow nearer, close enough to cup in her hands.

She decided she would take enough of the krael to Milatum first. She doubted the city would match the memory of the stories her father brought back; no matter, she would have her own soon enough. After a few months she could sell enough krael to hire the men she needed to return to Scaldasaig and seize it before anyone else could. The tree-dwelling Limbs would not want it. Most of them would be back in their villages, or rebuilding those the Wardens had destroyed.

She would fill a tower room with the krael and soon everyone would come to her, because the word would spread about a woman with black hair to her waist who rules a wilderness stronghold that can never be taken; who was once a swallow of the Red Turret in Draica but had found something far more lucrative to sell than herself. So the rumors would go. She might even spread them herself.

By the time a king sought to end her dream—*who does that common swallow think she is?*—she would meet his army with a force she'd trained herself, as only the shadden-daughter of Tranch could. She hoped one of her adversaries would come from Myrcia so that she might add it to the kingdom she established here, if only for views of windwhippers like her father's coming into Castlecliff. And by then Cassenite dreacons and the Vasper they served would be long dead, their fhold destroyed. She would personally see to that…

But first things first: Falca Breks.

Going down she thought about how she would do it.

All of them would likely be in the hall for a while yet, perhaps with food and drink. She wouldn't show her intent immediately. Best to keep the sword at her belt, the dagger hidden. Take the measure of this Ossa and Raleva, see if they had weapons. They'd be tired, not having slept yet, and possibly wounded. But any wounds would be insignificant; otherwise how could they have made it across the lake and through the yards to the keep?

Falca loomed as the biggest threat though he didn't have the falcata. Stakeen wasn't worried about the Limb—Styada—if he was there, too. That left…Ossa and Raleva as the means to chasten Falca by wounding them first, bettering the odds and giving him a dilemma with only one solution. A dagger at the throat of the bloodied graylock or the woman should convince him to tell her where the krael was if he wanted to save their lives. He would. After what she'd seen of the man—his foolish loyalties and wasteful mercies—she knew that as a certainty.

When she strode into the hall she passed the Limb as he was going out. "Kehsu," he said, whatever that meant. She nodded and smiled. *One less to worry about*, she thought.

The others were at the other end of the dimly-lit hall, heading toward the other stairwell, leaving a scattering of cups, flagons and food on a table. She didn't see Falca. So much the better. The graylock limped along, helped by the woman. A twisted ankle? Bruised knee?

She was younger than Stakeen expected. The mismatched eyes had to be a shadow cast by the few lunelings and torches illuminating the hall. She carried a bow, an empty quiver across her back, and was saying something to the graylock at the portal of the stairs. She noticed Stakeen first.

"Falca…" the young woman said.

The graylock turned with this. Stakeen walked on quickly.

It had to be now.

She moved her hand to the hilt of the sword at her belt. First the woman, then the other…dun the legs…pull the woman away…get a back to the wall before Falca, beyond them, knew what was happening.

The graylock dipped his head, squinting, as if the meager light in the hall was too bright. He withdrew his arm from the woman; she let him go. He faltered but hobbled toward Stakeen.

She recognized him now, and not only because his face no longer had the mask of hideous scars. His unsteadiness instantly recalled her first memory of watching him leaving the ship docked at a Heap o'Heads quay in Castlecliff. She'd thought the long absence had crippled him, but it was only his sea-legs unaccustomed to the solidity of land.

She knew it was her father before he whispered the name she hadn't heard in so many years.

"Flury?"

Chapter Forty-Six:

LAST GIFTS

FALCA AND RALEVA left them to their embrace and the tears. He led the way up the stairwell, luneling in hand, thinking that it might never have happened if Ossa hadn't the sense to keep himself—and Raleva—out of the worst of the fighting after freeing the Limbs from the stockade. Two more would not have made a difference along the shore against the last of the groods.

Ossa had come to the Bounds to die and found his daughter. No one would be getting much sleep tonight, least of all the two who had so many years to recover. Raleva must have been thinking the same thing: "How long was it? Do you know?"

"About twenty years, I think."

"You looked almost as shocked down there as they were."

"I had no idea."

"What're we going to call her?" Raleva said.

"Whatever she decides."

"Well, I like Flury better, though it doesn't seem to fit her as well as the other name. But one can't change and not the other. It's both of them, either way."

Falca smiled. "I think you're right. They're probably talking about that right now."

He wondered whose story was closer to the truth. Did it matter now? No…nor did the names. The father had changed his for a good reason and so must have the daughter. Memories changed too. Everyone, himself included, changed the truth of the past to better suit the present; some more, some less, depending on what the Fates had woven for them at their Loom Eternal.

✵

LANNID HOSTER COULD move his head and arms, feel the itching in his legs, and if he could whisper for water he could swallow it, so Tolo had given him what was left in the ewer.

Tolo had his tongue but said only this to him before snuffing the candle and taking to the bed Cossum had never lain in: "You're thinkin' about it, I know. You need my help. You'll not have it."

Lannid had indeed been thinking about killing Falca Breks—-as soon as he realized he was recovering more quickly from the floka's Claw than Breks said he would. Later tonight? Breks would be sleeping in one of the other rooms nearby, and while he might bolt the door he might not think to do the same with the outside entry from the allure.

The Draican had been a busy fellow. Conquering in less than a day what took five years to build had to tire a man. He'd be sleeping soundly, secure in his belief there was no threat from the last and least formidable of the Hosters whose dream he had stolen—the father's and mother's, anyway. Was there a better potion for deep sleep than fatigue, the smugness of mercies, and a triumph that would become legend in the Six Kingdoms? And surely he would be sleeping in the bed where Culldred Hoster roused to his brief resurrection.

So why then would he need Tolo's help to cut the man's throat with his own falcata? In the dark Lannid didn't have to close his eyes to imagine hearing Maldan's taunting voice:

You are *going to do it, or at least try, aren't you, brother? If not for me, then mother and father and Cossum. There's only you now to do what has to be done—if you have the belly for it.*

Lannid heard other voices now beyond the partially opened door to the room, then saw the flickering of passing light: Breks and a woman, not Shar Stakeen; the voice seemed younger, perhaps that of a Cruthin serving girl he'd found cowering somewhere, whom he was taking to bed, the victor's spoils.

Lannid sat up clumsily on the window ledge, sliding off something to the floor with a thump—that book of his mother's he'd earlier seen. Or was it his father's, written in the gliff he'd taught them? He'd read it soon enough, but first he had to finish with Falca Breks.

On a second try he got to his feet, shuffled toward the door. The Sisters' light lessened the darkness in the room. It wasn't so much his unsteadiness as the sight of Tolo's golden eyes that caused him to knock into the table, toppling the empty ewer with a clang.

"You'll wake him, too, going for his blade," Tolo whispered. "Won't matter he sees you first with empty hands. He'll kill you."

"Thank you again for that water," Lannid said. "It helped."

He was at the door, holding on to steady himself for a moment, expecting Tolo to stop him, but he heard only: "You want him to kill you, that it?"

Lannid didn't see Breks and the woman go into a room down the corridor, but luneling light shone from the edges of the partially opened door. The room was his, with all his books, treatises and somewhere Furka Vat's rough sketches of the river fortifications—designs that Lannid was supposed to finish yet hadn't even examined. His father brought the books for him, all except *The Vale of Dramare*, which he'd thrown away. "Don't pout, Lannid. You need only what can contribute to our plans for Scaldasaig, and you're a big part of them."

He expected the door to close any moment, and thought he'd have to wait until the morning…then Breks came out. Only when someone bolted the door from within—a dull snapping sound in the quiet—did he leave. So the girl, whoever she was, meant something more to him than a slide or two in the night.

Breks had only the luneling in his hand, nothing else. Lannid wondered what he would do if he had something in his, had the strength to use it and the legs to quickly set upon the Draican. Even so, Breks could easily choke the life out of him with those big hands.

Breks turned quickly, startling him. "You're doing better than I thought."

How could he have been aware of his presence, his breathing halfway down the corridor?

"Why?" Lannid said.

"Why what?"

"You know my meaning."

Breks took a moment, nodded. "You could have asked me in the morning."

"I'm leaving tomorrow. No doubt you'll be off inspecting your prize here. Or you could change your mind and decide it's best if *all* the Hosters are dead."

Breks glanced behind him.

"You think the question an ambush?" Lannid said. "Does the new lord of Scaldasaig think he's still in some alley in Draica? Is the answer something no one else should hear?"

"Where's Tolo?"

"In the room. He told me I'd need his help to kill you; he refused to give it—well?"

"Closer to the light, so I can see your hands."

Lannid shuffled ahead. "If I stood any chance it would have been while you slept; I'm no soldier."

"That was one reason."

"Another?"

"Amala. You would have saved her life at the falls. I remembered that much."

Lannid's legs were weakening, but there was nothing to hold onto here. He backed against the wall, found a luneling spit and held on. "I would have killed you so I could take her back to Draica."

"Killing me would have been the easy part."

"I would have brought her back to her mother and father, however long it took."

"You didn't know then that you'd never be able to go back, did you?"

Lannid could say nothing to that; it was true.

Breks shrugged. "They would have been very grateful. Who knows, maybe in time Amala would have realized she was better off without a ditchlicker who would only impoverish her, or leave her a widow long before our children were grown; who couldn't read his own name much less write it."

"We'll never know now, will we?"

"Nor whether you could have gotten safely back to Draica with her. But unless you took her back a prisoner I doubt you would have succeeded. You would have woken one morning to find her gone. I loved her, Lannid, and I believe she loved me, but there was also another reason why she chose to come with me to the Bounds, to do what we could to help the Limbs. I was a means for her to leave Draica…forever, but she would have left if she hadn't known I existed."

"I don't believe…"

"How well did you know her?"

"I…I knew her. I knew Alatheus…and the family well enough to pay a visit to them before I left Draica with my brother. Enough to promise Serisa I would do what I could to bring her back. Her father didn't…" His voice trailed off.

"Didn't what?"

"It was obvious he didn't think much of my chances for doing so."

"No, he would have sent someone else."

"All of this means…what matters now is that they should know what happened to her."

Breks shook his head. "You wouldn't last a week there, nor would I for different reasons, even if we survived the journey back through the Bounds."

"We did it once."

"Oh, I'd return if I thought Amala would want them to know. But she was prepared to never see them again. I'll be leaving for Myrcia soon. There will be at least one other going with me. Then I'm for Milatum."

"You're lying. Leave this? Scaldasaig is yours, you took it."

"Just because I did—with a lot of help—doesn't make it mine. I did think that one must follow the other, but no longer."

Lannid's legs gave way, and as he fell he cut his hand on the luneling spit. Breks made no effort to help him; Lannid was glad for that. The Draican watched him struggle to get up, a puppet without the strings. Just when one twitching leg felt good enough to bear weight, the other gave way. Finally the spasms passed and he stood, leaning back against the wall.

"I don't think you are," Breks said.

Lannid bent over, using his arms to lock his legs. "I'm not what?"

"Your brother was wrong about you—you're no strutterman."

"I have no idea what you're talking about but I could use a strutter now."

Breks' eyes narrowed. "You never heard him call you that?"

"Maldan never knew I'd bought a strutter, and I certainly wouldn't have told him I left it at the Damarr manse; it was bad enough the father knew I had, that I was too embarrassed to go back and get it—me, the fool who thought he could bring his daughter back."

Lannid was about to ask him what was so important about Maldan calling him a strutterman, but Falca Breks turned without another word, the luneling light vanishing as he hurried away, as if Lannid had brought his brother back from the dead, with a blade in his hand, to do what he never could have done himself.

FALCA FELT BETTER with the falcata in his hand. But there was something else he needed, too. As he quickly left the room to get it he told himself to slow down.

Had he tangled this skein?

She'd called Lannid a strutterman, must have lied about that when Falca asked because Lannid never heard his brother call him that; Maldan didn't know he had a strutter. Could that mean she was at the Damarr manse after Lannid and saw the strutter he said he left? If so, there could only be one reason why she'd been there.

He felt the lure of another explanation: he misinterpreted what Lannid said. Or maybe Maldan *had* said it but only Shar Stakeen heard him. Still, Falca had used and heard others use expressions for dandies and strutter-carrying festaloons but never…*strutterman.*

And maybe she had a past besides that of a shadden, that needed the lie about four brothers and apprenticeship to a Bastian healer.

No…

Everything became clear if Shar Stakeen was the shadden Damarr hired. That explained so much of what she'd done and how she'd done it—and also the differences in what she and Ossa had said of their pasts. How could he possibly have neglected to mention four sons supposedly responsible for the daughter's extraordinary confidence, composure and martial skill? If she'd lied about that, she would have lied about the reason for being in the Bounds.

Lies upon lies.

The simplest explanation was that she had come into the Bounds not to gather herbs and plants in the western Bounds but to kill him and bring Amala back. His impression was that she'd been taken by Lambrey Tallon not too far from Scaldasaig. So what was she doing *this* far east?

He'd tangled no skein here. She'd been at the falls, had to have been, and so she'd seen Amala's death and what happened with the krael Gurrus gave him afterwards. That changed everything. Here was something that could potentially far exceed what Havaarl Damarr had given her for his daughter's return. Why go back to Draica carrying naught but news of failure?

So she followed.

There was a reason for her odd protectiveness, her willingness to risk her life and help him: to make sure he wouldn't die before she learned of the krael secret. That's what she was after. Everything she'd done, including that hour at the embrasure, was to coax the source of the krael from him.

And now, Ossa made that a certainty. He had only to tell his daughter. Why wouldn't he? If he didn't, she had Raleva.

The moonlight was more than enough to see the kinnet was gone from the embrasure—and with it any remaining doubt that Shar Stakeen was the shadden sent after him and Amala. The kinnet hadn't been blown off; Falca could scarcely feel the wind in his face. She'd known it was here, figured it might be something to bargain with, if all else failed.

Now, he wouldn't have the protection of the kinnet wrapped around his belly and chest.

He and Raleva wouldn't last the night. Stakeen knew he was leaving tomorrow with her—the only ones besides Ossa and Styada who knew where the krael was. She was a shadden, averse to trusting anyone except herself—and her father now—with the secret. She certainly wouldn't trust a ditchlicker like himself—or a young woman—not to have second thoughts about coming back for more krael, as she no doubt intended.

Ossa had changed everything.

Stakeen could explain the two killings—fix the blame—by touting the menace of a Warden hidden somewhere in the keep. Or better yet, conjure a seething Lannid Hoster eager for revenge. Of course, she would avenge the deed, killing Tolo as well, leaving no one to tell Styada differently so he wouldn't gather enough Limbs to kill her.

And she'd stay at Scaldasaig until they all left. Why would they remain here, where so many of them had died? The Isle had been theirs, the Kalaleks' anyway, but all that was gone now, replaced by shitcatcher stone. It would be many months, a year or longer, before anyone else might hear about this abandoned fortress in the wilds of the Bounds, and march to seize it.

But when they did they'd find the walls garrisoned by men Shar Stakeen had bought with all the money from selling krael.

It wasn't hard to think like her; he had before.

She wouldn't call herself Shar Stakeen anymore. She'd be Flury Demoul, daughter once again of Mott Demoul. The krael would give them more years to make up for those they'd lost.

Falca thought of waking Raleva, fleeing with her in the night after alerting Styada. Let him and a hundred Limbs do the killing.

No…

He had to finish this himself.

And Ossa?

Falca couldn't kill the shadden without killing the man who had, in such a short time, come to be as much of a father as Barla Breks had managed to be in all the years before he disappeared—or abandoned his family.

Falca would have to do it quickly; he couldn't wait for more lies—that would give Stakeen time. Quickly then, while they were still in the embrace of those lost years. She was a shadden. He'd seen what she could do. His surest weapon was the fact she didn't know yet that *he* knew what she was.

He never would have known if it hadn't been for the chance meeting with Lannid Hoster.

Falca left the battlements, forming his own lie to explain the falcata: Tolo's urgent warning about the last of the Hosters hiding in the cellar somewhere. Falca had to find and kill him—*and would they help him look for the strutterman?*

The lie would gain him the moment he needed to kill her, the woman he'd nestled with only hours before; caressing her, tasting her, listening to her murmuring about growing her hair long again so he could brush it for her every night…

And then…Ossa.

There was no way around it.

If he was to kill one, he would have to kill the other.

FALCA TOOK THE allure—the way he'd gone down to greet Ossa and Raleva earlier—but stopped when he heard them talking below, coming out from the hall to the landing.

They went ahead to one of the embrasures, Ossa ahead of her. There was enough light from the moons to cast shadows on the landing.

Stakeen had the kinnet. "We won't need this after all. Poor Falca, he couldn't make up his mind whether it was a blanket or some oh-so-important relic."

"Whichever—it's useless for us," Ossa said. "We should give it to the Limb afterwards, though. He'll want it."

She tossed it away, as if it needed a washing, and leaned forward in the narrow embrasure, her father close behind her, a hand on her shoulder.

Neither of them had weapons that Falca could discern. It would be an execution. He would have to kill Ossa first to get to her. Four or five steps across the landing past where the allure stairwell met the other that lead to the hall—and it would be all over. He wouldn't need the lie.

"I haven't as yet told you the half of what I went through for this moment," she said. "Where is it, father? You said it was close."

Cassena's broader ribbon seemed like a ghostly road through the shimmering field of the lake, leading directly to the islet of krael trees.

"It's up there," Ossa said, nodding at the moons.

One hand stayed on her shoulder; the other dropped to the back of her knee, then below. When he moved a leg back—not the injured one—to brace himself, Falca realized what Ossa was going to do the moment she did.

She struggled but her father was taller, heavier and strong. He kept his weight forward, pressing against her: one last embrace. She couldn't get her arms around, to strike him.

He lifted her kicking legs over the embrasure.

Falca bolted for the door to the stairwell, taking the steps two at a time, skidding over the last of them, tumbling into the hall. He lost the falcata, left it spinning on the hilt as he rushed out to the landing.

Ossa knelt on the embrasure, on the verge of joining his daughter below in death. He hesitated when he saw Falca, shifted to face him, shoulders and chest rising, falling.

"You...should be asleep," he said, "not sounding like...you're halfway up the rigging."

Falca wanted to wait until his own panting subsided, until he found the words to say to him—if there were any that might bring him back. He felt as if a rag had been stuffed down his throat, but he managed: "Ossa...come back... into the hall." He was close enough now to extend a hand. "We can talk there."

Ossa didn't seem to hear him. "I...I even told her there wasn't enough light from the moons to see where it was, that it could wait until morning, but...she was so eager. She had to see it now. My eager Flury... always so quick to forgive my long absences at sea."

Falca thought of grabbing him, pulling him back—yet what of the next hour, or day, or week? Ossa had to want to come back. Maybe if he kept him talking... "Here then...tell me here."

"Why I had to do this now before she killed you and Raleva? How she patted me on the hand, as if only she knew what was best for us, when I told her that wasn't necessary?

"What? That I had her back for too short a time? That it turned out to be too *much* time; enough for her to tell me she'd been forced to become a shadden, that she'd remembered me telling her once that nothing was ever truly wasted; you could always learn from a mistake or misfortune and...it wasn't because what she learned proved useful when she went back to the Cassenite fhold and killed the Vasper for what he'd done to her.

"She thought that lie would somehow make me feel better. She said it before I could tell her I'd killed the Vasper myself. It was then I shut up, wanting to see if there was anything of my lovely daughter that had survived my longest absence. I as much as killed her before with those."

"Ossa..."

"You wanted me to talk and I am. She said that for all that had happened to her something was owed her—was owed the both of us—and that was the krael and…and as I listened to her tell me what had to be done about you and Raleva, I was thinking of all the years that were taken from us, when I might have helped her see that nothing is ever owed any of us merely because of our existence, however troubled that may be. That's the kind of gift a father should give his child, but all I had to give her tonight was the dream she was determined to have, no matter the cost…a dream for us both, she said, to replace what we'd lost."

"Ossa…you have more…maybe even Rohaise, if…"

"That was long ago, all of it was."

Falca had come down with a lie to gain the moment to kill them. Now, there was another one: "You don't have to do this. We will leave here, you and I, and Raleva. We'll go on to Milatum after we see her home. In time…this will pass…"

"Time? I've had much more than I thought I would, thanks to you—is she sleeping now…Raleva?"

Falca nodded, thinking of what she said earlier about which names they'd choose.

It's both of them, either way.

"Of course she is," Ossa said. "My daughter was going to kill you both tonight while you slept. She said the sooner it was done, the sooner I'd get over it. Your deaths were necessary because only she and I could have the secret of the krael."

He looked up at the moons, then back at Falca. "I've meant to ask you: did Raleva ever tell you about her grandfather? About what he once did? Oh, what am I thinking? You're not Myrcian. Why should you care?"

"Maybe I do."

"Then ask her on the way south. Lukan Barra will be so proud of what she did here. And Falca…"

"Yes?"

"I see your right hand is empty."

"It wasn't before."

"How did you find out about her?"

"I…it doesn't matter."

"Make no mistake; I still would have tried to stop you."

Falca nodded.

"Then you understand a father's instinct to protect his own, no matter how little time he's had with them."

In his rush down from the allure, Falca hadn't heard Shar Stakeen striking the water far below, but heartbeats after Ossa pitched forward, he heard his end: a sharp, cracking that from this height sounded like that of stone hitting stone.

EPILOGUE

SOMEWHERE ALONG THE way with them all, Styada lost the fear that had once stricken him as surely as a floka's Claw. Freaca never had that fear of venturing out, and now that his was gone he felt a sadness that he could not go with Falca, Raleva and the two other men. He lifted his spirits by imagining that Gurrus would tell him he could keep her closer if he stayed. He once would have thought that a mehka's riddle he'd never understand. He did now.

Still, the desire to leave with them was strong. That was why he had to stay here at the top of the tower after the farewell below and watch their boat cross the lake. Thankfully, the wind had lessened since dawn, though it still frothed the water white against the ruins of the bridge near and far.

Supplies, weapons and their Kelvoi escort had already been brought to the shore. The ferrying took most of the morning as only two of the boats that once supported the bridge could be used; by now the wind had swept the lake clear of what was left of the rest, piling splinters large and small on the strand.

The two men—Lannid and Tolo—repaired a partially charred cart as best they could for the journey south to Raleva's home. They'd also found a horse to pull it—a lucky horse indeed to have survived the battle and ensuing victory feasts.

Many Kelvoi survivors had already left, yet enough remained for Styada to pick the twenty-five to escort the group for three days—wherever that took them—before returning. It would be useful to know what lay beyond Kelvarra and the river to the south. Styada knew better than to accompany the twenty-five for the three days; the temptation to keep on with Falca might well have proven too powerful to resist.

The kinnet had to stay here, though the Tapestry could not be found. Over a hundred Kelvoi searched everywhere, including Amala's Keep, Falca called it; and below in the tunnels and red-water cavern. Falca had shown the kinnet to Lannid and Tolo. Neither had seen the like; neither had ever heard Heresa mention a Tapestry. Nor could they ask her about it. She was presumed dead though they hadn't come across the body down there where Lannid threw something into the water: his father's book, he told Falca.

Styada was sure the Kalalek ketheras must have taken the Tapestry when they fled before the shitcatchers' arrival years before, to hide it in some remote corner of Kelvarra. As Kelvoi spread the news about the victory at the Isle, the Kalaleks would return, the Tapestry made whole again.

Styada intended to ask the ketheras what the words on the kinnet meant. He'd earned the right to the knowledge. But he doubted they would know. Falca could neither read nor write his own language—yet—but he'd known those words on the kinnet were not of his own people. And Gurrus knew it wasn't Kelvoi writing. That didn't exist. If the Kalalek ketheras had that skill, their secret would have been discovered long ago.

One thing was certain: things would never be the same—for anyone.

Styada persuaded many Kelvoi to stay here a while; survivors who, like him, had no home to which to return. He got help with this from a Skeel mehka who agreed with him about the importance of Kelvoi remaining in this place of stone, enslavement and death. Even so, it took a day and well into the night for Styada to convince others of that necessity.

Some had to stay. If they all left, shitcatchers would come back—perhaps not Warden shitcatchers, but others, inevitably. And the destruction of Kelvarra would resume. Many Kelvoi had died to reclaim the Isle and it had to be guarded now, so that elsewhere the clans could rebuild villages and Roads. It was, Styada told them, better to keep this place as a stronghold that could never be burned or cut down. It would become someone's stronghold; better it be a Kelvoi stronghold.

He hoped they understood there could be no going back to what once was, not completely. Much might be lost of who they were if they stayed here. Yet if they didn't keep what they had won, they would eventually lose what had been gained by such a victory.

Styada had pressed on with them by the fire on the shore across from the islets. He suggested that in time each village might be required, by general agreement, to send contingents of soldiers to protect the Isle, relieving those who were serving, each clan thus taking its turn. If some came to believe they could use the stronghold to rule over all, they should think again—especially Kalalek ketheras if they sought to reassert their power. Walls could defy attacks by shitcatchers, but walls would always be vulnerable to a summoning of flokas.

Yet the Isle would always remain the revered site of the greatest Kelvoi victory, a place to honor all those who died here. There would be pilgrimages and not solely for the krael when the trees returned.

When Styada was done speaking by the fire, some praised him for this... kesslakor, calling him a mehka. He insisted he was nothing of the sort; anyone could shape the future by...carving holes in flenx horns, for instance—which completely confused them, and so they left convinced he had to be a mehka.

Still, if there was a vision to be had, it was that of a tree planted in what was once the meadow of the ketheras here; a tree whose branches would spread to the walls and grow above the towers, high enough, perhaps, for a floka's nest...

Falca and the others were at the shore now. Soon, they would be going up the road that led to the vale between the bluffs. Styada wondered if Falca would ever find a place where he would choose to stay...a home. He had come farther than the shitcatchers to Scaldasaig, but his purpose had only been to keep promises to those now dead.

He had been quiet for these past two days yet Styada believed a reluctance to leave was not among the reasons.

Styada had his own promises to keep.

More days would pass, given the coldness of the lake water, before the two bodies rose from the depths. When that happened, their remains would be carried to the meadow and buried beneath the seedling of a krael tree taken from an islet. Falca had not hesitated when Styada asked him about Ossa's daughter: "Her, too. They should be together."

And there was the adornment—Falca called it a swan's-wing brooch—that Styada promised to also bury under the seedling of the krael tree. It was a common bauble, Falca said, pressing it into Styada's hand, made by Kelvoi refugees in the place where he was born. But it had been Amala's most valuable possession, and it was his also, besides the falcata she'd given him.

"Even if the wing wasn't broken, it still wouldn't be worth stealing," Falca said, "but who knows how desperate thieves are in Milatum. It will be safer here. Wherever I go I'll always know where it is."

Before they pushed off in the boat from the ruined landing, Falca asked him if he knew why the flokas had come, why so many had answered Gurrus' summoning. Who but Falca would want to know, and so that was why Styada gave him the answer Gurrus had given him, before the flokas took them away toward the Isle: "We are descendants of the flokas and if we die, our lands laid waste, so will the flokas in time. To see them is to see who we were, and what we cannot be though we may sometimes wish that. They have spoken of the same to me…"

Whether or not this was true, it was what mehkas believed; what Gurrus believed, as did Styada now who passed it on to Falca.

When they were all specks in the distance, then finally gone, Styada turned away, the swan's-wing brooch tight in his hand, to go and see where in the courtyard below the meadow might have been.

About the Author

Bruce Fergusson's novels in the Six Kingdoms series—*The Shadow of His Wings,* and *The Mace of Souls*—were nominated for Nebulas and the former was a finalist for the Crawford Award for best first fantasy novel.

A psychological suspense novel, *The Piper's Sons*, was a *USA Today* and Barnes & Noble bestseller and was nominated for best novel by the Pacific Northwest Booksellers' Association.

His other novels include *Morgan's Mill,* which weaves history of the Civil War and Underground Railroad into a contemporary narrative of suspense; and *Two Graves for Michael Furey,* a literary thriller. Following *Pass on the Cup of Dreams,* the fourth novel in the Six Kingdoms series will be *Kraken's Claw.*

All of Bruce's books will soon be available, including the *Six Kingdoms Codex*, a companion volume for the series that includes an introductory short story, backround and glossary.

He lives in Edmonds, Washington, with his wife, Angelica.

Find out more about Bruce and his books at www.brucefergusson.com. To be notified when *Kraken's Claw*—the fourth book in the Six Kingdoms series—is published, sign up for Bruce's email newsletter.

CPSIA information can be obtained at www.ICGtesting.com
Printed in the USA
LVOW06s2218301213

367533LV00001B/257/P

9 781939 051493